New York Times and *USA Today* Bestselling Author

KELLY ELLIOTT

Holding You

HOLDING YOU
Book Three in the Love Wanted in Texas Series
Copyright © 2015 by Kelly Elliott
Published by K. Elliott Enterprises
Visit my website at *www.kellyelliottauthor.com*

Cover Designer:
Lisa Jay with Lisa Jay Studio

Cover Photographer:
Glass Jar Photography

Editing:
Nichole Strauss with Perfectly Publishable

Design and Formatting:
Christine Borgford with Perfectly Publishable

BOOKS BY

KELLY ELLIOTT

WANTED SERIES
Wanted
Saved
Faithful
Believe
Cherished
A Forever Love
The Wanted Short Stories

THE BROKEN SERIES
Broken
Broken Dreams
Broken Promises

JOURNEY OF LOVE SERIES
Unconditional Love
Undeniable Love

LOVE WANTED IN TEXAS SERIES
Without You
Saving You
Holding You

STANDALONES
The Journey Home

JOINT PROJECTS
Predestined Hearts

WANTED
family tree

Garrett & Emma

Jack & Grace

Sharon/Philip

Brian

GUNNER & ELLIE
ALEXANDRA
COLT

Jeff & Ari
Luke
Grace

Mark & Sue

Matthew

Greg & Elizabeth

josh & heather
will
libby

Brad & Amanda
Morgan
Taylor

Scott, Senior & Melody

Bryce

Scott & Jessie
Lauren

Drake

Dewey

Aaron & Jenny

DEDICATION

    This book is dedicated to all the *Wanted* fans out there. The entire time I wrote this book, I was thinking back to where it all started. With a football player named Gunner and a lost young woman named Ellie.

    This book is for y'all. Happy reading.

PROLOGUE

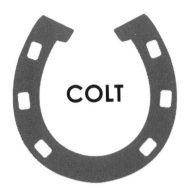

COLT

STANDING BEHIND LAUREN as I pushed on her back lightly, I watched the swing take her up higher. "I hate high school," Lauren said.

Smiling, I asked, "Why?"

Dragging her feet on the ground to slow herself down, she came to a stop. Twisting the metal chains of the swing, she turned to face me. "Boys."

My heart dropped. If someone did anything to Lauren, I'd bash their head in. "Did something happen?"

A part of me was scared to hear her say that she liked someone. Holding my breath, I reached out and spun her some, twisting the chains even more. Letting go, Lauren began spinning as she laughed and dropped her head back. Coming to a stop, she looked at me. Her blue eyes danced as the sunlight hit them. We had both just started our sophomore year of high school, and I hated the way some of the guys stared at Lauren.

"No, nothing's happened. That's part of the problem."

Swallowing hard, I asked, "Is there anyone you like?"

The air between us seemed to spark with something I'd never felt before. Lauren slowly smiled as she tilted her head. "Is there someone you like, Colt?"

Allowing my grin to grow bigger, I said, "Oh yeah. There's this blonde, blue-eyed beauty that has this thing for skipping around instead of walking. Also has a fondness for swings." Lauren's face turned from amused to something different. For a brief moment, it felt as if we both shared a connection that I'd never experienced before. My heart felt like the wings of a hummingbird; it was beating so fast. "I kind of think she's into her horse more than guys though."

Lauren's eyes turned dark as she broke our stare and looked to the ground. "Smart girl. I'd pick my horse over a guy any day." Glancing back up, she winked at me.

Reaching my hand down to Lauren, she closed her eyes as if anticipating my touch. My stomach dropped like always when I thought about kissing Lauren. I did what I always did though. I ignored my feelings and chickened out. Pushing a loose curl back behind Lauren's ear, I whispered, "Lucky horse."

Dropping her mouth slightly open, Lauren was about to say something when her father called for her.

Closing her eyes, she stood. Opening them back up, I saw nothing but sadness. I wanted to see the sparkle that was there a few moments ago. Giving me the sweetest smile ever, Lauren said, "I um . . . I guess I've got to go help with dinner. Thanks for helping me with the new horse."

Nodding my head, I grinned. "Anytime."

"See you tomorrow then?" Lauren said as she walked backward.

"Yep, see ya tomorrow, Lauren."

Standing there, I watched Lauren skip over to her back door. Pushing my hand through my hair, I walked back over to the barn. Climbing on top of my horse, Samson, I took in a deep breath of air. A cool fall breeze was blowing and the birds were chirping away in a nearby tree. Opening my eyes, I smiled as I thought about Lauren skipping to her back door. Letting out a chuckle, I headed for home. Glancing back over my shoulder, I noticed Lauren looking out her kitchen window. Lifting her hand, she smiled and waved. Raising my hand, I waved back to her as I whispered, "Someday, Lauren Ashley Reynolds, someday I'm going to ask you to be my wife."

ONE

LAUREN

G LANCING AROUND, I smiled when I saw Luke and Libby kissing as the waves crashed around their feet. Their wedding had been thrown together in record time and was probably the most romantic wedding I'd been to yet.

Leaning against the rail, my eyes caught sight of Colt. I watched as he talked to one of Libby's cousins. The way she was flirting with him turned my stomach. I'd like to pull her by that tight bun on the top of her head and slam her against . . .

"Lauren? Are you okay?"

Pulling my eyes from Colt and the blonde, I turned to face Grace. "Yep. I'm fine. Why?"

Grace gave me a knowing smile. "Well, to start with, you look like you want to kick that blonde's ass from here to Timbuktu. Second, you're gripping that bottle so tight your knuckles are turning white."

Glancing at my hand, I loosened the grip on the bottle. Sighing, I looked back to Colt and the blonde. "He drives me crazy."

Grace chuckled. "Why? Because a hot girl is attracted to him? Poor Colt can't help it if he is a mini version of his daddy, Lauren. Girls are going to flock."

Rolling my eyes, I looked away. "He sure looks like he

is interested in her."

Grace sucked in a deep breath and let it out. "You know what I see, Lauren?"

Turning to look at Grace, I asked, "What?"

Not taking her eyes from Colt, Grace smiled. "I see a guy who is being polite and talking to one of his friend's cousins. I see that every time she takes a step closer to him, he takes a step away from her. His smile isn't touching his eyes, and he looks bored out of his fucking mind. I think you need to go save him from what clearly is a conversation he doesn't want to be in."

My head jerked as I looked to Colt. It was then, for the first time, I noticed he was wearing a fake smile. When the blonde threw her head back and laughed, she took a step closer and Colt turned his body away from her and took a small step back.

Lifting his Coke bottle to his lips, his eyes caught mine, and I couldn't help but smile. I wasn't smiling because Colt looked at me. I was smiling because I saw how miserable he was. Colt didn't want to be talking to the blonde and in that moment of realization, I was ecstatic. Okay, so maybe I was also smiling because Colt looked at me.

"See what I mean?" Grace said as she nudged me with her shoulder.

Colt smiled back, and this time it reached his eyes. They lit up for the first time in weeks, and I loved that it was because of me smiling at him. Ever since he moved into the house we were all sharing, all we did was argue about the stupidest things or avoid each other all together. I knew my frustration toward Colt was from him turning me down the night I asked him to make love to me.

Then, of course, there was the fact that my father seemed to think I couldn't take over the family business without Colt's help. Part of me knew I was being unfair to him. Colt's love and knowledge of horses would be an asset to our breeding business and my father could see that. And Colt explained his reasons for not making love to me that night. He said he wanted to make the first time we made love special and the back seat of his truck was not how he was going to do it. Even with that explanation, it still didn't lessen the blow when he turned me down. The embarrassment from that night still clung to my heart and was the main reason I avoided Colt. That, and the fact that anytime I was near him, I wanted to jump his bones.

Well, I'm not going to avoid Colt anymore. Tonight I would be a good friend and save him from the blonde who clearly wanted more than just a casual conversation.

"Excuse me, Grace. I can't pass up this moment. I'll be able to rub it in Colt's face later how I rescued him from this situation."

Grace laughed as I walked toward Colt. His grin turned to a full-blown smile as his eyes never left mine. His smile had always been my weakness. My heart raced faster the closer I got to him. Seeing the blonde out of the corner of my eye, I glanced to her. She was staring at me with daggers as I made my way over to them. Frowning, her eyes moved over my body. I knew I looked good. The chiffon, platinum-colored bridesmaid dresses that Libby picked out for us to wear fit me like a glove. Even Meg said my breasts looked killer in the dress. Colt couldn't keep his eyes off of me when I walked down the aisle.

Walking up to Colt and the blonde, I smiled bigger. "Hey, Colt."

"Hey, Lauren."

Turning, I smiled at the bitch. I mean, the blonde. "Hi. I'm Lauren. You are?"

Flashing me a fake smile, she said, "Tina."

I nodded my head. "Nice to meet you, Tina." Tilting my head slightly, I looked back at Colt. "You promised we would dance."

Colt's mouth fell open as he gave me a dazed look. He, of course, hadn't promised this. He hadn't even talked to me since last night when we got into another argument over something stupid. I didn't even remember what the fight was about, to be honest.

Quickly coming to his senses, Colt placed his hand on my arm. I prayed like hell he hadn't felt my whole body shudder under his touch. "Right. I wouldn't want to go back on a promise."

We started to walk off when the blonde reached for Colt's arm. "Wait! Is Lauren your girlfriend or are you ... free later?" Moving her eyes over his body while biting her lower lip, Tina gave Colt a naughty as hell smile.

What. A. Bitch.

Pulling his head back, Colt gave her an incredulous look. Good. I'm glad to see he was as shocked by her advance as I was. "Yes. Yes, she is, Tina. See you around."

Colt's hand slid down my arm as he took my hand in his. My heart jumped, and my stomach felt like I had just gone through about ten loops on a roller coaster. Leading me out to the dance floor, I turned and gave Tina a dirty look. "Oh my glitter! How rude. I mean . . . holy sheets! She practically asked you to screw her later. In front of me."

Colt's laugh was a low rumble as he spun me around and pulled me into his arms. I couldn't take my eyes off of Tina as we danced.

Placing his lips to my ear, Colt spoke. "Thank you."

Looking into Colt's eyes, my breathing increased. It was then I realized where I was. In Colt's arms. Up against his body. Really, really up against his body. How many times had I dreamed of Colt holding me in his arms again?

Too many times. Asshole. Ugh. I hate that he makes my body feel like this.

"Thank you for what?" I asked, lifting an eyebrow.

"Saving me from what was probably the worst conversation of my life."

Stifling my giggle, I couldn't help but glance at Colt's lips. He noticed because the bastard licked them.

Oh God. Oh God. Calm yourself, Lauren. Quickly looking away, I tried to focus on something else. Anything else.

"You look beautiful, Lauren."

Shit. Deep breaths, Lauren. Stay strong.

"Thanks. You look pretty handsome yourself," I said as I continued to scan the dance floor.

"How would you know? You've barely looked my way all morning."

My head snapped to him. "Are you kidding? I've been

staring at you for the last . . ."

Shit. Shit. Shit. Way to play it cool, Lauren. Hello, world. The Lauren who throws herself at Colt has finally shown up, and she's looking to get her heart stomped on again by him.

Closing my eyes, I dropped my head to Colt's chest. I wanted to crawl under a rock.

"Hey, Lauren. Please look at me."

Colt's voice was a whisper. A hot sounding whisper. A whisper that I imagined would sound pretty damn amazing in my ear as he made love to me.

Ugh! Stop this, Lauren.

I pulled my head back but didn't look up. Placing his finger under my chin, Colt lifted my eyes to him. "Lauren . . ."

His eyes fell to my lips as I instinctively licked them. Finally finding my voice, I whispered back, "Colt."

Colt leaned closer to me, and I felt his hot breath against my lips. I moved my hands to his arms and gripped them tightly. Feeling his muscles flex under my grip, I let out a small moan.

"Tell me what you want me to do, Lauren," Colt said as our eyes found each other again.

My heart was pounding so loudly, I barely heard his words.

Swallowing hard, I said, "Kiss me."

When Colt smiled, my entire world lit up. Swiping his lips across mine caused a tingling sensation to rip through my body. Colt slipped his hand behind my neck and pulled me to his lips. The kiss was soft and ultra slow. When he finally slipped his tongue into my mouth, I melted on the spot.

Moaning, I squeezed his arms as Colt pulled me even closer. I was totally lost in the kiss. Never mind the fact that my father and mother were somewhere in the same room as me. Or the fact that my heart was beating so loudly in my ears, I couldn't hear a thing. I enjoyed every single second of his lips on mine. When Colt finally pulled back, he bit down on my lower lip and sucked it gently before dropping it.

My chest heaved as I attempted to calm my breathing down. *Colt kissed me. Holy shit. He finally kissed me.*

Leaning my head against his chest, I smiled as Colt rested his chin on top of my head. My blonde hair was pulled up into a French twist with a few strands of curls framing my face. Colt reached up and played with a curl. My body was still trembling from our kiss.

Closing my eyes, I silently prayed Colt wouldn't break my heart again.

"I'm headed back to A&M shortly, Lauren. Come with me."

Pulling back, I looked into his eyes. They were filled with passion. My mouth opened but words wouldn't form. Clearing my throat, I asked, "What are you saying, Colt?"

If there was one thing Colt Mathews could do, and do well, was swoon the hell out of me with his smile. And boy was he swooning me right now. My knees felt weak as Colt flashed me the smile that I had fallen in love with a few years back. That stupid crooked smile I dreamed about every single night.

"I'm asking you to let me make you mine, Lauren."

Holy mother of God. Play it cool, Lauren. Play. It. Cool. Colt wants to make me his!

Swallowing hard, I asked . . . again, "What are you saying, Colt?"

Colt chuckled. Pulling me closer to him, he moved his lips to my ear. "I've been wanting to make you mine for so long, Lauren. I can't bear to wait any longer."

My lips parted open. "Me? I . . . um . . . I've never . . . ahh . . . what about . . ." For the love of all things good. My mind was swirling with images of Colt making love to me. Colt naked. Colt kissing my body. Colt touching my body. My eyes widened in horror. The one thing I wanted so badly for the last few years I was about to lose because I couldn't form a damn sentence.

Colt lifted his hand and gently brushed the back of it down my face. "I'm scared too, Lauren. You're the only woman I've ever dreamed of being with." Closing his eyes for a brief moment before opening them again, he whispered, "I've never been with anyone, Lauren. My first time I wanted to be with someone I cared about, someone I loved."

Oh. My. Glitter. Swoon alert! We have a major swoon alert. My legs gave out, and Colt grabbed a hold of me. "Lauren, are you okay?" Colt asked as concern swept over his face.

"You waited for me? I mean, you're . . . a . . . um? Wait, someone you love?"

Colt pulled me closer as he nodded. I felt his desire pushing into my stomach. Something washed over me, and I found my senses. Grabbing onto his arms again, I smiled. "I've waited for you too, Colt. Every time I dreamed of being with someone, I dreamt it was you."

Taking a few steps back, Colt winked at me as a wicked grin grew across his face. "Follow my lead."

Turning quickly, he walked off. As if nothing amazing had just happened between us. He just said he loved me. *Well wait. Did he say he loved me? He didn't come right out and say it, but he implied it. Didn't he?*

Looking back, Colt motioned for me to come on. Snapping out of my stupor, I quickly followed Colt. He was headed over to Gunner and Ellie. Grinning, Gunner looked at Colt, then me. I wondered if my face looked like it felt. Hot and on fire.

"Hey, buddy, enjoying yourself?" Gunner asked as he reached out his hand for Colt.

Shaking his father's hand, Colt answered, "Yes, sir, I am."

Ellie turned toward me and gave me the sweetest smile. "Lauren, sweetheart, how is school going?"

As much as I would have liked standing there and chit-chatting with Gunner and Ellie, I really wanted Colt to take me home and make me his. "Good. It's going good. Busy, but I'm really enjoying my second year."

"That's wonderful. Your daddy was talking about you the other night. He's so proud of you."

Ellie mentioning my father right then was kind of putting a damper on things. Nodding, I gave her a weak smile in return.

"Dad, I'm going to head back to A&M and bring Lauren. There is a project she's never done before, and she needs my help."

Snapping my head over to Colt, I felt my face turn red. Gunner glanced at me and then back to Colt and gave Colt a wink. "Y'all aren't going to kill each other on the way there, are you?"

Colt and I both let out an awkward laugh. "We're gonna try not to," I said as I peeked over to Colt.

Feeling them before I saw them, I turned to my parents who had walked up and stood before me. "Hey, sweetheart. Are you coming back to the house with us or staying with the girls?" my mother asked as she reached over and pushed one of my blonde curls from my eye. I looked just like my mother. Blonde hair, blue eyes. Everyone said I was a mini version of my mother on the outside, but inside I was all my dad.

"I'm actually going to head back to A&M with Colt. I've got a . . . um . . . a project I've got to get done."

Nodding, my father looked over to Colt. "Y'all have to leave now? You don't want to wait until tomorrow morning?"

Remembering I had a class first thing Monday morning, I quickly said, "No! No, I can't because I've got a test first Monday morning, and I missed Thursday's class for the wedding."

"All right, well let me have a kiss and a hug. We'll see you in a month for spring break, right?" my father asked as he pulled me into his arms.

Giving my father a hug and kiss good-bye, I turned to my mother and repeated the process. "Yep, as of now, I'm still planning on spring break at home," I said with a smile.

Daddy reached for Colt's hand and shook it as he said, "Be careful driving, Colt; that's a long drive back."

Nodding his head and giving that damn smile of his, Colt said, "Always, sir." Turning to his parents, Colt kissed his mother good-bye on the cheek and told her how much he loved her, as he shook his father's hand. Glancing over at me, Colt asked, "Shall we, Lauren?" as he began leading me away from our parents.

Oh my glitter. Oh my glitter. Oh my glitter. I'm leaving with Colt. I'm heading back to A&M with Colt. Breathe in through the mouth. Out through the nose. Looking down at my hands as I wrung them together, I took a deep breath. *What am I, in junior high?* This was insane. I needed to chill the hell out.

Colt placed his hand on the small of my back and butterflies ignited in my stomach. "We need to find Luke and Libby and . . ."

"No we don't," I practically shouted, "we need to get out of here, now."

Colt leaned over and asked, "Lauren, are you okay?"

Stopping, I looked into Colt's eyes. They were breathtaking. Blue like the sky behind him. "I don't think I can wait until we get back to A&M, Colt." Shaking my head, I whispered, "I want to feel you inside me."

Colt's face beamed as a wide grin appeared and my heart began to race with excitement. "Luke and Libby know we love them; we'll chip in and buy them a great gift."

Nodding my head quickly, I said, "Perfect!"

Reaching for my hand, Colt pulled me toward his truck. "Colt, all my stuff is at Josh and Heather's house."

Colt practically pulled my arm out of its socket. Looking back over my shoulder, no one even paid attention to us as we quickly left the reception. No one that is, but Grace. Lifting her hand and giving me a wave, I waved back and smiled. Shaking her head, she turned on her heels and walked off.

Colt stopped and opened his truck door as he took my hand and helped me up and into his truck. Leaning into the truck, his eyes captured mine. They were on fire as I sucked in a breath. "Where we're going, Lauren, you're not going to need your purse, or clothes."

My eyes widened as I simply said, "Oh." Swallowing, I cleared my throat and said, "What about my cell phone? Or money?"

"I have a phone and I have money."

Slowly nodding, I whispered, "Clean panties for tomorrow?"

Colt lifted his eyebrows as he attempted not to laugh. "Do you want your bag, sweetheart?"

"I'd feel better knowing I had my stuff. If that's okay?"

Reaching in further, he kissed me on the nose and my stomach dropped at the sweet gesture. "Of course it is."

Moving quickly, he buckled me in, shut the door and made his way over to the driver's side of his truck.

I wasn't sure how Colt and I went from totally avoiding each other, to fighting like cats and dogs, to leaving our best friends' wedding to go somewhere so we could be alone. Smiling, I shook my head because I didn't care. I wanted this. I'd wanted it for so long. I was just too stupid and stubborn to admit it to myself. Libby and Alex had found love and happiness. I wanted that too, and I knew Colt was the only one who would be able to give me both.

Ten minutes later, I was running up the stairs to Josh and Heather's house. I used the key I had and ran as fast as I could in my heels and dress up the stairs and to Libby's room. Gathering up my things, I shoved it all into my overnight bag. Turning, I looked around for Alex's bag. Seeing it on the floor, I smiled as I reached down and picked it up. Overhearing Alex early this morning, I heard her tell Grace she had packed two outfits for Will, but she wasn't sure she would get to use them if the parents didn't all stay in one house.

Something blue caught my eye as I reached in and pulled out a beautiful blue satin, barely there, piece of lingerie. Clutching it to my chest, I whispered, "Perfect."

Shoving the lingerie in my bag, I skipped down the stairs and out to Colt's truck. *Finally, Colt was going to make me his.*

TWO

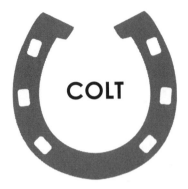

COLT

S ITTING IN MY truck, I tapped the steering wheel to calm my nerves. What had happened in the last hour? I went from observing Lauren from across the room, to asking her to let me make love to her.

What if I fuck this up? What if I don't make it special enough for her? My father's words from three years ago invaded my mind.

"Colt, make sure it's something you both want. Be gentle and think about her one hundred percent of the time. Show her how much she means to you above all. Remind her how much you love her. The moment can never be repeated."

The door to Josh and Heather's beach house opened, and Lauren came bouncing out. Shaking my head, I couldn't help but smile. Lauren was so full of life. She made sure to live each day with as much zest as she could.

As she moved closer to the truck, my heartbeat increased. I wanted to take her back to A&M, but when Lauren said she couldn't wait, I knew I had better check us into a hotel. The last thing I wanted to do was end up taking her in my truck.

The door opened and Lauren threw her bag onto the back seat. Hopping up into the truck, she shut the door and turned to me with a look of sheer panic on her face.

"I'm scared shitless, Colt."

Laughing, I nodded my head. "Me too, Lauren."

Her smile would have knocked me off my feet had I been standing. "I know you want to wait until we get back to A&M . . . but I don't think I can." Her eyes glanced down. "Colt, I've wanted you for so long, and I'm tired of fighting it."

Swallowing hard, I started the truck and made my way to the ferry. Luke had told me about a new hotel in Rockport that he had looked into for their wedding night, but something fell through and they weren't going to be able to stay there. It would be perfect for Lauren and me.

"Do you know where you're going?" Lauren asked.

Reaching over, I grabbed her hand as I nodded. "Yep, if we can't be home, I think I've got the next-best place."

PULLING DOWN A long driveway, I stopped in front of a giant white plantation-style house. Lauren leaned over and let out a gasp. "Colt, this is beautiful." Turning back to me, she wore a radiant glow as she looked in my eyes. "It's perfect," she whispered.

Placing my hand behind her neck, I pulled her to me as I gently kissed her lips. The driver's side door opened and I heard someone clear his throat. Lauren smiled against my lips and said, "I think they're waiting for us."

"Let them wait." Kissing her again, I sucked her lower lip into my mouth as Lauren let out a soft moan. When our kiss finally broke, Lauren turned and stepped out of the truck. With my heart racing, I followed.

"Good afternoon, sir. Welcome to the St. Claire. How many nights will you be staying with us?"

"One," I said as I opened the back door and reached in for my backpack that I always carried in my truck, and Lauren's bag.

Turning to the valet, I reached for his arm. "Dude, take care of her. She's my life."

Glancing to the truck and back to me, the valet nodded

14

his head and gave me an understanding smile. "I'll be sure to keep her in a safe spot for you, sir."

Giving him a quick handshake, I said, "Perfect. I appreciate that."

Walking up to Lauren, I placed my hand on her lower back and gently guided her into the hotel. Seeing my father do this to my mother all the time, I knew women must like it from the reaction my mother always had.

As we walked up to the front desk, Lauren turned and gave me the sexiest look I'd ever seen. My dick jumped in my pants and I prayed to God I didn't come the moment I saw her naked. My hands shook as I reached for my wallet in my back pocket.

"Good afternoon. Welcome to the St. Claire. Do you have a reservation?"

Nodding my head, I smiled. "Yes, I called not too long ago. Colt Mathews." After pulling up their website, I had called and booked the reservation as we rode over on the ferry and Lauren watched the dolphins.

"Yes, I have it here. I see y'all are celebrating a special occasion."

Lauren's head jerked up as she looked between the desk agent and me as excitement danced in her eyes. My hands began to sweat as my heart pounded in my chest. *Lauren and I were finally going to be together.* "Yes we are, indeed. Tonight is a very special night for us."

The desk agent gave me a tender smile as she typed away on her keyboard. "Looks like I have the perfect room for you."

After giving her my credit card and getting our key, Lauren and I headed up to the third floor. As we stepped off the elevator, we stood before one door. "Is this the only room on this floor?" Lauren asked. Shrugging, I looked around. "I guess so."

Lauren jumped as she clapped her hands. "Oh my gosh! I can't wait to see it."

Smiling, I handed her the key and watched as she rushed to the door, inserting the key card, Lauren let out a gasp as she walked into the room. Following behind her,

I almost let out a gasp myself. We were in the St. Charles room. I'd seen it on their website. It occupied the entire third floor of the hotel and had a view of the bay.

Lauren turned and looked at me, her mouth parted slightly open. "This is beautiful," she whispered.

Fist pumping internally, I walked over and pulled her to me. "Not as beautiful as you, Lauren."

Closing her eyes tightly, she opened them. They were filled with tears and my breath left my lungs. "Sweetheart, what's wrong?" I asked as I dropped the bags I was carrying and cupped her face.

"I'm so sorry, Colt."

Looking at her with a confused look, I asked, "Sorry for what, Lauren?"

Placing her hands on my arms, she was barely able to speak. "I'm so sorry for pushing you away, for hurting you with the things I said and did, and for Roger."

Roger. Oh God. She slept with Roger. I felt sick to my stomach and I wanted to take a step away, but I didn't.

"Roger?" I asked as my voice cracked.

Her eyes widened in horror. "No. Oh God no, Colt. I never slept with him. I knew it would drive you crazy if I dated him and that's why I did. He tried a few times to get me to sleep with him, but . . ."

My heart slammed in my chest, and I made plans to beat the fuck out of that asshole when I saw him again.

"But?"

"I always knew my heart belonged to you. As much as I tried to fight it . . . it only grew stronger. I'm so scared of my feelings for you and then everything with my father and the ranch. I thought it was easier to push you away than admit you were everything I've ever wanted."

Her words flowed through my mind as I let them soak in. My heart felt like it might explode with Lauren saying I was all she's ever wanted.

You were everything I've ever wanted.

Leaning in to her, I brushed my lips against hers. "Tell me, Lauren. Tell me what you want, baby."

Closing her eyes, she held onto me tighter. "You, Colt.

I want you."

Reaching behind Lauren's back, I began to unzip the dress she wore. She had looked beautiful today and I was pretty sure my pants grew ten times too small when I watched her walk down the aisle. Her beauty was unlike anything I had ever seen before.

"Lauren, are you nervous?"

Nodding her head, she whispered, "Yes."

Taking a step back, I looked into her eyes. "I used to dream about being with you, Lauren. I had everything planned out in my mind on how I wanted it to be for us." Closing my eyes, I thought back to my dreams. Opening them, I reached up and pushed the dress off of her body and watched as it pooled on the floor.

Lauren stood before me, dressed in a white strapless bra and matching lace panties. Her body was beyond anything I could have dreamed of. Lauren appeared to be confident, yet shy. I could see she wanted to look away, but she held her gaze. "And how do I compare to your dreams?"

Taking a step closer, I kissed her neck as she let out whimper. Between each kiss, I spoke. "Oh, Lauren." Kissing along her neck, I moved down. "My dreams could never have prepared me for your perfection."

Reaching behind her, I unclasped her bra and watched it fall to the ground. Letting out a moan, I took her breasts into my hands. They fit perfectly. I rubbed my thumbs across her nipples as she dropped her head back and moaned. My body felt as if it was on fire. "Colt, your touch is amazing. My body feels like it is on fire." Smiling, I kissed her lips quickly.

Dropping to my knees, I kissed around her belly button. Slipping my fingers into the top of her lace panties, I slowly took them off of her as she lifted each leg to remove them.

Taking a look at her, I fought like hell not to come in my pants. Jesus H. Christ. She was perfect. Lifting my eyes back up to hers, I could see she was nervous. I wanted to ask her how far she had gone with Roger, but I also didn't want to ruin the mood.

Lifting her leg, I placed it over my shoulder as I watched her eyes widen in anticipation of what I was going to do. My body tingled all over at the idea of being so intimate with Lauren. It was as if she could read my mind. Wetting her lips, she whispered, "I've never . . . I mean no one has ever . . ."

Smiling, I moved in closer and gently blew on her sensitive skin. "Never, Lauren?"

Frantically shaking her head, Lauren closed her eyes and said, "Never. It never felt right."

I placed my lips above her clit and gently kissed her as she sucked in a breath of air. Knowing I would be the first to do this made me happier than I thought. I was dying to taste her. Moving her leg off of me, I quickly stood up, and scooped Lauren into my arms. She let out a playful scream as I carried her across the room. "I need to know what you taste like, Lauren."

"Oh, God," Lauren whispered as I gently placed her down on the king-sized bed.

Looking at Lauren laid out on the bed, I let out a moan. I quickly undressed myself as Lauren watched. Pushing my pants down, I watched her eyes as they landed on my hard dick, hidden behind my boxer briefs. Lauren sat up and quickly moved to the edge of the bed.

"Wait," she said as she knelt before me. "I want to remove them," she said as her voice cracked. As she lifted her hands, I couldn't help but notice they were shaking. I knew she was nervous, and I'm sure she was scared out of her mind. Hell, I was scared out of my mind.

Placing her hands on my stomach, she smiled. "Your body, Colt . . . it's amazing."

Closing my eyes briefly before opening them again, I held my breath as Lauren bit down on her lip as she stared at my dick. Slowly pushing my briefs down, she never stopped staring. I was beginning to have a complex. Surely she'd seen a dick before. I couldn't imagine with her dating she had never gotten a guy off with her hand.

Fuck. Why am I thinking of Lauren being with other guys? What the hell is wrong with me? Shaking my head to clear my thoughts, I kicked my briefs off to the side. My body jumped when Lauren took me in her hand.

Please don't come. Please don't come. Fuck . . . think of something else, Mathews. Lauren's hand slowly moved up and down my rock-hard shaft. I was so hard, I actually ached.

Movies . . . I wonder what movies are coming out this weekend? The moment she took me into her mouth, I about lost it. Pulling back, I dropped down to my knees. "No! Holy fucking shit, Lauren."

Lauren jumped back. "Did I do something wrong? Oh God, I've never done that before, Colt, but I really, really wanted to, and I'm so sorry if I did something wrong. Shit! Shit! Shit!"

I looked into her frightened eyes, and I was elated knowing she had never given a guy a blowjob. Attempting to find my voice, I smiled the same smile I noticed seemed to make Lauren's eyes light up. "No, sweetheart. God no, you didn't do a damn thing wrong. I don't want to come before I even get a chance to be inside you."

The fear in her eyes was replaced with desire. "Really?"

Letting out a small chuckle, I nodded. "Really."

The blush that moved across her cheeks was the sexiest thing I'd ever seen. "Now lie back, baby. I'm going to get that taste of you now."

Lauren's chest heaved up and down as she scooted her ass up the bed and laid her head down on the pillow. Crawling onto the bed, I pushed her legs open to me. I'd never seen anything so amazing in my life.

I began to kiss her inner thigh as Lauren made the sweetest little noises. Reaching her lips, I licked up from the bottom of her pussy to her clit. Lauren's back arched off the bed as she cried out in pleasure.

Grinning, I was about to make Lauren completely mine. Burying my face between her legs, I moaned as I worked her with my tongue.

Finally, Lauren is mine.

THREE

LAUREN

T HE MOMENT COLT'S tongue touched me, it felt as if I left my body. Okay . . . not really . . . but it was the most amazing thing I'd ever felt. The furthest I'd ever let a guy go was finger fucking me. It had been nice and the orgasms pretty good, but this. Oh God, this was going to rock my world.

Placing my hands on Colt's head, I moved my hips as he continued to work his magic. It wasn't going to take long before I came and came hard.

Whispering his name over and over, my eyes about rolled into the back of my head as I felt my build up. I'd never experienced anything like this before. Colt slipped his fingers inside me, and I lost all control. My orgasm felt as if I was taken to utopia and left to float around for a bit.

Colt did something with his fingers and I felt a spilt second of pain, but my orgasm was too intense for me to really notice.

When he finally pulled his face away and looked at me, my breathing was so erratic I couldn't speak. I was pretty sure I didn't have just one orgasm, but two.

"Colt . . . that . . . was . . . so amazing!" I panted between breaths.

Moving up along my body, Colt placed gentle kisses as he softly spoke to me. "Lauren, I've never experienced such bliss as I am being with you right now. The taste of you was sweeter than I could have ever imagined."

Oh God. I'm going to come again just from him talking. Colt wasn't just handsome as hell, he was utterly the most romantic man I'd ever met.

My body shuddered as he moved further along. Settling between my legs, he placed his hands on the sides of my face. "May I kiss you, Lauren?"

Swallowing hard, I asked, "After you just did that?" I wasn't too sure how I felt about Colt kissing me after oral sex.

His smile lifted on the left side as Colt stole more of my heart. His blue eyes pierced mine as if he was looking into my soul.

"I won't if you don't want me to, baby."

Did I want him to? It was kind of gross thinking about it, but I put his dick in my mouth and I knew he would have kissed me afterward. Chewing on my lip I realized I was way overthinking this.

"Kiss me, Colt."

Pressing his lips to mine, I opened my mouth to him. Colt moaned when our tongues began to dance with each other. Not being able to describe the taste in my mouth, I let myself get lost in his kiss and decided I liked this. It felt as if it brought us closer together.

I could feel Colt's dick pressing against me, and I began to grind my hips against him. I knew he didn't have a condom on, and we would need to be careful. "Colt, you feel so good, oh God. It feels so good." I'd always imagined it would be magical being with Colt. But this . . . this was beyond anything I could have imagined.

He was rubbing against my clit and it didn't take long before I was moaning into Colt's mouth as another orgasm raced through my body. Pulling my mouth from Colt's, I panted out, "More. Colt, I want more of you. Please."

Running his nose lightly across my jawline, Colt let out a soft low moan. "Baby, the more orgasms you have, the more relaxed you'll be."

"Colt, please."

Pulling back, Colt gazed into my eyes. I wasn't sure, but something had changed between us, and I knew we would never go back to the way things were. Gone were the days of fighting and pushing each other away. Something in Colt's eyes caused me to tear up. Placing his hand on the side of my face, Colt lightly brushed his thumb across my skin. "Lauren, I want you to know something before we do this."

Nodding my head, I barely spoke above a whisper. "Okay."

"I saved myself for you, because I knew the first time I made love to a woman, it was going to be with the woman I loved more than the air I breathed. My heart wants no other woman but you, Lauren."

Wow. I've died and gone to heaven. I have officially been swept off my feet. I've. Been. Swooned.

A single tear slipped from my eye as Colt's eyes followed it. Reaching down, his lips gently kissed my cheek. "I love you, Lauren Reynolds. Please, will you be mine?"

Wrapping my arms around Colt, I cried harder. Colt moved and sat on the bed as he pulled me into his lap and held me. When I was finally able to form words, I spoke. "Colt, you've made every one of my dreams come true today. I love you, too, and I want nothing more than to be forever yours."

Colt's eyes lit up and I swore they sparkled like diamonds. He laid me down gently and kissed my lips before turning and reaching for his wallet and pulled out a condom. Standing over me, he never took his eyes from mine. Oh how I've longed for Colt to make love to me. Although I was scared as hell, I was excited, curious, and full of questions that I needed him to answer for me, not only with his mouth, but with his body as well.

Wetting my lips, I watched as Colt rolled the condom on. Instinctively, I opened my legs as Colt moved back onto the bed. He slipped his fingers inside of me and slowly pushed in and pulled out. "Fuck," he hissed through his teeth. "You're so wet, Lauren."

Hearing those words fall from Colt's lips did something

to me. I wanted to hear Colt talk to me like that more.

Moving over me, Colt leaned in and kissed me again. When he bit down on my lower lip, I lifted my hips and felt his dick pushing against me.

I was finally going to be with Colt. No more waking up in the middle of the night with my hands down my panties as I dreamt of his touch. He was finally taking what was his all along.

Kissing along my neck, Colt moved his lips to my ear and nibbled on my earlobe as he spoke in the most seductive voice I'd ever heard.

"I'm going to make love to you now, sweetheart. Please promise me you'll tell me if I hurt you."

The moment I had been dreaming of was finally here. I felt as if I was already on cloud nine and my mind was in a whirlwind.

Would it hurt? Would it feel good? Colt was thick . . . and long . . . and thick. Oh fuck. It's gonna hurt like a son-of-a-bitch. Squeezing my eyes shut, I attempted to quiet the voices in my head as Colt continued to build me up with his kisses and the touch of his hands on my breasts. If he pulled and twisted my nipple once more, I was going to scream out in ultimate pleasure.

"Lauren . . . promise me."

Gasping for air, I quickly said, "I promise! Colt, I promise. Please, I can't wait a second more. Do it now!" I knew I sounded desperate, but I didn't care. I'd waited too long for this and I wanted it now.

Colt chuckled and said, "My impatient girl. You always were bossy, Lauren."

Positioning himself at my entrance, Colt pushed in some and I sucked in a breath of air.

Fuck. This. Is. Gonna. Hurt.

Pulling back out, Colt pushed in again, this time going further. Gripping his arms, I attempted to relax.

"Baby, relax and let me in."

A tear fell from my eye as I watched Colt's face fall. "I'm trying, Colt. I'm so scared though."

Kissing me, Colt whispered against my lips. "Sweetheart,

please don't be scared."

Taking in a deep breath, I slowly let it out. "I'm more excited than scared, but what if I do something wrong, Colt?"

Pulling back, Colt looked at me and winked. "If you did, baby, I wouldn't know."

His expression beamed and the fluttering in my stomach took off as I laughed. Colt pushed in more as I laughed, causing me to call out, "Oh God."

Placing his hands on the sides of my face, Colt kissed me as he gently moved in and out of me. Going deeper with each push in. Relaxing a bit, I let my legs fall open more as Colt let out a long deep groan. "I'm all the way in, Lauren, and you feel so incredibly amazing. It's like nothing I could have ever imagined."

Pain mixed with pleasure as Colt's words filled my mind. "Colt, I love you."

Pulling out slowly, he pushed in again a bit harder. Moaning, he whispered, "Baby, I love you. Oh God, Lauren. I don't want to ever stop."

It didn't take long for my body to finally adjust to Colt's thickness. The pain slowly faded away with each movement, although the dull ache seemed to hang on. As Colt moved, I started to meet him, thrust for thrust. It was the most amazing feeling in the world, Colt making love to me. Kissing me as if I was the very air he breathed in. I would never forget this day for the rest of my life.

Never.

FOUR

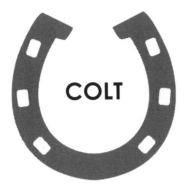

COLT

N OTHING COULD HAVE ever prepared me for the way it felt to make love to Lauren. I was in utter bliss. The sounds of her soft moans, the feel of her meeting me with every movement was magical. Feeling her body shudder, I knew she was about to come. The moment she clamped down on my dick, I was going to explode inside her.

Arching her back, Lauren called out my name as I felt her pussy squeeze around my dick. "Colt! Oh God!"

I fought like hell to hold off until I didn't feel her pulses around my dick anymore. Jesus H. Christ, I was going to come hard.

Pushing in harder and faster, Lauren's eyes rolled back and she called out my name again. *Holy fuck, she was coming again.* Pushing in as far as I could, I let out a moan and felt my cum pouring into the condom. I'd never had an orgasm last that long.

Coming to my senses, I looked down at Lauren. Her eyes were filled with tears, but she wore the most beautiful smile. Her face blushed from the round of lovemaking we had just shared together. Our bodies were covered in a sheen of sweat as we both breathed shallow. "Did I hurt you, Lauren?"

Slowly shaking her head, she whispered, "Colt, that was . . . it was so magical. Not even in my most wildest dreams . . . did I ever think it would be so . . . beautiful."

My dick twitched inside of her, but I didn't want to pull out. Not yet. Placing my lips against hers, I kissed her softly. "You're mine, Lauren. My everything."

Wrapping her arms and legs around me, she giggled. "And you're mine."

Slowly pulling out, I instantly missed her warmth. Looking down on the bed, I saw the evidence of Lauren's virginity. *Shit, we should have put a towel down first.*

Lauren's eyes widened in shock as she looked at the blood-covered condom and then down at the bed. "Oh God," she whispered.

Quickly removing the condom, I tossed it in the trash. Reaching down for Lauren's hand, I pulled her up and brought her into my arms. "I'm going to run us a hot bath so we can relax in it."

Lauren's entire body flushed at the mention of us taking a bath together. "Okay, sounds good," Lauren said as her eyes glanced around the room. We hadn't even taken a look around first.

"Are you okay, sweetheart?" I asked as I took Lauren's hands in mine.

Nodding and flashing me the most beautiful smile I'd ever seen, Lauren replied back, "I've never been better, Colt. My body feels . . . alive."

Looking around, I asked, "Where in the hell is the bathroom?"

Laughing, Lauren pulled the sheet from the bed, wrapped it around her body, and began skipping around the room. Walking around a corner, I heard her let out a squeal.

"Colt! Holy sheets! You have to see this bathroom."

Reaching down and grabbing my briefs, I quickly put them on as I made my way to where Lauren was. Walking into the giant bathroom, my mouth fell open.

"Mother of all bathrooms," I whispered as my eyes roamed the room. Directly in front of me was a giant soaker tub that was perched up on a step platform. Beyond that were three sets of French doors that led out to a balcony that overlooked the water.

Walking into the bathroom more, Lauren spun around and looked up. My eyes followed her gaze and I saw the tray ceiling with a huge chandelier hanging right over the tub. To my left along the entire wall were distressed white cabinets with granite countertops. The bowl sink sat in the middle of the cabinets and further down toward the window was a long bench with a leather cushion on it. The opposite side of the bathroom had matching cabinets, countertops and sink but there was a small vanity at the end by the French doors. I'd never in my life seen a bathroom this big.

Lauren had made her way over to the French doors and pushed them open as she said, "This is bigger than both our bedrooms back at A&M!" She was about to step out onto the balcony when I quickly grabbed her and pulled her to me.

"Where in the hell do you think you're going naked and wrapped up in a sheet?" Lauren spun around and gave me the sweetest smile. My heart slammed against my chest as I gazed upon her beautiful face. Her blue eyes reminded me of the sky right after a rainstorm. Her hair, the color of straw with small streaks of darker blonde running through it cascaded over her shoulders. I loved when she pulled her hair up into a messy bun and piled it on top of her head. Walking into the house on more than one occasion, Lauren had been on the sofa studying. I had to fight the urge to take her every single time. She was beyond attractive, and the fact that she had no clue made her even more beautiful.

Reaching up, I pulled the sheet off her body and threw it to the side. "You're too beautiful to cover up."

Biting down on her lip, Lauren reached up on her tiptoes and brushed her lips against mine as she whispered, "Please tell me I'm not dreaming, Colt. Tell me this is real and that we are together. That we're not fighting or pushing each other away."

Cupping my hands on her face, I kissed her with everything I had. Lauren's hands gripped onto my forearms as we both moaned into each other's mouths. Needing air, I pulled slightly away from Lauren and looked into her eyes. "Let me prove to you, sweetheart, that you're not dreaming."

"O-okay," Lauren whispered as the most beautiful rose color moved across her cheeks.

Dropping my hands, I walked over to the tub and began filling it up. There was a small bottle of jasmine bath gel that also read bubble bath, sitting next to the complimentary soap and shampoo. Opening the cap, I poured some gel into the hot water as I glanced over my shoulder. Lauren was standing before me, gloriously naked. Jutting her lip out into a pout, Lauren said, "You still have your briefs on, Colt. That doesn't seem very fair."

Standing, I never took my eyes off of Lauren as I pushed my briefs down. My dick was instantly hard as Lauren's eyes meandered over my body. Her nipples perked and I found myself moving to her and placing one in my mouth as she dropped her head back and whimpered.

Stepping back, I took Lauren's hands and walked her up the two steps to the bathtub. "Sit down on the edge of the tub, baby."

Watching Lauren's chest as it began to heave up and down and knowing it was because of me, was the greatest feeling in the world. I wanted to make her feel cherished always.

Lauren sat on the edge of the tub and chewed on her lower lip. Going to the side of her, I kissed her gently on her neck as she let out a small whimper. "Colt."

Moving my tongue along her jawline, I whispered into her ear, "I've never been so happy, Lauren. I've dreamed about being with you for so long, but nothing could have prepared me for how amazing it felt to be inside you."

Dropping her head back, Lauren let out a contented sigh. "I firmly believe that I am *not* dreaming."

Laughing, I pushed her back into the giant soaker tub. Lauren came up from the water laughing as she pulled me into the tub with her. Water splashed everywhere as Lauren and I tangled up within each other. Pulling her toward me,

I leaned against the back of the tub while Lauren sat between my legs. The warmth of the water felt like heaven.

Placing my lips on the top of her head, I kissed her gently as her whole body relaxed into mine as bubbles popped while Lauren moved her hand lightly around in the water.

"Thank you, Colt."

Wrapping my arms around her, I asked, "For what?"

Dropping her head back and tilting her head so that she could look me in the eyes, she said, "For making this the most magical day of my life. I'll never forget it as long as I live."

Grinning, I gave her a wink and kissed her forehead. She looked forward and settled back into me. Closing my eyes, I wanted to ask her to pinch me to make sure I wasn't dreaming. The one girl whom I had fallen in love with in high school, who I had fought for the last two years to push my feelings away from her, who I had spent countless nights dreaming about, was finally in my arms.

My plan from this moment on was to love her with everything I had. I was never letting Lauren go.

She was mine.

Finally.

FIVE

LAUREN

T HE MOMENT I sank down into the hot tub, I wanted to sigh in relief. My body had never felt so blissful. Yet at the same time, I was sore as hell.

I wonder if anyone will be able to tell? Like when I walk down the street, will they look at me and think, that girl lost her virginity last night. To a very well endowed man, I might add.

Sighing contently, I let the feeling of being in Colt's arms sink in. The way Colt spoke to me while he made love to me had my heart beating almost out of my chest. I'd never felt so loved. So admired. Roger never made me feel like he was taking care of me. The most he ever did was suck on my breasts and finger me. Once he realized I was not giving him what he wanted he gave me an ultimatum. Either move on from my so called, infatuation with Colt and have sex with him, or walk away. I choose to walk away and continue to admire Colt from afar.

Dropping my head back against Colt's chest, I let out a sigh. "We wasted so much time, Colt."

Holding me tighter, he whispered, "I know."

Leaning forward, I spun around in the tub. The hot water felt heavenly on my poor va-jay-jay. "I don't want to waste any more. Now that you're mine, I don't want to miss a single moment of time, Colt."

Giving me that crooked smile of his that has melted my heart since I could remember, Colt nodded his head. "Not a single moment."

Reaching under the water, I grabbed his dick and began moving my hand. Colt dropped his head back and moaned. Listening to him make those sounds was such a turn on.

I wonder if I could be brazen enough to crawl onto him and sink down on his dick? *Why not? I can do this.*

Smiling, I watched him get worked up. Moving quickly, I positioned myself and sank down onto him. The burning sensation caused me to take a sharp intake of air, but I pushed past it and quickly began riding him.

Colt's head snapped forward. "Shit! Lauren, baby, what are you doing?"

Giving him a sexy grin, I purred, "I'm riding my cowboy."

Water splashed all around us as I moved liked I was an expert and knew what I was doing. Maegan would be so proud of me. This was one of the hottest moments of my life. Colt's eyes danced with a desire I'd never seen before and it was because of me.

Dropping my head back, I played with my breasts. Colt mumbled something I couldn't understand as he placed his hands on my hips and helped me. Pulling me and up and slamming me back down onto him, I let out a moan. This way felt so different. It felt deeper and Colt felt bigger. Pulling on my nipples and twisting them, Colt gripped onto me harder. "Motherfucker, Lauren. Hottest fucking thing I've ever seen is my girl riding me and playing with her breasts."

Smiling, I went faster, harder. I was sore, but the hot water seemed to be helping, or maybe the friction of the water was making it feel more amazing. Whatever it was, I didn't want this feeling to end.

"Tell me what you want me to do, Colt."

Colt's eyes turned dark and my mouth parted open slightly. "Fuck me, Lauren."

Mother of all things good. Colt talked dirty to me. And

I liked it. I liked it a lot. "Yes," I called out as I did what he asked.

Placing my hands on the sides of the tub, I used the leverage to lift up and slam back down onto Colt. My body was being worked up into a frenzy. Colt leaned forward and took a nipple into his mouth and began sucking and pulling on it. "Jesus, what is happening? Colt! Oh God, Colt!"

"Fuck yes, Lauren." Dropping his head back, Colt let out a low growl from the back of his throat.

My orgasm began to build in a painfully slow way. *Would it always feel like this? I wonder why it feels so good? The water? The way I was positioned over him? Colt's amazing penis? Oh God . . . I can't believe I just called it a penis! I hate that word. Focus, Lauren! Focus!*

Shaking my head, I focused on squeezing myself around Colt's dick and that's when it hit. "Ohmygod! Colt!"

My whole body trembled as my orgasm hit me full force. I wanted to scream out *Yes! Yes! Yes!* But all I could think of was a cheesy porn flick. So I screamed out Colt's name.

The next thing I knew, I heard Colt. "Fuck! Fuck! Fuck!"

Okay, if Colt can do it . . . so can I! "Yes! Yes! Oh God, yes!"

Pulling me off of him, Colt jerked back and let out a grunt. His face was amazing and I was pretty sure he was coming, but why did he push me away?

Oh no. He didn't like the porn movie talk!

When he finally seemed to come to his senses, I felt embarrassed for the way I had acted.

Looking away, I said, "I'm sorry. I didn't mean to act so . . . brazen like that, Colt."

Standing up, I stepped out of the tub and grabbed a towel. Shit. It was soaking wet from our little fucking escapade. Glancing around, I carefully walked across the room and pulled another towel down from the shelf. I was so embarrassed, I didn't want to even turn and face Colt. Taking a chance, I peeked over my shoulder. Colt was sitting in the tub, staring straight ahead with a stricken look etched on his face, trying to catch his breath.

Wrapping the towel around myself, I cleared my throat. "I'm sorry, I didn't mean to act so . . ."

Colt turned and looked at me. Shaking his head, he asked, "Wait. What?"

Looking down, I barley mumbled, "I'm going to guess you didn't like that? I just got so turned on and it felt so incredible. I'm so sorry, Colt."

His eyes widened as he stood up. I let out a whimper as I let my eyes roam across his body. My God. He had the most amazing body I'd ever seen. The way his muscles moved as he moved was hot as hell. I wanted to run my tongue along his V under his abs and take his dick into my . . .

Shaking my head, I pushed my naughty thoughts away. *Stay in control, Lauren. Control is the key here.*

Colt stepped out of the tub and walked directly over to me. Placing his hands on my arms, Colt looked into my eyes. "Lauren, that was fucking amazing. I mean . . . I don't even have words to describe how fucking hot that was."

Slowly letting a smile play across my face, I whispered, "It was, huh?"

Chuckling he said, "Yeah, it was. I know why it felt so fucking good."

Standing up straighter, I purred, "Cause I know how to ride?"

Colt tried to keep a straight face, but rolled his eyes. "Baby, we forgot a condom."

My smile immediately fell and I'm sure my face turned white as a ghost. "What? Colt, how could we forget?"

Swallowing hard, Colt closed his eyes and shook his head. "Lauren, I'm so damn sorry. I know better than to ever risk something like that. It's just, you took me by surprise, and it felt so damn good and I didn't want to stop, and I wasn't thinking. The moment I realized why it felt so good I pushed you off of me and came. I wasn't in you when I came."

Dropping my shoulders, I couldn't help but smile and do a little jump. "Oh, thank God!"

Nodding, Colt said, "I know."

"No, I thought you were turned off by my porn talk. I'm so relieved that's not why you pushed me away."

Colt gave me an incredulous stare. "Wait. What porn talk?"

Dropping my eyes some, I said, "You know. When I yelled out yes, yes, yes."

Looking back into Colt's eyes, he narrowed them as he continued to look at me with a confused expression. Then he started laughing. "Lauren, how is you calling out yes over and over . . . porn talk?"

Shrugging my shoulders I said, "I don't know. Isn't it?"

"Fuck no. And if at anytime you want to talk dirty to me, baby, I'm all for it."

Sucking in my lower lip, I felt the pull in my lower stomach. "Really?"

Pulling me to him, Colt wrapped me in his arms. "Really, sweetheart."

I loved being in Colt's arms. There was no other place I'd rather be than right here. Up against, his cold, wet, naked body.

"Colt?"

Taking a step back and running his hand through his hair, I saw the worry on his face. "You need to dry off, and stop worrying. You pulled out before you came inside me. Plus, I got on birth control not too long ago."

Colt's face instantly relaxed, but then was quickly replaced with a look of horror. "Oh. Really? You got on birth control? How come?"

Tilting my head, I said, "Well, a certain hot football player from Texas A&M moved into the house I am living in. He has a very bad habit of walking around with no shirt on and let me tell you, his body is hot. *Very* hot."

I'd never seen such a smile spread across Colt's face. "Is that right? A hot football player?"

"*Very* hot, good-looking football player."

Reaching behind me, I took a towel and handed it to Colt as he asked, "So, why the birth control?"

Shrugging, I turned and headed back out to the other

room. Turning and walking backward, I purred. "Because I secretly hoped that one day, I'd get to ride this hot good-looking football player and fuck the hell out of him."

Colt dropped the towel and stood there stunned. Spinning around, I headed toward the bed, giving myself an imaginary pat on the back.

Me, one point. Colt, zero. Hugging myself, I fell onto the bed and wondered how long it would take for Colt to recharge for round three.

SIX

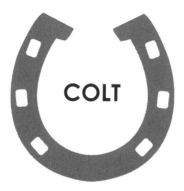

COLT

WATCHING LAUREN WALK out of the bathroom, my mouth was gaped open. I wasn't sure how I should feel. Lauren admitting that she had hoped we would end up together had me wanting to jump for joy like a girl. Lauren talking dirty had me wishing my damn dick would get hard again. Looking down at my guy, I pinched my eyebrows together. "Of all the times I need you to perform at top level, it's now."

"What did you say?" Lauren asked from the other room. She sounded sleepy.

"Um . . . nothing. Give me a minute or two to dry off."

Quickly running the towel over my body, I dried off in record time. Walking back over, I unplugged the tub and let it drain. Turning to head to the other room, I stopped as I looked at the shower. "I'm gonna jump in the shower real quick to get this jasmine smell off of me, Lauren."

Lauren responded back with a simple, "Mkay . . ."

Turning the water to hot, I stepped in and let it run over my body. I still couldn't believe that Lauren and I were together. Shaking my head, I thought back to the night when our relationship turned. The night she wanted to make love and I said no.

SITTING IN MY truck, Lauren stared off in the distance. Turning her body toward me, I looked at her and smiled. "I don't want to hide my feelings anymore, Colt. I'm . . . well . . . I'm attracted to you and I think you're attracted to me."

Grinning, I took her hand in mine. "Lauren, you're all I think about."

A blush swept across her cheeks as her eyes intensified. "Make love to me, Colt. I want you so much. Please."

I wasn't expecting Lauren to ask me to make love to her in my truck. I had no condom first off and there was no way in hell I was having sex for the first time in my truck, with the girl I loved more than anything.

Looking away as I gathered my thoughts, I turned back to Lauren. "Lauren, I don't want our first time together to be in my truck. I want it to be special. I want to make you feel desired and show you how much I want you. Fucking you in my truck is not what I pictured."

The moment I saw the hurt flash across her eyes, I wanted to take everything back and just take her in my arms and kiss her. I could have given her an orgasm and then maybe told her we needed to wait to make love.

Giving me a smile that did not reach her eyes, she turned back and looked out the front window. "I understand. Colt, if you don't want to be with me . . ."

"What? Lauren, that's not what I said. I want more than anything to be with you. It's all I think about."

Holding her hand up for me to stop talking, she looked my way. Tears formed in her eyes. "I think I'm tired and it's been a long night. Will you please take me home, Colt?"

TURNING OFF THE water, I pushed all memories of that

night away. It didn't matter anymore. Lauren was mine. She would forever be mine.

Stepping out of the shower, I reached for a clean towel and wrapped it around my waist. Inhaling a deep breath, I got ready for round three.

The moment I saw her asleep in the bed, my heart about burst from my chest. Her beautiful blonde hair was spread out over the pillow and her hand was tucked up under face. She wore a slight smile as she slept peacefully. I chuckled when I noticed the towel underneath her.

Walking over to her, I gazed upon her beautiful body. Turning, I walked to the closet in the hall and opened it. There was an extra blanket that I pulled down and took out of the bag. Heading back to the bed, I picked up my cell phone and checked it. I had two text messages.

> *Dad: It wasn't unnoticed son how you and Lauren were kissing while you were dancing and then you both left.*

Blowing out a breath of air, I hit Reply.

> *Me: Is there a question or something in there dad?*

> *Dad: Remember how we raised you.*

> *Me: I would never hurt Lauren. I love her dad.*

Holy shit. I just told my father I loved Lauren. Dropping my head back, I stared at the ceiling until I heard my phone beep. Seeing my dad's reply, I rolled my eyes. "Oh man."

> *Dad: Use protection.*

> *Me: Dad, really. Are we going to go there?? I'm not irresponsible!*

My heart was pounding in my chest. Here I was telling my father I wasn't irresponsible and I forgot to wear a damn condom the second time I'd ever had sex. Fuck!

> *Dad: I know. It's my job to pester you. How far are*

y'all from A&M?

Oh shit. *Shit. Shit. Shit.* Scrubbing my hands down my face, I paced back and forth. Glancing at the time on my phone, we had left the reception almost three hours ago. I never lied to my father. Ever. Okay, that's not true. I may have told a white lie every now and then.

Get a grip on yourself, Mathews!

Me: *We aren't that far away.*

Not a lie. We're not that far away.

Dad: *Okay. Be careful driving and kiss Lauren for me.*

Letting out the breath I had been holding, I typed back my response.

Me: *Will do! Later. Love ya, Dad.*

Dad: *Love you, Colt. Later.*

The next message was from Will.

Will: *Did my eyes deceive me or did I see you and Lauren kissing?*

Me: *No asshole, they did not deceive you.*

Will responded back within seconds.

Will: *So?*

Me: *So . . . what?*

Will: *Don't be a dick. Are y'all together?*

Me: *Maybe. Define together.*

Will: *Holy fuck. Y'all slept together? Where in the hell are you 'cause if you're at one of the beach houses you're about to be caught!*

Letting out a chuckle, I shook my head and glanced over to my sleeping beauty.

Me: *Nope, took Lauren to St. Claires in Rockport. Told our parents we were heading back to A&M for Lauren to work on a project.*

Will: *Please let me tell Luke! You've got to let me tell Luke.*

Shaking my head, I set my phone back down on the coffee table, but not before I turned it to silent. Taking the blanket I still had in my hand, I draped it over Lauren. She mumbled and let out a contented sigh. She looked happy.

Crawling in bed, I pulled the cover over me and brought Lauren up against my body. She fit perfectly. The feel of her naked skin up against mine was heavenly. Unlike anything I had ever imagined. It didn't take me long to completely relax as I listened to Lauren breathing in and out softly.

Pulling her closer, I whispered, "I love you, Lauren. I'm never letting you go."

FEELING LAUREN MOVE and stretch next to me, I felt my hard dick pressing into her back. "Mmm . . . I take it that means you're ready for round three, Mr. Mathews."

Opening my eyes, I saw goose bumps covering Lauren's body. Turning, she faced me as her hand rested under her cheek. "Are you sore, sweetheart?"

Scrunching up her nose, she whispered, "A little. But I want you, desperately."

I was hyper-aware of the warmth radiating from Lauren's body as she spoke. "I'll never get tired of hearing you utter those words from your lips."

A wistful smile spread across Lauren's face. Leaning in, I kissed her lips gently. The kiss was soft and slow at first. Pulling her over and onto my body, we both began to lose control as things heated up. Lauren began rubbing against my hard dick, and I was wishing like hell I had a condom on.

Breaking our kiss, I panted out, "Condom...Lauren...we need a condom."

Her eyes were lost in a need I wanted to satisfy. "Where? Colt, where are they?"

"Wallet, it's in my wallet."

Jumping up, Lauren searched for my wallet. "Where is it?"

Sitting up, I pointed to the coffee table. Lauren reached down and paused as she looked at my phone. Standing back up, she spun around. "Where's my phone? Oh my gosh, Colt where's my phone?"

"Um . . . I don't know. In your purse?"

Lauren ran over to her phone and my dick became so hard I was sure I could cut glass with it. Watching her breasts bounce as she ran was almost enough to make me come.

"What's wrong?" I asked as I pushed the covers off of me.

Pulling her phone out then swiping it open, Lauren glanced back at me with a panicked look on her face. "My dad was calling your cell phone. I had my phone muted from the wedding."

Scrubbing my hands down my face, I let out yawn. "Why are you freaking out, just tell him that. It was muted from the wedding and you forgot to turn it back on."

Placing the phone up to her ear she shook her head as she chewed on her lip. "You don't understand my dad, Colt. He'll think I'm irresponsible for *not* turning my phone back on."

I knew Scott was pretty strict when it came to Lauren, but I didn't think he was too terribly bad. He expected a lot from her. Just from our talks about the business, he felt like Lauren could do a good job running things, but he didn't think she was responsible enough to handle it all on her own. That's where I came in. I knew me being involved in Scott's business was a sore subject with Lauren, and I was not about to bring that shit up.

Making my way into the bathroom, I pushed the door open to the small room that held the toilet.

"Holy sheets! Motherfucker."

Smiling, I shook my head. Only Lauren would attempt to not use one swearword, only to follow it up with a larger one.

"Colt! We have to go! We have to leave now!"

Lauren came running in and grabbed my arm, mid piss. "Lauren! Wait, I'm using the toilet! Holy shit, what is wrong with you?"

Glancing down at me peeing, Lauren made a funny face and then looked back up at me. For one brief second I had a complex about my dick.

"My parents are leaving Port Aransas."

"So, why does that mean we have to leave our little heaven?"

Finishing up, I motioned for Lauren to step out so I could head over to the sink. Turning on the water to wash my hands, Lauren let out a frustrated breath. "No, you don't understand. They're leaving Port Aransas and heading to A&M."

Grabbing the hand towel, I wiped off my hands and nodded. "Really? What for?"

Placing her hands on her hips, she tilted her head and pursed her lips before she said, "They want to visit with me and see the house. See the project I'm working on."

It took a solid ten seconds for it to soak in. "Oh. My. God."

Nodding her head frantically, Lauren quickly found her bag and got dressed. I stood there stunned. My life flashed before my eyes as I pictured Scott's fist making contact with my face.

"Colt! What are you doing? Get dressed. We have to leave!"

Quickly running over to my bag, I grabbed sweats, a football practice T-shirt and my sneakers. Lauren was damn near almost done dressing as I let out a chuckle. Hearing my phone go off again, I reached for it. I had two missed calls, both from Scott. And three text messages, one from my mom and two from Will.

> **Mom:** *Hey darling. Dad and I are leaving early along with Scott and Jessie. We're gonna drive and get a place in College Station.*

Wait. What? My parents were coming to A&M . . . also? Looking back at my phone, I had two text messages from Will.

> **Will:** *Hey dude, you might want to think about heading back to A&M this afternoon. Your mom and dad are talking about road tripping it up there.*

> **Will:** *Code red! Your parents and Lauren's are headed to A&M. I have no clue what you're doing . . . well I do but . . .*

"Oh no. No. No. No," I said as I quickly threw everything into my bag. Lauren and I were both running around the room like maniacs. "What's wrong?" Lauren asked as she stopped right in front of me.

"My parents are leaving with your parents and heading to A&M."

A look of horror crossed over Lauren's face. "What? Why now? Why all of sudden do they want to know where we live or what we do? I mean they bought the house! They've seen it."

My phone buzzed in my hand. "Hello?"

"Hey, darling."

Hitting the speakerphone I said, "Hey, Mom. What's up?"

"Your father and I are on the ferry with Scott and Jessie. We are heading to College Station. I know it will be late by the time we get there, probably around eight or eight thirty, but let's plan on dinner, okay?"

My eyes widened as Lauren slowly shook her head and whispered, "We need to leave."

Holding up my hand and motioning for Lauren to calm down, I said, "Hey, Mom. Y'all aren't staying in Port A?

What's wrong? Did the party break up?"

Chuckling, my mother said, "Jessie and I want to see y'all. Besides, we hardly got to see you and Lauren before you both cried projects and homework and took off."

"So you're on the ferry?" I asked as my hands started sweating and I imagined what Scott would do to me when he found out I had stopped at a hotel and had sex with his daughter.

"Yeah, we are about to cross and head that way. Y'all are back, right? You left before noon."

Closing my eyes, I said a silent prayer we could pull ahead of our parents. Luke and Libby had decided to get married early in the morning and have the reception right after. Since they were working on the schedule of the baby. Lauren and I left the reception around eleven and it was now almost four. We wouldn't be back to A&M until almost eight.

"Yep, we are. Um . . . hey, Mom, I need to let you go. Y'all be careful driving and see you around eight."

"Sounds good. Love you."

"Love ya too, Mom."

Hitting End, Lauren and I stared at each other with blank expressions. "Our parents are on their way to A&M?"

Raising my eyebrows, I said, "Yep. And they think we're already there."

Turning and heading to the door, Lauren called out, "You better drive like you've never driven before."

Walking up behind her, I pushed the door closed as she went to open it. Turning her head, she gave me a confused look. "What's wrong?"

Dropping my bag, I grabbed her shoulders and turned her around. Pushing her against the door, I smashed my lips against her lips. Lauren dropped her stuff and wrapped her arms around me. The next thing I knew, her legs were wrapped around me and she was grinding on my hard dick.

Pulling her lips away, she dropped her head against the door. "Colt, I'm going to come. God, what are you doing to me?"

44

I watched the flush move across Lauren's cheeks as she fell apart. I wanted nothing more than to fuck her against this door, but I knew she was sore and we had zero time to be doing this.

Slowly lowering her down, I pushed her blonde hair from her face. "Will that keep you satisfied until later?"

Lauren's eyes were intense as they searched my face. "I think so."

After checking out of the hotel, we got in my truck and headed to A&M. The drive back was amazing. It was like old times with Lauren and I talking, laughing and enjoying each other.

Lauren cleared her throat and said, "So, maybe we should talk about the elephant in the truck?"

Quickly peeking at her, I tried to keep my out of control heart from racing so fast. "What do you mean?"

Smiling sweetly at me, Lauren turned and looked out the front window. "The reason I've been pushing you away, and frankly just being a bitch to you."

"I don't think you've ever been a bitch, Lauren."

Looking back at me, Lauren raised her one eyebrow and lowered her head at me. "Seriously, Colt. It's okay, I know how I've behaved. That night I walked away from you at the party, I saw the hurt in your eyes and it killed me. I was mad and acting like a little spoiled brat."

I kept my eyes on the road as I listened to Lauren talk. Things were amazing between us right now, and I didn't really want to risk the chance of us getting into a fight over something that happened in the past.

Lauren fiddled with her ring. It was a small diamond and emerald ring her parents had bought her when she turned sixteen. She'd spin it one way, and then the other. It was a nervous habit she had since she got the ring.

"Lauren, we don't . . ."

Holding up her hand, she sucked in a shaky breath. "Colt, please let me say this."

Giving her a weak smile, I motioned for her to keep talking. We had been driving with the sunroof open and I couldn't help but notice how the wind was sweeping around in the truck and blowing Lauren's curls around. She didn't seem to care one bit.

"My dream, since I've been a little girl, is to run Daddy's breeding business. I swear I remember the first time Daddy put me up on a horse. The smell of leather, to this day, reminds me of it."

Chuckling, I knew how she felt, because I felt the same way.

Clearing her throat, Lauren pulled her legs up and rested her chin on her knees as she kept talking. The smell of her perfume swept across my face and I inhaled deeply, feeling my dick jump in my pants.

"Daddy told me he thinks I can't run the ranch by myself. He says I'm not responsible enough and need someone like . . . someone like . . ." Her voice trailed off and my heart slowly broke as I listened to the sadness in her voice.

"Someone like who, Lauren?"

Lauren looked at me and my heart stopped beating the moment I saw the tear. Looking over my shoulder, I quickly pulled over to the shoulder and stopped the car. Putting it in park, I jumped out of the truck and ran around to the passenger side. Opening the door, I reached in and pulled her out. Holding her in my arms, Lauren began crying.

"I'm sorry. I'm not normally like this. I don't cry. Ever."

Running my hand along her back, I whispered, "Shh, Lauren, baby, tell me what has you so upset."

Pulling back some, I reached up with my hands and wiped her tears away with my thumbs. Lauren smiled the sweetest smile I'd ever seen.

"Daddy said he needed someone like you to run the family business."

Sucking in a breath of air, I took a step back. Everything all of sudden became clear. The night she walked away from me was the same day her dad hired me to help out on the ranch. All the times I talked about my ideas and pitched them to Scott, and Lauren would get so pissed of. It all made sense.

My eyes landed on her beautiful baby blues. They were anxious as she searched my face for some sort of a clue to how I was feeling.

I felt sick. Knowing I was the reason she had been so hurt and upset. I was the reason she had been pushing me away and fighting with me. All the things I said to her, I egged her on.

"Oh God." Turning, I leaned over and placed my hands on my knees and dragged in deep breaths. "I'm the reason you were so angry. I was the one who was pushing you away the whole time. It was because of me."

Lauren quickly started talking. "No, Colt I should have talked to you or Daddy. I should have told my father how I was feeling. Instead, I took it out on you and let my hurt and anger push you away. I was also upset about you turning me down that night in your truck." Tears streamed down her face as she attempted to keep talking. "If only I had stopped for two seconds to see that maybe we could do this . . . we could do this together."

I made a vow to myself that Lauren would always be first in my life. I'd wake up every single morning with one goal in mind. Make her happy always.

Pulling her into my arms, I held her tight. "Lauren, I love you."

Her body shook as she let out her tears. "I don't deserve your love, Colt."

Pulling back, I pushed her hair from her tear-soaked face. "Yes, you do. We deserve each other and I'm not going to let either one of us waste another second. Lauren, I want you to be happy and I need you to know that I will do whatever it takes to make you happy. If that means going and working for my father or Jeff, that's what I'll do, baby."

Shaking her head quickly, she wiped her nose. Her eyes lit up and she threw herself against my body. "Colt, I love you so much." She wrapped her arms around me tightly. "No, I want you to work for Daddy. You're so important to him, and he loves you like a son."

When she let her grip go, I pulled back and looked into her eyes. They were no longer sad, but filled with love. "Once he finds out I took his little girl's virtue, he won't love me like a son."

Laughing, Lauren dropped her head back. Knowing I was making her smile made the pain in my heart hurt a little less. "We better get going or he will be finding out tonight."

Quickly kissing Lauren on the lips, I started to walk but was stopped when she reached for my hand and pulled me back to her. "Colt, I don't want you going and working for your daddy or Jeff. I want to do this together. Me and you."

Relief coursed through my veins. "Baby, you have no idea how happy that makes me to hear you say that." Kissing her nose, I whispered, "Me and you. Forever."

SEVEN

LAUREN

PULLING INTO THE driveway of the house we shared with our friends, Colt and I quickly grabbed our bags and flew inside. Running upstairs, I dumped my clothes on the floor in an attempt to make it look like I had been here. Running in to the hallway, Colt and I slammed into each other. He had already changed his clothes as my eyes ran over his body.

"The project!" we both shouted at once.

Turning, we ran downstairs.

"Colt, I don't really have a project!"

Colt stood in the middle of the living room. Spinning.

God he looked so cute all freaked out. I had wondered what would happen if I just jumped on him right then and demanded he fuck me up against something? Women were always talking about being taken up against something. The whole orgasm against the hotel door was nice. Really nice. Really, really nice.

"Lauren! What are you standing there daydreaming about? Our parents will be here soon."

My eyes moved over Colt's body. The way he was walking around in those Wranglers was sinful. His ass looked amazing.

Focus, Lauren. Project. Parents on the way. Colt's ass. Taking me up against something. No, no, no! Focus.

An idea came to me, and I yelled out, "I got it!" Running upstairs, I looked around my room for the scrapbook paper I had bought for the baby book I made Luke and Libby. Grabbing a few pieces, I ran back down the stairs. Colt was still standing in the middle of the living room. Taking a quick peek at him, I attempted not to run into anything.

Yep. Still looking hot as hell.

"Colt, can you stop standing there looking all hot?"

Pulling his head back with a confused look upon his face, Colt said, "I'm not hot. Do I look hot? If I'm sweating, it's because I'm sure your father is going to see it all over my face. *I had sex with your daughter.* It will be like a giant imprint on my forehead."

Letting out a giggle, I opened the pantry and looked around. *There they are!* Reaching for the bag of pasta, I pulled it out and tossed it down on the paper. Shutting the door, I walked up to Colt, who was leaning against the island. "I mean you looked hot as in handsome, or I want you to take me up against a wall or a door. Oh! Holy sheets! In the shower!" My mouth dropped open and I looked at Colt. *Why hadn't I thought of that back at the hotel? Damn it! Oh, I'm so mad at myself.*

"W-what?"

"Yes! I totally want to have hot, fast, give it to me hard sex in the shower."

Colt wet his lips and let out a small moan. I was just about to kiss him when I remembered the project. "The project!"

Spinning on my heels, I quickly skipped over to the junk drawer, as Grace calls it. Pulling it open, I grabbed the glue stick.

Making my way back over to the scrapbook paper, I opened the box of pasta.

Looking at Colt through my eyelashes, I couldn't help but chuckle at his expression. I knew my sex in the shower comment probably had him going insane.

Using the glue I drew the number one and then started putting pasta on it. Colt continued to gaze at me with an incredulous stare. "Want to help?" I asked.

"Um . . . sure. What in the hell are you making?"

"My project."

Colt's head snapped up and he slowly tilted it as his eyes moved from the pasta to me, then back to the pasta. "Um . . . what is it?"

Drawing the number four with glue, I put more pasta on it. "Seriously? You don't know?"

Pursing his lips as he took in my project, he shook his head. "Lauren, I have no fucking clue what you are doing." Picking up the pasta, he began mindlessly pushing it onto the glue number.

Drawing the number three, we repeated the process. I held up the paper and smiled. "My project," I proclaimed with pride.

"It looks like something we had to do in grade school. What is with you and the numbers one, four, and three?"

Feeling my face blush, I started cleaning my hands to get the glue off. "You really don't know what it means?"

"Nope. I know I've seen you write it on a bunch on your notes in high school."

Closing my eyes, I shook my head. Another missing piece. That stupid idiot had no idea what I had been saying to him all through high school.

Turning and leaning against the sink, I gave Colt the sexiest smile I could. "I only wrote that in your notes, Colt. No one else's."

There went that damn smile of his. *God, does he have any idea how sexy that crooked smile is? Does he know it melts my panties instantly?*

"Oh yeah?" Colt asked as he pushed off the counter and made his way to me. Pulling me into his arms, he lifted me up and set me down on the countertop.

Slipping his hand through the leg of my shorts, Colt asked in almost a whisper, "What does it mean, Lauren?"

Dropping my head back, I felt him brush his fingers over my panties, causing my lower stomach to clench. "Oh, Colt. Yes."

Pushing on my clit, I jumped. "Tell me, Lauren or I'll stop."

"It stands for I love you!" I called out as I attempted to get more friction against my sensitive numb.

Colt let out a growl and slipped my panties to the side, pushing his finger into my hotness. Letting out a hiss between my teeth, I begged for him to take me.

"Colt, please take me. Oh God, take me right here, right now!"

His lips moved to my neck as he kissed me tenderly. "Sweetheart, I wish like hell I had known what the three numbers meant because what we did today would have been done about three years ago."

Placing my hands on his broad shoulders, I moved my hips. "More!" I panted out. Colt lifted me up and I wrapped my legs around him.

"Tell me what you want, Lauren. I don't want you to be sore, sweetheart."

Every time Colt called me sweetheart, my heart felt as if it was about to burst. No one had ever treated me the way Colt had in the last eight hours. I felt as if he adored not only my body, but my heart and soul as well.

"I want . . ."

Just as I was about to be brazen enough to tell him to fuck the shit out of me, the doorbell rang and Colt practically dropped me to the floor. "Your dad!"

Damn it all to hell! Just when I get all worked up. Letting out a frustrated moan, I walked somberly to the door, but not before I adjusted my panties and shorts. Stopping for a quick second to put my game face on, I pulled the door open. Standing in front of me was my mother, father, Gunner and Ellie. All four of them peering at me with wondering eyes. "Long time no see, family!" I said as I stepped out of the way and gestured for them to walk in. Looking over my shoulder, I did a double-take. Colt was walking down the stairs yawning, like he had just woken up.

Attempting not to laugh, I asked, "Did you sleep good, Colt?"

Giving me a naughty smile, he gave a jerky nod and said, "Yep."

Gunner and my father both walked up to Colt and

shook his hand. "How was the drive?" Colt asked as he flopped onto the sofa. I wanted desperately to sit next to him. To show our parents that we were together, and happy. Peeking over to my father, I couldn't help but notice how he stared at Colt. Glancing at my mother, she was staring at me.

Dear God. Do they know? Can they tell? Placing my hands up to my cheeks, I could tell they were on fire. One look to my mother's left and Ellie was staring at me. Swallowing hard, I jumped up. "I'm starved! Who's down for some pizza?" Looking around the room, everyone stared at me. Snapping my head over to Colt, I widened my eyes and tried to give him a signal. I had a feeling we needed to be in a very public place . . . and fast.

Colt stood up quickly. "Yeah, pizza, my treat."

As the two of us stood there, our parents just stared at us. Finally, the silence was broken.

My father cleared his throat and asked, "How long have the two of you been dating?"

Oh. My. Glitter. I'm pretty sure I just saw my entire life flash before my eyes. Taking one last look at Colt before my father beat him into the ground, I gave him a weak smile. Colt's eyes were calm. They didn't have the look of fear in them like I thought they should have. Returning my smile with a drop-me-to-my-knees smile of his own, he started walking over to me. The entire room seemed to have disappeared and it was only Colt and me. My senses went into overload as I smelled his musky scent before he even reached me. The memory of his lips on my skin caused my body to shudder. Walking up to me, Colt placed his hand on the side of my face and I instinctively rested my head in his hand. His thumb gently brushed across my skin, leaving a trail of tingles in its place. Colt's smile grew bigger, as if he didn't have a care in the world. His mouth parted open and he began to speak.

"For about nine hours, I would say."

Letting out a giggle, I found myself lost in his beautiful blue eyes. It was if he was looking into my soul with the way they pierced my eyes.

Hearing someone clear their throat, my eyes snapped over to my father, who was trying like hell to keep his smile hidden.

"That must have been an interesting drive home then," Gunner said with the same silky smooth voice Colt possessed.

Nodding my head, I spoke just above a whisper. "It was."

Walking up to me, my mother placed her hand on Colt's shoulder and gently looked into my eyes. I sucked in a breath when I saw tears in her eyes. "Mom, why are you upset?"

Colt took a step back and I wanted to yell out in protest. I instantly missed his warmth. "I'm not upset, darling; it's just that you're all grown up." Pursing her lips together in an effort to not cry, she said, "I just miss you I think."

Wrapping my arms around my mother, we held each other tightly. "I love you, Mom. I miss you and Daddy so much. I'm so glad you came to visit me."

Pushing me back at arm's length, my mother looked me up and down. She raised her eyebrow as if she was acknowledging something.

Out of the corner of my eye, I saw Gunner, my father and Colt all walking toward the front door. My heart began to race and my breathing picked up. Gunner was apparently going to keep my father from killing Colt.

Walking toward them, my mother took my arm. "Why don't you let the guys talk for a bit? Show me this project you had to rush home for?"

Glancing back at my mother, I gave her a dazed look before I turned back and watched the love of my life walk out the front door with my father leading the way. Colt glanced over his shoulder and gave me a quick wink, causing my stomach to flutter.

Turning back to my mother, I looked between her and Ellie with pleading eyes. My hands started to sweat as I thought about all the things my father could do to make Colt hurt. "You're just going to let them take him away?"

Ellie smiled and peeked over to my mother. Turning to

my mother, I grabbed her hands. "Mom, you have to stop Daddy. I love Colt. I've loved him for so long, but I've been so stupid by pushing him away. I was afraid Daddy would let Colt run the ranch because he doesn't think I can. I was afraid I wouldn't have any say in the business, but I see I was being stupid and acting like a spoiled brat and—"

Holding up her hand, my mother covered my mouth as I continued to talk in a muffled voice. "Lauren! My goodness, stop and take a breath."

My eyes darted back and forth between my mother and Ellie. "If I drop my hand, will you calm down?"

Slowly nodding my head, I closed my eyes in an attempt to hold back my tears. Opening my eyes, I saw something in my mother's eyes. Understanding. Compassion. Love.

Dropping her hand, she tilted her head. "Darling, where in the world did you get the idea that your father thinks you can't run the business?"

My mouth opened, but I couldn't talk. I didn't like to show weakness and right now, my voice was going to sound weak if I talked. I lifted my shoulders up and made a face. Ellie walked up to me and took one of my hands. "Lauren, you and Colt clearly have feelings for each other. It was evident when the four of us saw the two of you dancing. What threw us all was we had no idea either of you felt things for each other."

Feeling my cheeks flush, my eyes looked away. If they only knew. I wondered what would happen if I spilled my guts to my mother and Ellie? There were so many things I had wanted to ask them. Like, how long was it going to hurt after sex? Was it normal to already be wanting Colt, even though we had spent the most amazing afternoon together and made love twice? Did guys like dirty talk or was that something I shouldn't do? Was shower sex really all that?

Okay . . . maybe those types of questions I should save for the girls.

Chuckling, my mother pushed a curl behind my ear. "Your mind is spinning, Lauren. Calm it down, sweetheart.

My mother always said that to me. She could tell when

my mind was racing and she would always tell me to calm it down. Daddy said it was a sign of immaturity that I couldn't keep my thoughts clear.

"I've loved Colt since the day he punched Paul Hines in the face and threatened to kill him if he ever touched me again."

Ellie and my mother both let out gasps. "What did Paul do?" my mother asked.

"Colt punched him?" Ellie asked with her hands over her mouth.

Grinning when I probably shouldn't have been, I answered, "Yes! Paul Hines had wanted to have sex in high school and when I told him no, he slapped me and called me a whore. Colt punched him and told Paul he would kill him if he ever talked to me or touched me again." My mother had been looking past me, but her eyes snapped back to me when I said Paul had slapped me.

Ellie drew in a sharp breath and whispered, "That little bastard."

"That's why you hit Paul?"

Hearing Gunner's voice, I spun around. Colt, Gunner and my father were all standing at the front door. Not being able to read Colt's expression, I mouthed, *are you all right?*

Something moved across Colt's face. I'd seen that look before. It was the same look he had when he made love to me for the first time earlier today. My knees wobbled and I almost reached out for something to steady myself. Gunner stood in front of Colt, blocking my view of him. "Colt, is that what happened between you and Paul Hines?"

"Yeah, the bastard deserved more than just a punch."

My father's eyes were burning with anger. What did they talk about outside? What if he told Colt to stay away from me?

"It's a damn good thing I didn't know about this when it happened," my father said.

Shaking my head to clear my thoughts, I looked at my father.

"Daddy?" I wasn't even sure why I called out to my

father like I did. Questioning him, as if he could read the questions in my mind.

Giving me a slight grin, he looked around. "Take a deep breath, baby girl, everything is okay. Shall we go get that pizza before it gets too late?"

My mother reached for my hand and gave it a light squeeze. Pulling my eyes from my father, I attempted to smile. "Um . . . sure. Antonio's?"

Ellie flashed me a sweet smile as she walked by and over to Colt. Slipping her arm around his, she began to talk. "So, I want to hear all about how school is going this semester. Will you drive with your father and I over to the pizza place?"

I took a step back as my mother walked toward the front door behind Ellie. "Lauren, you can drive with your father and I. I hardly got to see you at all the last three days.

Oh God. They were separating us. Why? Shaking my head, I pulled my hand from hers. "What's going on? Why did you take Colt outside, Daddy? Why is everyone acting so strange?"

My father looked at me and smiled. "Everything is fine, Lauren. Colt's parents' just want to spend time with him like we want to spend time with you, darling. Everything is okay."

My blue eyes found Colt's. He quickly made his way over to me and placed his hands on my shoulders. The warmth of his touch calmed me instantly and I wasn't sure if that was a good thing or a bad thing. He moved his lips to my ears. "I promise you, sweetheart. Everything is fine. I love you, Lauren."

Pulling his head back just enough to look at me, I whispered, "Okay. I love you too, Colt."

Kissing me softly on the cheek, Colt made his way out the door, followed by his parents and my mother. Giving my father a fake smile, I walked toward the kitchen. "I better get my purse so I—"

Taking my hand, my father stopped me. "Lauren Ashley, stop for one second and look at me."

For some reason, I was afraid to turn around and look at my own father. I wasn't sure why. It was so quiet I could hear my heart beating in my ears. Slowly turning around, I looked up into my father's eyes. He gazed back upon me with nothing but love. "I simply asked him to take care of you." My father's voice cracked and he quickly cleared it before he continued talking. "Protect you, because you are the most important thing in the world to me. My heart belonged to you the moment I first looked into your eyes. You *are* my life, Lauren. It's hard for me to just give that to someone else, even if that someone else is like a son to me."

My lower lip trembled as I listened to my father talk. His mouth rose in a half smile as he looked at me. "Seeing the two of you on the dance floor earlier this morning, I saw something change. The way Colt looked at you is the way I see Gunner look at Ellie." Glancing to the floor, he barely spoke above a whisper. "I hope it's the way people see me look at your mother."

My heart hammered in my chest. To hear my father say that Colt looked at me like he looked at my mother brought tears to my eyes. "Daddy," I whispered as I threw myself into his arms. He held me tight as I cried. "Daddy, I'm so scared."

"Why, baby girl? Please tell me why."

"Is it possible to realize in one day how powerful your love is for someone? Daddy, my heart aches for him to just hold me in his arms. His touch calmed me down almost in an instant just now."

I wasn't sure this was what my father wanted to hear from my lips, but it was true. Colt's touch had calmed my nerves and that scared me.

Pulling back, I had to catch my breath. I'd never seen my father cry. One lone tear slowly moved down his cheek. "Oh, Lauren, I wish I had answers for you. Love is such a crazy thing. Do I think it's bad that Colt makes you feel safe? No, absolutely not. The person you are in love with should make you feel safe. Being in their arms should be the safest place in the world, Lauren."

"Was it like that with you and Mom? Was she your everything, Daddy?"

Placing his hand on the side of my face, he slowly nodded his head. "She still is, Lauren."

Grinning until my cheeks hurt, I took a step back. "I'm glad you didn't kill him, Daddy. Because I really love him."

Laughing, my father rubbed his hand on the top of my head. "Don't think the thought didn't cross my mind."

Draping his arm around my shoulder, my father led me to the front door. "Come on. I'll treat for dinner."

Walking outside with my father, I'd never felt so happy in my life. For once everything seemed to be perfect.

EIGHT

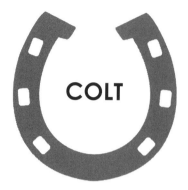

COLT

THE ENTIRE TIME we sat at the restaurant and ate pizza, I couldn't push the image of Lauren wrapped around my body out of my mind. I could see the lust in her eyes, and I was dying to know what she was going to say to me before the onslaught of parents showed up at our door.

Glancing across the table, I watched as Lauren talked her father's ear off about an idea she had for his breeding business. I knew how much she loved her family's business, and I was glad she shared her fears with me and the reasons why she had been pushing me away.

Scott caught my stare and I smiled politely. When he walked up and took my arm back at the house and said he needed to speak to me outside, I thought for sure I was dead. I felt better when my dad followed behind me.

"So, Colt, tell me all about what's going on in your world. I feel like I hardly get to talk to you anymore."

Turning to my mother, I couldn't help but smile bigger. My mother was breathtaking. An older version of my sister, Alex. Her blue eyes seemed to have a sparkle to them always. My father loved my mother with his whole heart. I can remember Alex and I sitting at the top of the stairs many a time, watching my father swoon my mother with something as simple as a dance in the living room. The way she would look at him is what I longed for with

Lauren. I saw it today when we made love for the first time. I'd do whatever I could to see that look as much as possible.

Bumping my shoulder, my mother asked, "Colt? Are you lost in thought?"

Letting out a chortle, I nodded my head. "I guess I was. School has been good so far. Hard to tell with it just starting up again for spring semester. I'm ready to start spring practice."

"We're really proud of you son," my father said as he placed his hand on my shoulder and gave it a squeeze.

Turning to him, I was overcome by the look on his face. I knew my parents were proud of me and Alex, but they never failed to tell us and show us that support. "Thank you, Dad. That really means a lot to me."

He nodded but then something changed in his eyes. "Don't get distracted with school or your commitment on the field."

Pulling my head back, I gave my father a blank stare. Why would he think I'd get distracted? Stealing a quick look toward Lauren, my father went back to eating. Did my father think my relationship with Lauren was going to be distracting? Hell, our push and pull game the last three years was a much bigger distraction. Everything would be better now that Lauren and I were finally together.

Picking up my pizza, I took a bite as I listened to Lauren telling her dad about a horse in Kentucky she had been following. Smiling, I took my surroundings in. My parents and Lauren's parents stopping by, I think, made things even clearer to me.

Life from this point on was going to be different. Things were finally turning around for me and I could see nothing but happiness in my future.

LAUREN AND I stood outside and said our good-byes to our parents. It was almost midnight and we had been at the pizza place until they closed. We came back here and talked for a while, Lauren showed her parents her project, and we made plans for spring break week. I had to admit, it was nice getting to spend some time with my mother and father. I knew Lauren felt the same way. She was an only child and super close to them.

As the two cars pulled off and headed to the Marriott Hotel, Lauren and I waved and watched until both cars turned and were gone.

Lauren grabbed my hand and dragged me back inside the house. The second the door closed, she jumped into my arms and pushed her lips against mine. Moaning as she pulled and sucked on my lower lip. "I never . . . thought they would . . . leave." She panted between kisses.

Walking over to the sofa, I dropped her onto it and crawled on top of her. Pushing my hard dick between her legs, we both moaned. Arching her back and giving me a sexy grin, Lauren pulled my shirt over my head.

Once my shirt was off, I reached down and pulled her shorts off of her body. Our kisses were frantic, as if we would never kiss each other again. I needed more of her; I needed to taste her. Feel her sweetness drip around my fingers. Nothing else mattered at this moment but being with Lauren.

"Colt, oh God. I'm so turned on. I don't want sweet and romantic. I want more."

Holy shit. My dick was so hard it hurt. "Lauren, baby, I don't want to hurt you."

Lauren pushed her hands up and played with her breasts. "Colt, please don't make me beg. I want to feel that you've been inside of me. Please!"

Jesus, just seeing her touch herself almost had me losing it in my pants. "Lauren, I need to go get a condom. They're up in my room."

Lauren's eyes turned dark and the electricity that flowed between us had me holding my breath. "Take me in the shower, Colt. Hard."

My eyes rolled to the back of my head as I whispered, "I've died and gone to heaven."

Standing up, I reached down and picked up Lauren. She was light as a feather. Turning, I had never run up stairs so fast in my life. Lauren laughed and held on tight as she yelled, "Don't drop me, Colt!"

Pushing open the door to my room, I walked in and dropped Lauren onto the bed. Crawling on top of her, our hands were everywhere. The sense of urgency to touch each other was overwhelming. Making love earlier had been amazing. But this . . . this was beyond anything I'd ever experienced. The absolute need to have her near me was out of control. The rest of our clothes were stripped off until there was nothing but the feel of skin on skin. Our teeth crashed together as we kissed each other senseless. Whimpers and moans filled the air as I slipped my fingers inside her. She was soaking wet and her sweetness coated my fingers, pulling out a deep growl from the back of my throat.

"Lauren, you're so wet, baby."

Her chest heaved up and down as the look in her eyes intensified. "I want you, Colt. Please don't make me wait any longer."

Lifting off of her, I reached into the drawer of the side table and grabbed a condom. Ripping it open, I slipped it over my dick. It was pulsing with need as I looked back at Lauren's glistening wet pussy. I'd never wanted anything so much in my life.

"Lauren, promise me if I hurt you, you'll tell me." Nodding her head, she wet her lips in anticipation. "Baby, I just want to fuck you."

Closing her eyes, she said, "Yes! Colt, yes!"

Moving over her, I teased her entrance with my tip as Lauren placed her hands on my shoulders. "Now, Colt. I'm so ready."

In one swift move, I pushed into Lauren. She called out my name and I tried like hell to control the animal in me. Each thrust went deeper as she dug her nails in my back.

Fighting to keep my orgasm at bay, I continued to push in deeper . . . trying to find her sweet spot. The sight of her body reacting to the coming orgasm was fueling me on.

Just as the orgasm hit her, she gripped my dick and I about poured myself into the condom. Lifting her limp, sedated body, I carried her into the shower. Wrapping her arms around me, she buried her face against my neck.

"Are you okay, baby; do you want to keep going?" I asked as I stepped into my bathroom.

"Yes . . . please don't stop, Colt."

The smell of our sweat and sex filled the air. It was a scent I wanted to smell every single day for the rest of my life. Never letting her out of my arms, I reached into the shower and turned it over to hot. Giving it a few seconds to heat up, I stepped into the shower and slowly let Lauren slide down my body. "Mmm . . . feels so good. Watching her head drop back, the hot water soaked her hair as it fell past her shoulders. Running my fingers through her hair, I grabbed a handful.

"I'm not done with you, Lauren."

Her eyes snapped open, and I was overcome by the seductive look she gave me. "Good," she whispered.

Lifting her up, I pushed her against the shower wall and pushed my dick back into her.

The feel of my dick slipping in and out of her combined with the hot water falling on us was heavenly. "Don't stop, Colt. So . . . close."

It wasn't long before Lauren began screaming out my name as I came hard right along with her. Still holding her in my arms, Lauren and I sank to the floor of the shower as we fought to pull air into our lungs.

"That. Was. So. Hot," Lauren said between breaths.

I nodded and whispered, "Very hot. So fucking hot." My heart dropped when I looked into Lauren's eyes. They were beckoning for me to be lost in them.

"Lauren, never in my wildest dreams did I think my heart could be so in love with one person. I'm captivated by everything about you. Your soft lips, I long to kiss. Your blue eyes, I find myself getting lost in every time I look into them. Your touch sends an instant bolt of electricity to my heart. But I think what I love the most is your heart. It is so pure and full of life." Closing my eyes, I whispered,

"I pray to God it belongs to me."

Lifting her hand and placing it on the side of my face, I leaned into it as I opened my eyes. "My heart is filled with love for you, Colt. Only you."

Slowly standing, I lifted Lauren up as we stood under the steaming hot water. Moving my lips to hers, I gently kissed her as I held her face within my hands. Pouring my love into her, I kissed her with every raw emotion I had. Life stopped in that moment as Lauren and I were lost in that kiss.

Brushing my lips gently across Lauren's, I smiled as I was overcome by the love I had for her. Smiling in return, Lauren giggled. "Think of all the showers we missed out on."

Chuckling, I pulled her to me. "Sweetheart, I'm never going to be able to take a shower alone again. You know this, right?"

Lauren's face softened as she gazed lazily into my eyes. "I love that you call me, sweetheart. It makes me feel . . . special to you."

My heart dropped into my stomach as Lauren's words filled my mind. Reaching over, I shut off the water. Walking Lauren out of the shower I took in her perfect body. Grabbing a towel, I slowly dried her body off. Starting from her feet up to her hair. Lauren looked completely relaxed as she dropped her head back and let out a contented sigh. Quickly drying myself off, I wrapped the towel around my waist and picked Lauren up. Carrying her back into the room, I pulled the covers back and gently placed her down. Lauren in my bed did crazy things to my heart. She stretched and my stomach did that thing where it flutters at the sight of her.

Covering her up, I kissed her forehead and spoke in a hushed tone. "Sleep, my beautiful princess."

"Hmm, Colt."

Lauren quickly drifted off to sleep. Knowing my name was the last thing to be whispered from her lips was amazing. The last twenty-four hours had been amazing.

Taking a few steps back, I sat in the chair that was in

my room. Watching Lauren sleep so peacefully in my bed, I knew things in my life would never be the same. Nothing else on Earth mattered except for her.

She was my life. My dreams. My entire world.

NINE

LAUREN

R EACHING UP WITH my hand, I rubbed my nose. Tickles.

Something kept tickling me. Not wanting to move, I swept my hand under my nose again.

Stretching, I let out a soft moan as I felt every single muscle in my body. Smiling at the knowledge of why I was so sore, I slowly opened my eyes. Expecting to see Colt, I was met by something far less pleasurable.

Grace and Alex.

Closing my eyes tightly, in hopes to erase them and make Colt appear, I slowly opened one eye and then the other.

Nope. Still Grace and Alex. "What are you two freaks doing in my room?"

Alex attempted to hide her smile as Grace lost it laughing.

"Bitch, please. You are nowhere near your room. Your ass is laying naked in Colt's bed."

Sitting up quickly, I pulled the covers with me and looked around. The memory of yesterday flooded my mind as I smiled. Turning back to Alex and Grace, I couldn't help but bite down on my lip and smile bigger.

Grace gaped her mouth open. "Oh. My. God. The cherry has been popped, and by the look of things, I'd say Mr.

Mathews did a good job of it."

Alex smacked Grace. "Eww. Really? I didn't need the visual thank you very much."

Covering my mouth, I attempted to hide my laughter. Alex and Grace both looked at me with beseeching eyes. Finally, Alex said, "So. Tell us everything that happened. I'm dying to hear about how y'all went from hating each other to Colt walking downstairs with the biggest smile on his face I'd ever seen."

Grace interrupted Alex with, "And you laying up in Colt's bed naked! Looking rather well-fucked, I might add."

"Grace!" Alex and I said at once.

Grace looked at Alex and then me with a smug look on her face. "What? Tell me she doesn't look . . . satisfied!"

Feeling my cheeks burn, I reached over and pushed Grace. "Shut up, you bitch!"

Alex laughed and handed me her robe. "Get up, I'm dying to talk girl talk. We'll be downstairs."

Both Alex and Grace gave me a warm smile that said they both knew how I was feeling. I was so blessed to have my friends in my life. Before they walked out the door, I called out. "Wait. Where is Colt?"

Alex looked over her shoulder. "He went for a run with Will. I overheard him telling Will he needed to get out of the house because all he wanted to do was wake you up, but he knew you were . . . tired."

Grace made some weird growl sound and wiggled her eyebrows. Rolling my eyes, I looked away. Once they shut the door, I climbed out of Colt's bed. Each movement reminded me of yesterday. I was sore, but deliciously sore. Walking into Colt's bathroom, his smell surrounded me. Seeing one of his shirts, I reached for it and brought it up to my nose and inhaled deeply.

Mmm, how I loved the smell of Colt. Who was I kidding? I loved everything about Colt. He had cut his dark wavy brown hair short, and I loved running my hands over it. It felt so soft. His sky-blue eyes that sparkled when he looked at me. His body . . . oh my, his body. Smiling, I closed my eyes and pictured Colt naked.

Dear God. I craved his body like nothing I'd ever experienced before. He was like the stick to my corn dog. Sliding my hand down between my legs, I gasped at how sore I really was.

Shaking my head to clear it, I set Colt's shirt back down. Realizing I didn't have anything to brush my teeth with, I headed out of Colt's room and into mine. After brushing my teeth and washing my face, I changed into some yoga pants. Wanting more of Colt, I skipped back into his room and began going through his drawers, looking for a T-shirt to wear. My eye caught something tucked under his shirts. Reaching for it, I sucked in a breath of air as I stared at the picture. I couldn't believe what I was looking at. My heart hammered in my chest as tears formed in my eyes. My hands shook gently as I attempted to wipe the tears from my eyes. Colt had a picture of me in his drawer. It was taken probably about three years ago when we were all playing football. I was standing with the football in my hand with it lifted above my head. Closing my eyes, I let the memory from that day engulf me.

TURNING AROUND, I waited for the signal from Colt. He gave it to me and I quickly cut back across the makeshift field. Colt threw the ball and I jumped. Catching it, I screamed with delight, only to see Luke and Alex running toward me. Spinning around, I took off for the goal line. Crossing over it, I began jumping as I held the ball up.

"We won! Holy sheets! I scored the winning touchdown!" Grace, Maegan and Taylor came running over as they tackled me to the ground. After they each congratulated me, I looked up. The sun was somewhat blinding, but I knew the person standing over me was Colt. Reaching down, he helped me up. His smile caused my stomach to flop around like a fish out of water. Reaching up with his hand, he brushed something off of my face. "I'll never forget that smile, Lauren. You sure were happy when you made that

touchdown."

Nodding my head, I said, "Couldn't have done it without you, superstar."

Winking, Colt leaned down and kissed my cheek before turning and yelling for his team to huddle up.

I'm never washing this cheek again.

I COULD ALMOST smell the fresh-cut grass from the field we played on. Or the smell of the bluebonnets that were in full bloom. Every time I smelled either one of those two things I thought about that simple kiss on the cheek. It had meant the world to me. Never would I have imagined Colt had taken my picture and had it printed out.

Clutching the picture to my chest, I whispered, "Please don't ever let me hurt him. Please."

Slipping the picture back under Colt's T-shirts, I took a shirt from the top. Slipping it over my head, I felt a warm rush run through my blood. Colt's smell surrounded me as I smiled, shut the drawer, and made my way out of the room and downstairs.

Walking into the kitchen, Alex and Grace stopped talking and stared at me. Glancing back and forth between the two I asked, "What's wrong with you two?"

Grace tilted her head and gave me one of her famous, *what in the hell are you talking about,* looks. "Yeah, no, Lauren Ashley Reynolds. You're talking. We want all the good shit. Like how both your parents showed up on your doorstep. Will told us how y'all had to beat it home before your parents."

Alex sat down and placed her hands on her chin. "I want to hear about the hotel in Rockport." Scrunching her nose, she gave me a small little nod of her head. "I'm dying to know, is my baby brother romantic?"

Leaning against the counter, I let out a contented sigh as his words flowed through my memory.

"Lauren, I've never experienced such bliss as I am being

with you right now. The taste of you was sweeter than I could have ever imagined."

Grinning until my cheeks began to hurt, I looked away from Alex and Grace.

"Holy hell. Look at how her cheeks are flushed. I'd dare say Mr. Mathews made our little Lauren blush a time or two."

Smiling bigger, I whispered, "Or three . . . or four."

Alex and Grace both let out yelps of happiness as they bounced around. "How do you feel this morning, Lauren? Was he gentle?" Alex asked with a look of concern on her face.

Dropping my shoulders and nodding, I said, "Oh, yes. He was gentle, romantic, caring, big . . . oh my gosh is he big."

Grace busted out laughing as Alex sucked in a breath of horror. "No, no, no, no! You don't ever say stuff like that, Lauren! Ohmygod! I have to bleach my ears." Alex's body shuddered as she kept sticking her tongue out like she was going to puke.

Grace wiggled her eyebrows and smiled with a Cheshire cat smile. "So he's packing, huh? Are you sore?"

Alex rolled her eyes. "Ugh."

Peeking back at Grace, I nodded my head. "Yes. To both."

Alex jumped off the stool. "I'm out. I'm so over this conversation. I can't handle this. He's my baby brother, y'all!"

Giggling, I turned and poured a cup of coffee. Turning back to Alex and Grace, I smiled and winked. "Let's just say he is the cream to my coffee."

Alex's face dropped and Grace busted out laughing. "Oh . . . oh man did I teach you good," Grace said as she walked up to me and pulled me into her arms. Pushing me back out, she gave me a once-over. "Seriously though, I'm happy for you and Colt, Lauren. You two were the only fools who couldn't see the truth. I'm glad you asked him to dance."

If it hadn't been for Grace, none of this would have

happened. Looking into her eyes, I couldn't help but notice how they looked lost. Empty almost. As if she longed for what I was experiencing right now. I wasn't sure why Grace never dated anymore. She was beautiful. Her long brown hair fell in waves across her chest as her chocolate-brown eyes gazed into mine. Her body was killer and she had a ton of guys constantly asking her out.

Giving her a warm smile in return, I barely spoke the words. "I'm glad I asked him to dance, too."

The front door opened and just like that . . . the air in the room became charged. It wasn't anything new . . . it had been like this for the last three years. Anytime he walked into a room, I felt him before I even saw him. The scent of sweat and Colt swept around me as he walked up to me. Leaning into me without a care in the world, he pressed his lips to mine and kissed me as if he hadn't seen me in weeks. "Good morning, sweetheart."

"Good morning," I softly spoke against his lips. My insides were going nuts as I internally fist pumped myself again for walking up to Colt yesterday and getting him away from that girl.

"You look amazing in my T-shirt."

Blushing, I placed my hand on my face. "It smells like you and I missed you this morning."

Colt his eyes were on fire while he searched my face. "Do you have plans for today?"

My heart had never beat so loudly in my chest. Raising his eyebrow as if he could hear it, Colt slowly calmed my beating heart with one smile.

Barely able to speak, I said, "To be with you are the only plans I have."

Grace made a gagging sound as Colt and I both turned to her. "Yuk. I think I liked it better when y'all were at each other's throats."

Giving her a smirk, I turned back to Colt. "What were you thinking?"

Placing a quick kiss on my nose, he said, "It's a surprise. I'm going to go take a shower and then take you for some lunch. Get dressed and meet me back down here."

My insides became inflamed when Colt mentioned taking a shower. Would it look obvious if I followed him up to his room? Then into the bathroom, then attacked him in the shower?

Shaking my head to clear my thoughts, I smiled. *Get yourself together, Lauren. Gesh. Within the last twenty-four hours you've turned into a horn dog.* "Okay, meet you back here in a few."

Colt dropped his hold on me and headed to the stairs. I missed his touch almost immediately. Flopping against the counter, I let out a long breath.

Waving her hand in front of my face, I looked at Grace. "Holy hell. You have it bad. Really bad."

Laughing, Will pushed Grace out of the way as he leaned down and kissed my cheek. "You were all he could talk about during our run, Lauren. That boy is head over heels in love with you."

Wrapping my arms around me, I grinned from ear to ear. "It feels like a dream. Like, something I've been wanting for so long but was so afraid to take that step for fear it would slip away again."

The smell of something sweet caught my attention as I turned to see Alex was making a fruit salad. Her eyes caught mine. "It's not a dream, sweetie. With the way my brother looks at you I would say he has been wanting this for as long as you."

Remembering the photo, my stomach dropped like I had just been on a roller coaster.

"I'm headed to the shower," Will said as he took off and ran upstairs.

Turning to Alex and Grace, I cleared my throat. "I found something in Colt's drawer when I was looking for a shirt of his."

Alex glanced up and asked, "What was it?"

The colors of the fruit salad were beautiful. I wasn't sure why everything seemed different to me today. Smells, sounds, colors. It was as if everything was clearer. "A picture of me from a few years ago. That day we all played football and I scored the touchdown."

Grace's head looked up from where she was cutting bananas. "He had a picture of you in his drawer?"

Alex's shoulders slumped and the goofiest smile spread across her face. "Oh my. How adorable is that? Lauren, he kept a picture of you." Looking at Grace, Alex smiled bigger. "I have goose bumps!"

Grace chuckled. "I have to admit, that got me right here." Pointing to her heart, Grace winked at me.

"He's . . . so romantic. What if I'm not doing something right?"

Alex's head jerked back. "What do you mean? Lauren, honey, from the look on my brother's face when he laid eyes on you just now, you are doing everything right."

Chewing on my bottom lip, I leaned in closer. "Sex wise I mean. I've never been with anyone."

Grace set the knife down and turned her whole body toward me. "Listen to me, Lauren. The fact that you saved yourself means more to Colt than anything. He's not going to expect you to be an expert."

Looking away, I wasn't sure if I should share this or not, but I wanted to talk to someone and who better but two of my best friends. "Um . . . Colt never . . . I mean . . . we were each other's firsts."

Looking back at Grace and Alex, I watched as they both melted and let out an "Ohh . . ." as they clutched their chests. "Lauren, how incredibly romantic!" Alex gushed. "Oh my, Daddy taught that boy right."

Grace smiled and shook her head. "Wow. I'm impressed. Colt is one of the major football players for A&M with girls throwing themselves at him all the time . . . and he saved himself for you, Lauren. That is so romantic, it almost makes me want to throw up."

Giggling, I nodded my head. Grace walked over to me and placed her hands on my upper arms. "Seriously though, Lauren, how perfect that you both get to learn with each other. What an amazing experience yesterday must have been for you both. Don't stress about this. Just be with the man you love and everything will take care of itself."

Walking into Grace's arms, she hugged me. Pulling back, I smiled at Grace. "Grace, you're going to make some guy very lucky someday."

Grace's smile faded and sadness swept across her face but as soon as I saw it, it vanished and she turned to Alex. "You're both very lucky to have the most amazing men in your lives. The gift that y'all have been able to give each other is so beautiful and rare."

Alex's eyes looked as if tears were building. Walking up to us, Alex wrapped her arms around Grace and me. Holding us tight she whispered, "I love you, Grace. You deserve this love and you're going to find it."

Hearing Grace sniffle threw me for a loop. Grace never cried. Stepping back, I looked at her. "Is everything okay, Grace?"

Laughing and waving her hand at me as if she was brushing off my concern she said, "Yes! Oh gosh, yes. I'm just all emotional for you, Lauren. It's been a hell of show watching you and Colt deny your feelings."

Alex gave me a little push. "Go get ready for your day. We'll talk later tonight when we can Skype with Libby, Maegan and Taylor! They're going to want to know all the details as well!"

Nodding my head, I turned and skipped toward the stairs. Taking them two at a time, I started thinking about what I was going to wear today.

TEN

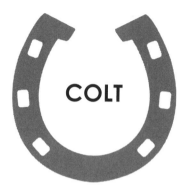

COLT

P ULLING INTO THE parking lot of Grand Station, Lauren
let out a squeal. "I've been dying to come here!"
Chuckling, I put my truck in park and turned to her. Lauren
had always been so full of life. It was as if she floated
through life just unaware of the bad shit and only con-
centrated on the good. She had no clue how beautiful she
was, and that made her more beautiful. We had stopped
at Longhorn Steak house for lunch and I wanted to punch
every guy who stared at her. But Lauren had no clue they
were all eye fucking the hell out of her. Her eyes never left
mine. When I talked, she gave me one hundred percent of
her attention. I'd never experienced that before with the
other girls I had dated.

"Do you know how beautiful you are, Lauren?"

Lauren had been staring at the front door, itching to
get out of the truck. When I spoke, she quickly looked at
me. Her eyes had been full of life, now they were dark with
desire. My pants grew two sizes too small as I attempted
to adjust myself. "Do you have any idea how handsome
you are, Mr. Mathews?"

My stomach fluttered and I felt my hands begin to
sweat. I didn't want this to be a dream. Waking up and
finding out it had been would devastate me.

Reaching over, I placed my hand on the side of her

face. "You're mine, Lauren."

Lauren's eyes filled with wetness as she placed her hand over mine. "Forever, Colt Mathews. I'm forever yours."

Lauren and I both jumped when someone banged on my truck window.

"Fucking yeah! Mathews where have you been?"

Rolling my eyes, I recognized the voice of Phil Lawson. Another Texas A&M football player. "Fuck," I said under my breath.

Lauren laughed as she looked around my shoulder and out the driver's side window. "Looks like he's happy to see you." Her smile quickly faded and my heart stopped beating.

Turning, I saw Phil, Roger, and Mitch. Roger and Lauren had dated off and on a few times. The fact that he tried to push her into having sex with him made me want to pound his face into the ground.

Roger wore a blank expression on his face as Phil kept telling me to roll the window down. Glancing back to Lauren, I asked, "Did you want to leave, Lauren?"

Shaking her head, she replied, "No. We came here to have fun, let's go have fun."

Leaning over, I kissed her quickly on the lips. "Let's go, let me get your door, sweetheart."

Lauren's eyes sparkled every time I called her sweetheart, and I loved it. Opening my door, Phil stepped back. "Hey, Colt." Looking back into the truck he smiled. "You want to hang with us?"

Taking a quick look over at Roger, I couldn't help but notice how he was staring into my truck at Lauren. "Nah, I'm here with my girlfriend, just hanging out for a while."

Roger's head snapped back over as he sent me a glaring look. Fucker. The idea of his hands on Lauren about drove me mad. Walking around my truck I headed to the passenger side. "You want to grab a couple lanes and hang out?" Phil asked.

Opening Lauren's door, I held my hand out for her. The moment her hand came in contact with mine I felt the rush of energy. Lauren sucked in a breath of air as her eyes met mine. She felt it, too. *God I loved this girl.*

Winking at Lauren, I said, "That would be up to Lauren. It's her day."

Lauren looked between Phil and me. "What is up to me?"

"Did you want to get a lane with these guys or hang out alone?"

Shrugging her shoulders, Lauren looked at me. "Um . . . I was kind of hoping to have you all to myself, if that's okay."

Giving her a smile that I hoped like hell knocked her socks off, I grabbed her hand and kissed the back of it. "Sounds perfect to me."

Glancing back to Phil, I said, "Maybe next time, dude."

Phil smiled and tilted his head to Lauren. "All right, but if you change your mind, there is a group of us playing."

Giving Roger a quick look before turning my attention back to Phil, I nodded. "Sounds good."

The three of them walked away as Lauren melted into my side. "Are you mad?"

Taking a hold of her tighter, we started walking. "Hell no. I see those guys all the time. I want to be with you."

Giggling, Lauren looked at me. "We live in the same house."

Grinning, I purred into her ear, "They don't make my dick hard with their smile though."

Lauren's mouth parted open slightly as she whispered, "Oh."

Throwing my head back and laughing, we made our way into Grand Station. The smell of pizza mixed with fried foods hit me right in the face. Taking a quick look around, the place wasn't too crowded, which was strange for a Sunday afternoon. Lauren began jumping with excitement. I loved how the little things in life made her so happy. "What should we do first, Colt? Bowl, miniature golf, or—Oh my gosh, they have laser tag!" Grabbing onto me, Lauren's face lit up. "Laser tag, Colt!"

Laughing, I walked closer to the check-in point. I wanted to see what Phil, Mitch and Roger were doing first before I decided what to do. They were getting three bowling lanes. Taking note of their numbers, I made a mental note not to be near them.

"How about miniature golf first? I've heard it is glow-in-the-dark."

Clapping her hands together, Lauren let out a squeal almost like what my mother did when she was excited.

I'd never had so much fun playing miniature golf as I did with Lauren. Her laugh was infectious and she truly just wanted to have fun. She never once got upset if I beat her on a hole. Unlike other girls I'd dated in the past, they expected me to just sit back and let them win. Lauren just enjoyed being with me and having fun.

After putting the ball into the last hole, Lauren walked up and wrapped her arms around my neck. "Let's go play laser tag now."

Taking her hand in mine, we headed out of the miniature golf section and made our way to laser tag. "Sounds like a plan."

Standing in the room, I held Lauren's hand while a young high-school-aged girl went over the rules. "We're going to break you up into teams. Red team verses blue team. Let's get your vests on."

Helping Lauren with her vest first, I slipped my vest on. I was about to say something when I heard someone call out my name. "Colt? Phil said you were here!"

Fuck. First Roger, now Marie.

Turning slightly to look over my shoulder, I saw Marie James standing next to . . . Roger. *What in the hell were the two of them doing together?*

Giving a polite smile, I said, "Hey, Marie."

Walking up to Lauren and I, Marie ran her eyes over Lauren. Her smile couldn't have been any more fake. "Phil said you were here with your girlfriend. I don't think we have officially met, I'm Marie. Marie James. Colt and I went out a few times."

Lauren's body stiffened next to me as I stole a quick peek at her. I've seen Lauren pissed plenty of times, but I've never seen Lauren pissed *and* jealous.

Sticking out her hand, Lauren smiled in return. "Lauren

Reynolds. It's nice to meet you."

Lauren quickly turned and looked at Roger. "Roger, how are you?" she asked.

"I'm doing good. How about you, Lauren?"

"Doing really good, thanks," Lauren said as she reached down and took my hand in her hand. I wasn't sure if she was trying to reassure me or give Roger the clear indication we were together.

"You're looking really good. I haven't heard from you in a while. You should give me a call sometime," Roger said as he winked.

That motherfucker did not just say that.

I was about to say something when Lauren squeezed my hand. "I don't think so, Roger. Much of my spare time will be spent with, Colt. My boyfriend."

Roger glared at me as I took a step forward. "You got a problem, Hanover?"

Holding up his hands, he let out a gruff laugh. "Nah, no problem at all, Mathews."

Anger zipped through my veins as I attempted to not pound his face in. "Good, I suggest you refrain from asking my girlfriend out again."

Lauren pulled back on my arm, "Colt, let's go enjoy ourselves. It's not worth it."

Roger flashed me a smirk as he draped his arm around Marie. "Have fun blue team."

Turning away from him, I took Lauren's arm and walked to the other side of the room. I was about to tell Lauren we needed to kick their asses when she looked up at me. "All right, Colt. You better get your game face on. We are taking those two down!"

Lauren and I planned out our attack and once we got inside the room we executed it. I had a feeling Marie would wimp out and basically hide in a corner and she didn't let me down. She cowered-down in a corner throughout most of the game. Lauren was a champ, and by the time the game was over, we had creamed Marie and Roger.

Taking off our vests and handing them back to the young girl, she congratulated Lauren and me for the great job we did in taking down the red team."

"Ready to head home?" I asked Lauren. Nodding, she took my hand and quickly led me to toward the exit.

"Where is the fire, Lauren?" I asked as she practically ran to my truck once we got outside.

Turning and walking backward her face lit up and I was instantly hard. "Do you really need me to answer that, Colt?"

ELEVEN

LAUREN

F EELING COLT'S WARM breath on my neck, I didn't want to move. The last two days had been nothing but bliss. After spending yesterday afternoon together, Colt and I came back to the house and spent the next few hours tangled up in each other.

Glancing over to the clock that Colt had on his side table, I silently cursed. I had a class I needed to go to. Gently picking up Colt's arm, I carefully slid out of bed so that I didn't wake him up. I knew he didn't have any classes until this afternoon.

Hustling, I slipped on Colt's boxer briefs and his T-shirt and headed to my room. I was almost to my door when I heard Grace. "Well, well, well. Look who decided to emerge from the blissfulness of amazing hot sex. At least I'm going to guess it's amazing hot sex with how messed up your hair is and the red chaffed skin on our face, and neck. Hmm . . . Colt does wear that five o'clock shadow well. In more than one way it seems."

Turning, I leaned against my door and looked at Grace. My smile was so wide, my cheeks were beginning to hurt. "Oh, trust me. The sex . . . oh yeah. Hot. Amazing for sure. And I'm sure I'm chaffed in other areas as well."

Grace closed her eyes and dropped her head back as she lifted her hands. "Thank you! *Thank you* for letting me rub off on at least one of them!"

Snickering, I pushed off the door and gave Grace a gently nudge. "Do you have a few minutes to talk? I really want to ask you something," I asked her.

"Sure I do."

Grace followed me into my bedroom and I shut the door after she walked in. Sitting on my bed, Grace looked at me. "What's up?"

Chewing on my lip, I wasn't sure how to ask this, but I knew I couldn't ask Alex. It would be too weird. I could ask Libby, but she was so busy with the baby. Maegan never answered her text messages and Taylor . . . well Taylor was in her own world right now."

"First off, stop gnawing on your bottom lip. You're freaking me out. Come sit next to me and just tell me what's on your mind."

Dropping my hands to my side, I flopped onto the bed. I would most likely be late for my first class, but that was okay.

"Well . . . I want to . . . I really want to make Colt . . . Okay well, I've never done . . . you know . . . to a guy . . . and well." Rolling my eyes, I let out a frustrated moan. "Colt is like the jelly to my donut and I just want to make him happy. I want to . . . well . . . I want to . . ."

"Jesus, Mary, and Joseph. Spit it the hell out, Lauren."

"How do you give good blow jobs?"

Grace's face fell. "Um . . . I don't know if I should be offended or honored you wanted to talk to me about this.

Placing my hands over my mouth, I sucked in a breath. "You've never?"

Grace started laughing. "Hell yes I have. And I might add, I think I'm pretty good at it." She rubbed her knuckles against her shirt as she spoke.

"Okay, so if you're good at it, how do I . . . you know. Do it?"

Grace leaned forward like she was about to share with me the most important secret in the world. "First, you make sure he's clean. Don't do it after he's been inside you. To me, that's just nasty."

I pulled back. "Why? I mean if a guy goes down on you, do you kiss him afterward?"

Grace's eyes widened. "Well, yeah. That's hot as hell."

Shrugging my shoulders, I asked, "So what's the difference?"

Grace sat back and looked up like she was thinking. "Well, hell. I guess there is no difference."

"Okay, so anywho, go on with what you were saying."

Grace was lost in thought for a moment before she started talking again. "Right. So scratch the clean thing because little miss nasty likes it." Pushing her over we both started laughing. "I don't know, Lauren. You just put it in your mouth and . . . suck."

"Suck hard? Suck soft? Do I move my hand up and down it while I suck?"

Grace rolled her eyes. "Okay, I think we need to have a 'how to give a blow job' class. I know the perfect person for it."

Sitting up, I let out a squeal! "Holy sheets! Really, Grace? Cause that would be so fun."

Chuckling, she stood up. "Yeah, girls night. I'll arrange everything."

Standing up, I hugged Grace. "You're the best! I've got to get ready for class, but I don't know how to thank you for this."

Grace gave me a sweet smile and headed out the door. Calling over her shoulder she said, "Ask and I shall deliver."

The rest of the day I couldn't get Colt out of my mind. We had sent a few text messages back and forth but his last one had me fidgeting in my seat and I wasn't even sure why.

Pulling out my phone, I read it again.

> **Colt:** *Every time I close my eyes I see your beautiful blue eyes. Can't wait to hold you in my arms tonight.*

Letting out a contented sigh, I closed my eyes and dreamt of Colt's touch. I could almost feel the scruff on his face between my legs as he took me to heaven and back. My whole body shuddered as I thought about it.

Opening my eyes, I sent Colt a text.

> **Me:** *Can't stop thinking about you. You are a delicious distraction Mr. Mathews and I miss your lips.*

Setting my phone down, I stared at it as I waited for his response. When nothing came after five minutes, I picked up the phone and pushed it into my pocket. Gathering up my books, I headed out of class. Making my way to the library to meet a study group, I heard someone call out my name.

Shit. Shit. Shit. Stay calm, Lauren. Don't punch her. Just smile and be nice to the little bitch.

"Lauren, wait up!"

Slowing down, I waited for Marie James to catch up to me. I hate her and that bothered me because I didn't even know her. The only reason I hated her was because she was the only girl Colt had dated steady since he broke up with Rachel in high school.

Marie came up and walked next to me. Turning slightly, I smiled weakly and said, "Hey there, Marie."

"Hey. How are you doing?"

Giving a quick nod of my head, I said, "I'm doing great. Late for a study group though."

"Oh, okay right. I'll be quick."

Staring straight ahead I waited to see what she wanted. "So you and Colt Mathews, huh?"

Smiling, I said, "Yep," as I popped my p.

"I have to say, you're a lucky girl. So many of my friends were dying to go out with Colt and they were so jealous when I was dating him."

Stopping dead in my tracks, I turned to Marie. *Okay, you little bitch. I'm not playing games with you.* "Marie, not to be rude, but was there something you needed?"

Marie's facial expression turned from one of amusement, to more of a stunned look. "Um . . . well, I just wanted to know like how serious are the two of you. I know you both grew up together and you live in the same house and all. But Colt mentioned you were his girlfriend and I was just wondering if he was saying that to push Roger back or something?"

My mouth gaped open. Taking in the sight of Marie James, I wondered what Colt ever saw in her. She was cute, don't get me wrong. But she just had an air about her that was off. Like she was trying to be something she wasn't. Her blonde hair was pulled up into a tight bun, and she looked like she had just stepped out of an interview with the CEO of some major company. Not what I pictured Colt would be into.

"Colt and I are dating, Marie." Turning to head to the library again, she reached out for my arm.

"Like as in exclusively dating?"

Rolling my eyes, I faced her. "Yes. We're exclusive."

Narrowing her eye at me, she asked, "How exclusive?"

"Are you kidding me? What is wrong with you? Colt and I are very much together, Marie."

"Uh-huh. Have you been . . . together?"

Shaking my head, I started walking. If I didn't get away from this girl now, I was going to punch her in the throat. "Damn it, Lauren I'm sorry. It's just Roger is wanting to know how serious you and Colt are. I really like Roger and I want to . . ."

I held up my hand as I stopped walking and turned to face her. "Oh. My. Glitter. Marie, don't do his dirty work for him. You could do so much better than him. I mean . . . he is having you ask me about my relationship with Colt. Doesn't that bother you?"

"Well, no. I mean, if I get the chance to date the quarterback of A&M, do you know how amazing that would be?"

My heart instantly hurt for this girl. Slowly shaking my head, I tried to understand how she was feeling but I couldn't. I wasn't with Colt because he was some star college football player. I was with him because I loved him. A light breeze blew as I pushed a curl away from my eye. "Okay, Marie. You need something to take back to Roger. Here ya go. Colt and I are very much together, the sex is amazing and every night I pray to God that I'm going to spend the rest of my life with Colt Mathews."

Marie's face fell. "Um . . ."

"I'm late, have a wonderful evening, Marie, and good luck with Roger."

As I walked away I felt my body shaking. How dare he? How dare that asshole recruit someone to dig information up on me? Hopefully Marie would go back and tell Roger what I said and he would move on to someone new.

Walking into the library, I took a quick glance around. Jimmy Mack, one of my chemistry lab partners, stood up and waved his hand. Giving him a slight smile, I headed that way. Everyone started talking about their notes for test that was next week but my mind was not focused at all. Pulling out my cell phone I checked for a message from Colt.

Nothing.

My mind began to drift off to last night as I thought about our date last night.

STANDING OUTSIDE THE movie theater, I glanced down at my watch. Colt had sent me a text and asked if I would meet him here at seven. It was now seven ten. Pulling my phone from my purse, I went to send him a text when a single red rose appeared in front of my face.

Spinning around, I smiled at the sight of Colt. "Hey," I whispered.

"Hey, back at ya, beautiful."

My stomach flipped and flopped as I found myself lost in those blue eyes. "So a movie huh?"

Smiling, Colt pulled me into his arms. "Not just any movie, it's a special movie."

Pulling back some, I gave him a questioning look. "What makes it special?"

Dropping me from his hold, Colt took my hand and began leading me into the theater. "You'll see, sweetheart."

As we walked up to the counter, a young guy stood there. It appeared he was waiting for us. "Colt, it's good to see you. How have you been?"

Nodding his head, Colt looked at me and then back at the guy. "How's it going, Mark? I've never been better. Lauren and I have been pretty busy with classes so I promised her a date night tonight. Is everything set?"

Wait. What in the heck is going on here? Colt knows this guy?

"I've got everything under control and set up," Mark said as he looked at me and smiled bigger.

"Wait, what's going on?" I asked as I looked between Colt and Mark.

Colt slapped Mark on the back and reached into his pocket and handed Mark a folded up envelope. Putting the envelope in his back pocket, Mark turned to another guy and motioned for him to do something.

"Theater six, Colt." Turning to me, Mark let out a chuckle. "Enjoy the movie, Lauren."

Colt took my hand and practically dragged me down to the last theater. "Colt, what did you give him? Money? Did you rent out the whole theater? I mean . . . if you want to make out, I'm down for a few people being in there."

Colt tossed his head back and laughed. "No, it wasn't money. They were box seat tickets for next football season. Let's hope Mark earned it."

"Box seats?"

Colt stopped walking when we got to the theater. "Yep, box seats. Are you ready?"

Pressing my lips together, I let the excitement of not knowing what was going on bubble over. Doing a little jump, I clapped my hands and said, "Yes! I'm ready."

"Close your eyes and I'll lead you in."

Narrowing my eyes, I chewed on my lip before doing as Colt asked. Taking my hands, Colt led me into the movie theater. He stopped and positioned me and placed his lips to my ear. "Open your eyes sweetheart.

Feeling my heart beating in my chest, I slowly opened one eye and peeked. Both eyes snapped open and I let out a *gasp as I looked around the movie theater.*

Oh. My. Glitter.

The entire place was empty, but there were bouquets of flowers going up each step to the middle of the theater.

"I know how you love to sit in the middle."

Turning to look back at Colt, I noticed a small table set up with an LED candle lit and placed in the middle. Walking up to it I laughed when I saw two popcorns, two boxes of snowcaps, and a package of licorice. Placing my hands over my mouth, I tried to hold back my tears.

"Colt. You did all this for me?"

Placing his hands on the sides of my face he smiled and my knees weakened. "There isn't anything I wouldn't do for you, Lauren. We can sit here at the table, or up in the seats to watch the movie. It's up to you."

My lower jaw began to tremble as I was overcome with a rush pure happiness. "What are we watching?"

Colt flashed me the sexiest smile I'd ever seen as he winked and said, "Your favorite movie, Brother Bear."

Stay calm Lauren. Don't jump his bones here in the movie theater. Stay calm.

"I think I want to watch the movie up there in the back corner," I said with a wicked smile.

Letting out a chuckle, Colt leaned in closer, "Why, sweetheart, you wouldn't think of doing something naughty while watching a Disney movie would you?"

Looking into his eyes, I shook my head and purred, "Never."

LEANING BACK IN my chair, I smiled. Colt and I had spent over half of the movie just talking about everything and anything. It was nice to just be alone together.

Excusing myself from the table, I walked between two rows of books and stared down at my phone. *Should I send him a text or wait? Gesh, Lauren, stop overthinking this.* Placing my thumb in my mouth, I began to chew on my nail. I don't get nervous. I don't play games so why is this throwing me for a loop?

Taking in a deep breath I typed out a message for Colt.

Me: I'm at the library studying for a chemistry test. I'll see you back home later

About to turn around and walk back to the table, my phone buzzed in my hand. Smiling when I saw Colt's name flash across the screen, I swiped the phone screen.

Colt: Chemistry huh? I bet I can teach you something about chemistry

The moan that escaped my lips was not intended. Looking around quickly, I began typing back. So Mr. Mathews wants to have some dirty texting? I can do that.

Me: Would it be hands on teaching?

Covering my mouth, I held my breath while I waited for his reply.

Colt: Very hands on. Hands on your beautiful face. Hands on your full lush tits. Hands all over your breathtakingly sexy body. Best of all would be my hand between your legs as I bring out the most intense orgasm you've ever had.

My hand dropped from my mouth to my side as I fell back against the bookshelf. Damn if he wasn't romantic and sexy at the same time. He gave new meaning to the words hot damn. Closing my eyes, I dreamed of Colt's hands all over my body. It was if I could almost feel him near me.

Running my hand along my neck, I attempted to control the raging desire I had. My body felt as if it was on fire as I stood among the archeology section of the library.

Taking in a deep breath, I was about to reply when I felt the air around me change. Turning quickly, I sucked in a breath as my eyes locked with the most beautiful blue eyes ever. Colt stood before me dressed in jeans, a light-blue T-shirt that made his eyes seem to shine brighter, and a smile that melted my panties in less than a second.

"Colt," I whispered.

"Your text to me earlier had my stomach in knots, Lauren."

Wetting my dry lips, I asked, "Why was your stomach . . . um . . . in knots?"

Colt took a step closer to me as my body shook with the anticipation of his touch. "All I could picture was my lips on your beautiful body."

A breath escaped my lips as my heartbeat began to beat faster. "That . . . would . . . be nice to feel. Your lips on my body."

Tilting his head, Colt raised his eyebrow at me. "Yes it would, Lauren."

Slowly nodding my head, I attempted to control my breathing. For some reason, Colt walking up on me in the library . . . surrounding by books talking about digging in the dirt . . . had me all worked up.

"Take a few steps back, Lauren."

Doing as he said, I found myself at the end of the aisle. Colt took my arm and led me around a corner. We were tucked back into a corner and the only way anyone would see us is if they came looking for a book back here.

"W-what . . . are you doing here? I thought you had a class?"

Lifting his hand, Colt brushed my hair back and away from my face. Sliding his hand behind my neck he pulled me to him. Fire ignited my body the moment our lips touched. My arms immediately went around his neck. I needed more. The feelings that Colt pulled out of me were unlike anything I'd ever experienced before. It was as if I needed him near me to breathe.

Colt's tongue danced with mine as we moaned softly into each other's mouths. Colt whispered against my lips, "Lauren, I want to touch you so damn bad."

"Yes! Please, Colt. Please!" I begged as his hand moved to my jeans. Unbuttoning my jeans he slipped his hand into my panties as I let out a gasp when his fingers plunged between my lips and into my body.

"Jesus, Lauren. You're so wet, sweetheart. Do you want me, Lauren?"

My breathing was erratic. This had to be the hottest moment of my life. Knowing that any moment someone might walk around the corner and see us had my libido in overdrive. "I want you, Colt. I want you so much."

Colt's lips moved to my ear. "I'm going to make you come, Lauren."

My eyes widened as his words rushed through my brain at the same time my orgasm rushed through my body.

Biting down on my lip, I attempted to hold back my whimpers. "Lauren, I feel you pulsing around my fingers."

Burying my face into his chest, I rode out my orgasm.

Barely coming back to my senses, Colt had my jeans buttoned back up and was staring into my eyes. "I love watching you fall apart because of me, Lauren."

Not moving my eyes from his, I couldn't help but notice how blue they were. Was it his T-shirt or was it because they seemed to be lit up with passion? Or love.

Closing my eyes, I took in a few deeps breaths before opening them again and capturing his eyes once more. "I love you, Colt. I've loved you for so long."

Yes. Oh, yes indeed. That was love I was seeing in his eyes. The way he stared into my eyes was like he was trying to stare into my soul. "I want you, Lauren. Now."

Nodding my head, I said, "Okay. Where?"

Colt took a step away from me and looked around. "Where is your stuff?"

"Um . . . it's back at the table."

"Do you need to study, baby?"

Shaking my head frantically, I said, "No! No, I'm ready for the test. I don't need to study."

Oh my glitter. Calm down, Lauren. Take a deep breath. Focus. At this rate I was gonna jump on him and screw him right here in the library. *Hmm . . . that actually isn't a bad idea. No no . . . focus Lauren.* There was no way I was passing up a chance to be with Colt to study for a damn chemistry test. The hell with that.

Attempting to not sound like a crazy, horny person, I

calmly said, "Let me grab my stuff."

Colt winked and stepped to the side, allowing me to go first. Glancing down, I held in my moan as Colt adjusted his hard-on.

I wanted to skip all the way back to the table knowing that I had Colt turned on like this. Walking up to the table, Jimmy looked at me and smiled. I felt Colt come up beside me and slip his hand around my waist. I loved how he made sure everyone knew I was his.

His. I was Colt's. The thought of it still amazed me and caused my stomach to drop. No one ever made me feel so amazing. Colt was for sure the stuffing to my Oreo.

Jimmy's smile faded as he looked down at Colt's arm. Thinking nothing about it, I looked around the table. "Hey, I hate to do this to y'all but something has come...up...and I need to take care of it."

Colt squeezed tighter on my waist and my insides exploded with the need to feel him inside me.

Jimmy looked away and didn't utter a word. Mindy Jackson, who had a crush on Jimmy and why he couldn't see that I had no idea, was the first to bid me good-bye. "No worries, Lauren. If you need any study help, give me a call and we can meet up."

Giving her a polite smile, I nodded my head. "Thanks, Mindy! I appreciate that. Later, y'all!"

Colt moved his arm out from around my waist and grabbed my bag and books. It wasn't until we walked away that I realized I didn't even introduce Colt to anyone. Shit.

"Hey, I wasn't even thinking back there. I didn't introduce you," I said as we walked toward the exit.

Colt smiled at me. "I didn't even notice. All I can think about is one thing."

Widening my eyes, I quickly looked around. A naughty thought occurred to me and I grabbed Colt's arm and began leading him in the opposite direction of the parking lot exit.

"Lauren, where are we going?"

Glancing back over my shoulder, I gave him a naughty smile and whispered, "You'll see."

Walking up to the main desk, I glanced down at the young girl's name on her name tag.

Leaning in close so I didn't speak too loud, I asked, "Hi, Candace. Is it possible to reserve a study room for right now?"

Candace looked up from her reading and gave me a weak, but polite smile. Then she glanced over to the god standing next to me and she perked up. Sitting up a bit taller, she flashed a beautiful smile toward Colt. "Yes, of course we have a few available."

"Perfect, my boyfriend and I have a huge chemistry test to study for."

Her smile faded a bit, but she quickly took down my student information and booked us a room. "I've got you booked for two hours in room two seventeen."

Flashing her a smile, I turned to Colt and winked. "Shall we?"

His smile made my knees wobble. Glancing over my shoulder back to Candace, Colt said, "Thank you, Candace. Have a wonderful day."

"Oh . . . um . . . yeah . . . you, too."

Poor girl. I knew exactly how she felt . . . Colt Mathew's smile had rendered me nearly speechless many times.

Making our way to the study room, I felt my heartbeat increasing. *Oh. My. Glitter. Was I really going to have sex with Colt in a study room . . . at school . . . with other people so close by? Yes. Yes I sure as hell was.*

Smiling a smile so big my cheeks started to hurt, I prepared to get my sexy on.

TWELVE

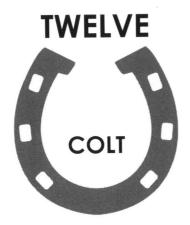

COLT

O PENING THE DOOR to the study room, Lauren walked in first as I followed. I was so turned on, it felt like my dick was going to explode. Giving Lauren an orgasm in the library was the hottest damn thing I'd ever done and I knew it turned her on just as much.

Shutting the door behind me, I watched as Lauren closed the blinds. The slight blush across her cheeks told me she was nervous. Lauren took a few steps back and leaned against the large table that sat in the middle of the study room.

"Please tell me you have a condom, Colt."

My body shuddered at the idea of taking Lauren in this room. I knew how thin the walls were and if anyone was on either side of us, they would hear us. The idea of it thrilled me. My dick was throbbing in my pants as I dropped her books to the ground and quickly made my way over to her. Before I even touched her, Lauren moaned.

Pulling her body to mine, I slammed my lips against hers. Our kiss was crazed. It was as if we couldn't get enough of each other. I wondered if it was all those years we had both desired each other but never acted on it that had us desiring each other so much now.

Pulling back, I quickly tugged my T-shirt over my head

as I watched Lauren do the same. Kicking her shoes off, she slipped her jeans and panties down in one fast move. "Oh fucking hell. You're so damn beautiful."

Lauren's eyes drifted down and I watched as her chest began to heave up and down. "Colt, oh my. That is so hot."

Glancing down to see what she was talking about, I saw I had my cock in my hand and was stroking myself. Looking back at Lauren, I studied her face as she watched me stroke myself. Her mouth was parted open and her eyes were wide with desire.

"Touch yourself, Lauren."

Her eyes snapped up as she quickly wet her lips. "W-what?"

Slowing down my movement so I didn't come, I motioned for Lauren to lie down on the table. "Touch yourself, Lauren."

"I . . . I've never done that in front of anyone, Colt."

Her eyes fell back to my hand on my dick. The next thing I knew, Lauren was laying on the wood table, her whole body shaking as she slowly slipped her hand between her legs. The moment she touched her clit, her body arched and she gasped. "Oh God!"

"Fuck . . . this is so hot watching you, Lauren."

Lifting her head she smiled. "Really? You like watching me do this?"

Nodding my head, I looked back at her hand. "Give me more, Lauren."

Lauren slipped her fingers inside her wet folds and began to finger fuck herself as I stroked my dick faster. "Faster, Lauren. Make yourself come, sweetheart."

Her head thrashed back and forth as she whimpered and moaned in pleasure. "Colt, this is so . . . naughty!"

Closing my eyes, I attempted to gain control, but I was quickly losing it. I knew the moment she came, I was going to explode.

Leaning up on her elbow, Lauren watched me as I watched her. "It feels so good, I'm so turned on watching you. I want to come together."

My breathing picked up as I watched her sweetness

coat her fingers. Walking over to her, I pressed my thumb against her clit and Lauren's eyes widened as her whole body began to tremble.

"Yes! Oh God yes. I'm coming! Ahh . . ."

My body shook as my orgasm began to build. I could feel my balls sucking up and I knew I was going to come hard. "Oh god," I called out as I came. Lauren never took her eyes off of me as I came all over her stomach. Looking at my cum on her body practically had my dick ready for round two.

Motherfucker. So damn hot.

Lauren collapsed back onto the table as she sucked in one deep breath after another. Placing my hand on the table, I slowly dragged in air.

"Oh my glitter, Colt. That was so amazing. So. Freaking. Amazing," Lauren said.

Looking around for something to clean my cum off of Lauren, I asked, "You wouldn't happen to have anything to clean up my . . . um . . . mess would you?" Leaning up, Lauren looked down at her stomach and smiled before her eyes pierced mine. "You came on me?"

Nodding my head, I whispered, "I did."

Giggling, Lauren pointed to her backpack. "I have some wipes in the front pouch of my bag."

Moving over to the bag, I reached in and grabbed the wipes. Quickly cleaning myself off, I moved to Lauren. Getting her stomach cleaned off, I helped her up and off the table. Wiping down the table good with more wipes, I threw them all in the trash and quickly got dressed.

Lauren stood before me with the sexiest grin on her face. "That. Was. Fun."

Laughing, I pulled her into my arms. "Yeah it was. I've never done anything like that before."

Gazing into my eyes, Lauren seemed sedated. Her eyes sparkled and I imagined taking her again on the table and just burying my dick deep inside her as I slowly made love to her.

Lauren's eyes filled with love as she spoke softly. "I've never done anything like that before either. We have lots of firsts together."

Rubbing her nose with mine, I whispered, "Yes we do. I have a lot more firsts planned for us, Lauren."

Burying her face in my chest, she said in a muffled voice, "I can't wait."

SPRING BREAK WAS finally here and I couldn't wait to get out of College Station and back home. Our parents had all decided to go on a cruise over spring break. The girls desperately wanted to spend time with Libby and Mireya, so the plan was for everyone to hang out in Mason. I just wanted to be with Lauren. It would be the first time we were home as a couple. So many ideas were floating around in my head for things I wanted to do with her. Spring football training started two weeks after we came back from break so I wanted to spend as much time with Lauren as I could.

Will came down the stairs carrying two duffle bags and a suitcase. Looking over at him, I chuckled. Rolling his eyes, he dropped the bags. "Why do they bring so much shit? They have clothes and stuff at home." Flopping down on the couch next to me, Will let out a long, frustrated sigh.

"Everything okay, Will?"

Smiling, he nodded his head. "I'm tired. School, planning the wedding, it's just got me all kinds of messed up."

Laughing, I looked back at the email I had received from one of my football coaches. "Yeah, but just think, one more year of school and you're done. Then it's work."

Will sat up and smiled. "Damn, I can't wait to marry Alex."

"She's really happy, Will. Thank you for loving her the way you do."

Will glanced at me. "She's my entire world, Colt. There isn't anything I wouldn't do for her."

Nodding my head, I turned back to the computer and started my reply email to my coach.

"What about you and Lauren? How are things going?"

The moment her name was mentioned, I felt the crazy dip thing in my stomach. Looking at Will, I flashed him a grin. "Amazing. Fun. Exciting, yet scary as hell."

Will pulled his head back and wore a surprised expression. "Scary? What's scary about it?"

Leaning back, I pushed my hand over my head and scratched the back of my head a few times. "The emotions I feel for her, Will. It's like I need to be near her all the time. I need her smile, her laugh, the silly little snore she does at night. Her perfume on my clothes drives me mad. I swear, sometimes I'll be sitting in class and I can't think straight because I smell her on my clothes. She's like a drug and I can't get enough of her."

Will put his hand on my shoulder and gave it a light squeeze. "Dude, I know exactly how you feel."

Nodding my head, I looked down. "I don't want to suffocate her though. You know?" Giving me a look that said he totally understood, I asked. "Will it always be like this?"

His grin widened and nodded his head. "Yes. It changes though. Sometimes Alex looks at me and I feel like I have to hit myself to make sure I'm not dreaming. Every morning I wake up and she looks at me, I fall more in love with her."

Glancing up, I watched as Lauren came running down the stairs, her cell phone pushed to her ear. "Maegan! You have to come home for spring break. Libby is planning a girls' night at her place! It won't be the same without you." She skipped into the kitchen, opened the refrigerator, grabbed a Diet Coke and skipped back to the stairs. Before she bolted up them she stopped and flashed me that beautiful smile of hers. "Hey! I'm almost packed." Blowing me a kiss, she took off.

Raising my hand, I gestured to where Lauren had been standing. "See. She enters the room and my whole body comes to attention. All I want to do is follow her upstairs and watch her pack."

Laughing, he stood up. "Damn dude, you've got it bad."

Letting out a small chuckle, I replied, "I know. My coach

told me my focus is not a hundred percent."

Will tilted his head and narrowed his eyes at me. "What do you mean?"

Shrugging my shoulders, I leaned back. "I don't know. We were in a team meeting yesterday and I couldn't focus. For once in my life, football isn't my number-one love. I'm not sure how I feel about it right now. I'm confused."

"Balance, Colt. That's all it is. You can love football and Lauren at the same time."

The windows were open and a breeze blew through. Inhaling a deep breath, I let the smell of the bluebonnets root inside me. Blowing out a deep breath, I closed my eyes quickly before opening them again. Looking back at the email I thought about how Coach had told me the NFL was looking to draft me early, they were that interested. That meant leaving Lauren. Frowning, I said, "I'm starting to feel like some things are just more important. I just need a few days at home I think."

Looking back at Will, he gave me a weak smile. "Probably. You need a night with the guys. I'll make plans with Luke."

Smiling from ear to ear, I said, "That sounds like a damn good plan."

Will dropped his shoulders and shook his head. "I guess I'll take these out to my truck."

Quickly finishing up my email to the coach, I hit Send and closed my laptop. The next nine days I wasn't thinking about anything but Lauren.

Sprinting up the stairs, I stood outside my bedroom and I watched Lauren move about the room as she sang a song from Brother Bear. She must have felt my stare because she stopped packing. Her blue eyes embraced mine as we stood there and took each other in.

Biting down on her lip, her eyes narrowed and I recognized the expression in those beautiful eyes. Walking into my room, I shut the door behind me as Lauren laughed and pulled her shirt over her head. "I've been waiting for you, Mr. Mathews."

Lauren and I were quickly lost in each other. Nothing

was more magical than the two of us making love. Running my finger along her arm, I felt completely relaxed. A part me didn't want to leave. I wanted to stay right here in my bed for the next week doing nothing but making love to Lauren and giving her orgasm after orgasm.

"I'm done packing," Lauren said, barely above a whisper.

Chuckling, I leaned into her hair and took in a deep breath and slowly released it. "Did you pack your whole closet?"

Playfully hitting my chest, she laughed. "Nope. Just half of it. You never know when a girl is going to need a certain outfit."

Smiling against her soft blonde hair, I grinned. "You're right. I've got a few things planned for us this week."

Turning, Lauren looked into my eyes as she raised her eyebrows. "Oh yeah? What kind of things?"

"The kind of things that are for me to know and you to find out."

Lifting up, Lauren turned and rested her hand and chin on my chest. "Surprises? Oh, I like surprises!"

Her eyes sparkled with excitement as she talked. Lauren had always loved surprises. Since I could remember she would beg her mom to throw her a surprise birthday party. Jessie never could get one planned because Lauren would snoop around for clues and always ended up finding out about the party. This year though, she would be surprised. Lauren's birthday was in July but because of football practice this summer, I was going to be gone over her birthday. I was throwing her a surprise party at the end of June, and there would be no way she would catch on.

Tapping the tip of her nose with my finger, I laughed. "I know you like surprises. Come on, the faster we leave, the faster we get home."

Lauren jumped out of bed and headed into the bathroom, but not before glancing over her shoulder and saying, "I'm taking a quick shower."

My dick jumped as I smiled and followed her into the bathroom. *This woman has bewitched me, heart and soul.*

THIRTEEN

LAUREN

HOLDING MIREYA IN my arms, I walked around the room talking to her. Libby was deep in conversation with Alex and Maegan. They had been talking about something that had been going on with Maegan at school. I wanted to pay attention to the conversation, but my heart was lost to a four-month-old blue-eyed beauty that was currently giving me a huge smile.

"That's right. You love your Aunt Lauren the best, don't you, baby girl?" Mireya began doing that adorable little baby talk as my heart melted even more. Luke walked up to me with the biggest smile I'd ever seen.

"She's addictive, isn't she?" Luke asked as he leaned over and kissed his daughter on the head.

Giggling, I said, "Very addictive."

Looking back down at the baby my heart did a crazy flip. *I wonder what mine and Colt's kids would look like? Wait. Whoa. Slow down on that line of thinking there, Lauren.* We had only been dating a month, but it seemed liked it had been longer. So much longer.

Colt came walking up behind Luke with a drop dead gorgeous smile on his face. Yep. If we had a little girl, I wanted her to have light-brown hair . . . curly . . . light-brown hair. Blue eyes like the sky right after a rain shower moves through. She would have her daddy's dimples and my nose. Oh, for sure she'd have my nose. Closing my eyes, I thought about my stomach growing with Colt's baby. Snapping them back open, I got control of these crazy thoughts.

Peeking over to Colt, my stomach dropped. The way he was looking at Mireya had my insides turning all gooey. His hand came up as he pushed her hair back and chuckled. "She has so much hair, you could put those little Velcro bows in it."

Dear God. He knew about the little Velcro bows? My heart was gonna explode. He kept talking and my insides kept melting. "Wow! Her eyelashes are so long." Glancing at me quickly, he gave me a wink. "Isn't she so precious?"

If I hadn't been holding the baby, I would have dropped to the floor and told Colt to take me. The throbbing between my legs was unreal. I was ready to blow off this little party Grace had organized and take Colt back to my house and have my wicked way with him.

Licking my lips, I couldn't pull my eyes from Colt, who was now gazing down at Mireya and talking baby talk to her.

I felt someone come up next to me. Hot breath was next to my ear as Grace whispered, "Don't even think about it."

Snapping my head to her, I asked, "What?"

She narrowed her eye at me as she tilted her head. "Please, I see it all over your face. This party is for you, missy! Calm the hormones and put them to rest."

Colt's head bolted up, "What? What's going on?"

Grace scooped the baby from my arms and gave her a kiss on the cheek. "Nothing for you to worry about, Colt." Snuggling her nose into the crook of Mireya's neck, Grace went on. "Isn't that right my sweet little niece? The big bad boys have to leave so the girls can get their party on."

Luke chuckled and asked, "Why am I worried, Grace?"

Grace looked up at Luke, lips parted open in a state of surprise. "I have no idea what you are talking about, big brother. I simply planned a little get-together with all my girls. We need some one-on-one time. Besides, Lauren asked me for a bit of advice a few weeks back, so I've invited a friend of mine to help her with the subject."

Looking at Grace with a confused expression, she moved her tongue in her mouth and pushed her cheek out.

Sucking in a breath, I knew instantly what she was talking about. Blow jobs! Grace was having a Blow Job workshop party. Oh my glitter! This just turned into something totally different.

"Shut up!" I said as I smiled at Grace.

Giving me a slight pop of her head, she said, "I told you I wouldn't let you down."

"Wait, what is going on? I'm confused. Y'all are having a study group?"

Grace slowly turned and looked at Colt as I attempted to hold back my laughter. "Yeah, Colt. We're having a study group party." Grace shook her head and rolled her eyes at Colt.

Colt frowned and looked at me. "That doesn't sound like fun."

Luke started laughing as he took Mireya from Grace. "If I know my sister, Colt, they are in for more than just fun tonight."

Grace dropped her mouth open and placed her hand on her heart like she was stunned. "That hurts. I'm being falsely accused."

Luke made a face and said, "Uh huh. Just don't get into trouble. No drinking and driving and don't get my wife trashed. I intend on making love to her when I get home tonight."

Grace slammed her hands over her ears and began singing, "La la la la!"

Luke walked over to Libby and let her kiss Mireya goodbye. She was spending the night at Grace and Jack's, Colt's grandparents' house. They offered to take Mireya so that Luke and Libby could enjoy a night out with all of us.

Colt pulled me into his arms and searched my face. "You sure you want to stay for a study group?"

I giggled at how naïve he was being. "It's a blow job workshop, Colt."

His eyes widened in surprise, and he went to talk but

nothing came out. "A w-what?"

"Blow job workshop."

Swallowing hard, he whispered, "Holy fuck."

Winking, I leaned up on my tippy toes and kissed him. "Maybe tonight I can try out what I learn on you."

The lust that danced across Colt's face had me needing him desperately. "I just came in my pants."

Throwing my head back, I laughed. Looking at him, I hit him lightly on the chest and gave him a little push. "Go have fun with the guys. Be careful, Colt."

Kissing me hard and fast, Colt smiled against my lips. "Always, sweetheart. I love you."

"Love you too, Colt."

After the guys left, Libby clapped her hands and said, "All right! Let's get this workshop going!"

Libby walked around with a bottle of wine as she filled up each of our glasses. The only person who didn't have any wine was Taylor. She never was much of a person for drinking.

Maegan was about to say something when the doorbell rang. Alex, Libby and Maegan all jumped up and squealed. Rolling my eyes, I drank half the glass of wine. I was going need it to get through this night.

Grace's friend, Anna, walked through the door pulling a dolly behind her and carrying a small cooler. Grace began all the introductions.

"Anna, meet Libby, this is her house."

Anna smiled and reached for Libby's hand. "The new mom. I have some wonderful gadgets for you."

Libby's eyes widened. "Thank God, Jack and Grace took Mireya tonight."

Everyone laughed.

"Next we have Alex. She's getting married this summer."

Anna smiled bigger. "Ohh . . . I have some fun little tips for the wedding night that will rock your new husband's world."

Alex blushed. "Next we have Maegan who could probably have taught this class herself."

Maegan shot Grace a dirty look. "Fuck you, Grace."

Anna chuckled. "It's a pleasure, Maegan."

Grace walked over to Taylor who looked scared to death. "This is the virgin of the bunch." Looking at Taylor, Grace pulled her head back and asked, "You are still a virgin, right?"

Red washed over Taylor's face as she pushed Grace. "Yes, and I wear the title proudly."

Anna clapped her hands. "Oh good!" Reaching into her bag, she dug around and pulled out a sash. Placing it over Taylor's head, we all started laughing.

The sash read *Proud Virgin.*

Grace turned and held her hand out for me. Placing my hand into Grace's, she pulled me closer to her. "This is the girl who requested your help, Anna. Lauren has recently popped her cherry—"

"Hey!" I said as I looked at Grace, who continued to talk.

"She would like to know the proper way to please her man in the area of blow jobs."

"I'm going to be sick," Alex said as her face drained of all color. Pursing my lips together, I attempted to not start laughing.

Anna walked up to me and smiled. It was almost a motherly-type smile. I liked Anna instantly. Her smile was infectious and when she smiled really big, she had a dimple in each cheek. Reaching for my hand, Anna gave it a firm shake. Her nails were flawless. "Lauren, it's a pleasure to meet you."

Shaking her hand, I nodded as I felt my cheeks light up on fire. "The pleasure's all mine."

Anna gave me a wicked grin. "Oh not yet, honey. But it will be this evening when I'm done with y'all."

Turning, Anna began pulling everything out of her bags. She put down flavored condoms, flavored lubricants, sex toys, which I had no idea what half of them were used for and some I didn't want to know what they were used for.

Then she pulled out a few different vibrators and these

silicone blob-looking things. Reaching over I picked up the pink one and turned it over. Sucking in a breath of air, I turned to Taylor with a horrified look on my face. Showing her, I whispered, "Does that look like a—"

"Vagina? Yes. Except I don't think all va-jay-jay's look like half a rose."

Giggling, I looked back at it. It did somewhat resemble part of a rose.

Anna looked at Taylor and me and smiled. "You're holding a masturbation sleeve. Better know as . . . your man's second vagina."

"Oh shit." Taylor and I both said as I dropped the sleeve back onto the table.

My cell phone rang and I quickly pulled it from my pocket. *Daddy* scrolled across the screen. Standing, I walked to the corner of the room.

"Hello?"

"Hey, baby girl."

Smiling, I shook my head. I adored my parents and was lucky to have a close relationship with them. They both still called me baby girl and even though I wouldn't ever admit it to them, I loved it.

"Hey, Daddy! What's up? Are y'all in a port?"

"Yeah baby, we just got off the ship. Is Colt with you?"

My heart dropped. Slowly taking in a deep breath, I blew it out. "No, why do you need him?"

Covering the phone, Daddy shouted something to someone. "I was gonna see if he might be interested in—"

Closing my eyes, I prayed he wasn't going to say something about the new stallion we had coming in tonight. I wanted my hands on that horse first and I had told Daddy that.

"Lauren? Are you still there?"

Shaking my head, I said, "Um, yeah. Sorry what did you say?"

"I need a fence repaired tomorrow and wanted to see if Colt would be around and could help with it."

Relief flooded my body. "Oh. He should have his cell phone."

"Text me his number again will you, Lauren. I must have lost it."

"Sure, I'll do it right now."

"Have fun tonight, baby girl. Love you."

Feeling my face flush, I said, "I'll try. Y'all too and love you back."

Hitting End, I sent the text to my father and pushed the phone back into my pocket and made my way back over to where everyone was. Taking my seat next to Taylor, I looked down at the coffee table. There were all kinds of little packets spread around the table. Grace, Maegan, Alex, and Libby were picking everything up and talking about how they wanted to try it. Then the Altoids caught my eye. Thank God. I was starving.

Reaching over, I grabbed a container. Reaching in, I grabbed two mints and threw them into my mouth then handed the container to Taylor.

"Thanks!" Taylor said with a smile.

Looking around, I noticed everyone was staring at me. "What?"

Anna let out a small squeal. "You're jumping ahead, Lauren. But by putting Altoids in your mouth while you suck off your man, it gives him another sensation. The men I've done this with have loved it. They come so much faster."

Anna wiggled her eyebrows up and down as I choked on the Altoids. *Holy shit. Oh my glitter! Eewww! I need bleach after that mental image. Stat!*

Taylor began slapping my back as she laughed. Glaring over at her, I gave her the finger.

Libby started laughing. "Just don't eat like ten of them and then try it. I did that with Luke and all he did was start screaming. I thought he was screaming because it felt good, so I sucked harder. He jumped up and started yelling, 'My dick is on fire!' as he ran to the bathroom. He turned the water on and just kept repeating how it burned. I think ten Altoids was a bit overkill."

We all laughed except for Grace. She wore a look of horror the whole time Libby told the story. "I will never be able to unhear that, Libby. Ever."

"Now ladies, let's get this started. Shall we?"

Everyone nodded and got settled in, ready for our lesson. Libby had a huge sectional sofa that we sat on. All the . . . goods . . . were spread out on the barn door coffee table. The suctioned dildo looked scary as hell to me, but I found myself thinking of places to stick it. Did it stay stuck to the surface when you used it? I wondered why you would need it to suction on something.

Shaking my head to clear my thoughts, I listened to Anna tell us all about herself. She was thirty-one, married with three kids. Two boys, twin three-year-olds, and one little girl who just turned five. She had been doing sex party's for Pure Romance and decided to branch out on her own and start her own company. Taylor hit me on the leg when Anna said the name of her business was *Blow by Blow*.

Reaching into her cooler she began taking out . . . cucumbers? Grace and Alex busted out laughing as Libby and Maegan stared at the cucumbers with I'm sure the same shocked expression Taylor and I both wore.

"Cucumbers? You expect me to suck off a cucumber?" Maegan asked.

Anna nodded her head as she flashed Maegan a smile and gave her a wink. She dug around and pulled out the biggest, thickest cucumber I'd ever seen. Handing it to Maegan she said, "I think you need this bad boy." Taking a closer look, I noticed the blue balls at the end of the cucumber were water balloons and the tops of the cucumbers were made out to look like the head of a dick.

"Jesus, what are you trying to do, choke me to death with this monster?"

Everyone laughed as Grace poured more wine and Libby brought over a small little cooler filled with beer. Reaching for a beer, I popped it open and took a long drink. I was gonna need a strong buzz if I was going to be sticking a cucumber in my mouth and pretending it was a dick.

Taylor leaned over and said, "If she gives me one that big she is going to scar me for life!"

Letting out a chuckle, I pushed Taylor with my arm as she giggled.

Once all the cucumbers were passed out, Anna stood. "Now, is everyone pleased with their dicks?"

Grace sat back and stared at her dick . . . I mean cucumber. "If I was only so lucky to have a dick this size."

Alex gasped and told Grace to stop. "What about Noah?" Libby asked. Grace's face fell and Libby shook her head. "Shit, Grace I'm sorry. Have you seen him at all this year?"

Grace leaned forward and finished off her glass of wine. Setting it on the table she shrugged. "Nope. I guess he decided to either quit school or move schools after he got married."

My heart broke for Grace. Alex and Libby said that Grace must have fallen hard for Noah because she hadn't been out with anyone since him. Maegan told Alex today that it was time for Grace to move on but I wasn't so sure Grace was going to feel the same way.

Smacking her hands together, Anna pulled me from my thoughts. "Okay ladies. Now I'm going to use a cucumber dick as well. First off let's talk about the penis." Anna spent about five minutes giving us a run down of the penis. I didn't think I really needed to know about the anatomy of a dick, but Anna said it would help. "Now, the first thing you are going to want to discuss is the yes and no's. Every couple has them. By talking about this first, you'll both be more relaxed."

Maegan huffed. Anna looked over at Maegan and said, "Maegan, did you have something to add?"

Maegan shrugged. "I mean, if you're both hot and bothered and you decide to go down on a guy, are you really going to stop and be like, wait, we need to discuss this?"

Anna smiled sweetly. "You're right, you probably wouldn't. But, if you're in a relationship with someone you care about, you're more likely going to be able to have that conversation together."

Grace pointed to Maegan. "That counts Meg out. She's a wham bam thank you ma'am kind of girl."

Maegan glared at Grace. "Again, fuck you, Grace. You're one to talk."

Alex let out a frustrated moan. "Stop arguing, you two. I want to know how to give Will a good blow job."

Libby snarled her lip. "Gross. That's my brother you're talking about, Alex."

Anna let out a chuckle. "Shall we continue?"

Taylor practically shouted, "Yes!" I couldn't help but notice she was now drinking a glass of wine. Looking at me she winked. "I needed to loosen up a bit."

Anna started talking again. "Remember fast isn't always best. Start off slow. Kiss around his stomach, hips, and inner thigh. Remember to breathe and relax. No one enjoys rushed oral sex. Take your time and I promise it will be worth it in the end." Giggles encircled the room and you would think we were all sitting in a high school sex education class.

"The next tip is to make sure your man's dick is wet enough." Anna spit on her cucumber, so we all followed her directions. "Whether you use your spit or lubricant, make sure it is good and wet before you begin playing with it. You could even attempt to take your man all the way to the back of your throat as it releases more saliva."

Libby attempted to take her cucumber all the way in but started gagging. "Nope. No way, this baby is not going in any more."

Glancing over to Grace, she was licking all over her cucumber. "Damn, I want a salad now." She mumbled as everyone started laughing.

"The next tip is if you get tired or your jaw begins to ache, take a break and use your hands. Slowly move them up and down the shaft with a relaxed wrist. You'll want to add a little twist to your movement but not too much of one." Anna began to show us the proper way to use our hands. Moving my hands up and down my cucumber seemed silly at first, but one quick peek around the room and everyone was totally focused on their cucumber dicks. Alex was staring at it as if she was concentrating hard.

Continuing to work her cucumber, Anna continued

talking. "Now the next thing to talk about. To spit or swallow."

Grace let out a moan as she slowly pushed her mouth over the cucumber. The way she worked it had me and Taylor leaning forward to watch her. Grace pulled it out and looked at us. "Sorry girls, it's been too long since I've even touched a penis. This cucumber is starting to look pretty damn good."

Laughter broke out around the room as Anna talked about letting your partner know if you wanted to be warned ahead of time in regards to him coming in your mouth. Taylor leaned over and asked, "Spit or swallow?"

Shrugging, I looked back out at everyone. "What does it taste like?"

"Ass," Maegan quickly said. "Spit that shit out as soon as you can. Better yet, let him jiz on himself." My mind was flooded with the memory of Colt and I in the study room as he came on my stomach. Chewing my lip, I pushed the memory away.

Libby laughed. "No it doesn't, Lauren. It depends on what they eat. If they eat a lot of Kiwi or Pineapple, the cum tastes better, sweeter almost. Most of the time it's kind of salty."

"Huh," I said as I let it soak in.

Taylor downed her wine as she sat back and laughed. "Nope. He is just gonna have to come somewhere else, salty, sweet, or peanut butter tasting. That shit is not going in my mouth."

Everyone died laughing as Taylor made her announcement.

Anna took a sip of wine and went on with her presentation. "Now the most sensitive part of man's dick is the head. Be sure to pay particular attention to this area. To start you should lick up and down his shaft. Get to know his sensitive areas."

Anna began licking up the cucumber and motioned with her hand for us to do the same. "Now, put your mouth on the top of the head. No teeth ladies. Using a sucking sensation, go down a little ways." Anna started moving her mouth up and down her cucumber dick.

"Move your head some ladies . . . like a corkscrew."

Okay this is awkward.

"Keep that dick wet, ladies." Libby and Grace were giggling as they took their cucumbers and hit them together like they were toasting each other.

Alex cursed, "Damn it. I took a nipple off my cucumber!"

"Don't forget the balls, but be mindful if he is overly sensitive in that area. Don't be afraid to play with them. Sometimes right before they come, a slight pull on the scrotum will heighten his orgasm. Some men don't like a lot of sucking. Listen to him. Learn what pleases him and what doesn't."

"What if the penis is too big to fit in your mouth all the way?" Taylor asked.

Anna smiled. "Great question, Taylor! If that is the case, use your hand in that up and down relaxed motion I showed. Apply a little pressure with the hand but not too much."

As we continued to practice on our cucumber dicks, I was growing more and more confident I would be able to give Colt a good blow job. Anna kept talking as we all laughed, practiced and drank.

Maegan cleared her throat and said, "Let's talk deep throating."

Anna picked up a dildo and began talking. "For me, I practiced on a dildo. The deeper you go, the better you train your throat. The best position for deep throating is a sixty-nine."

"Yeah," Grace said as she and Alex high-fived each other. Libby made a shuddering move as she rolled her eyes and said, "Again, don't need that visual, Alex."

Maegan nodded her head and placed her cucumber dick in her mouth and moaned.

Grace looked at Maegan, "Yeah, Meg, get into that shit!"

What Maegan did next had all of us gasping.

"Oh my glitter!" I shouted. "You just bit off the head of your dick!"

Anna's mouth dropped open, as she stood there stunned. "Maegan. Why?"

Taking another bite of her cucumber, she shrugged. "I was hungry damn it! You can't have us sucking on cucumbers all night and not expect us to get hungry for Christ's sake!"

Grace reached over and hit Maegan. "I cannot believe you just ate your dick!"

Maegan smiled and said, "I'll tell you one thing, it sure as shit tastes better than any cum I've tasted."

"Gross," Taylor said as she took another drink of wine and rolled her eyes.

"Jesus, Meg, what in the hell is wrong with you?" Grace asked as she busted out laughing.

We spent the rest of the evening laughing, drinking, and learning tricks to please our men. My favorite part of the evening was learning how to apply a condom with your mouth. Taylor kept gagging every time she tried until she finally gave up. "That's it. I'm not meant to be the type of girl who gives blow jobs. I'll end up puking on the poor bastard."

Laughter echoed through the room as Libby said, "Don't worry, Tay. You can't help it if all that knowledge went to Meg!"

Maegan raised her glass of wine and smiled proudly. "Hell yeah it did!"

After taking a break and eating some food and chatting, Anna got back down to business. Picking up one of the silicone looking blobs she held it up. "Now, for the masturbation sleeve. This can be a lot of fun for your man, especially if you're not feeling it, maybe it's that time of the month, or you both want to just play, this can be a great tool to use."

Taylor reached for one and said, "What if he likes this better than you?"

Grace grabbed it from Taylor. "Tay, if any guy ever tells you he wants to use this thing rather than stick his dick in your pussy . . . you better kick him in his junk and walk out the door."

Anna chortled and pointed to Grace. "That was way better than my answer."

B Y THE TIME I walked Anna to the door and thanked her for everything, I was feeling pretty damn good. My buzz was borderline being tipsy, which probably meant I was drunk. Taylor for the first time ever had a pretty strong buzz going on but she wasn't drunk. She knew when to back off and quickly began drinking water for the rest of the night.

"Thank you, Anna for the fun evening. I haven't laughed that much in a long time."

Anna reached for my hand and gently shook it. "It was my pleasure, Lauren. Have fun tonight."

Giving her a naughty grin, I responded. "Oh I plan on it."

Turning to walk back inside I heard someone coming down the driveway. My quickening heartbeat left me feeling breathless as that familiar ache between my legs began growing. "Colt," I whispered.

Pulling up and parking, he jumped out of his truck and gave me that crooked smile of his. My grin was so big I couldn't contain it. Wetting my lips, I tried to push the naughty thoughts of taking him with my mouth away.

"Hey," Colt said as he sauntered up to me.

"Hey," I whispered back.

Stopping right in front of me, I inhaled a deep breath. His cologne swept around my body and instantly had me walking into his arms. "I missed you," I said into his chest as he wrapped his strong arms around me.

"Yeah? Well I missed you too, sweetheart. Did y'all have fun?"

Pulling back I gazed up into his eyes. How in the world did I ever push this man away? Why in the world did I push this man away? "I did. I learned a lot on my practice dick and then I ate it."

Colt's eyes widened in disbelief as he tilted his head and said, "Come again?"

Giggling, I placed my cheek on Colt's strong broad chest. I loved his body. He was built, but it had nothing to do with playing football. It was from all of the hard work he would do on the ranch. "Colt?"

Running his hand over my back softly he asked, "Yeah, sweetheart?"

"Will you take me home? I want to be wrapped up in your arms."

Holding me tighter, he whispered against the top of my head, "Nothing would make me happier."

FOURTEEN

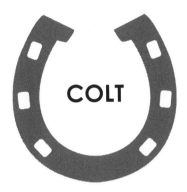

COLT

I T FELT LIKE I was wiping the palms of my hands on my pants every few seconds. Lauren was sitting next to me in my truck talking a mile a minute. She was for sure tipsy. I heard all about their cucumber dicks, Maegan eating her dick, Taylor drinking wine and getting a buzz, and how there was a suctioned dildo on the table. That you never want to have more than two Altoids in your mouth before giving a blow job and that if I ever liked a fake vagina she'd kick me in the balls. The last one still had me thrown for a loop.

Trying not to chuckle at some of Lauren's innocence, my mind drifted to what I had been doing the last few hours.

Luke and Will had decided to go out for dinner and meet up with a few guys from high school. I headed on over to Lauren's house and spent the next few hours transforming her room into what I hoped would result in a romantic evening.

Candles had been placed all around the room. Rose petals started from the door through the house and up to her room. I had made a playlist of some of Lauren's favorite songs and had that ready to go.

Gripping the steering wheel tighter, I started getting nervous and I had no idea why.

Dropping her head back against the headrest, Lauren started laughing. "Man oh man. I'm just talking your ear off, aren't I?"

Reaching for her hand, I brought it up to my mouth as I placed my lips on her soft skin. "Don't stop. I love hearing you talk."

Lifting her eyebrows she asked, "Why?"

Shrugging my shoulders, I pulled into her driveway and replied, "I love everything about you, Lauren. The way you laugh when something really tickles you. Or how you hum when you brush your teeth. The way you do a little dance when you get excited, or how you skip around without a care in the world. The list is endless."

Parking in front of her house, I turned to look at her. Lauren stared at me as I watched her eyes fill with tears.

Reaching over I placed my hand on the side of her face. "Baby, are you feeling okay?"

Biting on her lower lip, she nodded her head and quickly wiped a tear that began to fall. "It's just . . . I mean . . . I love you so much, Colt and I know we've only been dating for a month." Looking away, she wiped another tear. Turning back to me her eyes were on fire. "I don't think I could survive a day without you now that you're mine. I need your touch every single morning or something feels off for the rest of the day. It scares me how much I love you, Colt."

Moving my hand behind her neck I pulled her to me. Unbuckling her seat belt Lauren leaned closer to me and pressed her lips to mine. "I love you, Lauren. I love you so much."

"Colt, please make love to me. I need you."

Opening the door to my truck, I unbuckled my seatbelt and hopped out. Lauren crawled over my seat and right into my arms. Giving the door a kick, it shut as I walked up to the front door. Unlocking the door with the key that Scott had given me two years ago for emergencies, I walked us into the house and straight up to Lauren's room.

It was hard trying to walk, carry Lauren, and climb the stairs all at once. Her sweet little whimpers and moans

had my pants feeling too small. Stopping outside her bedroom, I slowly slid her down my body until her feet hit
the ground. Cupping the sides of her face, I looked into
her beautiful baby-blue eyes. "Lauren, you have and will
always be, my forever love."

Closing her eyes, I watched a tear roll down her cheek.
Slowly opening her eyes she smiled. "Colt, you have and
will always be *my* forever love." My heart slammed against
my chest. I knew Lauren knew how special those words
were to me and for her to repeat them back to me meant
more than anything.

"I'm going to make love to you all night, Lauren."

Nodding her head, she sucked in her lower lip. "Um . . . I
do want to try out some things I learned tonight though."

Letting out a moan, I reached behind her and placed
my hand on the doorknob. "Give me two minutes, baby."

Looking at me with a confused expression, Lauren fur-
rowed her eyebrows. "What?"

Holding up my fingers and making the sign for two, I
repeated, "Two minutes."

Scooting around her, I slipped into the room. Grabbing
the lighter, I quickly began lighting all the candles. Walking
over to the small ice chest, I pulled out the container full
of chocolate-covered strawberries. Reaching down, I felt
the pouch in my pocket. Taking a look around I smiled. It
was perfect.

There was a knock on the door and I quickly walked
over to the door. "Turn around and close your eyes,
Lauren."

"O-okay."

Slowly opening the door, I smiled when I saw Lauren
standing with her back to the door. Walking around to the
front of her, I brought her to me and kissed her. Her arms
immediately went around my neck as I walked her into her
room. I wasn't sure how long we stood in the middle of her
room, completely lost in our kiss.

Pulling back some, I smiled at her. Lauren smiled and
looked around. Her hands dropped from around my neck
and went to her mouth. "Oh . . . my . . . Colt." Spinning

around, she took everything in. She wasn't expecting this and by the look on her face, she was beyond happy.

"When did you do this?" Lauren asked as she walked up and ran her hands over the baby-blue lingerie I had laid out on the bed. Picking it up, she looked over her shoulder at me. "Did you buy this?"

Nodding, I smiled. "While you were at your . . . study group. I came over and set everything up. And yes, I bought that for you."

Clutching it to her chest, she walked up to me. "It's beautiful."

"Do I get to see it on you?" I asked as I pushed a long curl from her face.

The air in the room instantly changed as Lauren gazed up at me with nothing but desire in her eyes. "Do I get to see you naked?"

Letting out a soft chuckle, I said, "I bet you will as soon as I see you dressed in this."

Narrowing her eye at me she said, "Mmm . . . playing hardball, huh? Okay, give me a second to change."

Spinning on her heels, Lauren walked into her bathroom. Glancing back, she gave me a wink and a sexy smile then closed the door.

Placing my hands on my face, I ran them up and down and tried to calm my beating heart. *What in the hell is wrong with me? I feel like it's our first time.*

Looking around the room, everything looked perfect. *Was it perfect though? Was it romantic enough? Shit.*

Sitting down on the end of the bed, I let out a frustrated moan. What if I was moving to fast? We'd only been dating for one month exactly. Maybe I should I wait? The last thing I wanted to do was scare Lauren away. My heart was pounding against my chest as my head and heart duked it out. My heart eventually won.

The door to the bathroom opened and I jumped up. Lauren was standing there with her hand up high on the doorjamb as she gave me the sexiest smile I'd ever seen.

Barely being able to even speak a word, I whispered, "Wow."

Lauren licked her lips and looked down at the one-piece teddy. The blue brought out her eyes so much they looked as if they were lighting up the whole room. I could see her hard nipples through the lace material and my dick throbbed in my pants.

"How does it look?"

"Better on you than the girl at the store."

Lauren's face dropped and I started laughing. Holding up my hands I said, "Sorry! Shit! I'm nervous as hell and I was trying to make a joke."

Giving me a dirty look, Lauren walked closer to me but stopped just short of my reach. "That was a very bad joke, Mr. Mathews."

Lacing her arms around my neck, my eyes traveled all over her body. "Very bad," I mumbled.

Lauren gave me a seductive look. "Do you know what today is?"

Walking up to her, I placed my hands on her hips and pulled her to me. Making sure I pressed my hard dick into her stomach. Lauren closed her eyes as she dropped her mouth open slightly and let out a deep breath. "Today marks one month since we've been together."

Lauren's eyes danced with happiness as a beautiful little crooked smile moved across her face. "You totally just redeemed yourself from the bad joke."

Tossing my head back, I laughed.

Lauren's hands moved to my jeans as she quickly began to unbutton them and tried to push them down. "Colt, I can't take it any longer. I need to feel you."

Grabbing her hands, I smiled. "I have something else to give you first before we go there."

Lifting her eyebrows, she asked, "What?"

Dropping my one hand, I reached into my pocket and pulled out the small velvet bag. Lauren looked down at it and smiled. "Colt," she whispered as I dropped her other hand and opened up the bag.

Before I took the ring out, I looked into Lauren's eyes. "I wasn't sure how you'd feel about me giving you this since we just started dating, but I want everyone to know you're mine, Lauren."

Her eyes widened as she wore a shocked expression on her face. Opening the bag I took the ring out and held it up for her.

Her mouth fell open and she let out a small chuckle. "The ring I wanted."

Almost three years ago we had all been in Austin shopping and Lauren had pointed to a belt buckle ring that she wanted. When we all walked out of the store and headed to lunch, I doubled-back and bought it for her.

Swallowing hard, I said, "I bought it that day. The day you looked at it in James Avery."

Placing her hands over her mouth, Lauren slowly shook her head. "You've had it this whole time?"

Letting out a gruff laugh, I said, "Yeah, I know it was stupid but—"

Lauren's eyes gleamed as she threw herself into my body and kissed me. Wrapping my arms around her, I deepened the kiss until we were completely lost in it . . . again.

Lauren barely pulled back as she talked against my lips. "You'll never know how special you make me feel, Colt Mathews. I've never felt so loved and desired in my entire life."

Breaking our contact, I took a step back and reached for Lauren's hand and slipped the ring onto her left ring finger. "I'm yours forever, Lauren. No matter what, I'll never leave your side."

"Forever," Lauren whispered.

Reaching out, Lauren pushed my pants down as I pulled them off of my feet and tossed them to the side. "I know you want to try what you learned tonight, but right now, sweetheart, I just want to hold you."

Placing her hand on my chest, Lauren's face beamed with happiness. "That sounds perfect."

Pulling my T-shirt off my chest and throwing it onto the floor, I reached and picked Lauren up. Carrying her over to her bed, I pulled back the covers and gently set her down. Crawling over her, I slid in next to her and pulled her body up against mine. "I love you, Colt."

Kissing the back of her head, I pulled her closer. "I love you more, Lauren."

Everything in this moment felt perfect. It felt right.

"Never stop holding me, Colt."

"Never," I whispered.

FOOTBALL PRACTICE IN the spring was closed to the public, but players' girlfriends were allowed to attend the practices, as long as they were not a distraction. Glancing over to the stands, I saw Lauren with her nose buried in a book. She had a huge test she had been studying for.

Lining up, I got ready for the play. Roger seemed to have moved on since he found out how serious Lauren and I were. We'd been dating over two months and I couldn't believe how amazing things still were between us.

Roger called hike and I took off running. Roger threw and I jumped and caught the ball and took off down the field. Making the touchdown, everyone ran up and gave me a high five.

Coach nodded his approval and told the team to huddle up.

"Great practice. This was our last spring practice. We have a scrimmage this weekend and I expect a repeat of what I saw on the field today."

Everyone hooted and hollered. "Now go shower up and get out of here."

Walking toward the locker room, I turned to find Lauren. She was talking to a girl I'd never seen before. She must have sensed me watching her because she looked up and smiled at me. Smiling, I gave her a wave and then held up both hands telling her to give me ten minutes.

Nodding her head, she blew me a kiss. Laughing, I turned and headed into the locker room. After taking a quick shower I got dressed and was about to head out to meet up with Lauren.

"Good catch, Mathews," Roger said as he walked over

to me with a towel still wrapped around his waist.

"Thanks. Good throw."

Roger smirked. "Now that everything seems to be settled between us, friends?" Roger stuck his hand out for me to shake it. Grabbing his hand tightly, we shook. I didn't trust the look in his eyes. Lauren had told me about Marie stopping to talk to her and how Roger had been digging for information and using Marie to gather it all up. What a dick.

"Friends it is."

Turning, I headed to the door. "Oh hey, Mathews, one more thing."

Glancing back at him I asked, "What's up?"

"Stay focused in the game."

Pulling my head back and giving him a confused look, I said, "I always am."

Pushing the door open I headed out of the locker room area and up to Lauren.

That was three times now someone had told me to stay focused. *Was I not focusing?* I hadn't dropped a single ball, I made every play. What in the hell was wrong with everyone?

Running my hand over my short hair, I dreaded this fall. For some reason coach did not like me having a girlfriend. I was going to have to learn to balance both and I didn't think I would have a problem doing that. Lauren knew how much I loved football and she would never get in the way of that. Ever.

I just wasn't sure how much I loved football.

FIFTEEN

LAUREN

GRACE AND I were walking out of the library laughing when Grace smacked right into a guy. "Oh shit! I'm so sorry." Grace said as she bent over to pick up her books. I couldn't help but notice how the guy was staring at Grace. She was, of course, oblivious to it.

My heart broke for Grace. As much as she tried to brush off the fact that Noah had pretty much dropped off the face of the Earth, we all knew it killed her. Noah had been texting Grace and she would text back but her fear of committing to anyone stood in the way. Then when he didn't tell her he was getting married and he kept texting her, that just reaffirmed to Grace that men sucked. She stopped texting him back, yet she wouldn't date anyone. It was as if her heart had been given to Noah, even though she denied it, and she wasn't sure what to do about it. Then, Noah just stopped texting.

Handing Grace her last book the guy flashed a smile at Grace. "Grace Johnson, right?"

Grace stared at the hottie standing in front of us. His light-brown hair was a mess, clearly he just got done running, and his emerald eyes had Grace's eyes pinned in on him. "Um . . . do we know each other?" Grace asked as she tilted her head.

Laughing, he said, "Yeah, Hunter. I'm in your psychology

class."

Recognition moved across Grace's face as she pointed to him and said, "Oh yeah. Well, so sorry for running into you like that."

Seeing he was losing the moment he ran his hand through his hair and asked Grace out. "Hey, you wouldn't want to go grab dinner and a movie would you?"

Grace never missed a beat. She kept her smile sincere as she turned the poor guy down. "Awe, thanks for the invite, but I'm going to have to pass. I'll see you in class though."

Hunter's smile faded some as he nodded his head. "Right. Okay sure. See ya in class."

Grace walked off and I fell into step next to her. The hot breeze made me wish like hell I had worn shorts today and not jeans. May in Texas could be a hit or miss as far as the weather went. It could be sixty-two one day, and eighty-two the next. It just so happened yesterday was six-ty-two and today felt like ninety-nine.

"Grace, why didn't you take him up on his offer?" I asked.

Rolling her eyes as she glanced over at me she laughed. "Lauren, school's out for summer in a few days and I'll be heading home for the summer. Why would I want to go out on a date? If he wanted to ask me out, he should have done it like three months ago."

Frowning, I nodded my head. She did have a point there. I never did understand why guys waited so long to make their move. Glancing down at my ring Colt had given me, I smiled. Even Colt, buying this ring so many years ago and hanging on to it as long as he did. My heart felt as if it skipped a beat whenever I thought about Colt being in love with me for so long.

Pulling my books closer to my chest, I smiled.

"Oh dear lord, you're thinking about Mathews aren't you?"

Chuckling, I asked, "How did you know?"

Grace reached out and gave me a playful push, causing me to stumble a few steps. "It's all over your damn face.

What, did you have hot sex last night or something?"

There was no way I could hide the happiness I felt. "Sex with Colt is hot every time."

"Ugh. Gag me, Lauren."

Laughing, I laced my arm around hers. "I can't wait to get home. I'm so over school."

Grace waved to some guy who walked by and said hello to her. "Me too. I just want to dig in the garden with Grams and not have to worry about anything."

Grace and Alex were both going to school for Horticulture. They loved getting their hands into Grams garden. Me? I enjoyed gardening, but I preferred to be with the horses. This summer Daddy was going to train me on the books and I was beyond thrilled to be able to gain knowledge on a piece of his business. But I wanted to gain more on the horse side of the business. Daddy even had a few trips planned to take a look at some horses and Colt and I were both going. Smiling slightly, I couldn't believe how threatened I was before about Colt working for my father.

Grace and I walked back to the house instead of taking the bus. It had felt good to get fresh air and just talk about stuff. Colt only had one final left, while Grace, Alex, Will and I all had two left. Once we all finished with our finals, we would be heading back to Mason. Will and Colt had been packing up stuff and getting the house ready to lock up for the summer. Colt would be coming back for football early and I was trying to figure out a way to let my parents know I'd be heading back early with him. They were not going to be happy about that. Colt was the first really serious relationship I was in. Roger was just . . . fun times. We hung out, the kissing got hot and heavy a few times, but my mind wasn't consumed with him twenty-four hours a day like it was with Colt.

"Besides the hot sex, things seem to be going good between you and Colt," Grace said as we walked up the driveway to the house.

"Amazing. Perfect. Amazing."

Grace laughed. "That bad huh?"

Stopping, I turned to Grace as she stopped and stared at me with a goofy smile. "Grace, sometimes . . . well sometimes I feel like I'm living this dream and I'm so scared that I'm going to wake up." Glancing down, I shook my head before looking back up at Grace. "I pushed Colt away for so long, fought feelings that I had just because of my pride. I guess I'm just scared that this is to good to be true. Like I'm waiting for the floor to be ripped out from underneath me."

Grace reached out and took my hand as she rubbed her thumb back and forth. "Lauren, what you and Colt share is amazing. The fact that three of my very best friends have found this amazing love makes me so happy for y'all. Honey, you can't keep worrying about the what-ifs. Look at Will and Alex. Luke and Libby. They are so in love and happy. Sweetie, if it's meant to be it will be. Enjoy every single day together, Lauren. Each day is a gift so don't ever take it for granted or think you can put something off until tomorrow because you might not get the chance."

A breeze blew as I watched it toss Grace's long hair around. Why hadn't Grace, Maegan, and Taylor been as lucky as the rest of us? Grace and Maegan were both battling demons they both insisted on fighting alone, and Taylor was so caught up in being the perfect student for her parents, she wasn't enjoying her life.

"Thank you, Grace. I really hope that your time is coming next. You deserve to be in love and happy. To find the frosting to your cake!"

Grace laughed as she rolled her eyes. "You and your damn sayings, Lauren."

As we walked back to the house I finally got the courage to talk to Grace about Noah. "Grace, may I ask you something personal?"

"Of course you can, Lauren."

Worrying my lower lip, I asked, "Grace, why did you push Noah away? Alex and Libby said you seemed to really like him a lot."

Grace's whole body tensed as we continued to walk. "I do really like Noah. Or did like him anyway. He's married now, so it doesn't really matter."

Knowing Grace needed to talk about this, I pressed on. "But that doesn't answer why you pushed him away."

Grace chuckled. "It's pretty simple. I was scared of my feelings. That seems to be a common thing in our little group."

Nodding my head, I whispered, "Yeah, it sure is."

Grace pushed her hair behind her ear as she inhaled a deep breath and slowly let it out. "When I was in high school I let a guy have almost complete control over me, Lauren. I vowed to never let that happen again. Actually, I vowed to never get lost in another guy again. One night with Noah and I was completely and utterly lost. He brought out feelings in me that I had never experienced before. The way he looked into my eyes was as if I was the very air he breathed. It felt like it was too much too fast. If that makes sense."

Smiling, I said, "That's how Colt looks at me."

Grace glanced over to me with a weak smile. "He does look at you like that. And my brother looks at Libby like that, and Will does the same with Alex."

"And that scared you, Grace?"

Nodding her head, her face looked distraught. "Yeah, it scared the piss out of me, because I knew I was looking at him the same way. The last thing I wanted to do was open my heart up again. What if Noah ended up breaking it? I'm not sure I could have survived it."

The wind was picking up and the temperature was dropping. Grace and I both picked up our speed. A cold front had been about to blow through. Glancing back over my shoulder to the north, I saw the storm clouds building. I swear the weather in Texas could change faster than Grace could get to a sale at Nordstroms.

"We better hustle and get home before we get drenched," Grace said as she attempted to give me a reassuring smile.

It started sprinkling, so Grace and I started running. We were only two houses down from our place. As we ran up to the front porch, we both started laughing. "We made it!" Grace said just as it began pouring.

Before we walked into the house, I took Grace by the arm and asked, "Do you regret pushing him away, Grace?"

Tears formed in her eyes as she closed them. Opening her eyes, she slowly nodded her head. "Every single moment of every single day I regret not taking that last phone call from him. I'll never know what he was going to say." Letting out a fake laugh, Grace looked into my eyes. "I know I need to move on. My heart won't let me though."

Pulling Grace into my arms, I held her as she cried. It was the first time in my life I'd ever seen Grace Johnson cry.

LEANING MY HEAD back, I let the warm sun beat down on my face. A light breeze was blowing, giving just enough relief from the hot sun. We had been out of school for two weeks and summer was already heating up.

Taylor let out a frustrated moan. "Sometimes I swear, I want to move to Montana."

Grace sat up and looked at Taylor. "Tay, that's a great idea!"

Looking toward Grace, Taylor asked, "What's a great idea?"

Grace jumped up. "Oh my gosh! A road trip! We should totally go on a road trip."

Pulling my head back, I looked at Taylor and then Grace. "To where?"

Rolling her eyes, Grace laughed. "To Montana! We should go to Montana."

Taylor and I both busted out laughing as I shook my head while I dropped it back down.

"You're crazy, Grace."

Grace kicked my foot as I snapped my head back to her. "Hey!"

"Come on y'all! How much fun would it be if we all went on a road trip?"

"What about Libby? She won't leave the baby."

Panic set in as I thought about Colt. "What about Colt! I can't leave Colt."

"Oh Jesus, Mary, and Joseph. You can go a week or two without seeing Colt."

My eyes widened. "Two weeks!"

Grace slapped her hands together and started back to her horse. "Come on, let's head back. I'm calling an emergency meeting at Lib's. Get on your horses, bitches."

Standing, both Taylor and I looked at each other. The idea of going on a road trip with all the girls sounded like fun. But could I leave Colt for that long? Yes. Of course I could. I was a strong independent woman. This would be good for us.

As I climbed onto my horse, I actually got excited about this idea. I just had to worry about what Colt thought about the idea. Or worse yet . . . my parents.

TWO HOURS LATER we were all walking into Libby and Luke's house. The race to get to Mireya was a close one, but Taylor won out. Bitch. She was like a racehorse when it came to moving quickly.

Sticking my tongue out at Taylor, she chuckled as she settled onto the floor with the baby.

"So what's the big emergency meeting, Grace?" Alex asked as she flopped onto the couch next to Libby. Maegan sat next to Taylor as they both began trying to make Mireya laugh.

Looking around Libby's house I couldn't help but smile. Luke and Libby had settled into family life perfectly. Glancing over to Libby her face glowed with a sense of contentment. Since we had been home from school I'd been dreaming of me and Colt and us married and in our own little house.

Alex pulled me out of my thoughts as she stood up. "Are we here to talk about the wedding?"

Smiling, Grace shook her head. "No, Alex. We are not

here to talk about your wedding."

Jutting her lower lip in a pout, we all laughed as Alex fell back onto the couch.

Before my mind could drift off to the idea of marrying Colt, Grace slapped her hands together, startling not only me, but also Mireya. She had started crying when Taylor scooped her up and began dancing around the room with her, instantly making her laugh.

"Shit, sorry about that, Lib." Libby smiled and motioned for Grace to go on. "Now that Tay has Mireya all settled, we are here to talk about our girls' trip."

Alex, Libby, and Maegan all wore confused expressions on their faces. "Girls' trip? What girls' trip?" Alex asked.

Taylor let out a chuckle. "The girls' trip to Montana that Grace is planning."

Libby busted out laughing. "When did this come about?"

Grace placed her hands on her hips and looked around the room to each of us. "It came about this morning. Just think how fun it would be if we all drove up to Montana."

"Um . . . Grace, I have a slight problem with that. I have a seven-month-old baby. I can't go to Montana."

Grace pressed her lips together tightly. "Is it the distance? Too far?"

Libby offered Grace a bemused smile. "You could say."

Grace narrowed her left eye as if she was devising a new plan. "Okay, I'll give you that Montana could be a bit far to go with a baby. How about Colorado?"

Maegan perked up. "Durango? I've always wanted to go to Durango!"

The air in the room quickly changed to excitement. "How far is the drive?" Libby asked, clearly thinking more seriously about this.

Grace pulled out her phone. Asking into her phone for directions from Mason to Durango, it came back with thirteen hours. Libby chewed on her lower lip. "I don't know, Grace. Luke isn't gonna go for it."

"Go for what?" Everyone turned and looked at Luke. He was covered in sweat as he took a long drink of water.

Peeking over to Libby, I attempted to hold back my smile. She was looking at him like she wanted to pounce on him. He was for sure the salt to her nuts.

Standing, Libby made her way over to Luke and gently kissed him. "You look hot."

Luke smiled and I found myself looking away. Turning back I let out a gasp when I saw Colt standing there. He was wearing a white T-shirt that was soaking wet from sweat. It clung to his body, showing off the muscles he earned while doing work around his daddy's ranch. Will walked up to Alex and went to kiss her as she laughed and pushed him away. "Gross, Will. You are covered in sweat!"

Glancing back to Colt, I smiled. Winking he took a drink of water. Sighing, I wondered how in the world he made getting a drink look so damn sexy. My eyes traveled all over his body as a shiver ran across my skin. Colt never took his eyes off of me while he finished off his water. Setting the glass down in the sink he tilted his head and slowly flashed that smile of his. God help me to control myself because right now I couldn't care less who was in the room. I wanted Colt's hands on my body.

"Hey big brother! I'm trying to talk the girls into a girls' trip."

Luke, Colt, and Will all looked at Grace. She looked between each of them and laughed. "Holy hell. You'd think I just told the three of you that you were never going to have sex again. I'm just asking for five days with my girls. Five damn days of not having to stand here and watch the love fest between y'all."

"Amen!" Taylor and Maegan both said at once.

"Five days of just girl fun. Maybe a little responsible drinking, hiking, river rafting."

Libby's mouth dropped open. "Wait! I can't do any of that if I have the baby."

"Wait. What? You want to bring the baby, Libby?" Luke asked in a shocked voice.

Shrugging her shoulders she raised her eyebrows. "Well, you work every day so what else would I do with her?"

Will held up his hand, "Hold on. When and where?"

Grace smiled. "Durango and as soon as we can book the hotel we can leave!"

Colt's eyes were locked onto mine. I couldn't tell what he was thinking. A part of me really wanted to go on this girls' weekend, even though I'd miss Colt something fierce. What if he said no? The idea of Colt saying no had me getting upset. I was still my own person, and if I wanted to go on a trip. I'd go on a trip.

Motioning with his finger for me to come to him, I headed his way. Stopping just short of him he placed his hand on the side of my face. "I want to hold you in my arms but I'm sweaty."

His eyes burned with love as he gazed upon my face. "Kiss me then," I whispered.

Leaning down he did just that. Gently placing his lips on mine, he kissed me softly. Colt's kisses were like the sweetest candy I'd ever tasted. They were addictive and I craved them always.

"Ugh, see what I mean. Love fest example number one from Colt and Lauren."

Smiling against my lips, Colt whispered, "I'm going to miss you."

Sucking in a breath of air, I instantly felt relief wash over my body. "You wouldn't mind?" I asked as I searched his baby blues.

Smiling bigger he shook his head. "Of course not, Lauren. I think it would be fun. I'll worry about you and the girls but I certainly don't mind."

I threw myself into his sweat soaked body as he laughed and wrapped his arms around me.

"Lib, baby you don't have to take Mireya. I'm sure between my folks and yours, they would love to spend more time with her."

Dropping my arms from Colt, I spun around. Libby was grinning at Luke as tears filled her eyes. "You wouldn't have a problem with it?" Luke shook his head. "Of course not baby." Libby turned and looked at Taylor who was still dancing around as Mireya giggled. "I mean, I'm not sure how I'll do leaving her for so many days but it sure would be nice to get away for a few days."

Luke walked up to Libby and placed his finger on her chin and pulled her face back to him. "You deserve a break."

Grace started jumping. "Okay, so I'm going to guess by Lauren jumping into Colt's disgusting sweat-covered arms, he is down for this trip." Glancing at Colt and I, I nodded my head enthusiastically. Grace jumped for joy and that caused me to jump for joy. Turning her attention to Will, Grace raised an eyebrow. "William?"

Alex started laughing. Will reached down and kissed Alex again. "Of course I don't mind. That's not saying I'm not going to be worried. I want y'all to be careful. Like no driving at night and all of that."

"I agree with, Will." Luke said.

Colt wrapped his arms around me as I felt a sense of warmth invade my body.

"Same here," Colt said.

Grace beamed with a sense of accomplishment. "Then it's settled bitches. We're going on a girls' trip!"

Grace and Maegan grabbed hands and jumped around as Taylor bounced Mireya all over as she said, "Yay! Girls' trip!"

As I looked around the room at my friends I was overcome with happiness. Everything just seemed to be falling into place. Peeking over my shoulder to Colt who was still holding me, my body shook. I had a feeling things weren't always going to be so smooth. Looking back ahead I tried to smile as I attempted to push the uneasy feeling that overtook my happiness.

SIXTEEN

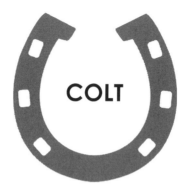

WALKING DOWN THE stairs, I headed to the front door. "Hey, where are you going?" Stopping, I peeked into the living room. My mother and father were both sitting on the couch watching a movie. Heading over to them, I couldn't help but smile when I noticed they were holding hands.

"I'm headed to go pick up Lauren. We're gonna spend some time together before the girls leave tomorrow for Colorado."

My mother glanced down to the bag I was carrying. Motioning with her head, she asked, "What's in the bag?"

Smiling, I opened it slightly. "Let's see, a blanket, a gift, and an iPod filled with Lauren's favorite songs. Oh and a small speaker to hook the iPod up to."

"Do you mind if I ask what the gift is?" my mother asked with a sweet smile.

Shaking my head I said, "Of course not. It's an Alex and Ani bracelet that I'm going to give Lauren. It is a heart with a keyhole in it. You know, since she holds the key to my heart and all."

"And what do you need the blanket for?" my father asked.

"To watch the stars."

Both my parents looked at me with raised eyebrows.

"Watching the stars, huh?" They both asked at once.

"Yeah, I'm taking Lauren somewhere special after dinner to look at the stars. Then I'll give her the bracelet."

My mother smiled and said, "Awe! How romantic, Colt!" Turning to my father, she nudged him with her shoulder. "Sounds so familiar. Like father, like son."

My father smiled at my mother and kissed her gently, yet quickly on the lips. "I taught the boy everything he knows."

Laughing, I shook my head. "Whatever, Dad. Hey I have to go. I have reservations for dinner."

Turning to leave my mother called out. "Where in the world do you need to make reservations in Mason for dinner?"

Turning around and walking backward to the door I said, "When you pay to have Lauren's favorite restaurant in Fredericksburg come to set up dinner for you and you're told to be there by a certain time . . . you have reservations."

My mother's mouth dropped open and father's chest puffed out as if I had just scored the winning touchdown in a championship game. "Oh, darling. You're going to sweep her off her feet. Be careful!"

"That right there is my son. Yep, I taught him everything he knows."

Laughing, I quickly headed out the door to my truck. I couldn't wait to see Lauren's face when we pulled up to where I had planned for dinner to be. Turning my truck on, I put it in drive and headed to Lauren's.

WALKING TO LAUREN'S front door, I rang the doorbell. As the front door opened, I was greeted by Jessie, Lauren's mom. "Hey, Jessie!"

Giving me a warm smile, Jessie motioned for me to come in. "Hey there, Colt. Come on into the kitchen."

Following Jessie into the kitchen I looked around.

Cupcakes were everywhere. "Um . . . what's with all the cupcakes?"

Rolling her eyes, Jessie let out a frustrated moan. "Jenny, Aaron's wife. Her baker told her at the last minute they couldn't make the cupcakes for a wedding she is planning tomorrow. So I'm helping her bake and decorate them."

Glancing around the kitchen there were at least a hundred cupcakes. "Wow, Jessie. You've done an amazing job." Each cupcake either had a dove on it, or an initial of what I was guessing was the last name of the married couple. "I may have to hire you for a certain surprise birthday party."

Jessie's eyes lit up. "Oh Colt, don't be silly. I would never charge you but I would love to do that. I think it would be fun. I actually kind of enjoy doing this."

Licking my lips, I eyed a chocolate cupcake as my stomach rumbled. "They look good."

Placing her hands on her hips, Jessie lifted her finger. "Don't even think about it Mathews."

Holding both hands up, I chuckled. "I wouldn't think of it."

Jessie winked and then whispered, "Scott's been down in the barn, supervising."

"Does she suspect anything?"

Jessie chuckled. "She's been so busy packing for their trip, I've only seen her twice all day today."

"Good. I figured she would be."

The hairs on the back of my neck stood before I even knew Lauren was in the room. Turning, I saw the most beautiful woman in the world standing before me. Lauren was wearing a light blue T-shirt that brought out the blue in her eyes even more. Her jeans shorts were just short enough to cause me to moan internally as my eyes traveled down to her baby-blue Nike sneakers. Her wrist was adorned in her vast collection of Alex and Ani bracelets and I couldn't help but smile.

Walking up to me she reached up on her tippy toes and kissed me sweetly on the lips. "Hey there."

My heart began to beat rapidly as I looked into her eyes. "Hey."

Peeking over to her mom, her face blushed. "Mom, these cupcakes are killing me."

Jessie laughed. "Why?"

"They smell like heaven and I want to eat them all!"

Jessie laughed as she tossed a dishtowel over her shoulder. "I've got two dozen more to decorate so if y'all will excuse me, I've got some birds and some initials to make."

Lauren giggled as she looked at me. "I'm so hungry I could eat my horse."

"Guess I better get you some food then huh?" I said as I wrapped my arm around her waist and led her to the back door.

"I thought you parked out front."

Grinning from ear to ear, I replied. "I did, but we are going to the barn."

Lauren attempted to stop walking but I guided her on with my arm. "No seriously, Colt. I'm really hungry and I'm not in the mood to go to the barn."

Opening the back door, I motioned for Lauren to head outside. Rolling her eyes and letting out a frustrated breath, she marched down the steps and to the barn. She was walking ahead of me so I couldn't see the adorable pout I was positive she was wearing.

"Hey, Lauren, before you go in will you wait for me please?"

Lauren instantly stopped walking and turned to me. Yep. There was that cute little pout of hers. God I loved her.

Stomping her foot, Lauren whined. "Colt! I'm really, really, *really* hungry!"

Taking her hand, I walked us into the barn. The first person I saw was Scott. Smiling from ear to ear he gave me a thumbs-up as Lauren placed her hand over her mouth. "Oh, Colt."

Every single horse had their heads leaning out of the stall doors. Scott had set up a small round table in the middle of the barn. We didn't want to use real candles so he had LED candles sitting in the middle of the table. There were two place settings and the salad had already been placed onto the table. Turning to me, Lauren slowly shook her head. "Did you plan this?"

Grinning, I nodded my head. "I did."

Wearing a dazed look on her face, Lauren whispered in a disbelieving voice, "Why?"

Cupping the sides of her face with my hands, my thumb wiped away a lone tear making its way down Lauren's beautiful face. "Because I love you, sweetheart. And I'm going to miss you fiercely while you're on your girls' trip."

Lauren placed her hands over mine as she closed her eyes. "Colt, I love you so much. You make me feel as if I'm living in a fantasy."

Clearing his throat, Scott walked to us. Taking a step back, I broke the contact between Lauren and I. Placing his hand on my shoulder; Scott gave it a slight squeeze. "You did good, son. Now don't keep her out too late. They're leaving early in the morning."

Nodding my head, I said, "No, sir, I won't keep her out late."

Glancing back to Lauren, Scott leaned down and kissed her on the cheek. "Enjoy your evening, baby girl."

Sniffling, Lauren whispered, "Thank you, Daddy."

Reaching for Lauren's hand I led her over to the table. Pulling out her chair, I waited for her to sit down and then pushed her chair in. Making my way over to my chair I couldn't help but notice Lauren's face. She wore the most amazing smile. "Tell me what you're thinking this very moment."

Pressing her lips together, she took her napkin and placed it onto her lap. "That Grace would call you an overly romantic bastard . . . or something along those lines . . . if she saw this."

Laughing, I nodded in agreement. "Yeah she probably would."

"Colt, I love this so much. I was starting to feel a little down about leaving you and—" Wiping a tear away she continued. "Well, you just do something like this and make me fall more in love with you if that's even possible. I'm going to miss you so much."

Reaching for her hand, I moved my thumb across her delicate skin. My heart felt as if it was about to burst. "I'm going to miss you too, but you're going to have so much fun, it will fly by."

Looking down, she whispered, "I hope so, cause right now, I don't want to leave you."

Squeezing her hand, Lauren looked at me. "I have a fun night planned for us. I promise, tomorrow the excitement to go on your trip will be there." Nodding, Lauren gave me a weak smile. "Eat up, sweetheart, the night is young and I promised your daddy I wouldn't keep you out late!"

Giggling, Lauren picked up her salad fork and went to town. It didn't take Lauren long to figure out that I had the food catered from her favorite restaurant in Fredericksburg, Pasta Bella. The second they placed the manicotti with garlic mushroom and alfredo sauce down in front of her she snapped her head up at me with her mouth gaped open in surprise. "Pasta Bella?"

Winking, I motioned for her to eat. "I know how much you love that place."

Taking a bite, Lauren rolled her eyes and let out a moan. "Oh my glitter. This is so good. It gets better every single time. How did you do this?"

"I have my ways."

Tittering, Lauren shoved a hefty bite into her mouth. We spent the rest of dinner talking about the girl's trip. I was scared shitless and I know Luke and Will were also, but we couldn't treat them like little girls. They were grown women and I had to just let go of the fear.

Leaning back in her chair, Lauren looked full and happy. "You feel like going on an surprise adventure?"

Watching her eyes light up, she leaned forward and rested her chin on her hand and asked, "What kind of adventure?"

"It wouldn't really be a surprise if I told you what kind of adventure it was, now would it."

"Mmm . . . that's true but I'd be willing to forego the surprise part of it."

Laughing, I stood and held out my hand. "Come on, let's get the second part of the evening started."

Taking my hand, Lauren and I walked to the truck. "Oh wait, Colt what about all that stuff in the barn. Don't we need to help them clean it all up?"

Shaking my head I kept walking. "Nope, I've got it all taken care of." I'd worked the two weekends we'd been back home by hauling hay for one of my father's friends. He paid me handsomely, even though I busted my ass working for him for four days. The money I made hauling and loading the hay I used to pay for this evening's meal.

Opening my truck door, I helped Lauren in. Reaching across I pulled the seat belt around and buckled her in. "If I didn't think your daddy might be watching I'd totally slip my hand up those shorts of yours."

Licking her lips, Lauren squirmed in her seat. "Baby, are you horny?" I asked as I winked.

Glancing up at her house, Lauren looked back at me. Her eyes pierced mine and I could see just how much she wanted me when her blue eyes turned dark. "Just tell me we'll be together tonight, Colt. I miss being with you."

We'd only managed to make love twice since we had been home from college, mostly because I was splitting up my time between my father's cattle ranch, and Scott's breeding business. I wouldn't change any of it though. I loved the work. It just kept me away from Lauren. Which really sucked. Tonight I planned on being with Lauren come hell or high water.

We drove along in silence for a bit before Lauren spoke. "We're heading into town?"

"Yep."

"Where to?"

Grinning, I kept looking ahead. I knew what she was doing. "You'll see when we get there."

Letting out a frustrated breath, she asked, "Have I been there before?"

Turning to her, I didn't know the answer. It had never

occurred to me that another guy might have thought of the same thing and taken her up there. I had almost taken Rachel once, but decided against it. I knew it was because I had always wanted to take Lauren. "I'm ah . . . I'm not sure. If you have, it wasn't with me."

Lauren's eyebrows pinched together, as if the idea of being somewhere without me bothered her.

"Oh," she said as she turned and stared out the front window. I could almost feel the anxiety practically pouring off of her.

"Have you been to this place with anyone else?"

"Nope."

Peeking over to her, she was smiling.

We remained silent until I parked near the cities main water tower. Putting the truck into park, I reached into the backseat and grabbed the bag that contained everything I needed to complete this evening.

Glancing out the window, Lauren turned back to me. "W-what are we doing here? I thought we were going on an adventure."

Giving her my best panty-melting smile, I nodded my head. "We are. There is a reason I told you to dress in sneakers, sweetheart."

Jumping out of my truck, I jogged around it and stopped when I saw Lauren looking straight up. I wasn't sure if it had clicked yet or not.

"Wow, look at the stars tonight. Even with the lights from town, you can still see the stars so good."

Nope. She had no clue. Taking her hand, I walked over to the ladder. Pulling on my arm, Lauren attempted to get me to stop walking. "Colt. Oh my gosh no! We'll get in trouble if we climb the water tower!"

Giving her a slight pull, I laughed. "No we won't. Blake is working tonight and I gave him a heads up my truck would be parked here and that I was taking my girl on an adventure." Blake was one of Luke's best friends from high school. He was one of the sheriffs working for Mason County. And he owed me a favor. I saved his ass one night when his truck broke down and he wanted to take Colleen

Mitchell out on a date. He begged to borrow my truck and I let him.

Stopping at the ladder, I held my hand out. "Ladies first." I could see the excitement dancing in her eyes. Lauren started up the ladder as I followed. Once we got to the top, Lauren let out a gasp. "Wow, look at the stars from up here! It's beautiful."

Smiling, I dropped my head back. The light breeze blowing kept it cool, but not too cool. "Thank goodness you're not afraid of heights," I said with a chuckle.

Lauren nodded her head and said, "Yeah, you lucked out on that one."

Reaching into the bag, I pulled out the quilt and spread it down. The lower deck of the tower was wide enough for us to practically lie down up here. Once I got it spread out, Lauren sat down and looked all around. "Colt, this is perfect. I feel like it's just the two of us."

Reaching down, I lifted her hand and placed the back of it softly against my lips. Using my tongue I drew a pattern onto the back of her hand. Lauren's lips parted open as her tongue darted out to lick her lips.

Keeping my eyes on her, I kept up the motion. Lauren clearly enjoyed it. The moon was casting light onto her beautiful face as her eyes watched my tongue move across her skin. "Colt," she whispered.

Slowly and gently, I placed soft kisses up her arm. Pulling her closer to me, Lauren straddled me as she wrapped her legs around me. "Don't . . . let me . . . fall," she said as her eyes met mine.

Smiling softly, I whispered, "Never."

Lauren leaned in and took my lower lip between her teeth and gently bit down on it. Letting out a moan, my dick pressed between her legs. Lauren's hand moved gently up and down my back as she rocked against me.

"Fucking hell, Lauren. I want you." Slipping my fingers in her shorts, Lauren let out a whimper.

Moving faster, Lauren pressed her lips to mine again as our kiss turned hungry. I had no idea if anyone was walking by and if there was, could they tell what we were doing? Lauren began whimpering softly into my mouth.

"Oh, Colt. Colt, I'm going to come."

Pulling her in closer, Lauren fell apart as I swallowed her moans. My dick was throbbing in my pants I wanted her so damn bad. This was about Lauren, not me. Pulling her lips from mine, Lauren dropped her head into the crook of my neck as she attempted to gain control of her breathing.

"I love you, Colt Mathews."

Shutting my eyes tightly, I pulled my hand out of her shorts and I wrapped my arms around her tighter. "I love you too, Lauren."

Sitting like that for about five minutes longer, neither one of us spoke. Lauren finally moved off of me and sat back down next to me. Her face flushed from her orgasm still. Letting out a nervous laugh she looked away. "I'm sorry. You just do things to me, Colt. Sometimes it feels like I can't even control my own desire for you."

Placing my hand on the side of her face, she nuzzled into my palm. "I feel the same way, sweetheart. You're my life, Lauren. You always have been, and you always will be."

Sliding onto my side, I wrapped my arm around her as we dropped back onto the quilt and looked up at the stars. "Colt?"

"Yeah?"

"I still can't push away the fear I have about Daddy's business."

Closing my eyes I sucked in a breath before slowly blowing it out. "Lauren, I can tell Scott I'm going to be helping out my father this summer if—"

Lauren quickly sat up. "No! No, I don't want you to do that. I want you working for daddy. It's just, I know him and I know he's gonna be pushing me away and telling me I'm not ready and I don't want to take that out on you. I'm so scared I'm going to pull away again."

Pulling her back down next to me, Lauren rested her head on my chest. "I won't let you, Lauren."

"Promise me, Colt. Promise me you won't let me push

you away again."

Holding her tightly, I whispered, "I swear to you, Lauren. I'm never letting you go. Ever." Reaching into the bag I pulled out the bracelet and took Lauren's hand in mine.

"Because I hold the key to your heart, and you hold the key to mine." Slipping the bracelet over Lauren's hand she let a sob escape between her lips.

Holding it up, Lauren smiled. "Colt, this is perfect. So perfect."

Smiling, I pulled her to me and held her.

"Are you excited about Colorado?" I asked.

Nodding her head, Lauren said, "Yes. At the same time I feel sad though. I mean I really want to spend time with the girls, but I also want to spend time with you."

Kissing the top of her head, I smiled to myself. "I know what you mean. But y'all are going to have fun, sweetheart."

"I know. I'm so glad Taylor is going. She needs to cut loose in a big-time way."

Chuckling I held her tighter as we lay under the stars and talked about everything and anything. I'd never felt so whole in my life as when I was holding Lauren in my arms.

"Colt?" Lauren whispered.

Taking in a deep breath, I smelled sweet flowers from Lauren's shampoo. Smiling, I kissed her head. "Mmm?"

"Are you going to make love to me?"

My heart dropped to my stomach and my dick instantly hardened. "I take it you've had enough of the stars."

Laughing, Lauren pushed herself up and gave me a naughty smile. "I'm kind of in the mood for seeing stars of a different kind."

Standing, I reached down and helped Lauren up. Honestly, it felt too good having her in my arms, I didn't want to move but I still had another surprise for her. "Come on, I've got one more place I want to go."

"Somewhere private I hope."

Wiggling my eyebrows, I said, "Oh yeah baby. When you come, you can scream to your heart's content."

Biting on her lip, Lauren whimpered.

Climbing down first, I kept reminding Lauren to watch her step and to take it slow. Stepping off the ladder I reached up and grabbed Lauren by the hips, lifting her off the ladder. Letting out a small yelp, she spun around and I about fell over. Her smile would always be my undoing. There was something magical about it. It filled my body with love and hope.

Taking her hand, we walked to the truck. Lauren jumped in as I threw the bag into the back seat. Making my way over to the driver's side of my truck, I jumped in, started my truck and hit play on my iPod. "Smoke" by A Thousand Horses began playing. Smiling, I reached over and turned it up. Taking Lauren's hand in mine, I made a plan to make sure my shirt was covered in her perfume by the end of the night. Pulling out onto the street I turned and headed to our spot.

SEVENTEEN

LAUREN

M Y HEART WAS still beating like crazy as Colt drove toward what I thought was his families cattle ranch. My mind was spinning as I attempted to take it all in, the orgasm, the height of the water tower, the stars in the sky, Colt holding me in his arms as we just talked endlessly.

Colt pulled down his driveway and waited for the gate to open. I watched as the giant black-iron gate opened. The words *Mathews Cattle Ranch* stood out in bold letters. Glancing over to Colt, I asked, "Where are we going? To your house?"

Smiling, he shook his head. "Nope, we're going to our spot."

Pulling my head back in surprise, I asked, "Our spot? We have a . . . spot?"

Tossing his head back, Colt let out a rumbled laugh. "Yes ma'am we do."

Facing the front, I desperately tried to think of where in the hell our spot would be. *We had a spot? I don't remember ever having a spot? Huh.* Chewing on my lip, I turned back to Colt. "We have a spot?"

Colt turned down one of the older dirt roads. This road ran behind the main barn of the ranch, just down from Grams and Gramps house. Looking all around, I tried like hell to remember our spot.

Oh. My. Glitter. I'm the worst girlfriend in the world. Placing my thumb in my mouth, I chewed on my nail. We have a spot and I don't even remember it. Lifting my eyes, a thought occurred to me and I snapped my head over and looked at Colt.

That bastard. He's probably thinking of Rachel! It's probably *their* spot. Not our spot. Slowly facing the front, I folded my arms across my chest. Oh, if he thinks I'm letting him make love to me in someone else's spot, he has another thing coming.

Bastard. Oh wait until I tell the girls this one.

Sitting in the passenger seat, I began to plot my revenge on Colt. Maybe I'd give him a blowjob and *accidentally* sneeze and bite down . . . just a little. I bet that would hurt. Maybe my foot would make contact with his balls . . . by mistake of course.

Not paying attention at all to where Colt was going, I didn't even notice when he stopped driving.

"We're here."

Humph. *I'm not moving one inch.*

"I know it's dark, but do you remember what you said to me when we were standing in this very spot when we were six years old, Lauren?"

Blowing out a fast breath, I blew a blonde curl from my eye. "No."

Wait. What? Six years old?

Looking out the window, I let my eyes adjust. Sucking in a breath, I opened the truck door and jumped out. My hands came up to my mouth as I walked over to the tree. The tree that held the treehouse Gunner made for all of us. I hadn't been here in years. Truth be told, I had forgotten all about it.

Stopping just short of the tree, I looked up. It looked like it was in perfect condition. Like the years hadn't even touched it at all. It stood only a few feet off the ground, but when I was six, it seemed so high.

Closing my eyes, my mind drifted back to that fall day.

"COLT, YOU WATCH Lauren and make sure she doesn't fall," Momma yelled out. Colt turned and smiled. "I won't, Aunt Jessie! Promise!"

Colt took my hand and helped me climb up into our new treehouse. Looking around, I started jumping. "Is this all ours?"

Colt started jumping, too! "Yes! And Luke's and Grace's and Libby's and Will's and my stupid sister Alex's! Oh and Daddy said it's for Maegan and Taylor, too!"

Letting out a scream, I hugged Colt. "I can't wait to show them," I said as I stopped jumping and spun around.

Colt stopped me from spinning. "Or, we could tell my momma and daddy and your momma and daddy that this is our spot."

Grinning so hard my cheeks hurt, I nodded my head. "Yeah! Our special spot forever, Colt. You can even marry me here."

Colt wasn't smiling anymore. "You want to marry me, Lauren?"

Shrugging my shoulders, I scrunched up my nose and looked up to think about it. Looking back at Colt, I nodded my head and said, "Yep. You ain't gonna marry anyone else, Colt Mathews." Placing my hand on my hip, I took my other hand and pointed at Colt. Like Momma does when she wants me to listen real good. "You hear me? If you do, I'll beat you up 'cause I ain't afraid of you."

"I ain't afraid of you either and girls can't beat up boys, Lauren."

My lip began to shake and I felt sad. "Does that mean you won't wait to marry me, Colt?"

Colt laughed as he spun his body around. "Ah heck, Lauren. I'll marry you. I don't think any other boy could like you more than I do anyway. I will love you forever. That's what Daddy says to Momma."

Standing up straight, I nodded my head as I stomped

my foot. "Then it's settled. You're gonna marry me and be-come Mr. Lauren Ashley Reynolds."

"Cool!" Colt smiled and winked. I had to look away cause my face felt funny. "Come on, let's play hide and seek before the others get here! You're it!"

Covering my eyes, I counted to twenty-five before I jumped down out of Colt and mine's special spot and start-ed looking for him. I couldn't wait to grow up and marry Colt.

A TEAR SLOWLY slid down my cheek as I opened my eyes. *Our spot.* How could I have forgotten about our spot? Oh my glitter. I'm the worst girlfriend in the world. I was plan-ning on biting Colt's dick!

My body instantly warmed as tingles raced across my skin. Colt wrapped his arms around me and whispered in my ear. "You thought I was taking you to some spot I had with another girl, didn't you?"

Pulling away from his hot breath, I barely said, "No."

Colt began nipping my earlobe. "Really? Cause you sure looked pissed off when I was driving through the fields."

The pull in my lower stomach was growing as the sec-onds ticked off the clock. "N-no I didn't."

Colt's hand slipped down my chest, over my stomach and into my pants and panties. *Oh God. Yes.*

"Really? Are you sure about that, Lauren?" Colt's fin-gertips brushed across my lips and clit as my legs wob-bled.

"W-what are we talking about?" I panted.

Much to my disapproval, Colt pulled his hand out of my shorts and stood in front of me. Cupping his hands on the sides of my face, Colt stared into my eyes. "This is our spot. Forever and always. I'm going to make love to you in our spot, Lauren. You stole my heart that day you stomped your foot down and declared I was to marry no one but you. I promise to make that come true, sweetheart."

Brushing his lips softly against mine, he smiled and said, "I want nothing more than to become Mr. Lauren Ashley Reynolds." Smiling, I let out a chortle. Colt pulled back, his hands still cupping my face as he pierced my blue eyes with his.

Placing my hands on Colt's strong arms, I fought to hold back my tears. Damn it all to hell. I have never cried as much as I have since I started dating this incredibly sexy and handsome man standing before me.

Closing my eyes, I whispered, "Colt."

Lifting me up, Colt carried me over to his truck. Slowly setting me down, he pushed me against the tail-gate. Running his hand through my hair, he took a handful and gently pulled back until my neck was exposed to him. Moving his lips across my sensitive skin, Colt spoke in a low sexy voice. "Tell me you're mine, Lauren."

My insides were melting, and not like they were melting the day Colt mentioned Velcro baby hair bows. They were melting in a completely new way. Pulling harder on my hair, I moaned as Colt spoke again. "Tell me . . . you're mine, Lauren."

Closing my eyes, I attempted to speak. My heart raced, my hands began to sweat and I found myself holding my breath. Finally gaining some composure, I whispered, "Yours. I'm yours, Colt. I've always been yours."

Pressing his lips against mine, Colt kissed me like he had never kissed me before. I was lost in a euphoria that had my body feeling like it was lifting off the ground. The cool night breeze was blowing and it was as if every exposed area of my skin tingled. Before I knew it, I was in the bed of Colt's truck, on the quilt, as he quickly undressed me. A shiver ran across my skin as Colt asked, "Are you cold, sweetheart?"

Shaking my head, I placed my hand on my chest. My heart was slamming against my hand as I swallowed hard. "I won't be for long."

Colt began to kiss me, on the bottom of my foot, slowly working his way up my leg, one painfully slow kiss after another. When he reached the inside of my upper thigh, I attempted to push his head between my legs. Wanting him to taste my desire, I lifted my hips to him.

"Lauren, baby. Do you need something from me?" Colt asked as his fingers slipped into my body. Pulling out a long deep hiss between my lips, I jerked my hips, craving more of his touch.

"Yes, more," I panted.

And more is exactly what Colt gave me. He took me to heaven with his mouth not once, but twice. Feeling him over my body, I opened my eyes and saw nothing but a sea of blue staring at me. "I want to feel you, Lauren. No barriers, just you and me."

Nodding my head I knew it would be okay. Neither of us had ever been with anyone else, and Libby made sure to tell me to get on stronger birth control pills as soon as she found out Colt and I had been together.

"Please, Colt, please make love to me. I need you."

"Lauren, are you sure?"

The concern on his face only made me realize how much I'd wanted this. How much I had desired this connection between the two of us.

"I've never been so sure of anything in my life, Colt."

Spreading myself open to Colt, he slowly pushed into me. Once he was all the way in, he didn't move. Wrapping my legs around him, we both moaned.

"Does it feel different?" I asked.

Lifting his head, Colt placed his hands on the side of my face. "It feels like heaven."

Smiling, I whispered, "It does for me too."

Colt slowly pulled out as I watched his eyes roll to the back of his head before he shut them. "Lauren—"

Pushing back in I felt my orgasm building. Colt was moving slow. Too slow. "Colt, for the love of all things, go faster! Please go faster!"

Shaking his head, he kissed my lips as he talked. "Can't. Feels. Too. Good."

Bucking my hips, I whined. "I know! It would feel better if you just moved faster."

Ugh, I sounded like a little whore, but I didn't care. Colt

began to pick up speed and I didn't think it was possible, but it felt even more amazing. Something was happening between us and I had no words to describe it. My body trembled as I watched Colt's face. My orgasm was growing faster and I was about to come, but I couldn't pull my eyes from his face. Snapping his eyes open, Colt pierced my eyes with his. I gasped as I saw nothing but love in his eyes.

Oh. My. Glitter. Screw the glitter, this is no time for glitter! Holy fucking shit. This was going to be big.

My orgasm hit me as I called out Colt's name. He kept his hands on the sides of my face, pinning me so that I was looking directly at him as I came. "Oh God. Colt!" My body trembled as I called out his name into the darkness as one of the most intense orgasms rolled through my body.

"Lauren, look at me," Colt panted. Opening my eyes, Colt's face gazed upon me with adoration. He slowed down as he moved gently inside of me.

Grabbing onto his arms, our eyes were lost in each other. "Lauren," Colt said as he pulled out and pushed in hard, pouring himself into me.

"I love you, sweetheart. Oh God, I love you so much." Pressing his lips to mine, I felt our connection change. It grew stronger. Deeper.

This moment would forever be etched in my memory. The moment Colt and I became one . . . at our spot.

EIGHTEEN

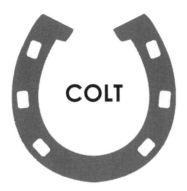

COLT

SITTING ON THE tailgate of my truck, I stared out over the pasture. Feeling a bump on my shoulder, I turned and looked at my father as he gave me a smile, letting me know he knew exactly how I was feeling.

"You know, Colt. She's only been gone for two hours, yet you're sitting here like someone just ran over your favorite dog."

Frowning, I looked down. "Feels like it. I don't understand it, Dad. It's not like I don't want her to go and enjoy herself, because I do. I really honestly do. I guess I'm feeling . . . lost . . . which kind of freaks me out a little bit."

Letting out a slight chuckle, my father jumped up and sat next to me on the tailgate. "I'll never forget the first time I saw your mother. She had just punched a guy right in the face after she found out he had been cheating on her."

Pulling my head back, my mouth dropped open. "What? Mom punched a guy?"

A smile slowly grew on my father's face. "The little fucker deserved it."

Laughing, I shook my head. "Damn, somehow I can't picture Mom hitting anyone."

My father looked out over the pasture and nodded his head. "Your mother is a very strong person, Colt. She rocked my world that day and nothing was ever the same after that."

"It scares me sometimes, Dad."

Turning back to me, my father asked, "What scares you?"

Blowing out a deep breath, I rubbed my hand across my hair and shook my head. My father and I had always been close. I knew I could talk to him about anything and that was an amazing feeling. "Love I guess."

Laughing, my father bumped my shoulder. "Love scares you, Colt? Why?"

Shrugging my shoulders I looked into my father's eyes. One thing about my father, he was always there for me. When we talked, I could see it in his eyes, at that moment, I was his only concern. "I feel like I crave her, Dad. Her touch, her smile, her laughter, and the silly way her blue eyes light up in the mornings when she comes skipping into the kitchen to get a cup of coffee. She is so full of life and I'm drawn to it like a moth to a flame. When I'm not with her, I feel lost. I keep thinking it's because we're fairly new in our relationship. Puppy love phase maybe?" I let out a nervous chuckle.

Clearing his throat, my father nodded slightly. "It's not a puppy love phase, Colt. That is something special. Rare, that not everyone is blessed to experience. It never stops, it only grows. There are times when I'm away from your mother and nothing seems to go right." Laughing, he shook his head. "It's like I can't think right or function right because she's not there. She is almost like my energy source sometimes." Glancing back at me his eyes glassed over. "That is scary, son. But at the same time, it's the most precious gift in the world. Never take that feeling for granted."

Placing my hand on his shoulder, I gave it a squeeze. "Lauren and I would be blessed if we had a marriage as strong as you and Mom."

My father smiled, then dropped it. "Marriage? Um . . . are you two . . . ah." Shaking his head as if he needed to clear his thoughts, my father looked straight ahead. "Marriage."

Tossing my head back, I let out a laugh. "You should see your face right now, Dad. Don't worry. Lauren and I have not even talked about that step. Wipe the look of panic off your face."

Scrubbing his hands down his face he whispered, "Thank God. I was trying to come up with some kind of plan to keep Scott from breaking your legs."

My smile faded. "Huh?"

Still looking straight ahead, my father blew out another breath as he slowly moved his head back and forth. "Man oh man, that was a close call. You really scared me there, buddy."

Jumping off the tailgate, he took his cowboy hat off, ran his hand through his hair, and placed the hat back on his head. "I need a cold beer after that."

My eyes widened as I watched my father walking to his truck. Jumping off the tailgate, I attempted to catch up to him, but I stumbled and had to catch myself from falling flat on my face. "Dad! Wait. Why would Scott want to break my legs? I thought he liked me?"

Looking over his shoulder, he let out a stronger laugh. What the fuck?

Stopping at his truck, he turned and watched me as I made my way to his truck. My legs felt like rubber. "What in the hell is wrong with you? Are your legs asleep?"

Stopping in front of him, I glanced down to my legs. "No! You just gave me the image of Scott breaking them and I'm a little concerned. Why would he break my legs? I mean, Alex and Will are engaged and you didn't want to break Will's legs."

My father's eyes grew dark. "Please, if you only knew the different ways I was going to torture that boy, your eyes would pop out of your head."

Taking a step back, I tried not to look stunned. "Dad. Will's like your son."

Pursing his lips together he nodded in agreement. "He is, just like you're like Scott's son. But I can promise you one thing, Scott cares more about his little girl than he does you. You mention marriage right now and all I think about is you're wanting to get married because of a baby. " Leaning closer, my father looked around, then looked back at me and talked in a hushed voice. "Don't forget, his best friend was a trained killer. One shot and how in the hell am I gonna explain it to your mother?"

Sucking in a breath of air, I said, "Wait! What? There is no baby! No baby . . . none. None! Seriously, Dad you'd let someone kill your own son?"

Pulling his head back in surprise he widened his eyes. "Hell no I wouldn't. But as much as Scott loves that girl and she is their only child, I'm almost positive he'd find a way to hurt you in some way."

Swallowing hard, all I could think about is how Lauren and I had made love last night with no condom. Sweat began to build on my forehead as I reached up and wiped my brow. Tilting his head, my father stared at me. Then he started laughing his ass off. "Seriously, Colt. You have always been so easy. Scott's not going to kill you. Can't promise he wouldn't hurt you if you ever hurt Lauren though, so don't."

Closing my eyes, my shoulders dropped. "I hate you right now, Dad. You scared the piss out of me and I wasn't even sure why. I didn't say we were getting married."

Pointing at me, he said, "You said the M word and that's close enough." Opening the door to his truck, my father climbed up into the driver's seat. Starting the truck, he looked at me. "Seriously though, Colt. Always use protection, you're both too young to be starting a family right now."

Feeling my face heat up, I nodded my head. "Yes, sir."

"Stop staring at the pasture and go find something productive to do. I'm sure Scott's got something he can put you on. When do you start working for him?"

"Next week. He wanted to give Lauren and me a couple weeks off. I'll head on over there now and see what he's got going on."

"Good, it will keep your mind off of Lauren and before you know it, she'll be back," my father said as he smiled big. Nodding in agreement I took a step away from his truck. "See you for dinner, Colt."

Lifting my hand I said, "See ya later, Dad. Thanks for the talk."

Laughing, he started pulling off but not before sticking his head out the window and shouting, "You should have seen your face! Priceless!"

Letting out a chuckle, I turned and headed to my truck to make my way to Scott and Jessie's place. A part of me didn't want to head over until Lauren came back. I knew she was still struggling with her father and the business. I made a mental note to talk to Scott about it before Lauren came back.

WALKING INTO THE barn, I heard Scott talking to someone. "You honestly think this horse can't be trained?" My interest immediately piqued.

"Listen, Scott, I appreciate that you've been doing this for years and your daddy did it for years before you. I think on this one you need to stick to what you do best. Find a good match to breed him to and leave it at that."

Scott huffed and he shook his head as he let out a frustrated sigh. Glancing over he gave me a quick head pop and turned back to the older gentleman in front of him. "He's fast, Jon, and he's got it in him to be a damn good racehorse. He just needs the right hand when it comes to training him."

I'd never seen the man standing before Scott. He looked to be about the same age as Gramps. His cowboy hat and boots had seen better days. I was almost positive the man was worth a few million, most of Scott's clients were. Scott had some of the best stallions and mares in central Texas, almost all from bloodlines that would make the queen of England envious.

"I don't know, Scott. He's temperamental and won't for the life of him breed with a mare. He acts like he has no interest in them at all. That's why I brought him to you.

I'm not interested in racing a horse who won't even move to breed."

Clearing my throat, both men looked at me. "You've got something to say young man." Looking to Scott for permission to speak, he smiled and motioned for me to speak.

Walking to Jon, I reached out my hand and gave him a firm handshake. "Colt Mathews, sir."

Raising his eyebrows he asked, "Gunner Mathews' boy?"

Smiling wide, I replied. "Yes, sir I am."

Looking me over he nodded his head. "Well speak, son; I'm eighty-two years old and don't got all day."

Chuckling, I nodded my head. "Your stallion, you say he isn't interested in the mares. Could it be it's because he's interested in something else? Say for instance, taking off around that track? I heard my Uncle Jeff tell a story about a stallion who, every time they walked him by the track, he'd go insane. Wouldn't have anything to do with the mares and carried on day after day in his stall. My uncle took him to the track and the horse stood there and stared at my uncle. Taking a chance, he climbed up on him and next thing he knew, the horse was running the fastest lap he'd ever recorded on his track."

Giving me an incredulous stare, Jon slowly nodded. "So, are you willing to climb onto this big boy's back and prove to me what you're saying?"

My heart began to beat faster as I looked over at the bay colored stallion. His nostrils flared as we made eye contact. I felt something there though. Not really sure how to put it into words, I walked over to the horse and ran my hands down his neck. Feeling the horse shudder, I slowly made my way around him. Touching him the entire time. It was something Lauren had taught me to do. Connect with the horse on every level, she would always say.

"Has he ever had anyone sit on him?"

Laughing, Jon said, "He has yes. He doesn't mind you getting the saddle on and climbing on top, but the moment you try to get the stubborn ass mule to move, he just stands there."

Looking over my shoulder back to Jon and Scott, I smiled. "Let's saddle him then." Scott's face beamed with pride and I knew this was showing Scott I could step up to any challenge. I wished Lauren had been here though. She would have been able to show her daddy how ready she was to take on more of the business.

Fifteen minutes later I was climbing up onto the back of Mighty Mike. Good name for this horse. He sure was Mighty Mike. Scott checked everything on the saddle once more and shook his head. "You got a feeling, Colt?"

Smiling, I nodded my head with confidence. "Yes, sir. I very much do. Look at how the muscles in his legs are twitching. He wants to be let loose."

"Be careful, Colt. No telling what this horse is capable of."

Giving Mighty Mike slight pressure with my legs, he started walking. The closer we got to the track the more I could feel his body reacting. Placing my hand on his neck, I leaned down. "Steady there big boy. I know what you want. Let's show them what you've got."

Walking the horse onto the track I held him for a few seconds. "You ready, buddy?"

Mighty Mike started bouncing his head up and down as I laughed. "Let's go." One small kick and he took off in a full-on run. All I did was hold on and let the horse take control. He needed to get this out of his system and I was gonna let him.

Four and half laps later, he finally slowed down and began trotting. Giving him a good pat on the neck I looked over at Scott. The smile on his face was all I needed to see to know I had just earned respect from him. I couldn't wait to tell Lauren.

Walking up to Jon and Scott, I couldn't wipe the smile from my face. Jon shook his head and let out a laugh. "Cocky little bastard, just like your daddy. You proved your point. I want you in on Mighty Mike's training, if that is all right with you, Scott. I like his instinct with this horse. They seem to have a connection." Mighty Mike bobbed his head as we all laughed.

Turning to look at me, Scott gave me a grin and said, "I'm more than all right with that, Jon. Colt here is wanting to come on board after college and help with the business."

Clearing my throat, I said, "Helping alongside, Lauren." Scott looked at me with a surprised expression before turning back and talking to Jon more about getting Mighty Mike started right away on a training schedule.

I handed the reins off to one of the high school guys Scott had working for him. Scott started walking Jon to his truck. "Give me a couple weeks with him and I'll put him out to pasture with one of my broodmares and we'll see if Colt's theory is correct."

"If you can make it happen and breed that stubborn ass horse, I'll let you have a ninety percent control of the racing," Jon said with a nod and smile before closing his truck door. Scott and I watched as Jon drove down the driveway.

Turning, Scott started laughing. "I want to kiss you right now! Holy shit, Colt. That damn horse ran four hundred forty yards in twenty-one seconds."

My mouth dropped open. "Shit, I knew he was fast, but I didn't think he was that fast."

Scott rubbed the back of his neck as we headed back to the barn. "Could have been a fluke. Just him itching to get it out of his system, but I want you on his back every time that horse takes the track."

Attempting to hold my excitement back, I played it cool. "Will do."

"Now go muck out the stalls, Colt. Dinner's at six. Your parents will be joining us."

I stopped walking and stared at the back of Scott's head as he continued to walk on. Once he turned the corner, I fist pumped and did a jump. Pulling out my phone, I sent Lauren a text.

Me: Hey sweetheart! Are you having fun?

Not a minute later, Lauren texted back.

Lauren: *I am! I'd have more fun if Grace and Maegan would stop arguing about everything! What are you doing?*

Me: *About to muck out stalls but your daddy let me get a stallion on the track today. It was amazing. I can't wait to tell you all about it.*

Lauren: *Awesome! Can't wait. Love and miss you.*

Me: *Love you more! Miss you the most.*

Walking into the barn, I grabbed a pitchfork and got to work on the first stall. I couldn't wait to get started on Mighty Mike. I had a feeling this was going to be the best summer yet.

NINETEEN

LAUREN

PULLING UP TO the Strater Hotel, we all let out an "Oh!" The hotel was beautiful. "Nice pick, Libby!"

"Thanks. Wait until you see the rooms." Libby pulled up to the front of the hotel. "I booked three rooms so we'll draw names to see who is bunking with who," Libby said as she parked the Tahoe we rented for the trip. Once we all got out of the car, we started stretching.

Taking in a deep breath of clean mountain air, I slowly blew it out as I smiled. Taylor came walking up to me and was about to say something when she stopped. Holding up her hands she gave me a weak smile. "Now, Lauren. I don't want you freaking out."

My eyes widened as I stared at her. "What? You can't start a conversation saying that. What's on me?" I started jumping around as Taylor yelled for me to stand still. I immediately stopped moving. Alex walked up and put her hand over her mouth.

"Oh my glitter. Somebody tell me what is on me! Where? Get it off!" I screamed. That's when I felt it. There was something crawling on my neck. Grace walked up with a bellhop. They both looked at me and Grace rolled her eyes. "There is a bee on your neck, Lauren."

Screaming, I tried to get it off. The only thing I did was piss it off. The sting felt like a knife in my neck. Okay, maybe not that bad, but pretty damn close.

"It stung me! It stung me!"

Now it was the bellhop's turn to chime-in. "Well yeah, I mean you tried to get it off your neck, but dude, he's still there on your T-shirt."

Screaming, I pulled my T-shirt over my head and began running around the car. *Oh my glitter! I hate bees! I really hate bees!* Of course my show wouldn't have been complete if I hadn't been swinging the T-shirt around like a mad woman.

"She's gonna get us kicked out of here!" I heard Maegan yell. Alex walked in front of me and stopped me.

"Lauren, get it together woman! Put your shirt back on. I can see the bellhop's hard-on from over here."

Stopping, I looked around, then looked down. Thank God I had my pretty beige lace bra on. Quickly shaking out my T-shirt, Alex handed it to me as I pulled it on and covered myself. "Damn it! It hurts already."

Grace laughed. "Well, yeah it hurts. Your damn adrenaline pumped that shit through your body in record time."

"Grace!" Libby said as she gave Grace a push.

"Okay, well I'm going to start getting your luggage now," the bellhop said as he walked to the back of the Tahoe.

Maegan followed him as she batted her eyes. He was probably close to our age and for sure easy on the eyes. "Bet you didn't wake up this morning expecting to see a free show today, did you?"

The bellhop started laughing and said, "No, ma'am, I didn't."

"She's taken, so stow away the woody," Grace said over her shoulder as she walked with me into the lobby.

Dropping my mouth open, I glared at Grace. "Do you have no filter, Grace Johnson?"

Looking at me like I was the one who was insane, Grace smiled and gave me a wink. "Yes. I'm just picky about when I use it."

Rolling my eyes, I followed Grace into the hotel. While Libby checked us in, someone brought me out some ice,

Advil, and Benadryl.

"Okay, y'all, huddle up. Pick a number from the bag."

After we each picked a number, we were teamed up. Grace and Libby were in one room, Alex and Meg in another and Taylor and I in the last room. Taylor and I high-fived each other and did a chest bump.

"All right, calm down. Let's get settled, then go get something to eat." Turning to me, Libby pressed her lips together. "Lauren, can we trust that you'll keep your shirt on?"

Snarling my lip at Libby, I raised my middle finger and mouthed *fuck you.*

WALKING INTO THE Salon Bar, I glanced around. "Grace, Taylor and I aren't twenty-one."

Waving me off, she headed to a table. "Just sit, drink Coke and no one will say anything."

Worrying my lower lip, I did what she said. We spent most of our first evening in Durango in that little saloon bar. We danced, laughed, danced some more and just had fun. Taylor and I were currently attempting to ignore the two guys who would not go away. *If this guy tells me one more time how pretty my eyes are, I'm gonna junk-punch his ass.*

Libby, Alex and Meg were all dancing together and Grace was cutting a rug with a very good-looking cowboy who sure did know how to move. It was nice to see Grace smiling and enjoying herself. When a slow song came on, I couldn't pull my eyes away from Grace and the cowboy. He lifted his hand and placed it on the side of her face and leaned in to kiss her. Leaning my own body closer, I noticed Taylor was doing the same thing. "Oh my gosh. Is she gonna kiss him?" Taylor gasped.

Shaking my head, I said, "No! She's in love with Noah. She can't."

Making a grunting sound, Taylor said, "Please. He's

married. There is no Noah."

Taylor and I both leaned forward more. One of the guys started talking and we both said, "Shh!"

They finally got the hint and got up and left. "She's moving in. She is moving in!" Taylor said.

"What are y'all doing?" Maegan asked.

"Hush, we're watching Grace. I say she's not going to kiss the cowboy, but Tay says she is."

Everyone sat down and all eyes were on Grace. "I'm with Lauren. I say she isn't," Libby said.

"Bullshit. Look at the way she is looking at him. She's got that cowboy wrapped around her finger. I say she kisses him," Maegan said with a chuckle.

Alex said, "I'm with, Meg and Tay. I'm going with lips touching."

Libby and I looked at each other. Glancing back over to Grace I quickly said, "A hundred bucks, she doesn't."

"Deal!" Alex, Maegan, and Taylor all shouted.

Holding my breath I watched the slick cowboy slide his hand down to Grace's waist. "He's pulling her in! He's pulling her in," I said with panic laced in my voice. "Don't do it, Grace. Resist the hot, muscled-up, tattooed cowboy!"

"Fuck that, she needs to get with that shit!" Maegan said as Alex and Taylor started laughing.

"Meg! She's not going to screw some random guy she just met," I said as I glared at Maegan.

Raising her eyebrow, she smirked. "I'll add another hundred that she not only kisses him, but she ends up in his bed before this little vacation is over."

Libby leaned in close to my ear. "She's looking weak, Lauren. I have a feeling Grace is about to break her silent vow of chastity."

Whipping my head around, I looked back out on the dance floor. *No. Oh no. Don't do it, Grace. Stay strong!* "Don't do it, Grace! Noah is the cream to your coffee."

Maegan let out a gruff laugh. "No, he's the cream to someone else's coffee now, Lauren."

Flashing Maegan a dirty look, I glanced back to Grace. Throwing her head back and laughing, she dropped her hands and took a step back. Leaning in, she gave him a quick kiss on the cheek and walked to us. I had to admit, I felt bad for the cowboy. He couldn't pull his eyes from Grace as he watched her walk away from him. Smiling, I turned to Maegan and said, "I do believe you bitches owe some money."

Libby started laughing and Maegan glared at me as Grace walked up. "What's going on? Meg, why are you looking at Lauren that way?"

Smirking I said, "She's just mad she lost a bet that's all."

Grace reached for her drink and took a sip. "Jesus, that cowboy had his dick pushed all into my body the entire time we were dancing. Felt like a big motherfucker." Raising her eyebrows, Grace smiled.

"Grace!" Taylor yelled out as everyone started laughing. Grace being Grace just shrugged it off and sat down. Leaning toward me she asked, "Missing, Colt?"

Giving her a weak smile, I said, "Yeah, but I'm having a ton of fun."

"Good! As it should be. Girls weekend!" Grace yelled out as she held up her drink. Everyone yelled out, "Girls weekend!" and took a drink.

TAYLOR AND I both collapsed onto our beds and let out a long sigh as I said, "Holy hell. I can't believe how wasted those girls got."

Giggling, Taylor rolled over onto her stomach and looked at me. "I know! Thank goodness the bar was right here in the hotel."

Taylor had helped Maegan and Alex back to their room and I helped Grace and Libby. Libby wasn't too wasted, but she was for sure feeling good.

"That's why I don't want to drink. I mean, all four of them are going to be bears tomorrow. You know this, right?"

Giggling, I flipped onto my stomach. "Yeah, I know."

Taylor placed her elbow on the bed and then rested her head on her hand. "So, tell me what it's like. We haven't even had a chance to talk."

Grinning, I asked, "What do you mean?"

"Sex. Did it hurt? Was Colt amazing? We never even got to talk about any of it." Taylor frowned. "Remember all the times we talked about what we thought our first time would be like? Sometimes I hate being at UT."

I nodded my head. "I know, I miss our talks."

Giving me a wicked grin, Taylor said, "So . . . tell me! Did it hurt?"

"Yes it hurt but at the same time, it didn't hurt."

Laughing, Taylor said, "That doesn't make any sense."

Sitting up, I crossed my legs and laughed. "I know it doesn't but I don't know any other way to explain it. It burned like a bitch but once I got used to him, it felt heavenly."

"Are you glad you waited?"

My smile faded. "Yes. There were a few times I didn't think I was going to wait."

Taylor chewed on her lower lip as she moved and sat on the bed. "I met someone."

Sucking in a breath of air I said, "What? Taylor! Who is he? What's his name?"

Giving me an innocent smile, she said, "He doesn't even know I exist."

Pinching my eyebrows together, I pulled my head back. "What do you mean?"

Shrugging her shoulders she cleared her throat. "His name is Jase. He's in my English Lit class."

Raising my eyebrows up, I smiled. "Really? This Jase, what does he look like?"

Closing her eyes and sighing, Taylor licked her lips and smiled big as she opened her eyes and looked at me. "Oh my gosh, Lauren. He looks like . . . like . . . like a Greek god."

Slamming my hands over my mouth, I began hopping on the bed. Dropping my hands, I whispered, "Tell me all about him!"

Blushing, Taylor bit down on her lower lip and chewed on it. "Well, he's smart, funny, and did I mention he looks like a Greek God?"

Snickering, I said, "Yes, you did mention that already. Have you talked to him?"

Dropping her smile, Taylor shook her head.

"What? Why, Tay?"

Wringing her hands, Taylor looked away and let out a nervous laugh. "Lauren, this guy is amazing. He hasn't even looked twice at me. I mean, look at me."

My mouth dropped open. "Taylor, you are beautiful. Inside and out. Any guy would consider himself lucky to even catch your eye."

Rolling her eyes Taylor laughed. "There is this other girl. She's in Italian with me. She speaks it really well and she flirts with Jase. Talks to him in Italian all the time and the stuff she says turns my stomach."

Inching closer to the edge of my bed, I swung my feet around and looked into Lauren's eyes. "Does he know what she's saying?"

"No, he just smiles at her. The way he looks at her though is like he wants her." Shrugging her shoulders again, she gave me a weak smile. "I've never been attracted to a guy like this before or had feelings like this. I'm sure it's just a silly crush."

My heart hurt for Taylor. She was beautiful. Her light-brown wavy hair was pulled up in a ponytail. Her green eyes glossed over with sadness. Reaching over, I motioned for Taylor to give me her hands.

"Taylor, please don't ever sell yourself short or think you don't deserve someone. This Jase guy, if he hasn't noticed you yet, then fuck him. You don't need the Greek god. There are other ones out there. He probably has a small dick anyway with a name like Jase."

Taylor started laughing. "He probably does!"

My phone rang as I pulled it out and saw it was Colt. "Speaking of Greek gods—"

Taylor jumped up and headed into the bathroom. "I'm

taking a quick shower."

Smiling, I answered my phone. "Hey, baby."

"Hey, sweetheart."

My heart melted. The tenderness in Colt's voice caused a pulling sensation in my lower stomach. "I miss you, Colt."

"Damn, baby. I miss you, too."

Swallowing hard, I nodded my head. Closing my eyes I pictured Colt lying on his bed in nothing but a pair of boxers.

"Where are you?" I asked in a husky voice.

"In my bedroom."

I could hear his smile in the way he talked. "What are you wearing?"

There was a moment of silence before my phone beeped. Smiling, I pulled my phone back and saw I had a text from Colt. Putting him on speakerphone, I opened up the text and gasped. It was a picture of Colt lying in his bed . . . naked.

Good lord, his body was perfect. Licking my lips, I stared at the picture. I wondered if I could get it printed out and carry it around with me. Feeling sad . . . pull out Colt's picture. Feeling angry . . . pull out Colt's picture. Feeling horny . . . oh yes. Pull. Out. Colt's. Picture.

"I'm saving this forever," I whispered as I began biting on my thumb as I stared at it.

"Lauren?"

"Mmm?"

"Baby, will you take me off speakerphone now?"

Look at his abs. Oh my . . . it's getting rather hot in here. What did Colt say?

"What? I mean . . . um . . . did you say something?"

Laughing, Colt said, "Sweetheart, take me off speaker-phone."

Colt's laughter snapped me out of my trance. "Right. Speakerphone."

Putting the phone back to my ear I said, "Okay, you're off speakerphone. Tay couldn't hear you anyway."

"Where is, Tay?"

My heart started beating faster and my hands began

171

to sweat. I knew where this was going and I was for sure going to let it go right down that path. "She's um, in the shower."

"Get your headphones baby and call me back on FaceTime."

Hanging up my phone, I quickly ran over to my purse and dumped it out to find my headphones. Something red caught my eye. *There you are!* Running back over to my phone, I pushed my headphones into the jack and called Colt back on FaceTime.

Seeing him lying on his bed, naked, caused me to smile. "Colt," I whispered.

"Can you go anywhere, Lauren?" Glancing back to the bathroom door I wanted to cry. There was nowhere I could go. Then I remembered I had the keys to the rental.

"The car!" Jumping up, I ran to the bathroom door and yelled, "Tay, I left something in the rental car. I'll be right back!"

"Oh. Okay, Lauren. Be careful, it's late."

Grabbing the keys, I made it out the door and to the elevator. "I'm going to lose my signal. I'll call you right back."

Colt winked. "I'll be waiting, sweetheart."

The screen went blank as I pushed my phone into my pocket and practically ran to the elevator.

The whole way down, I couldn't wipe the smile off my face. My phone pinged as I stepped out of the elevator. Pulling it out, I saw it was Grace.

Grace: *Bitch, I saw you running with the rental car keys. Get your freak on!*

Rolling my eyes, I deleted her message and walked out front. The valet came running over to me. "Yes, would you like your car?"

Oh shit. I didn't think this through very well. "Um, no! I just need to get something out of it. We parked it ourselves."

Giving me a smile he, asked, "The Tahoe right? It's parked right next to our valet parking lot."

Nodding my head, I smiled. "Okay. Great! Thanks so much."

Giving me a sweet smile, the valet said, "Would you like me to run and get it for you?"

"No! It's personal and all that."

I took off running toward where Grace had parked the Tahoe. Calling back over my shoulder, I yelled, "Thanks!" Adrenaline raced through my veins as I thought about having phone sex with Colt.

Hitting the panic button to find the car, I heard the horn going off. Smiling, I hit the button again and skipped over to Tahoe. Jumping into the front driver's side seat I looked around. *Nope, I'm gonna need more room.* Crawling over the console, I flopped down onto the back seat, opened up my phone and hit Colt's number to FaceTime him. The moment I saw him my stomach flipped.

We stared at each other as we smiled. "Lauren, make sure no one can see you."

Nodding my head, I looked around and slid further down into the seat so no one would see me.

Licking my lips, I whispered, "Touch yourself, Colt."

TWENTY

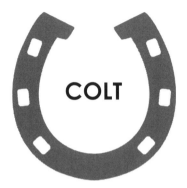

COLT

MY DICK JUMPED when Lauren whispered for me to touch myself. I'd never done anything like this before, I knew Lauren hadn't either. There was something very hot about what we were about to do.

Reaching down, I grabbed my dick and began moving my hand up and down my shaft. Closing my eyes, I pictured Lauren's lips wrapped around my dick.

I could hear Lauren's breathing increase. "Does it feel good, Colt?"

Nodding my head, I moaned. "Lauren . . . touch yourself, too. I want to hear how wet you are."

"Colt," Lauren hissed and I imagined her hands slipping into her panties and between her lips. "How wet, Lauren?"

Panting, Lauren whispered, "Wet. Very wet. Colt, let me see you touching yourself."

Moving my phone down, I showed Lauren what I was doing. I heard her gasp. "Hottest thing I've ever seen, Colt. Go faster."

Fuck. Is she trying to kill me? "Lauren, if I go faster I'm going to lose it."

"Faster, Colt. I'm so close." My eyes snapped open as I watched her. Desire washed over her face as I picked up the pace. "Yes," she hissed through her clenched teeth. My heart was racing as I watched Lauren making herself feel good.

"Ahh . . ." Lauren said as she arched her body. I felt my balls sucking up and I was about to lose it.

"Lauren, baby, I'm going to come."

Lauren's mouth dropped open as her breathing increased more as I came all over my own stomach.

"Oh, God yes," I moaned.

Lauren closed her eyes as she said, "Talk to me."

"Baby, you look so hot touching yourself. I want to hear my name when you come, Lauren."

"Shit! Colt! Colt! Colt! Colt!"

Smiling, I watched her come undone. I'd never seen anything so damn sexy in my life. Standing up, I made my way into my bathroom and grabbed a washcloth. Throwing it into the sink, I turned on the hot water. I couldn't pull my eyes from Lauren. Her chest was heaving up and down still. Opening her eyes, Lauren looked at me and started giggling. "I can't believe we just did that. We had phone sex!"

"FaceTime sex, really."

Lauren was about to talk when I heard what sounded like someone knocking on the car window. Lauren jumped and screamed. "Fuck! I think it's the valet," she whispered.

Looking around, Lauren reached down for something, then opened the back door. I could hear a male's voice talking to her.

"So that's two free shows I've gotten from you in the last twenty-four hours."

What the fuck did he mean by that?

"Um, Colt, I'm going to call you right back."

Feeling a sense of panic, I yelled, "No! Lauren stay on the—"

Lauren disconnected the FaceTime and I stood there stunned. She hung up. She just hung up.

Pushing my hand over the top of my hair I let out a frustrated sigh and then hit her number.

Voicemail.

What the fuck? Dropping my phone on the counter, I cleaned up and quickly put on a pair of pants. Grabbing my phone, I was about to hit Lauren's number when my phone began ringing.

Swiping to answer, I practically yelled, "Why in the fuck would you hang up on me?"

"Colt, give me two seconds to get back into the hotel."

"No, Lauren you were fucking giving yourself an orgasm when some asshole walked up. Was he watching you? It sure sounded like it and what does he mean this was his second free show? What in the hell have you been doing?"

Silence.

"Lauren! What. Is. Going. On. There?"

"Colt, shut the fuck up for thirty seconds!"

Stunned, I sat down on my bed as I attempted to calm down.

Hearing a door shut, Lauren cleared her throat. "He didn't see anything, but it was obvious what I was doing, Colt. It was the same valet that helped us when we checked in. I had an . . . incident."

Pinching my eyebrows together, I quietly asked, "What kind of an incident?"

"I got stung by a bee and I kind of panicked and pulled my shirt over my head in the front of the parking lot."

Closing my eyes and shaking my head I tried to understand what she was saying. Looking out my window I felt sick to my stomach. "You did what? Why would you pull your shirt off? Did you have a bra on? Did that asshole see you in just your bra?"

Letting a deep breath out, Lauren sighed. "Are you finished asking me all your questions?"

Slowly taking in a deep breath, I blew it out just as slow. "I'm sorry, Lauren. It's just I heard this stranger talking and I kind of freaked out and then you hung up on me. Why did you hang up on me?"

Letting out a gruff laugh, Lauren said, "You were on FaceTime naked, Colt. I didn't want this guy seeing you."

Oh. I hadn't thought of that. Shit.

"Damn it. I'm sorry, Lauren. I wasn't even thinking about that."

"No kidding. I wanted to wait until I got to the hotel before I called you back. The stupid guy walked me back to the hotel."

Balling up my fists, I had the urge to hit someone. Fucker. I prayed to God he hadn't seen anything. "Did he, I mean are you sure he didn't?"

Lauren remained silent for a little too long. "I can't say a hundred percent, but he knew what I had been doing."

"Fucking asshole. Don't talk to him again, Lauren. Don't even go near him."

Letting out a giggle, Lauren said, "Why, Mr. Mathews, are you jealous?"

"No I'm not jealous. You're mine, Lauren. I never want another man to see what's mine. Ever."

Letting out a slight moan, Lauren whispered, "I love you, Colt."

My heart dropped at her whispered words. What was it about this girl? She had my stomach in all kinds of knots and I wouldn't have it any other way.

"I love you more, sweetheart."

"So, tell me about this stallion."

Grinning like a fool, I started to tell Lauren all about what had happened. My adrenaline began pumping again as I talked about it.

"Wow. That's awesome, Colt."

Something was off in Lauren's voice. I could hear it. "I can't wait for you to take a look at him, Lauren. He's amazing."

"Yeah, I'm excited to see him. Listen, I better get to bed. We're going on a train ride tomorrow, early."

Yep. I could hear the disappointment in Lauren's voice. I made a mental note to talk to Scott tomorrow about Lauren.

"All right, baby. I love you and I miss you. I hope y'all have fun tomorrow. No more taking your shirt off, okay?"

Laughing, she said, "Deal! Don't get too crazy with that stallion either, Colt. Be careful, okay?"

"Always. Night, Lauren. Sweet dreams, baby, and I love you."

"Sweet dreams, Colt. Love you."

Closing my eyes, I could almost smell her perfume. Pulling the phone away from my ear, I set it on my side table. Dropping my head back, I let out a frustrated breath.

"Lauren," I whispered as I formulated a plan to have her help me with the stallion. We were going to do this together and she was going to prove to her dad that she was more than ready to take over more control of her families breeding business.

Falling back, it didn't take long for sleep to win me over.

WALKING INTO THE barn, I saw Scott leaning against one of the stalls looking over a piece of paper. "Hey, Scott what's going on?"

Glancing over to me, Scott smiled. "Colt. Thanks for meeting me down here." He handed me the piece of paper and I began to look over it.

Shaking my head, I looked at him. "What is this?"

"This is your schedule for this summer. You are officially part of Reynolds Breeding, Colt. Welcome aboard son." He held out his hand for me to shake it. I wasn't sure how I should be feeling. I was happy but at the same time, I wasn't sure how Lauren would react to this new development. "Jessie is booking your tickets this afternoon for the trips to Kentucky and New York. Those two are strictly for the racehorses Jeff and I are interested in."

My mouth went dry. Scott wanted me to travel with him to look at potential racehorses. Holy shit.

"Um . . . I'm not sure what to say, sir. It is an honor that you would take me under your wing like this."

Scott winked and motioned for me to follow him as he walked out of the barn. "Colt, I see great potential in you. The way you nailed it on the head with that stallion really proved to me that you know your shit. You were meant for this and I don't want to waste a second with your training."

Nodding my head, I swallowed. "What about Lauren, sir?"

Scott snapped his head over and looked at me. "Lauren? What about her?"

"Will she be joining us on these trips?" Glancing down I saw there were three trips planned. Two trips to Kentucky and one to New York.

Shrugging his shoulders, Scott let out a chuckle. "I guess if she wants to join us she can. I figured she'd spend some time with her mother learning the books and—"

Stopping, I closed my eyes. This could go two ways. Scott would listen and agree with me, or he would tell me to mind my own business about his family and his business.

"You have something to say, Colt?"

Opening my eyes, I nodded my head. I loved Lauren more than anything and if it meant walking away from the one thing I dreamed of doing for her love, I would do it.

"Yes, sir. I do have something I'd like to talk to you about. May we go to your office?"

Scott raised his eyebrow and nodded his head. "Sure. Let's go."

My heart was beating like crazy in my chest as I followed Scott to his office. Opening the door, we stepped in and I looked around. Pictures covered the walls. They were a mixture of Scott's prized horses, pictures of Jessie and Lauren and pictures of all of us on trips we had taken together. Walking up to one picture, I smiled. The moment I saw her smile a warmth rushed through my body.

"You really love her don't you, Colt?"

Smiling, I nodded my head. "Yes, sir, I love her very much."

Turning, I looked at Scott. He had always been like a second father to me. Really, all of my father's friends were like second fathers. Each of them had taught us boys lessons that I would cherish forever. Letting out a quick breath, I got ready to talk. My hands began to sweat so I rubbed them against my pants. "Take a seat, Colt and tell me what's on your mind."

Worrying my lower lip, I sat down. Clearing my throat, I looked Scott right in the eyes. "I want to start off by saying I hope you know how much it means to me that you have faith in me. I've always dreamed of helping you with your business for as long as I can remember. I feel like I have some fresh ideas to add to the smooth operation of the breeding business as well as the racing side of your business."

Leaning back in his chair, Scott gave me a slight grin and nodded his head. "Why do I feel like there is a but in there somewhere, Colt?"

"Sir, this is a bit awkward to talk about it since this has to do with Lauren."

Scott moved a little in his seat. "Go on."

"Lauren loves this ranch sir. She dreams of running it one day alongside of you and the last thing I want to do is stand in the way of that."

Scott's eyebrows raised and I wished like hell I could read his mind. Was he angry with me for speaking about this? Was he going to tell me to get out of his office? I couldn't read his eyes at all.

"Lauren has expressed some concerns with me, sir."

Clearing his throat, Scott moved about in his chair again. "Concerns?"

Nodding my head, I kept talking. I was in too deep now to turn around and drop it. "She feels like you don't think she can run this ranch without um . . . well, without help from . . . ah."

Narrowing his eyes at me, Scott leaned forward. "Spit it the hell out, Colt."

"Well, um, she said you told her she needed a man to help her run the ranch and she fears you're going to stick her in the office with her mother and that is the last thing she wants. If you take me on these trips and keep Lauren out, she's gonna think I'm pushing her out of what she considers her position within Reynolds Breeding. Sir, the last thing I want to do is have Lauren feel like I'm taking something from her. I love her too much to do that to her."

Leaning forward, Scott placed his elbows on the desk.

His eyes were burning with something. Anger? *Yep. That sure looked like anger to me. Fuck. He's going to give it to me. Good-bye trips to Kentucky and New York.*

"She told you I said she needed a man to help her run the ranch?"

"Um . . . yes, sir, she did."

Something passed over Scott's eyes. It was gone before I could really tell what it was.

"Tell me, Colt. Where do you think Lauren's position is in *my* business?"

Ah hell. He stressed *my*. Swallowing hard, I thought about how I wanted to answer this question. "Scott, it's not my place to say where Lauren belongs, or even where I belong. I do know that she loves this ranch. She loves every single one of these horses and I've witnessed her first hand with some of them. They love her just as much as she loves them. She has a gift that I don't really know how to explain. She can calm them with a single touch. She seems to know things about them before she even works with them." Letting out a chuckle I shook my head. "I've even seen her talking to them, and I swear they understand her."

Looking back to Scott, he was smiling as he listened to me. "Scott, let Lauren help me train the stallion."

Dropping back in his seat he shook his head. "No. No way do I want her near that horse. No."

Looking down, I thought about the first time Lauren told me her fears about me and why she pushed me away from her. I would not stand in the way of her dreams, but I knew if Scott didn't give Lauren the chance to prove herself, it would always be someone in her way regardless of if it was me or some other guy Scott hired.

"Scott, please forgive me if I'm speaking out of line, but you're making a terrible mistake holding Lauren back from what she was clearly meant to do."

Scott narrowed his eyes and if looks could kill, I'd have been dead on the floor right now. "That's my daughter, Colt. My everything. Do you understand that?"

His fists were balled-up as he glared at me. "I understand,

sir, but I still think you're making a mistake and it will ultimately lead to you pushing Lauren away." Standing, Scott's chair flew back and hit the set of cabinets behind him. "Do you think because you're dating my daughter that gives you the right to tell me what she should and shouldn't do with this business? Son, you are more than stepping over the lines here. You're just her boyfriend. I'm her father and I have nothing but her best interests at heart. There is no way I'm putting her in harm's way."

It was my turn to stand up and ball my fists. "Just her boyfriend?" Shaking my head, I felt the heat move across my body. "I'm sorry, sir, but I love Lauren with my whole life. She is *my everything,* and if that means standing up to you on this and arguing for her, I'll do it. Even if it means you ask me to leave. I have faith in Lauren. I believe in her and I know she would do better at taking over this ranch and running it over any guy you bring in here."

Pointing to me, Scott asked, "Does that include you? Can she run this business better than you?"

Staring into Scott's eyes, I felt the frog forming in the back of my throat. Clearing my throat, I said, "If given the chance to prove what she can do, and I don't mean organizing files—"

Scott glared at me when I made that last comment. "I really think, sir, you would be surprised by some of the ideas she has for things." Letting out a quick breath, I said, "Scott, she is your daughter. This has been her entire life. I can remember watching her follow you around and asking you everything she possibly could about the horses." Shaking my head, I looked down, then back at Scott.

"Sir, don't hold her back. She has so much more to offer than sitting behind some desk being unhappy and miserable. The stallion. That is in her blood."

Reaching back and grabbing his chair, Scott pulled it in close to him and sat down. Motioning for me to sit, I did as he asked. Beads of sweat began to form on my brow, and I was waiting for Scott to chew my ass out.

Looking down at his desk, Scott pursed his lips together and nodded his head. "I'll never forget the first time

I walked into the barn and saw Lauren dragging a stool over to a stall. She couldn't have been more than four or five years old. She climbed up onto the stool so she could reach Blazin' Fire. Damn that horse was a bitch of a mare. Hated everyone but she had some of the best racing bloodline in her than any other horse I had before or since her. Blazin' walked up and looked over the stall door at this tiny little curious thing. Lauren reached up and said, "Fire Girl, let me touch you."

Smiling, I saw tears fill Scott's eyes as he paused. It was as if he was drinking in the memory. "Blazin' leaned as far down as she could and Lauren rubbed her neck. Then she wrapped her arms around Blazin's neck and that damn horse lifted Lauren right off the stool. My first instinct was to run in there and grab Lauren, but something held me back. Lauren held on for dear life as her laughter filled the barn. A few other horses snickered as if they knew what was passing between Blazin' and Lauren. Slowly setting her back down on the stool, Blazin' snickered and bobbed her head at Lauren who laughed again, then proclaimed that she was going to love Fire Girl for the rest of her life."

A tear threatened to spill from Scott's eyes before he quickly wiped at his eyes. "She's always been fearless like that, Colt. Always. The first horse she was ever one, was Blazin' Fire. That damn horse moved like she was walking on a cloud anytime Lauren was on her. No one else could ride her. I mean no one. I came out of the barn one day when Lauren was around eleven. She was riding up from the pasture on her Fire Girl. Those two were inseparable."

Nodding my head, I whispered, "I remember."

Glancing at me, Scott said, "Yes, you would remember because wherever Lauren was, you were there, too. The two of you, training horses and pushing things always to the limits. It's always scared me."

Scott let out a chuckle. He was about to say something else when a look of fear crossed his face. Dropping his face into his hands he let out a frustrated moan. "Dear God, what have I done?" Slowly shaking his head, Scott dropped his hands. "I did tell Lauren that." Scott's face was pained and my heart broke for him. "I also mentioned you when I told her that. I mentioned you taking over the ranch someday."

My mouth went dry and I had a hard time swallowing. *Shit.*

We sat in silence for a few minutes. "All right. Have Lauren help with the stallion. I'm trusting you on this, Colt. That girl is my . . . she's . . . if anything ever happened to her." Scott's voice cracked.

Standing, I nodded my head as I attempted to push down my own fears. "Believe me, sir. Lauren is the very air I breathe. Without her with me, I honestly don't think I could go on. I will do everything in my power to always keep her safe."

Getting up, Scott reached for my hand. His grip was firm and he shook my hand quickly before dropping it. "I know you will, Colt. I appreciate your love for my daughter. I want to tell you how lucky you are to have her, but I'm sure you know that. Just know, Colt, she is also the lucky one as well."

By the time I walked out of Scott's office, it felt as if a huge weight had been lifted from my shoulders. Scott wasn't holding Lauren back because he thought she couldn't handle the task. He was holding her back out of fear of something happening to her.

Pulling the baseball cap out of my back pocket, I slipped it on and headed back to the barn with a smile plastered on my face. All I could see was my future with Lauren. Her and I together, working on the ranch and starting our own family here. Watching our own daughter someday fall in love with the horses.

Stepping into the barn my happiness quickly disappeared when I saw Rachel and her father standing there talking to Ryan, Scott's trainer.

Fuck. Just when life seemed to be going in the right direction. Rachel glanced over to me and smiled as she winked, then licked her lips. Rolling my eyes, I turned and headed into the tack room. Shutting the door, I pulled out my phone and sent Lauren a text.

Me: *Talked to your dad. He loves the idea of us working on the stallion together!*

Lauren: *What? Are you serious?*

Me: *Yep. And we are going to Kentucky twice this summer and New York.*

Lauren: *That's amazing Colt! I can't wait to get home now!*

Smiling, I dropped my head back against the door and prayed like hell Rachel would be gone by the time I stepped out of this room.

Jumping when someone knocked on the door, I heard her voice. "Colt? Colt are you in there?"

Glancing back down at my phone I knew what I had to do.

Me: *Rachel is here at your dad's. Looks like her father is dropping off a horse*

Lauren: *Yeah, I know. I scheduled it before I left. I love you, Colt Mathews*

Letting out a chuckle I whispered, "Damn, I love you."

Me: *I love you more.*

Opening the door quickly, Rachel let out a yelp and jumped back as she looked behind me into the room. "Who were you talking to?"

Walking past her, I hurried over to a stall to start cleaning it out. "Lauren."

"Right. Little sweet Lauren. How's that working out for you, Colt?"

Turning around, I glared at Rachel. "Considering I'm planning on asking her to marry me, I'd say it was working out pretty damn good."

Rachel sucked in a breath of air as she took a few steps back. Glaring at me with that look that used to make my skin crawl, she lifted her chin and whispered, "Your loss."

Letting out a chuckle, I said, "Enjoy your afternoon, Rachel." Turning back around, I began cleaning out the stall. Scott cleared his throat behind me and I glanced over my shoulder.

"Tell me what I just overheard was just simply a way of you getting Rachel to leave you alone."

Laughing, I set the rake up against the stall door. "Yes sir, but, there is one other thing I needed to ask you now that we are on the subject." Walking closer to Scott I gave him a huge smile.

Scott closed his eyes and let out a pain filled moan. "Oh, son-of-a-bitch. I was not ready for that one."

TWENTY-ONE

LAUREN

S PINNING MY ALEX and Ani bracelet on my wrist, I closed my eyes and felt the heat move across my body. Colt had given me the locket bracelet the night before I left for Colorado after we had made love in the bed of his truck. Letting out a long sigh, I felt someone bump my shoulder.

"Daydreaming of a certain blue-eyed cowboy?" Alex asked with a smile.

Nodding my head, I let out a chuckle. "Oh, Alex. I'm so afraid I'm going to wake up and this is all going to be a dream."

Grinning, Alex looked out at the beautiful Colorado countryside that was passing by us. We were riding the Durango train back down the mountain after spending the day on it. We had stopped at a few little towns to shop along the way.

"It's not a dream, Lauren." Turning back to me, she took my hands. "I've never seen my brother so happy, Lauren. It's almost like you can feel the love just pouring off his body. He was actually singing in the shower the other day. My mother and I walked into his room and stood there giggling as we listened to him singing. It was kind of cute."

Feeling my cheeks blush, I squeezed Alex's hands. "What about you and Will? How are things going?"

The smile that spread over Alex's face was contagious.

I smiled back at her. "The wedding?"

Letting out a sigh, Alex's face lit up. "I'm so excited, Lauren. Everything is just falling into place."

My heart was bursting with happiness for Alex and Will. They went through a lot the first year they were together, but their love pulled them through it all.

"I think it is so romantic that you're getting married under the same tree your parents did."

Placing her hand over her mouth, tears formed in Alex's eyes as she stifled her sob. "Me, too. It's beyond perfect. I mean, when my parents got married there, our house wasn't there, but there is something magical about that tree. I feel it in my heart."

Reaching up, I wiped a tear from Alex's cheek. "Why are you crying, Alex?"

"Because I'm so happy, Lauren and at the same time I'm so afraid the floor is going to fall out from underneath me because I'm so happy."

Pulling her into my arms, I held her tight. "Alex, everything is going to be perfect. Don't worry about a thing."

Sniffling, Alex nodded into my chest. "I'm so scared, Lauren."

"Oh, honey. Why? Why are you scared?"

Pulling back some, Alex worried her lower lip. "I don't know. I love Will so much and I really can't wait to start my life as his wife but at the same time . . . I'm getting married in a little over a month." Letting out a nervous giggle, her eyes widened. "Married. As in Mrs. William Hayes."

Staring at Alex I tried to hold it back, but I couldn't. I busted out laughing. It didn't take Alex long to start laughing also. Before long, we had tears streaming down our faces and I wasn't even sure why we were laughing. Grace and Maegan walked up and looked at us with smiles.

"What's so funny?" Grace asked as she walked up to us.

Wiping my tears away, I winked at Alex. "Just being silly and we lost control of our giggles."

We spent the rest of the train ride planning our evening. We were going to dinner, then dancing at a local club that would allow Taylor and me in.

THREE HOURS LATER, Grace was grinding up against yet another cowboy as we all sat at the table and watched. After the song ended, she meandered her way back over to us.

"Whew. Damn, that boy was hot! I was pretty sure I was one move away from getting his number."

Maegan jumped up. "That's it! Okay, the first one to get a guy's number wins!"

We all looked around at each other and then back to Maegan. "What in the hell are you talking about, Meg? I thought we all agreed no getting wasted tonight," Libby said with a wink.

"I'm not wasted, I've only been drinking water all night. Come on y'all! It's innocent fun."

Taylor shouted over the loud music. "What do we get if we win?"

Maegan looked around at each of us. "If we all chip in fifty bucks, that would be three hundred dollars."

Alex jumped up. "I'm in! I have a wedding to pay for."

Libby started laughing. "Okay, but for those of us with guys, no kissing is allowed so those who are single, no kissing either."

Grace rolled her eyes. "That is totally not fair, Libby."

"The only lips my lips touch are Colt Mathews.'"

Alex gave me a wink and mouthed, *thank you.*

The air in the dance club suddenly became thick. The music was a mixture of country, hip-hop, and pop. My stomach tightened and I wasn't too thrilled about this bet, but the way Maegan was eyeing me was starting to piss me off. Turning to Grace, Maegan said, "This is in the bag for either you or me. Let's do this." They both slapped hands and I seethed with anger.

How dare Maegan think that just because we had boy-friends we couldn't still pull a number from a guy.

"Who's up first?" Grace asked.

Alex jumped up. "Me. I've got this. I see my victim, too." Taking a drink of her lemon drop, Alex started walking over to the blond-haired guy who had been sitting at the bar with three other good-looking guys. Alex walked up and placed her hand on his shoulder and whispered something into his ear.

"Ah hell. Look at my girl go!" Grace shouted as we all laughed. I was silently thanking God they didn't come up with this bet last night when they were all drunk.

The blond stood up and wrapped his arm around Alex's waist and moved her to the dance floor. "My brother would be going through the roof right now if he saw this," Libby said.

Some hip-hop song I'd never heard of began playing as the bass thumbed in my chest. Had Colt been here I would have been turned on by the idea of dancing all up on him. But he wasn't, so I needed to stow away my naughty thoughts of him.

Alex wrapped her arms around the guy's neck and went after it with everything she had. She smiled, she tossed her head back and laughed, she whispered against his ear. She even turned and placed her backside to him. When he brushed his hand down her side and dangerously close to her breasts, she quickly turned around.

"Oh! Nice move, Mathews!" Maegan shouted. Glancing to Taylor, she was watching Alex closely but smiling.

The song ended and Alex walked back over to the bar with him. Less than thirty seconds later, she was walking back with a napkin and the guy's number on it.

Grace and Maegan's smiles dropped. "What? No fucking way!" Maegan yelled as Alex walked up and smiled as she waved the napkin around. Grace shook her head and placed her hands on her hips and glared at Alex.

Alex leaned over and whispered in Libby's ear. Pulling back, Libby smiled and winked.

"All right bitches, let's see what the married one with a baby can do," Grace said as she pointed to Libby.

Libby stood up straighter, adjusted her breasts and

said, "All right. Watch and learn ladies. Watch and learn."

Libby walked over to the same group of guys, but she zeroed in on one of the other guys. Turning, Libby pointed and four guys all turned and looked. The guy Alex danced with smiled at Alex as she gave him a flirty wave.

"Shit, that guy wants in someone's panties," Grace teased Alex.

One of the guys got up and followed Libby to the dance floor. Smoke began engulfing the dance floor as the song changed. All I heard in the song over and over was *I want to fuck you all night long.*

Waving a hand in front of her, Grace picked up her water glass and ran it along her neck. "Shit if that song don't turn you on!"

Glancing back to Libby she was talking to the guy as they danced. His hands moved down to her hips as she placed her hand on his chest and bit down on her lower lip.

Maegan laughed. "Oh my gosh! She's still using the move she had in high school." We all started laughing until the guy moved his lips to Libby's neck. Dropping her neck back she let him kiss her.

"Oh my God! What is she doing? She's kissing," Taylor shouted as she jumped up.

Not really liking where this was going, I turned to Alex and she winked at me. Something was up with those two. Grace and Maegan were shouting and hollering as the guy pulled back and said something to Libby that caused her to start laughing. The song ended and he reached into her back pocket and pulled out her cell phone.

"Oh. My. God. Are you kidding me?" Grace shouted as she stood there stunned. Libby gave the guy a flirtatious wave a she walked back over to us. Holding up her phone she showed everyone the number.

Greg was his name and the moment Libby showed Maegan and Grace, she deleted the number. Sitting down next to me I turned to her. "How could you let him kiss your neck, Libby?"

Leaning closer to me she said, "If you looked closely,

his lips were nowhere near my neck. He was telling me about a kids' show his daughter loves to watch on TV."

Wait. What? A kids' show?

I was about to ask what she was talking about when Grace announced it was her turn. Making her way back over to the guy she had just danced with, he took her hand and began dancing her around on the dance floor to a Luke Bryan song. She spun around and made sure at one point when he pulled her back in she was flush up against his body. Her hands were moving everywhere on his body and Alex yelled, "Slut!"

Grace must have heard her, because she lifted her middle finger in Alex's direction.

The song ended and she handed him her phone. He punched his number in and she reached up and kissed him on lips. It wasn't just a quick kiss. They were practically crawling into each other's mouths. Laughing I turned to Alex and Libby and rolled my eyes. "I guess it doesn't count since she had already gotten the number.

Grace walked back up and declared she was keeping that cowboy's number. Reaching for my water, I took a sip. It felt extremely hot in the dance club and I began feeling light headed. *Gesh Lauren. Get it together. It's just a bet. It's not like you're cheating on Colt. It's just a dance. Simple as that. One dance.*

Maegan was next. She must have had her sights on someone because she walked up and whispered in the guy's ear. He pulled back and nodded his head. Maegan glanced over her shoulder and winked.

The guy pulled her into his arms as a slow song started to play. "Damn. Meg is all up in that shit!" Grace said as she tossed her head back and laughed. Staring out at Maegan dancing my heart broke for her and Grace. They were both so beautiful and I knew they could easily walk out of here tonight with a guy. The both wanted to have fun, but that was as far as it went.

The song ended and Maegan followed the guy back to his table. I strained to see them through the crowd of people and for one brief second I began to worry. We had all agreed not to split up. What if this guy had taken Maegan off to a corner or something? Grace was trying to stand on her tippy toes to see Maegan. She turned and looked at Alex with a concerned look.

"Why would she walk off with the guy?" Grace shouted.

Maegan came walking up and pulled Grace's hair as she said, "Because I needed to get my cowboy's room number along with his phone number. I'm half tempted to go to his room tonight!" Maegan wiggled her eyebrows up and down and said, "He's from Montana."

Grace laughed and said, "Montana dick. I bet it's nice."

"Gross, Grace!" Taylor said as she pushed Grace, causing her to stumble a bit.

Grace lost it laughing but pointed to Taylor. "Tay. You're up."

Taylor began pulling and pushing her lower lip in and out of her teeth as she stood up and looked around. Maegan pointed to a guy standing near the bar. "He's got a killer ass and I got a look at him earlier. The guy is fucking beautiful."

Taylor nodded her head and made her way over to the guy.

"Fifty bucks she turns around before she even gets to him," Alex yelled over the song now playing.

Grace nodded her head. "I'm voting she's gonna do it. I feel it in my bones. Our little Tay is growing up, y'all."

Standing up, I watched Taylor walk up to the guy. She placed her hands on his shoulders and stood up on her tippy toes, attempting to talk into his ear.

"Oh my glitter! She didn't even get a frontal view! She went in blind!"

We all started yelling out Taylor's name as the guy turned around and smiled. Taylor's smile dropped instantly. Oh my. The guy was for sure *very* good looking. "Did he just say her name?" Libby asked.

"Wait. Does she know him?" Maegan asked. My smiled faded as the guy took Taylor's hand and led her to the dance floor. Taylor turned and looked at me with nothing but panic on her face. I mouthed, *are you okay?* Shaking her head she mouthed back, *it's Jase.*

"It's, Jase! What are the odds?" I said out loud as four sets of eyes turned and looked at me.

Grace took my arm and pulled me out of my trance. "Lauren, does she know him?"

Nodding my head, I turned back to watch Taylor. "Yes! Oh my gosh she was talking about him last night. He's in one of her classes at UT, and she has a massive crush on him, y'all. She said he has never given her the time of day before."

All four of them said, "Wow," at the same time. "Holy hell. That would never happen again if you planned it," Grace said.

Jase leaned down and spoke into Taylor's ear. I could see the flush on her cheeks from where I was standing. Reaching her hands up, she placed them on his chest and smiled.

"Look at that smile," Libby said.

The song ended and Jase and Taylor stood on the dance floor for a few minutes and talked. I was silently willing him to ask her out. For him to ask Taylor for her number. She glanced over to us and shrugged her shoulders as she flashed us a weak smile before looking back at Jase. Taking out his phone, he handed it to her. Taylor did the same. After another minute or so of talking, Jase placed his hand on Taylor's arm and smiled as he leaned down and gave her a quick kiss on the cheek. Taylor just stood there as he walked away.

"W-what is she doing? Taylor, walk. Honey move your legs," Maegan shouted.

Grace threw her hands up in the air. "She's breaking a major girl code right now y'all. She's letting the guy see he affected her. Code red!"

We all jumped up and went out to the dance floor and surrounded Taylor as we danced. Pulling her to me, I shouted, "What are the odds?"

She giggled. "I know! But, Lauren he knew who I was. He knew who I was!"

Pulling Taylor into my arms we both began jumping in

excitement. "And y'all exchanged numbers!"

Nodding her head Taylor did another little jump. "I know! Holy shit I know! He asked me for mine first!"

Grace made her way to me and said, "Okay, Miss Striptease. It's your turn."

Rolling my eyes, I glanced around the club. No one here held a candle to Colt. One of the guys that was sitting with the two guys Alex and Libby walked up to was looking out on the dance floor at us. I decided he was going to be my target. Making my way over to him, the girls were chanting my name as I walked his way. His smile caught me off guard. It was breathtaking. I hadn't really noticed how cute he was until I got right up to him. "Hey, you need some help with that bet?"

"What?" I asked in a shocked voice.

The other guy who Alex danced with said, "Your two other friends already told us what was going on."

Glancing over my shoulder back at the girls, they were all watching. Turning back to the guys I laughed. "Yes. But I need to make mine bigger than just a number or a room number." The two guys that Libby and Alex danced with held up their hands. "Sorry, we're married."

Laughing, I shook my head and shouted, "No, I don't mean anything like that."

Turning to the guy I had originally noticed, I sucked in a breath of air. He was looking at me like he wanted something more than to pretend he was giving me a number. Leaning in closer to him I asked over the loud music, "You married, too?"

His eyes smoldered as he shook his head. "Just tell me what you want me to do, baby, and I'll do it."

Oh shit. Shit, shit, shit. That can't be good to have a guy say that to you.

"I was just thinking you would give me your number and give me a little striptease on the bar."

The guy almost choked on his drink. "What? Are you serious?"

Smiling, I gave him a taste of his own medicine. Giving my best innocent sexy look, I said, "Yeah. Totally serious."

Tilting his head, he asked, "Are you with someone?"

Although the guy was drop-dead handsome, I felt nothing even though he was looking at me with nothing but lust in his eyes. All I could think of was Colt. I'd never do anything to hurt Colt. Not even for a bet.

"Yes, I am with someone. I love him very much."

The guy nodded his head and gave me a sweet grin. "He's a lucky guy."

Okay, so that made my stomach drop a little. "How do you know?" I shouted over the song. "You don't even know me!"

Nodding his head slightly, his eyes turned sad. "I know enough. How far you want the striptease to go?"

Giggling, I leaned closer to his ear, "As far as you want it to go, but no penis shots. I may be taken, but I'm still a girl." Pulling back, I winked as he started laughing.

Standing he asked, "What's your boyfriend's name?"

"Colt."

The air around us changed for one brief second as the guy turned and grabbed a napkin and wrote his number down on it before turning to me. "Well, angel eyes, if things don't work out with Colt, you know where to find me. By the way, my name is Grayson."

Looking down, I felt my face flush. Glancing back up, I gave him a smile. "Lauren, it's a pleasure to meet you, Grayson."

"Let's do this!" He shouted as he jumped up on the bar. Leaning over, he yelled something to the bartender. She gave him a thumbs-up and walked to the other end of the bar. When she came back, she was holding a microphone.

The DJ stopped the music as Grayson held up his hand. "All right, y'all. I've got a special request from my new friend, Lauren. DJ give me something sexy for my new girl."

My face blushed as everyone started yelling out. An older song played as Grayson started dancing to it. My eyes widened as I turned back and looked at the girls. All five of them had their mouths hanging open as they watched Grayson.

Turning back, I watched Grayson move. Holy shit. Good lord this guy was hot. He was going to make some girl *very* happy someday. Chewing on my lower lip, I couldn't pull my eyes off of him. His T-shirt was already gone as girls were screaming all around me.

The guy who Alex danced with yelled close to my ear. "He's a professional stripper. You couldn't have picked a better thing for him to do."

Snapping my head to look at the guy, I shouted. "Are you kidding me? He's a stripper?"

The guy threw his head back and laughed. "He sure is."

Slowly looking back at Grayson, I watched as he worked the crowd on top of the bar. He turned and looked at me as he unzipped his pants.

Oh wow. Look away Lauren. Look. Away. My eyes slowly made their way up Grayson's chest to his eyes.

A girl next to me screamed out, "He isn't wearing underwear! Take it off, baby!"

Grayson smiled as he winked at me. Glancing down he had his pants pulled down just enough to leave the rest up to your imagination.

Snapping my eyes back up to his eyes, he shook his head no and yelled out, "No penis shots!"

Laughing, I gave him a thumbs-up as I turned around and smiled at the girls. Grace and Maegan were yelling out for Grayson to pull his pants all the way down.

"Fuck that! Penis shot! Penis. Shot!" Grace yelled out.

The song ended as I turned back to Grayson. He zipped his pants back up and the bartender handed him back his T-shirt as every female in the place began booing. Jumping down off the bar, Grayson took me by the arm and pulled me closer to him. "How was that?"

His touch did nothing to me, which had me breathing a sigh of relief because the bastard's body sure had a slight effect on me. Taking my hand and fanning myself I said, "Perfect! I'm going to guess you're good at your job?"

Laughing he said, "It gets me through college."

Grinning, I said, "Thanks so much, Grayson."

His smile faded slightly as he nodded his head. "Sure.

It was fun, Lauren. Enjoy the rest of your night."

"I will! Thank you again and sorry for getting all the girls worked up. Maybe you'll end up getting lucky tonight!" I said with a chuckle. Grayson's eyes turned dark as he shook his head.

"I'm afraid the only girl I have my sights on is already taken."

Giving him a wink, I said my good-byes and made my way back over to the girls as I held up the napkin with Grayson's number on it. Grace grabbed it out of my hand as she looked over my shoulder back at Grayson. "Fuck, Lauren! You got the guy to strip on the bar."

Maegan threw her head back. "I declare Lauren Reynolds the biggest dick-tease of the night and the clear winner of this bet!"

Alex, Libby, Taylor, Grace, and Maegan all busted out in cheer. Laughing, I shook my head. "Dick-tease? Please! He's a stripper, so that was nothing for him."

Grace pulled me closer to her and said, "Lauren, you have no idea how much that guy wanted you. I could see it in his eyes from over here."

Laughing, I pushed Grace away. We all started dancing as I took a chance to look back over my shoulder only to see Grayson staring at me as two girls talked to him. Raising his hand to me, I lifted my hand in return and gave him a slight smile.

Yeah, he may have been good looking and had a nice body, but he didn't even come close to Colt.

Colt.

Turning away, I smiled as I pictured Colt hauling hay out of the barn with his T-shirt off and sweat covering his body. That familiar burning low in my stomach began to build as I closed my eyes. I could practically feel Colt's hot breath on my neck.

Turning to everyone, I shouted. "I'm ready to head on back to the hotel room."

Everyone agreed to call it a night as we made our way back to our table. Taking the napkin with Grayson's name on it, I tossed it down onto the table. Pulling my cell phone out of my back pocket, I sent Colt a text message.

Me: *I miss you and I love you.*

Colt: *I miss you and I love you more. See you in a few days!*

Me: *I can't wait!*

My heart felt as if it would burst within my chest. Nothing or no one would ever come between us.

On the way back to our hotel, I made plans to talk the girls into leaving early. I wanted Colt. The sooner. The better.

TWENTY-TWO

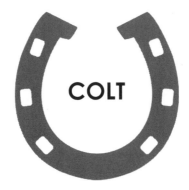

COLT

S ITTING ON MY porch, I jumped up when I saw her car. Yesterday Lauren had sent me a text saying the girls were headed back early. I had been beyond thrilled when I got it. Luke and Will were with me and they had gotten the same message from Libby and Alex. I could see the relief wash over their faces and I wanted to tease them, but I felt the exact same way.

I needed Lauren. Those few days with her gone felt as if a part of me was missing. I couldn't wait to hold her in my arms.

Pulling her car up and parking, Lauren jumped out and made her way over to me. Her blonde hair was blowing in the wind, and the second I smelled her perfume, I let out a moan. The moment I hit the last step, Lauren ran to me. She jumped right into my arms as I picked her up and she wrapped her legs around me. Her lips pressed against mine as I felt her tongue slide along my bottom lip.

"Colt," she whispered.

Holding her closer to me, I whispered against her lips. "Fuck, I've missed you, Lauren."

Our kiss quickly turned into something deeper. Frantic almost. "I need you to fuck me, Colt. Hard and fast. Now."

Swallowing hard, I pulled back and looked at her. "Jesus," I spoke barely above a whisper. "Okay," was all I could say.

Lauren giggled as she looked into my eyes. Her eyes were such a beautiful blue as they sparkled in the sunlight.

"Where?" she asked.

Turning, I headed back up the stairs. "My parents are gone." Opening the front door, I kicked it shut with my foot as I smashed my lips to Lauren's and started up to my room.

"What if your parents come back?" Lauren asked as she pulled her lips from mine. My dick was painfully hard, and at this point I didn't care if the damn Pope walked in on us.

"They won't; they went to Austin for the night. We're alone."

Lauren wiggled her eyebrows as I pushed the door to my bedroom open and kicked it shut. Slamming Lauren against the door, I pushed my hand up under her T-shirt and pulled her bra down, exposing her nipple to me. Dropping her head back, Lauren hissed between her teeth. I pulled and twisted her nipple as I kissed her again. I'd never been so rough with Lauren before, but I could tell she needed it as much as I did.

"Oh, God yes," she whispered against my lips. "Colt, don't stop."

Dropping her legs to the floor slowly, I panted between deep breaths. "Get undressed, Lauren."

Ripping my T-shirt over my head, I watched as Lauren took her T-shirt off, followed by her shorts. She stood before me in nothing but a pink lace bra with matching panties. I needed her. I had to have her and I couldn't wait a second more. Unzipping my pants, I pushed them down enough for my dick to jump out in excitement. My heart was pounding in my chest. It seemed like I would never be able to get enough of this girl.

Lifting her up again, I pushed her thong panties to the side as I slid my fingers inside her. Coating them with her wetness. "Jesus, you're soaking wet, Lauren."

"More. Colt, give me more!"

With that, I slammed my dick inside her, causing

Lauren to scream out. "Are you okay, sweetheart?" I asked as I began pumping.

"Faster, Colt! Harder."

I gave her exactly what she wanted. "Lauren, I'm not going to last long, baby. You need to come."

Her panting was pushing me over the edge, and quick. "Feels. So. Good."

Burying my face in her neck, I moved in and out of her body with such fierceness, even I was surprised. Being with her without a condom was more than I could take. The feeling was just as amazing today as it was the night before she left.

"Colt!" Lauren screamed out as her orgasm raced through her body and she squeezed down on my dick.

Pulling almost all the way out, I slammed back into Lauren. "Oh, baby," I whispered against her neck as I poured myself into her.

My dick twitched inside her body as I held her up against the door, our breathing erratic as we both attempted to regain our speech.

"Jesus, Lauren. I can't seem to ever get enough of you."

Pulling back, I looked at her. Her eyes were half closed as she wore a lidded look of satisfaction. "Colt," Lauren whispered as I slowly pulled out of her and carried her over to my bed. Laying her down, I stood and removed my pants. Sliding in next to her, I pulled her into my arms as she let out a satisfied sigh.

Whispering against the back of her head, I smiled as I said, "I missed you, sweetheart."

"Mmm."

Chuckling, I held her tighter. "I take it you needed that."

"Mm hmm."

Moving my hand down between her legs, I rubbed her clit through her lace thong.

"Can you not speak?"

Giggling, Lauren responded, "Nope. Too relaxed."

Turning over, Lauren faced me as we looked into each other's eyes. "Colt? I'm scared."

Frowning, I placed my hand on the side of her face. "Of what?"

Closing her eyes for a brief moment, she opened them again as she pursed her lips together. "I'm so happy and everything seems to be falling into place. When I got home, Daddy gave me three horses to tend to this summer. I don't just mean brushing and tending to their stalls; I mean, he wants me to build a breeding and workout schedule for each of them. He's taking me tomorrow to meet some of his contacts and well . . . I . . . I just don't . . ."

A tear rolled down her face and my world stopped. Reaching with my thumb, I wiped it away. "Baby, what? Tell me."

Sniffling, Lauren said, "I just don't want this to be a dream. Everything is so perfect right now."

Smiling, I kissed her softly on the tip of her nose. "Everything is perfect and it's going to stay perfect. I promise you though, you're not dreaming."

Giving me a weak smile, she narrowed her eyes and asked, "Did you talk to him, Colt?"

My heart felt as if it had stopped beating. I would never lie to Lauren, but I wasn't sure how she would feel about me talking to her father about her. Closing my eyes, I whispered, "Yes."

Soft lips touched mine as I opened my eyes. Lauren barely pulled her lips back from mine as she spoke. "Thank you."

Feeling my heart slam against my chest, I was overcome with the sense of relief that she wasn't mad at me and also with my love for her. "There isn't a damn thing I wouldn't do for you, Lauren. I will forever be by your side no matter what."

Moving in closer to me, Lauren gave me a sexy smile. The air in the room was charged as my dick slowly came back to life. "No matter what?" Lauren asked as she moved her hand up and down my chest.

"No matter what, Lauren."

Snuggling her face into my chest, she let out a deep breath. "I feel so safe like this. Like nothing in the world could ever possibly tear us apart when you're holding me."

Pulling her in tighter, I whispered, "I plan on holding you forever."

"Mmm, I like the sound of that."

Lauren quickly fell asleep in my arms as I held her. We didn't leave my room the rest of the night. I woke Lauren up twice during the night to make love to her. After giving her body the attention it deserved, I soon fell asleep, finally able to push down the uneasy feeling that kept creeping up every time I thought of our future.

SMILING, I WATCHED as Lauren took Mighty Mike around the track at a slow and steady pace. It was almost as if the stallion knew how precious she was to me, so he was being extra careful.

Trotting up to me, Mike stopped on a dime and flared his nostrils at me. "He feels amazing. Powerful, yet I can tell he's holding back."

Nodding my head, I ran my hand down Mike's neck. "He is for sure powerful. Mr. Betrim, your dad's new trainer, said Mike's probably one of the fastest horses he's ever worked with." Lauren was running her hand up and down Mike's neck and I could almost see it in his eyes he was falling in love with her. Standing in front of him, I said, "She's mine, dude, so don't even think about it."

Lauren giggled. "Jealous are we, Mr. Mathews?"

Giving her a wink, I held up my hand to help her down. Sliding off with ease from the giant horse, she walked around him. Her hand on his body at all times. "He's built for speed that's for sure." Worrying her bottom lip, she kept walking while I held Mike's reins.

"What's running through your mind, Lauren?"

Glancing up at me, she said, "Breeding him. He needs to be with a broodmare that's built for speed as well." Picking up Mike's front left leg, she took a look and dropped it. Standing, she walked in front of the horse and brought his head down to hers. They stood there for a good three minutes, just staring into each other's eyes.

"Mia," Lauren whispered.

Pulling my head back I asked, "Lucky One Time, Mia?"

Smiling, Lauren looked up at me. "Yep. Mia. She's a beautiful sorrel quarter with the perfect temperament for this guy. Her fifteen hands and strong build will hold up to him I have no doubt."

Looking back at Mike, I nodded my head. "Who was the sire?"

Lauren smiled, "One Time Jack. Dam was Lucky Lady. I'm telling you, Colt, we put those two out to pasture and not only will they breed but I'm almost positive Mia will give him a run for his money. I think leaving them to be on their own, they'll work it out. I'm positive."

Damn I was turned on just listening to Lauren talk about horses. Reaching down, I adjusted my growing dick. Lauren followed my hand, then snapped her eyes up to mine. "Are you getting turned on Mr. Mathews by horse talk?"

Licking my lips, I slowly smiled the smile I knew melted Lauren's panties. I watched as her eyes darkened and her body perked up. Taking a step closer to her, I pulled her into my arms and kissed her. Wrapping her arms around my neck, we quickly got lost in our kiss. Before things got too carried away, the new man in Lauren's life put a stop to it. Mike nudged me with his head and pushed me away from Lauren. Laughing, Lauren quickly kissed me on the lips.

"Do you think if we put them out to pasture they could get it done on their own, Colt?" Lauren asked as she began to walk Mike back to the barn.

My heart felt as if it would burst out of my chest as we headed back to the barn. This was what I picture our future as. Lauren and me working and doing the one thing we both loved . . . and doing it together.

Walking into the barn a few other horses snickered as Lauren put Mike back in his stall and began taking off the reins and riding pad. "I don't see why we couldn't try. He's sixteen hands, so not that much bigger than Mia. I'm pretty sure she can hold her own like you said. Go with your gut, Lauren."

Lauren stared at Mike as she nodded her head. "Let's go talk to Daddy about it."

Grabbing her hand, we made our way out of the barn and to the house. I wasn't sure how Scott was going to respond to Lauren. I prayed like hell he didn't ask me what my thoughts were. He needed to trust Lauren on this one. Show her he believed in her.

Stepping into the kitchen, I smiled and looked away when we walked up on Scott kissing Jessie.

"Um, really Mom and Dad? Really?"

Jessie pulled away and smiled at Scott and simply said, "Really, Lauren."

The way Scott looked at Jessie was the way my father looked at my mother. You could practically see the love pouring off of him. Peeking over to Lauren, I smiled as I felt my heart and stomach do that crazy little act they put on anytime I looked at Lauren. Thought about Lauren. Kissed Lauren. Hell just anything to do with Lauren.

Scott whispered something into Jessie's ear and she blushed but quickly turned and headed out of the kitchen. "I'm off to go for a run. Colt, are you staying for dinner?" Jessie asked, peeking back around the corner.

"I wish I could, but I've promised Alex I'd go into Austin tonight to help her get some things for the wedding."

Jessie smiled big. "I can't believe Alex and Will are getting married in a few weeks. Unreal."

Nodding my head, I agreed. "Yes, ma'am. My mother has been an emotional mess the last few weeks, along with Alex. It's been hell for me and my father."

"Amen," Scott said as Lauren hit me, then her father.

"Stop it both of you." Scott glanced at me and gave me a wink as he sat down at the table.

"So, tell me what you thought about Mighty Mike, Lauren?"

Swallowing hard, I sat down and let Lauren do all the talking. Even though Scott had given me full control over

Mike, this was Lauren's show.

"He's amazing, Daddy. I could almost feel his power just as he trotted around the track.

Scott's eyes quickly snapped over to me. "You rode him? How'd he do?" Scott looked at me as he asked Lauren the question. My heart rate began to pick up and I imagined what it would feel like to have Scott beat the shit out of me for letting his daughter get up on a horse that we still weren't really sure about.

Wiping my sweaty hands on my pant legs, I turned to Lauren.

"He did great. It was as if he was holding back though. I could for sure tell he wanted to get something out of his system. I have a sneaky suspicion that Colt had Mr. Betrim run Mike before we got here this morning though."

Scott nodded his head and glanced back at me. I could see it in his eyes. He was thanking me for looking out for his little girl. What he didn't realize was that she was just as much my girl as his. The moment I found out Lauren was coming home, I made arrangements for Betrim to take Mighty Mike for a few laps around the track first thing this morning.

Scott rubbed his chin as he looked between Lauren and me. "Is that so?"

Giving him a quick wink and nod of my head, Scott smiled and turned back to Lauren. "Tell me what you're thinking, darlin.'"

Lauren sat up straighter. I knew she wasn't expecting that from her father. She was expecting him to ask me. "Oh, um, well . . . what I think is we should put Mike out to pasture with a broodmare."

Scott nodded his head. "You don't think we should try to control the breeding?"

Shaking her head, she continued. "No. I think Mike is the type of horse who is going to do things his way or no way. He needs that sense of freedom, I can see it when I look into his eyes."

My heart was soaring as I sat next to Lauren and listened to her talk. This is what she was meant to do.

Scott nodded and motioned for Lauren to continue talking. Clearing her throat, she kept talking. "With Colt taking the reins on training Mighty Mike for racing, I'd like to handle his breeding."

Scott pursed his lips together, attempting to hide the smile that I knew he was holding back. Glancing back at Lauren, I waited for her to continue.

"I'm thinking Lucky One Time Mia would be the perfect fit for Mighty Mike. She's tough and can hold her own so she won't take Mighty Mike's shit. He hasn't lived out with a mare before, but I think since he hasn't been used for breeding before it shouldn't be a problem. I think they will get along well and Mia's just come into season. She was trying to get Jumping Jack's attention this morning. She has an impressive lineage and I think together their foal would be something amazing. Putting them out to pasture is what I'd like to do first."

Lauren stopped talking and I could tell she was holding her breath. Reaching over, I took her hand in mine and gave it a light squeeze. Turning to me she gave me a sweet smile.

Scott nodded his head like he was taking it all in. I found myself holding my breath as well.

"I like it," Scott finally said.

"What?" Lauren asked with a stunned expression.

"Your plan, Lauren. I think it's a solid plan and I like the idea of using Mia as the broodmare. If we can get them to breed on their own, without him hurting her, I'd like to see that happen. Let's use the west front pasture. Just those two."

Lauren sat there stunned for a few moments before she jumped up. "Okay. Great. Yeah perfect. Right."

Turning, Lauren looked at me and smiled as she did a little jump then composed herself. Taking in a deep breath she quickly blew it out. "Then, um, Colt I'll just meet you in the main barn."

Smiling, I nodded my head. "Sounds like a plan."

Lauren quickly turned and all but ran out of the house. Standing, I walked to the window and watched her skip to the barn. Damn I love that girl.

"I'm glad to hear that," Scott said as he stood next to me and watched his daughter.

Looking at him with a confused face I asked, "You're glad to hear what?"

Scott laughed. "That you love my daughter. I'm guessing you didn't mean to say it out loud."

"Um . . . well I . . . I mean I do love her and well—" For the love of all things, Colt, stop talking.

Scott laughed as he slapped my back but continued to look out the window. "You know, Colt, you proved something very big to me this afternoon. Two things actually."

Scott started to make his way to the back door. "Walk with me, son."

Following him out of the house, I waited for him to continue talking. A light breeze was blowing and I inhaled a deep breath to relax myself. There was nothing I loved more than to smell horses, hay, dirt, and just good ole horseshit.

Nodding his head, he smiled and let out a gruff laugh. "Lauren is my entire life, Colt. In my eyes, no man was ever going to be good enough for her. He would never love her like I loved her. I was wrong about that though and you showed me that today."

My heart dropped to my stomach as I swallowed hard. "Sir, I'm afraid I don't know what I did."

Scott walked up to the fence of the small arena outside the main barn where a mare had just been brought up. Reaching down he grabbed a handful hay from a bale that was sitting there and gave it to the mare.

"You arranged to have Mighty Mike ran this morning before Lauren saw him. Why?"

Looking back at the barn, I saw Mr. Betrim talking to one of the stable hands. I knew he would report everything I did with Mighty Mike back to Scott.

Clearing my throat as I ran my hand down the neck of the mare, I said, "Well, I knew the first thing Lauren would want to do is jump up on Mike. I've come to know that horse the last few days. He likes to run and usually it's the first thing he wants to do. I figured if I had Betrim run Mike for a bit this morning, it would get it out of his system that way when Lauren got up on him he wouldn't be so damn high strung."

Grinning like a fool, Scott looked at me. "That's what I thought. That girl is like her mother. Stubborn and wants to do everything her way. Remember that."

Chuckling, I said, "I will, sir."

Turning and leaning against the fence, Scott scanned the area. Pushing my hand over my head, I wasn't sure why I was so damn nervous.

"The second thing you showed me is your respect for my daughter and your belief in what she is capable of doing. Something I wasn't doing until you and I had that little talk." Glancing at me, Scott's face was serious. "You sat there and let her take control of the conversation. You showed her that you would stand by her side no matter what and I respect the shit out of you for that, Colt. Your daddy is a fine man. One of the best men I've ever had the privilege of calling a friend. I have to tell you that . . ." Scott's voice cracked as he shook his head and cleared his throat. "I have to tell you, Colt. Your daddy should be damn proud to see the man he and your mother have raised. I'd be honored . . . um . . . I'd be . . . hell this is so damn hard to say."

Trying to get a grip on my emotions, I had no idea what Scott was going to say. I had approached him yesterday morning and asked for Lauren's hand in marriage. I wasn't sure when I was going to ask her, but I wanted to make sure I had Scott and Jessie's blessings. Scott had stood up and walked out of the room, leaving me standing there wondering why he left. Jessie had said it was hard for Scott to think of his little girl growing up and getting married. She told me to give him some more time.

"Scott, if I did something wrong with the stallion then—"

Scott lifted his hand and laughed. "No, Colt. You're doing everything right, son, don't stop what you're doing." Placing his hands on his knees he began taking in deep breaths.

"Um, do you have asthma Scott? Is everything okay?" I asked as I tried to figure why Scott suddenly went pale and was trying to take in deep breaths.

Holding up his hand and motioning for me to stop talking, I just stood there. Taking a look around, I saw Jessie standing on the back porch with a smile on her face.

Scott stood up and jogged in place. "I've got this. I can do it." Cracking his head from side to side I just stood there, trying to figure out what in the hell he was going to say.

Turning to me, Scott looked right into my eyes. "Colt, I'd be honored to have you ask for Lauren's hand in marriage. I see the two of you together and I know there is no other man that would make my little girl happier than you."

I bit down on the inside of my cheek to keep my tears at bay. *What the hell was wrong with me? I'm acting like a pussy. I'm not going to cry. I'm not. I'm not a pussy. Don't you dare cry, Colt Mathews.*

Reaching deep down inside, I pulled out the memory of seeing Luke naked that one time. My body shuddered at the memory and the tears quickly vanished.

Reaching my hand out to shake Scott's, I smiled. "Thank you, sir. That means the world to me to have your blessing."

Scott nodded, shook my hand fast and hard before dropping it. "Right. Okay then. That's done." Turning, he made his way back to the house. Jessie wiped a tear away as she watched Scott walk toward her. It wasn't lost on me the motion of Scott's hand coming up to his face and wiping a tear away.

Glancing back at the barn, I watched as the love of my life came walking out with Mia on the end of the reins as she told Mr. Betrim what her plans were.

Leaning against the fence I took it all in. The way the sun was shining on her hair, the smile that she wore that seemed to brighten the area around her. The way she laughed when Mia got excited about heading out. Everything about this moment was perfect.

Beyond perfect.

TWENTY-THREE

LAUREN

SITTING NEXT TO the fire, I watched everyone laughing. Alex was sitting on Will's lap and I could practically see the love pouring out of them.

Someone bumped my arm so I looked up. Libby was standing there. "Walk with me?"

Nodding my head, I got up and started following her to the river's edge. "These parties just don't seem as fun anymore." I said as Libby nodded her head in agreement.

"Yeah, I agree. I'd rather be snuggled up on the sofa in Luke's arms."

Smiling, I looked over at Libby. Her blonde hair was blowing softly in the breeze as she stared straight ahead. Taking in breath, I slowly blew it out as I said, "What's on your mind?"

Shrugging her shoulders, she peeked at me. "You."

Laughing, I pointed to myself and said, "Me? What about me?"

Taking my arm in her arm we started walking along the riverbank. "I see something in your eyes, Lauren. Something I saw in my own eyes not too long ago."

"Oh yeah? What would that be?"

Thinking Libby was going to say something about being in love, or being happy, I wasn't prepared for what actually came out of her mouth.

"You're not happy and I talked to Colt about it."

I stopped walking and glared at her. "What? How dare you tell Colt I'm not happy. I've never been so happy in my entire life, Libby! Why? Why would you do that to me? Why would you say something to Colt like that?"

My heart was beating like crazy because deep down inside, Libby was right. *No. No. No she was wrong. So very wrong because I'm happy. I am. I have everything I've ever wanted.*

Placing her hands on my shoulders, Libby chuckled. "Calm down, Lauren. I don't mean you're not happy with Colt."

Wait. What? I'm so confused. What in the hell is she talking about?

"What? Libby, are you like on crack or something because you aren't making sense."

Laughing, Libby slowly shook her head. "No, I'm not on crack, but I am tired. Mireya hasn't been sleeping very well through the night and I've been trying to figure out a way to get her to sleep and—"

Oh. My. Glitter. Is she serious right now? She tells me she told Colt I'm unhappy, yet she babbles on about her daughter not being able to sleep? I'm about to vagina punch her.

Libby continued to talk about some new lavender pillow she bought for the baby. Shaking my head, I held up my hands. "Stop. Oh my glitter, please stop talking. Libby! Focus, bitch. Focus!"

"Oh right, gosh I'm so sorry. Okay, focusing back to you not being happy."

Ugh!

"I am happy! Do I need to shout it from the rooftop?"

Libby tilted her head and gave me that look. The same look my mother used to give me when she's about to lecture me on something like, my shorts are too short, or I'm wearing way too much makeup or how guys like girls who are natural.

Oh holy hell. Now I'm not focusing.

"Lauren, honey I know you are so very happy with Colt.

And he is so happy with you and he loves you so very much."

Tears began to form in my eyes. *Ugh! I don't cry. Stop this, Lauren. Stop this now.* Why do I always cry when it comes to Colt? My voice cracked as I talked. "I know. He's the yummy marshmallow fluff to my hot chocolate."

Libby giggled. "Yeah, I know he is, sweetheart."

A tear slowly made it's way down my cheek. "Libby, I hate school. Oh my glitter . . . I hate it so much and I don't know what to do. I can't focus. I thought at first it was just because I was so wrapped up in Colt. You know. Pushing him away and always thinking about him." Rubbing my fingers under my nose, I kept talking. "Then when we finally got together I was thinking this would fix everything, but it didn't. I can't focus because I don't care about any of it, Libby! What am I going to do?"

Libby pulled me into her arms and held me as she ran her hand up and down my back. "Shh, it's okay, Lauren."

Shaking my head, I pulled back. "It's not okay, Libby. If my father and mother heard me say that, I'd get the biggest lecture of my life. You know how our parents are about college degrees. I mean, look at my mother. She could own her own Vet clinic! She's got all these stupid degrees and I . . . I just want to work on the ranch. I want to be with the horses everyday, not sitting in some stupid class learning about business." Slamming my hands up to my face, I let out a frustrated scream as I sank down to the ground.

Libby sat down next to me and took my hands in her hands. "Lauren, you only have two more years and that's it. Then you'll be back in Mason, working on your daddy's ranch and Colt will be by your side."

Nodding my head, I took in a shaky breath. "I know. I know, Libby. Believe me I keep telling myself that."

Reaching over, Libby pushed a piece of my blonde hair behind my ear. "Colt said your grades are amazing."

Chewing on my lower lip, I whispered, "I have a four point zero grade average."

Libby laughed. "You're with Colt, sweetie, and you both only have two more years. Take it a semester at a time and

I promise it will go by fast. Look, Alex, Will, and Maegan have just this year. It's gone by fast."

Nodding my head, I knew Libby was right. There was no way I could leave school, and leave Colt behind. Plus, my father would chain me to a desk at A&M and make me stay there.

"I promise to take it a semester at a time."

Libby smiled and stood up. "Good. Now that we've got that taken care of, are you ready for the wedding?"

Jumping up and down and letting out a squeal, I clapped my hands. "Yes! Yes! Yes! It's finally here. Seems like forever ago they got engaged."

Libby and I started walking back over to the party. It was a small get together with just a few friends from high school that we had invited. Libby and I talked about last-minute details that we were taking care of for Alex. My eyes caught a glimpse of someone and I looked to see it was, Rachel. Colt's ex-girlfriend. *What in the hell was she doing here?* She was talking to Colt and kept putting her hand on his arm. Balling up my fists, I stared at them.

Libby kept talking but I heard nothing. Nothing but the sound of my blood rushing through my veins as I watched Colt throw his head back and laugh at something she said.

"Lauren? Hello, Earth to Lauren? Are you even listening to me?"

"No, I'm not because I'm too busy looking at the little slut who's talking to Colt."

Grace walked up next to me and laughed. "Oh man, I love that you're turning more and more like me as the days go by."

"That truly does concern me," Libby said.

Holding up my hands to them both I shouted, "Hush up!"

Why is he laughing? What does he find so funny? If she touches him one more time I'm going to rip her eyes out.

Hot breath was near my neck as Grace whispered, "I'm going to safely say you're currently thinking you want to rip her hair out."

Swallowing hard, I whispered, "Her eyes."

Grace chuckled. "Lauren, take a deep breath and let it out. Colt loves you and only you. She knows by talking to him she's gonna get under your skin."

Dragging in a deep breath, I slowly blew it out as I released my fists. Right about that moment, Colt's eyes found mine. I could almost see the blue in his eyes from where I was standing. Moving my eyes back to his face, they landed on his lips. The same lips that had kissed my body tenderly last night as Colt made love to me under the stars again in the bed of his truck, our new favorite place to be.

Grace whispered in my ear, "Do you see how he's looking at you, Lauren? His whole face lit up the moment he saw you. Baby girl, you have nothing to worry about."

Smiling, I nodded my head. "I know," I whispered.

Giving me a nudge, Grace said, "Now get over there and show that little bitch who Colt belongs to."

Turning to Grace, I quickly hugged her. "I love you, Grace."

Holding me tighter her voice cracked as she spoke. "I love you too, Lauren."

Dropping her hold on me, Grace took a step back. Turning, I made my way over to Colt. Rachel was talking to him as he kept his eyes on me the entire time I walked over to him. As I got closer I remembered the last time I approached him like this. He was looking at me the same way he did the day of Luke and Libby's wedding. My heart began to beat faster in my chest as I stopped right in front of him.

"Hey," I whispered.

Giving me that panty-melting grin of his, my knees went weak as a rush of goose bumps covered my entire body.

The crooked smile grew bigger as Colt took a step closer to me. "Hey, sweetheart."

Rachel stopped talking as Colt pulled me into his arms. "I was wondering where the most beautiful girl in the pasture was."

Letting out a soft chuckle, I turned to Rachel. "Oh hey

there, Rachel. I didn't see you there."

Rachel gave me a dirty look, but quickly turned it to a smile when Colt looked at her.

That's right. He's mine bitch so just move along. Move. Along.

"Lauren, how are you?"

An evil thought entered my mind. Do I ignore said thought? No. No I don't think I should.

Giving a fake, but believable laugh, I looked at Colt, then back to Rachel as I let out a breath. "Well, I'm tired but that's to be expected. You know, first trimester and all."

Peeking back to Colt, his smile dropped and I actually could see the color drain from his face. Swallowing hard, Colt said, "W-what?"

Rachel also asked what. But her *what* was more of a shout.

"What? What do you mean? Oh my God. Are you?"

My eyes were still on Rachel, but I was watching Colt out of the corner of my eye as he leaned closer to me. "Lauren, baby, I need to talk to you."

It was taking everything I had not to bust out laughing. Rachel was now falling over her words as she attempted to ask me how far along I was.

"When . . . is the baby . . . don't you think you're a little young?"

Placing her hands on her hips she looked between Colt and me.

Tipping my head to the side, I placed my fingertips on my partially opened mouth. "Well, I don't know what my age has to do with anything."

Colt pulled on my arm. "Um, Lauren can I speak with you for a second?"

Snarling her lip up at me, Rachel shook her head. "Your parents must be utterly disappointed with you."

Colt stepped in-between us. Oh man. This was just too fun watching Rachel get her panties in a twist.

Looking around Colt, I asked, "Why do you say that, Rachel? My father is extremely proud that my first attempt at breeding was successful," I said with a wicked smile.

"What?" Rachel and Colt said at the same time. Colt pushed me away from Rachel. "Baby, I really think you and I need to talk."

Leaning in I kissed Colt on the lips softly but quickly. "Colt, I'm just happy about Mia being pregnant. I thought you were, too?"

Biting on my lower lip, I tired like hell to keep in my laughter. Taking a peek at Rachel, I saw the confused look on her face.

"Wait. What?" Colt said as relief washed over his face. Then he smiled. A really big smile that made my stomach flip. "Mia's pregnant?"

Smiling, I nodded my head and said, "Yep. My mom confirmed it this morning."

Pulling me into a hug and lifting me up, Colt spun me around. "Sweetheart, this is wonderful!"

Setting me back down, Colt placed his hands on the sides of my face as his thumbs brushed across my skin leaving a fiery wake in their path. "Lauren, I'm so damn proud of you." Leaning in closer, his lips brushed against my neck as he moved them up to my ear and whispered, "And you totally had me second-guessing our decision about no more condoms."

The moment his lips touched mine, I forgot everything and everyone. My hands reached up and held onto his arms as my knees wobbled. Colt's tongue danced in perfect harmony with mine as he deepened the kiss with a moan.

Rachel cleared her throat. "Um. Hello, you know I'm still standing here."

Colt pulled his lips back and whispered, "I love you so much."

Looking into his eyes I was lost within the moment we shared. Lost in his beautiful blue eyes that seemed to sparkle when he smiled. Lost in his blissful love.

"Take me to our spot, Colt," I said, barely above a whisper. Before I knew it, Colt was carrying me to his truck and we were on our way to our secret spot where we spent the rest of the night wrapped up in each other's arms.

"OKAY, IT LOOKS like I'm gonna have to be the one to say this. Alex is bridezilla. There. I said it."

Everyone turned and looked at Taylor. Raising her eyebrows and dropping her mouth open she asked, "Am I wrong?"

Maegan started laughing. "Hell no you're not wrong, baby sister. You're just the only one brave enough to say it out loud."

Shaking my head, I turned back around and finished putting the flowers in Grace's hair. "Cut her some slack, y'all. She's been really stressed. Weren't you stressed with your wedding, Libby?"

Libby chuckled. "It all happened too fast for me to get stressed." Libby twisted Maegan's hair up and began putting bobby pins in. "God, Meg, I'd kill to have your hair."

Maegan rolled her eyes. "I hate my hair. I wish Tay had gotten the auburn hair and I got the brown."

"Dye it," I said as I placed the last flower in Grace's hair.

Turning, I looked at Maegan. "Seriously, why don't you just change the color then?"

Maegan started chewing on her lower lip. "You think?"

Grace leaned forward and put more lipstick on. "Hell yeah, you should! Shake things up a little. Maybe it will throw the little bitches off at your school, too."

We all started laughing. Then someone knocked on the door and we fell silent. "It's her!" Taylor whispered as she moved away from the door with a look of fear on her face.

Brushing Taylor off with my hand, I moved to the door. Opening the door, my mouth fell open. Alex stood in the hallway. "Alex? Honey, are you okay?" She was just standing there, looking lost. Very lost. Reaching for her hand I looked up and down the hallway before I pulled her into the guestroom. We were in Gunner and Ellie's house since the wedding was right outside in their backyard practically.

"Alex, sweetie, what's wrong?" Libby asked as she walked up to Alex and led her over to the desk chair. We all gathered around Alex.

"She doesn't look like she's been crying," Taylor said in a whisper.

Maegan leaned down and waved her hand in front of Alex then snapped her around to look at us. "She's in shock."

Grace dropped down to the floor. "Alex. Did something happen?"

Oh no. What if Will changed his mind? I'm going to kick his ass if he changed his mind. Why would he change his mind though? No, he didn't change his mind. Oh my glitter! He cheated! No. No. He didn't cheat.

Kneeling down next to Alex, I noticed she was clutching something in her hand. Her hair was fixed, her make-up was done and all she had to do was get dressed. We all had the same matching robes on and had been in the guest room getting the finishing touches done to our hair when Alex quickly jumped up and raced out of the bedroom screaming she needed air.

Placing my hand on her clenched fist, Alex jumped and looked at me. "Alex, you're scaring us sweetie, please tell us what's wrong," I said as I moved my hand up to the side of her face. A single tear fell and rolled down her cheek as Alex held up what was in her hand. I heard Grace and Libby gasp as Taylor and Maegan both said, "Oh shit."

Glancing down, I saw what Alex was holding. Placing my hand over my mouth, I whispered, "Oh. My. Glitter."

TWENTY-FOUR

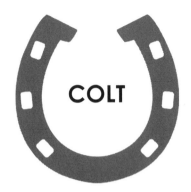

COLT

K NOCKING ON THE door, I opened it slightly. Will was standing at the window looking out. "Will? It's time."

Turning, he gave me a smile and walked toward me stopping halfway across the room. "Colt. I'm marrying your sister."

Giving him a smile, I nodded my head. "I know. I've gotta say I'm impressed my father hasn't come up and threatened you in some form."

Will's smile faded. "Oh, he has. Twice."

Letting out a chuckle, I shook my head. "Do you love her, Will?"

Closing his eyes he sighed. "More than anything, Colt. More than anything."

"Then you've got nothing to be worried about." Walking into the room, I headed over to Will. "She loves you, Will. Y'all were meant to be together. Just always take care of her and please don't ever hurt her." Looking down I let out a deep breath before looking back into Will's eyes. "Cause if you do, I'll tie you up by your balls and hang you from a rafter in the barn. Then I'll take a baseball bat to you and hit you like a piñata filled with Reese's peanut butter cups. You know how I like my Reese's."

Will's mouth dropped open as he stared at me. "What in the hell is it with this family and wanting to hang me up

222

by my balls in the barn? Your father and Luke have already bestowed the same threat on me today."

Placing my hand on his shoulder, I laughed. "Great minds think alike. Come on, let's gets down there so you can marry my sister."

By the time I finally got Will downstairs and out where he needed to be, the wedding was about to start. Glancing around, I smiled as I looked at everything. Alex had spent hours going through our parents' wedding photos and had set up her wedding almost the same. Everyone was sitting on square bales of hay as white lights hung from the trees. One of my favorite things Alex and Will did was take pictures from our parents' weddings and framed them in small white frames that hung from the tree and adorned the tables. Alex said she felt like it was good luck and I had to agree with her.

Will was rocking back and forth as he rubbed his hands up and down his pants. "Will, you're gonna rub a hole in your damn pants before she even gets here. Calm the hell down," Luke said to Will.

Pastor Roberts cleared his throat. "Boys, let's not do this again. I did it with your fathers. Please, no repeats."

Will, Luke and I all turned and looked at him. "What?" Will asked confused.

"Who is the best man, son?" Pastor Roberts asked Will.

Looking between us, Will said, "Both. I couldn't pick one."

Letting out a sigh, Pastor Roberts pointed to Luke and me. "Who has the ring?"

I turned to Luke and he turned to me. "Luke's got the ring."

Luke's mouth dropped open and I instantly knew we were both fucked. "Me? I don't have the ring. It's your sister."

Staring at him like he was insane, I whispered, "She's your cousin!"

Luke laughed. "Dude, sister trumps cousin every time."

Pushing Luke on his shoulder, I whispered, "Go to hell. You had the ring last night, dude."

"Boys," Pastor Roberts whispered.

"No, Colt, you had the ring last night and then gave it to . . ."

Will stood there staring at us as he held the ring in his hand. Grabbing it from his hand I shoved it in my pocket. "Bastard, you scared the piss out of me."

Pastor Roberts sighed. "Lord, give me strength to make it through another one."

Looking at Pastor Roberts, I leaned over, "Sir, are you feeling okay?"

Luke leaned over and asked, "Hey, where did you decide to take Alex for the honeymoon? Cause I still owe Libby a decent honeymoon, so don't be one upping me!"

Lifting his fingers to his temple Pastor Roberts let out a moan as I asked him again. "Pastor Roberts? Are you feeling okay?"

Nodding his head, he gave me a weak smile as he said under his breath, "The apple doesn't fall far from the tree."

The music started playing and we all turned and looked at the house. Smiling, I watched as Libby carried Mireya down the aisle. Mireya was nine months old now and she was having fun throwing rose petals everywhere.

"My God. She's beautiful. They're both beautiful," Luke said from behind me. As Libby walked down the aisle, she smiled at Luke the whole time.

Will cleared his throat. "I'm taking Alex to Belize."

"What the fuck?" Luke yelled out as everyone turned and looked at all of us. Smiling, I pointed behind me to Luke as Will chuckled. Libby narrowed her eyes at Luke and shook her head.

Next was Taylor, followed by Maegan. Smiling, I watched the girls all walk down the aisle and take their places. Will had asked a few of his college buddies to be in the wedding also to round out the numbers. Pulling my eyes from the girls, I glanced back to the house. Walking out was Lauren. Sucking in a breath of air, my mouth dropped open as I took her in. Her blonde hair was pulled up with red roses scattered throughout it. Her dress was a light-blue and hung straight down. It fit her curvy body like a glove.

"Motherfucker," I whispered as I watched her slowly smile at me. Luke leaned over and said, "I think Pastor Roberts is about to pass out if one of us swears again, dude."

Ignoring Luke, I had to force myself not to meet Lauren halfway down the aisle. Her beauty literally took my breath away. As she walked up, she gave me a wink and it felt as if the world shook. I reached out and grabbed a hold of Will who chuckled.

The music changed to the wedding march and everyone turned to watch Alex walk down the aisle. It took every ounce of strength I had to pull my eyes off of Lauren.

The moment I saw my sister, my heart felt as if it was about to jump out of my chest. Peeking over to Will, I watched him wipe a tear away as he watched Alex walk down the aisle on my father's arm.

"She looks beautiful," Luke and I both said at once. My father and Alex stopped at the altar and Pastor Roberts asked who was giving Alex away.

"I do, her father, the man who will always be number one in her life. Oh, and her mother." Everyone laughed, including Alex.

Alex reached up and kissed my father. "Daddy, I do love you so very much."

Placing Alex's hand in Will's, my father smiled, wiped a tear away and went to sit down next to my mother who was full-on crying.

Will smiled at Alex and leaned in and said, "You are the most beautiful woman I've ever seen."

Alex began crying as she reached up and kissed Will as everyone clapped. Pastor Roberts cleared his throat and began to speak. "Seems the couple is jumping ahead."

Alex and Will turned to face the Pastor. "It's hard for me to believe that I stood under this very same tree and married Alex's mother and father."

Alex rocked back and forth and I knew she only did that when she was nervous. She had done it for as long as I could remember. Will kept looking at her and at one point he leaned over and asked if she was okay.

Glancing over to Lauren, she looked white as a ghost. Her eyes caught mine and I mouthed, *what's wrong?*

Her eyes widened and she mouthed back, *it's big. Huge.*

Oh shit. Swallowing hard, I turned to my dad. He must have noticed the same thing I did.

Pastor Roberts was about to start with the vows when Alex turned and faced Will. The only thing anyone heard was five girls all whispering, "Oh shit."

Alex's lower lips trembled. "Will. I have to talk to you."

"Now, Lex? I mean, can it wait?"

Luke leaned over Will's shoulder. "Alex, if this is about the fart thing, really, you've got to move on."

Will and I turned and looked at Luke. "Shut the hell up, Luke," Will said.

"Will, it's important. I need to talk to you."

Will shook his head. "Have you changed your mind, Lex?"

Sucking in a breath, Alex frantically shook her head. "No. My gosh no, Will. I want to marry you more than anything but . . . but I need to tell you something before we do this. You *have* to know something. It will take like three minutes."

Looking back to my father he shrugged his shoulders.

Turning back to Will and Alex, I walked up and said, "Um, excuse me ladies and gentleman, we're gonna take a five-minute, um, intermission. Just stay in your seats and the bride and groom will be right back." Turning to Alex and Will, I motioned for them to step away. "Go, you've got five minutes."

Alex grabbed Will's hand and walked through the girls as she made her way away from everyone. All eyes were on them, watching as Alex talked and Will listened. The moment I saw Will's smile, I knew. Looking at Lauren, she was smiling at me. *Baby?* I mouthed. Lauren wiped a tear away and nodded.

"My father is going to kill, Will," I whispered.

Leaning in closer, Luke spoke to Pastor Roberts. "Pastor, you may want to say a quick prayer for William there, his life could very well be over." Turning to me, he said, "Damn, he was so close. So close to being safe."

Laughing, I watched as Will scooped Alex up in his arms. They were both crying as Will stood there and held my sister.

My father stood up and asked me, "Do you have any idea what is going on?"

Shaking my head slowly I said, "Nerves. I think she needed to talk to him." My father smiled, then looked back at my mother.

"I totally get it." Turning, he went and sat back down. Peeking at Luke, we both let out the breath we were holding.

Will and Alex walked back up and things moved along perfectly after that.

Once Will had about three bottles of beer in him, Alex and Will took my father and mother, and Josh and Heather, and led them into the house where they told them that Alex was about two months pregnant. Luke and I had been watching through the window. My father didn't even flinch, he stood up and walked up to Alex and took her in his arms, with my mother following my father.

"Well damn. That sucks." Luke pulled out his wallet and handed me five twenty-dollar bills.

Taking them from his hand, I said, "Thank you very much. I could have told you he was going to be okay. They're married. There isn't anything he can do. Now, had he found out last night? Will might have two broken legs right now."

Luke chortled and slapped me on the back. "Our little group is growing. You're next."

Feeling the blood drain from my face, I shook my head. "Ah, no I am not. I've got two more years of football to play."

Luke pinched his eyebrows together. "And college. Two more years of college."

Rolling my eyes, I looked away. "Yeah, that too."

The rest of the night was spent, dancing, eating, drinking, dancing some more and sneaking Lauren up to my room where I had my wicked way with her. Nothing was more amazing than holding the love of my life in my arms.

Before Lauren drifted off to sleep she whispered, "Love me forever, Colt."

Kissing her forehead, I held her tighter as my stomach did that crazy flip. "I promise, Lauren. Forever."

PULLING THE FENCE tight, Luke wrapped the wire around the post. "So have you thought about trying to plan another surprise birthday party for Lauren?"

Rolling my eyes, I shook my head. "No. I still can't believe she got the flu and we had to cancel the party."

Laughing, Luke shook his head. "You ready to head back to College Station? Get your football on?"

Just the mention of football had me all kinds of excited. "I sure as shit am."

Wrapping another wire around a post as I pulled the fence tighter, Luke grunted. "What about, Lauren?"

Letting the fence go after he got the wire to stay on, I felt my heart slam against my chest. Taking my gloves off, I mumbled, "I need a drink of water."

Luke looked at me. "Ahh hell. That can't be good."

Pushing past him, I made my way over to my father's old truck. We used it for the ranch now, but he still insisted she be taken care of. The damn thing was ancient and needed to be sold for scrap metal.

Opening the cooler, I saw Luke had packed a few beers. Reaching in, I grabbed one. Walking up to the truck, Luke leaned against it. "Talk to me, Colt. I don't think I've ever seen or heard about the two of you fighting since you got together."

Taking a long drink I closed my eyes and shook my head. "She doesn't want to go back to A&M."

"What?"

Nodding my head, I took another drink. "Yep, she wants to stay in Mason, work on her daddy's ranch helping horses fuck."

"Hey, Colt don't let your anger put words into your mouth."

Pushing off the truck, I turned to face Luke. "I'm not. The plain simple matter is she'd rather be on the fucking ranch than be with me. She says she hates school, she struggles with it which makes her stress out because she feels like she has to get good grades for her parents. She has a damn perfect grade point average." Pushing my hand through my hair, I let out a sigh. "She just doesn't want to go back early. There is nothing I can do about it, so I'll leave tomorrow and she'll stay behind for a few extra weeks." Tipping the beer against my lips, I finished it off. Crushing it with my hand, I threw it in the back of the truck.

Luke looked away for a second before he turned back to me and looked me in the eyes. "Do you want to hear what I think about all this?"

Letting out a gruff laugh, I held out my hands and said, "Sure. Why not."

"All right, I think you go back to A&M, do what you have to do for football."

Raising my eyebrow, I asked, "And Lauren?"

Luke shrugged. "Let her stay. I mean, you knew getting into this how much she loved being with the horses. It's no different than you loving football."

Looking away I let Luke's words soak in. "Fine, I guess I'm being a selfish prick about this."

Luke pushed off the tailgate. "Ya think?" Walking up to me he put his arm on my shoulder. "Come on, let's go sit by the river for a few hours with a six-pack and just kick back. We can call Will since we haven't heard all the details about the honeymoon. You leave tomorrow and I'd much rather spend my time with you doing that, than here putting up a fence.

Smiling, I said, "That sounds like a solid plan."

Luke and I began cleaning up. Luke had sent a text to Will telling him to meet us at the riverbank where we had our pasture parties and for him to bring the beer.

Climbing into the truck, I pulled out my phone.

Me: *Hey. I'm sorry I was a dick early. You don't have to come back with me*

I stared at my phone the entire drive to the riverbank. Then once we were there, I kept checking it but never heard back from Lauren. By the time I got home it was almost nine and I had to leave in the morning for A&M. Checking my phone one last time, I tossed it onto the bed and cursed. Closing up my suitcase, I dropped it to the floor.

"You ready to head back?"

Spinning around, I smiled when I saw my mother. "Yeah, I'm thinking of heading back tonight though." Taking a step into my room, she narrowed her eyes as she looked at me.

"This late, Colt? You wouldn't get into College Station until after midnight."

Giving her a weak smile, I nodded my head. "Yeah, that's crazy of me to even think it."

Grinning she placed her hand on the side of my face. "Did you and Lauren have a fight?"

Closing my eyes, I sighed. How did my mother always know what was wrong. "I was being a jerk and she won't answer my text messages or my phone calls."

Giving me a reassuring smile, she tilted her head and said, "I'm sure she will. She wouldn't let you leave without saying good-bye to you."

Nodding my head I smiled. I wasn't feeling so optimistic about it like my mother was. "Don't stay up too late, sweetheart. You have a long day ahead of you."

"Yeah, I'm gonna head to bed now. I'm exhausted."

Reaching up and kissing me on the cheek, my mother smiled tenderly at me. I could feel the love moving from her body into mine and I instantly felt better. "Get some sleep, Colt."

I watched as my mother softly shut my bedroom door. Not feeling like doing a damn thing, I stripped out of my clothes and made my way to the bathroom where I took a hot shower. The water felt amazing as it moved down my body, relaxing muscles that I had been working the hell out of the last three days while helping Luke with a fence.

Drying off, I walked into my room and crawled into bed naked. Exhaustion soon took over as I felt my eyelids growing heavier and heavier.

TWENTY-FIVE

LAUREN

D AMN IT ALL to hell. I couldn't believe I had lost my phone. I'd spent all day combing through my house, the barn, and the pasture I road in earlier today until I found it in my car. The second I saw all of Colt's text messages, I panicked. We had a fight the night before so he probably thought I was ignoring him.

Running into the house, I stopped the moment I saw my mother. "Mom, did Colt text you back on your phone?"

Turning and motioning with a head pop she said, "It's on the table. My hands are full of dough, can you check it? I haven't heard it go off."

Pulling up her text messages, my mouth dropped open when I saw the message. "Oh my glitter! Mom! You didn't even send the message!"

Turning, she looked at me like I was insane. "What? Are you sure?"

Facing the phone to her, I showed her the typed up message that she never sent. "Mom! Now Colt is going to think I'm mad at him."

"Oh, honey, I'm so sorry. I must have thought I hit send or maybe I got interrupted. Just send him a text and let him know what happened."

Feeling the tears building in my eyes, I closed them and pursed my lips together in an attempt to not start crying. "I did. He's not responding back."

Glancing at the clock my mother said, "Go see him. I'm sure he'll be leaving early in the morning."

My heart felt like it was ripping in two. I wanted to stay here for as long as I could before I had to go back to school, but I wanted to be with Colt also. Worrying my lower lip, I took off upstairs. "Lauren? What are you doing?"

Calling over my shoulder I said, "I'm packing. I'm going back early with Colt."

STANDING IN THE doorway to Colt's room, I couldn't help but smile. He was sleeping like a baby as his mother and I stood there. "Sleep in the guest room tonight, Lauren. That way the two of you can take off tomorrow first thing."

"Yes, ma'am. Do you mind if I wake him up? Let him know I'm here."

Ellie smiled and shook her head. "Of course not. He was rather upset when he came home. I'm sure he'd love to know you are here and decided to go back with him tomorrow. Don't stay up too late."

Feeling the blush move across my face, I looked away and said, "No, we won't stay up late. I just want to talk to him for a bit."

Placing her hand on the side of my face Ellie gave me an all-knowing look. "I was your age once. I remember a certain set of blue-eyes that used to cause the same flush across my own cheeks."

Placing my hand on the other side of my face, I dropped my mouth open slightly. "The Mathews men have that effect on us."

Grinning, I whispered, "Yes. Yes they do."

Ellie kissed me on the cheek and slowly shut Colt's door as she left the room. Turning, I made my way over to his bed. I'll just give him a kiss, let him know I'm here, then I'll head to the guest room.

Colt moved and turned just a bit, causing the sheet to

pull away from his body. Sucking in a breath of air I whispered, "Oh. My. Glitter." Colt was naked.

Waving my hands in front of my face I attempted to cool off. "My . . . is it hot in here?" I whispered as I looked all around. Colt moaned and whispered my name. Turning back to look at him, I stopped moving. I'm pretty sure I stopped breathing, too. Colt had his dick in his hand as he slowly moved it up and down.

Licking my lips, I turned back to the door. *Do I?* Shaking my head, I whispered, "No. Lauren you do not."

Chewing on my bottom lip, I stood there and watched Colt. Every time I whispered, he moaned out my name. *Okay, well I'm faced with two decisions. I could leave a note and head to the guest room. Or I could lean down and start whispering in Colt's ear while he played with himself in his sleep.*

Tapping my fingertip to my lips I decided I was going with option two. Tiptoeing over to the door, I locked it and then quickly made my way back over to Colt's bed. Stripping out of my clothes, I sucked in a deep breath. "Dear me oh my. I'm naked in Colt's bedroom and his parents are downstairs. What would my mother think?"

"Lauren," Colt moaned as his hand moved faster up and down his shaft. *My mother would think you're stupid if you don't crawl on top of him. Okay, so my mother wouldn't think that. But I think it therefore I'm doing it.*

Slowly pulling the covers all the way back, I couldn't contain my smile. Holy hells bells. He had the nicest body I'd ever seen. My eyes moved to his hand where he continued to stroke his dick. Quirking my eyebrow, I smiled. "Here goes nothing."

Climbing onto the bed, I straddled Colt with my legs. Ever so slowly I began to sink down. Colt was still working himself, so I carefully pulled his hand off of his dick as I took a hold of it. "Mmm," Colt moaned.

Positioning him at my entrance, I slowly sank down on him as Colt let out a long hiss followed by my name. Sitting there for a few seconds I enjoyed the feeling of Colt filling me to the max. My eyes snapped open and I looked at Colt. What would I have done had he said another girl's name? That would have sucked big time. Placing my hands on his chest, I moved up and down slightly. Dropping my head back when Colt moaned, I started moving faster. Holy hell. It wasn't going to take me long to come and I needed Colt to wake up. Feeling his hands grip my hips, I dropped my head forward. His eyes were still closed as he moaned softly again. Moving a bit more up and down, I realized that Colt was still asleep. *What in the hell?*

Leaning over, I kissed his lips then whispered against them. "Mr. Mathews, wake up. I'm riding you with your parents downstairs."

Colt moved, then opened his eyes. "W-what . . . where? What's happening?" Placing my fingers up to his lips, I gave him a naughty smile.

"I'm going to finish what you started."

Colt still seemed confused and began looking around. "My parents, Lauren!"

Sitting back up, I slipped my finger into my mouth and sucked on it before I slowly pulled it out and smiled. "Are downstairs, so be quiet."

Moving faster, I felt my build up. Closing my eyes, I placed my hands on my breasts and pressed my lips together. Oh my. This was going to be big. Opening my eyes back up, I looked into Colt's eyes. He quickly sat up and captured my mouth with his as we both came together.

When I finally came down from my high I rested my forehead against Colt's. "I lost my phone today and asked my mother to send you a text letting you know. She typed it up but never sent it. I'm so sorry you thought I was ignoring you. I'd never do that to you, Colt."

Wrapping his arms around me tighter, I let Colt hold me. Being wrapped up in his arms was one of my favorite things. I felt safe and loved. Like nothing in the world could ever pull me away from his love.

Pulling back, my blue eyes, met his. "I'm sorry."

Shaking his head, Colt closed his eyes briefly before opening them again. "No, baby, no it's not your fault. I was being selfish and I wanted . . ."

Placing my finger up to his mouth I smiled. "Shh. Let's just both agree that we were both wrong. I'm going back with you tomorrow." Colt went to talk and I shook my head. "Let me finish, please, baby."

Nodding his head, he moved a piece of my hair back and behind my ear. "My decision was made for one reason and one reason only. I want to be with you, Colt. You're the only thing in my life that makes me happy. I love you so much, Colt Mathews."

Flipping me over, Colt hovered over my body as he teased my entrance. When I felt his dick becoming hard, I wiggled my eyebrows. "Miss Reynolds, I'm going to make love to you while my parents are downstairs. Can you keep quiet?"

Pressing my lips together, I smiled as I nodded. "I think so, Mr. Mathews."

Colt slowly pushed into me and I was in heaven again.

PULLING THE SWEATSHIRT over my head, I tried to stop my body from shivering. The whistle blew and I looked down on the football field. It had only been two weeks since the fall semester had started back up, but Colt and I had been in College Station for about a month or so.

"Lauren? Honey are you okay?"

Glancing up, I saw Coach Johnston's wife who happened to be a nurse at Scott and White Hospital. "Um, I think I'm getting the flu or a cold or something."

Reaching out, she placed her hand on my forehead. "Lauren, how long have you had this fever? You're burning up."

Taking in a shallow breath, I blew it back out. "A few hours, but I didn't want to worry Colt. With practice and all. I've never had the flu hit me so hard . . . or so fast."

"You think it's the flu?" she asked as she looked at me closer.

Shrugging my shoulders, I closed my eyes. "I think. I'm

so achy. My head hurts so bad and my neck . . . my neck hurts so bad."

"Lauren, is the light bothering you? Are your eyes sensitive to it?"

Nodding my head, I barely said, "Yes. I'm just tired. I need to lie down."

"Chuck! Chuck I need you to come here right away!" I heard Mrs. Johnston yelling.

A few second later I heard Colt's coach. Opening my eyes, I saw him standing there. "What's wrong?"

"Chuck, she needs to get to a hospital right away. She thinks she has the flu, but she has all the symptoms of meningitis."

Hospital? No. No. I'm okay . . . the flu . . . I just have the flu.

I attempted to talk, but I suddenly felt so weak. "Colt," I whispered.

Touching my forehead I heard the coach talking to his wife. "Get her to the car and get her over to Scott and White Hospital right away. I'll get Colt and meet you there."

Feeling myself being moved, I opened my eyes. "Lauren, sweetheart, you're really sick. I'm going to take you to the hospital, okay?"

Licking my lips, I tried to talk but my mouth was so dry. "I think it's just . . . the flu."

My body was shaking and I had no way of controlling it. The more it shook the harder my head pounded and my neck hurt. Mrs. Johnston walked me up to her car and held the door open. I sat down and leaned my head back. Finally, I could rest my eyes.

"TWENTY-YEAR OLD FEMALE transferring to Brackenridge Hospital in Austin. Spinal tap shows bacterial meningitis, fever is one hundred and three, due to arrive in less than three minutes."

Opening my eyes I tried to look around. "Where?"

A girl with bright green eyes smiled at me. "It's okay, Lauren. You're in an ambulance being taken to a hospital in Austin. You're doing great sweetie. Just relax."

Voices. All I heard were strangers' voices. Opening my mouth I tried to speak but nothing would come out. I felt strange. Hot, but cold. Sore all over. What's happening to me?

"COLT," I WHISPERED.

My hand tingled and a warm sensation moved through my hand up my arm. Colt's voice swept through my body. "Sweetheart, I'm here. Lauren, I'm right here. Please, baby. Please open your eyes and look at me, Lauren."

I tried so hard to open my eyes but I couldn't. *Why can't I open my eyes?*

Then I heard my mother's voice. "Colt? We need to talk to you."

Momma? Oh thank goodness. The sounds of my mother's voice calmed me. She'll put the wet cold washcloth on my forehead and I'll feel better.

"Jessie, she said my name. She said my name."

My heart felt like it was physically hurting. Colt's voice was laced with fear.

"Colt, the doctors made us sign something."

Was my mother crying? Why is she crying? It's just the flu! Mom, I just have the flu!

"What . . . what did you sign?"

Sniffling, my mother started talking after the longest pause. "Her fever is now a hundred and five. They said her body could go into a coma and . . ."

Coma? My body was feeling funny as the voice of my mother slowly faded off into the distance.

Colt. I just needed Colt.

TWENTY-SIX

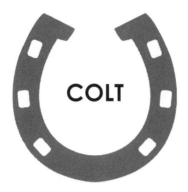

COLT

GRABBING ONTO THE bed, I listened to Jessie talking about Lauren. The hospital in College Station had transferred Lauren to Brackenridge once they diagnosed her with bacterial meningitis. Lauren's condition had only gotten worse.

Coma? Shaking my head, I whispered, "No."

Sniffling, Jessie placed her hands on my arms and forced me to look at her. "Colt, the bacterial meningitis is . . . it's not good. They can't control the fever and her temperature is so . . . it's so high and her body could put itself in a coma, so I need you to prepare for . . ."

Taking a step away, I shook my head as I felt my entire body start shaking. "No. No, she's not leaving me. She is not leaving me." Turning back to look at the love of my life, I whispered, "Lauren would never leave me." Glancing back to Jessie, my heart dropped.

Tears streamed down Jessie's face as the door opened and my mother walked in. Jessie turned and whispered, "Ellie—"

Giving me a weak smile, my mother moved closer to me. "Colt, honey let's step outside for some fresh air."

Shaking my head, I stood firm. I was not leaving Lauren. "She's not . . . she's going to be okay. She wouldn't leave me, Mom. She knows how much I love her and need her."

Turning to Lauren, I walked up to her and took her hand again. Kissing the back of it, I felt my tears begin to fall freely. "Please, baby. Please don't do this to me. Lauren, I beg you!"

Jessie quickly left the room as I buried my face down into Lauren's neck. Her skin felt so hot. So incredibly hot. "Lauren, please wake up. Don't leave me, sweetheart. I'm nothing without you, Lauren. *Please* wake up."

A woman began talking. "Sir, we need to put the ice-packs on her stat."

Strong hands took a hold of my shoulders and pulled me away from Lauren. *No. I can't leave her.* Turning, I saw my father. "Dad, no I can't leave her. She needs to know I'm here. She needs to know I won't leave her side."

"Colt, you need to get some food and some sleep."

Pushing him away, my father stumbled against a chair. "I'm not leaving her!" I shouted as my mother jumped. Covering her mouth, she began crying.

"Gunner," she whispered as my father took another step toward me. "Colt. Listen to me, son, I know how much you want to be here, but you need something to eat."

Warmth trickled down my cheeks as I felt my tears. "Dad, I can't lose her. She's my everything. The very reason I breathe."

Tears formed in my father's eyes. "Son, I'm only asking for two hours. Please."

Wiping the tears from my face, I slowly walked into my father's arms. "Dad, please tell me she's going to be okay."

Two nurses walked into the room as one cleared her throat. "I'm sorry, we can only have two people in here at a time."

Turning, I nodded my head. "What about her fever?" I asked.

The younger nurse gave me a weak smile. "We're going to be doing something called ice packing. We will place icepacks in key locations to bring her body temperature down, but we need to do it now."

Guiding me out of the room, my father said, "Your mother will be with her while we go get you something to eat."

Stopping in front of my mom, I attempted to talk but my voice kept cracking. "Mom . . . please . . . please don't leave her."

Shaking her head, she placed her hand on the side of my face. "I promise I won't leave her side."

My legs felt like rubber as my father guided me out of the room and to the waiting room. Looking up, I saw all of our friends sitting there. Grace jumped up and ran over to me and slammed her body into mine. "Colt," she whispered as she held me tight. My eyes moved across the room to see Maegan and Taylor with their parents, Brad and Amanda. Libby and Luke were now standing and I asked, "Where is Mireya?"

Libby wiped her tears away. "My parents have her back in Mason."

Grace pulled away and gave me a smile. "She's a fighter, Colt." Nodding my head, it felt as if someone was squeezing my heart.

When my eyes landed on Alex, I felt myself lose control as I started to cry. Alex quickly got up and walked over to me. Pulling her into my arms, I let it all go. The last two days had been hell as Lauren continued to decline. "Alex, she won't wake up. She won't wake up for me."

"Shh, she's going to, Colt. She's strong and she loves you so much."

Holding Alex as tight as I could, I tried to imagine my life without Lauren and I couldn't. I needed her.

Whispering in Alex's ear, I said, "Nothing else matters if I don't have her, Alex. Nothing."

Clearing his throat, my father walked up to me and placed his hand on my back. "Colt, let's go get something to eat."

Alex stepped away and looked into my eyes. There was something calming about the way she was looking at me. "You need to eat, Colt. If you want to be strong for Lauren, you need to eat. Let me take you to the cafeteria."

Nodding my head, I glanced over to Grace. Her eyes were red from all the crying. She looked how I felt. "Grace, are you hungry?"

Nodding her head, she smiled slightly. "Yeah."

Looking around the room I asked who was hungry. Amanda walked up to me and gave me a kiss on the cheek. "Um . . . we all just got back from eating something." Turning to Grace, Amanda smiled. "Grace, you go with Alex and Colt, sweetheart. I know you haven't eaten anything since yesterday."

Walking up to me, Grace laced her arm through mine as Alex stood on the other side of me. "Come on, let's get us some food," Grace said, barely above a whisper.

Turning to my father, I went to talk but he just nodded his head. I knew he wouldn't leave, but I just needed to know he would be here for Lauren if I couldn't.

The moment we stepped into the elevator and the door closed, I felt as if I couldn't breathe. "Maybe I should stay here and y'all go get food?"

Alex shook her head. "No, Colt, we're going to get food. Mom, Dad, Scott, and Jessie are up there. It's okay."

Nodding my head, I blindly let Alex and Grace lead me to the cafeteria.

Grace and I both ate chicken salad sandwiches and a bag of chips. I had to admit I felt better getting something into my body. Alex made me drink two bottles of water, then handed me a bag. "It's a change of clothes. Will brought them after Daddy asked him to grab you some clothes."

Reaching out for the bag, I nodded my head. I'd been in the same clothes I changed into after football practice a few days ago. "I'll um, go change in the bathroom."

Grace and Alex both nodded their heads and said they would wait for me by the elevator. After changing, I placed my clothes into the bag and zipped it up. Looking at myself in the mirror, I couldn't believe how terrible I looked. I hadn't slept in two days except for a few times when I nodded off for about ten minutes or so. Closing my eyes, I dropped my head back. "I swear to you, I'll do anything you want if you please just bring her back to me. *Please.*"

Looking back at myself in the mirror, I splashed cold

water on my face, reached for the bag and headed out the door. Alex and Grace were both waiting by the elevator as I made my way over to them. Swallowing hard, I attempted to push down the ache in my chest.

"Do you feel better?" Alex asked.

With a shaky voice I answered, "Yeah, a little. Alex, how are you holding up? I mean, the baby and everything?"

Giving me a sweet smile, Alex placed her hand over her stomach. "Everything is fine with the baby, Colt. Please don't worry about me. We're both fine."

Leaning over, I kissed Alex lightly on the cheek. "I love you, Alex," I whispered.

Fighting to keep her tears at bay, Alex whispered back, "I love you too, Colt."

Grace hit the up button and we waited for the elevator doors to open. Stepping inside, I glanced down at something Grace was holding in her hand. "Grace, what are you holding?"

With a trembling chin, she held her hand open and revealed a rock. "Lauren gave it to me when I left for college." Letting out a weak chuckle she shook her head. "I asked why a rock and she said it was the rock I threw at Thomas Wringer when he called her a tomboy. She had kept it . . . and . . ."

Grace turned away from me as she covered her mouth in an attempt not to cry.

The doors opened to the fifth floor. ICU was on this floor as well as the oncology unit. Stepping out of the elevator, I heard Grace and Alex both let out a gasp. Turning, there was a guy and a girl standing there.

"Grace?"

Wiping her tears away, Grace whispered, "Noah?"

"W-what are you doing here? Is everything okay?" Noah asked as he went to reach out for Grace. Taking a step back, she bumped into me. Taking a hold of her, I felt her whole body shaking.

"Lauren, she's here in ICU. Bacterial meningitis," Grace whispered.

Noah's eyes filled with compassion. "I'm so sorry."

Grace nodded her head but didn't say anything. Noah cleared his throat as he looked at Alex, then me.

"I lost my phone, and your number was in my phone, Grace. I tried to call but—"

Grace lifted her chin and stood taller as she looked at Noah, then the girl standing next to him. "Well, I'm sure you've been busy. Congratulations on your wedding. I hope the two of you have been happy."

Noah pulled his head back and looked at Grace with a confused expression. Turning to the girl next to him, Noah shook his head as he looked back at Grace. "Wait. Is that why you wouldn't return my calls, Grace? You think I'm . . ."

Noah's voice was cut off by a code blue coming across the speaker system. "Code blue room two thirty-two."

My heart dropped. *Lauren.* "That's Lauren's room!" I shouted as I ran down the hall to the double doors that led to the ICU.

By the time I got to Lauren's hospital room door, my heart felt like it was going to beat out of my chest. People were going in and out of her room.

Panic had already set in and I felt as if I was forcing the air to move in and out of my lungs. "What's going on?" I asked as nurses walked in and out.

Grabbing the younger nurse, I shouted, "Someone tell me what's going on?"

"Sir, I need you to let me go, she is in respiratory distress, let me go."

Dropping my hands, I started to head into the room when I felt someone pull me back.

"Colt, you need to let them do their job."

Turning I looked to see Scott had a hold of me. "No. No, she needs me! Let me go, Scott." The door opened and my heart stopped when I saw what was happening. The doctor was giving Lauren CPR. "Oh. My. God. Lauren! Lauren!" I screamed as someone yelled, "Shut the door and get him out of here!"

I was about to rush into the room when I felt more hands on me. "Colt, waiting room. We need to go to the waiting room."

My father's voice registered in my mind, but all I saw was Lauren. Lying on the bed as someone attempted to get her breathing again.

Respiratory distress.

Pulling against Scott and my father, I yelled, "Let me go! Lauren, please, God no! No!"

The next thing I knew, Scott, my father, Will and Luke were attempting to hold me down as I fought like hell to get to Lauren. I just needed to hold her. If she felt me, I knew she wouldn't leave me. She would never leave me.

Standing in front of me, Scott yelled, "Colt!"

My eyes snapped to his and I saw nothing but fear. "Scott," I whispered as tears fell from my eyes. "Please let me go. I need her. She can't leave me. She needs to know I'm here." Closing my eyes, I felt my legs give out as I fell to the ground. "Don't take her from me. I just want to hold her. She likes it when I hold her. Please. *Please* just let me hold her."

My sweet Lauren. I promise you . . . I'll spend forever holding you . . . even if it's only in my memories.

Dropping to his knees in front of me, Scott grabbed me and held me as my entire world fell apart.

TWENTY-SEVEN

C OLT. I HEAR Colt's voice calling out for me. Looking around, I couldn't believe my eyes. I was looking at myself in the hospital bed as the doctor tried to get me to breathe. The fever was gone. The aches in my body were gone.

Then I felt a warmth like I'd never felt before wash over my body as I turned and saw him.

"Grandpa?"

Smiling that brilliant smile, he moved closer to me. "My precious little Lauren."

"H-how am I talking to you?" Colt's voice continued to call out to me as the room grew brighter and I felt such a sense of peace.

Taking my hands, my grandfather smiled. "I've missed you, sweet Lauren."

Turning, I glanced over my shoulder. Nurses moved about in my room as I let out a gasp. "Grandpa, I'm—"

Slowly looking back at my grandfather, I felt a love I'd never experienced before. "Not now, Lauren. Not now, my sweet niña. He loves you too much."

Closing my eyes, I heard Colt calling out to me. Looking back at my grandpa, I smiled weakly. "I feel his love pulling me to him, Grandpa. I can't leave him."

My grandfather leaned over and kissed my cheek. "My

sweet Lauren, open your eyes. Open your eyes and go back to him."

The light slowly faded as the voices grew louder. "I've got a heartbeat, Dr. Wilker."

Another voice. "She's breathing. Her temperature is down to one hundred and one, doctor."

"Let her family know she's stable. Good job, everyone."

The voices slowly started to fade as I drifted off to sleep.

TINGLES. MY HAND was tingling. *Colt.* I could feel his warm breath on the back of my hand.

My sweet Lauren, open your eyes. Open your eyes and go back to him.

Slowly opening my eyes, I saw him. Leaning his head down, Colt had his lips to the back of my hand as he whispered against my skin.

"Baby, please. I want to hear your voice. I love you, Lauren. I love you so much and I'm not leaving until you wake up."

Tears stung my eyes as I watched the man I love pouring his heart out to me.

Opening my mouth, I tried to speak but nothing would come out. Colt continued to speak against my skin that was now on fire from his touch.

"I'm so scared, sweetheart. *Please,* I beg you to wake up."

My body felt so weak, but I needed to let him know I was here and I was never going to leave him. Lifting my hand, Colt jumped back as he stared down at my hand.

"I'm up," I whispered as Colt snapped his head to look at me. Jumping up, Colt wiped his tears away. He stared at me for a few moments before he leaned over and pressed his lips to mine.

"I love you. Oh God, Lauren. I love you so much."

Smiling against his warm soft lips, I whispered, "I love

you more."

Shaking his head he chuckled. "Never. Not possible, sweetheart."

Colt's blue eyes were red and the puffy dark circles told me he hadn't been getting much sleep. How long had I been in the hospital?

Licking my lips, I tried to talk.

"Are you thirsty?" Colt asked.

Nodding my head, I looked around the room. No one else was in here but Colt. Holding up a glass and a straw, Colt spoke. "Just a small drink, baby. I'm not sure you can have anything yet. I need to get the nurse."

Taking a small sip I let out a sigh. The cold water felt amazing as it slid down my throat to my stomach.

Speaking in a raspy voice, I asked, "How long have you been here, Colt?"

Smiling, he placed his hand on the side of my face and rubbed his thumb gently across my skin.

"You've been here at Brackenridge for four days." Glancing up at the clock he looked back at me. "Five days actually."

Swallowing, I closed my eyes, then opened them again. "You look so tired, Colt. Have you slept?"

Leaning over, he brushed his lips against mine. "I'm fine, sweetheart. Everything is fine now that you've come back to me."

Smiling at him, it felt as if my heart was going to burst in my chest. This man, who I loved so very much, had stayed by my side the entire time. He was indeed the tick to my clock. My everything. "I'll never leave you, Colt. Never."

Colt started to walk away when I called out. "Wait. Don't call anyone yet. I just want you to hold me. There was a moment when I felt like I was slipping away from you, but I closed my eyes and pictured you holding me. I could feel your warmth spreading through my body, pulling me to you."

Colt quickly walked over as I attempted to move myself over some. Crawling into the bed with me, Colt moved tubes out of the way as he pulled me closer to him.

Gently kissing me on the forehead, Colt began to talk. "For a few minutes there I thought I was going to lose you, Lauren. I'd never felt so empty in my entire life."

"I'm so sorry I scared you, Colt."

Pressing his lips to my head, he said, "Sweetheart, I love you. Marry me, Lauren."

Wait. What did he just say? Oh. My. Glitter. Pressing my lips together to contain my excitement, I slowly smiled. "What?" I asked in a whispered voice.

"Marry me. As soon as you get better and get out of here, let's go off somewhere and get married. Let me make you mine. I don't want to waste another minute, another second, in this life without you."

I tried to absorb what Colt was saying. "You want to get married? What about school?" Then it hit me. Colt had been by my side this last week; that meant he must have missed a football game and practices. "The game?"

Colt's head flinched back slightly. "The game? Lauren, this isn't a game. I'm serious, I want to get married the moment you get out of this hospital and get your strength back."

I began to blink rapidly in an attempt to hold back my tears.

Colt wants to marry me. Oh my. Mrs. Colt Mathews. Mrs. Lauren Mathews. That sounds so good. I feel like I should start practicing writing it down or something. I need paper right away.

"Lauren? Um, your silence is kind of scaring me."

My body felt on fire as my stomach dipped and my heartbeat increased. *Colt wants to marry me.* Grinning, I looked into his eyes. God those blue eyes were able to drown out everything else in the world when I looked into them. "I know it's not a game, I meant your football game, you missed it."

Colt's expression changed for one brief second before a grin spread across this face. "Nothing else matters to me except for you, Lauren. Football, school, ranches, none of it matters. As long as you're by my side, I'll forever be happy."

Feeling the tear slide down my face, I sucked in a shaky breath. "There is nothing more I want than to become your wife, Colt."

Leaning over, Colt pressed his lips against mine. His tongue ran along my bottom lip, asking for entry and I gladly gave it to him. Letting out a soft moan, I was quickly lost in Colt's kiss. His love for me felt as if it was pouring into my body and I was already feeling better.

The door to my hospital room opened and someone cleared their throat. Pulling back some, Colt whispered against my lips. "Our secret for right now?"

Nodding my head, I wiped my tears away. "Yes."

"Ms. Reynolds, I see you're awake."

Peeking over to the nurse, I smiled. "Yes ma'am."

Walking over to me, she gave Colt a polite smile as he crawled out of the bed. "Let's see how that fever is, shall we?"

Nodding my head, I let go of Colt's hand and kept my eyes on him as he took a few steps back. When he winked at me, I felt my insides melt and my face flush. That crooked smile of his was driving me mad with desire, even though it felt as if I had been in a train wreck. My body was aching and my head hurt with a dull headache.

Smiling, the nurse nodded her head. "Your fever is down to one hundred. That's amazing, considering it was one hundred and five the other day."

My mouth dropped open. "What? Wow. That's really high."

Colt and the nurse both chuckled. "You really gave your family a scare." Looking over her shoulder to Colt, she smiled. "And I must say, Miss Reynolds, you're very lucky to have someone love you as much as this gentleman standing here does." Glancing back at me, she looked into my eyes. "Not everyone gets a chance at a love like that. Don't waste a second of it."

Chewing on my lip, I thought of Colt's proposal to me. *Could I really run off and get married? Did I want a big wedding with the white dress and all the headaches that went along with it?* I'd been through two of them already with Alex and Libby.

Smiling bigger, I said, "No ma'am, I don't intend on wasting any time at all. Isn't that right, Mr. Mathews?"

Colt's smile grew bigger as he nodded his head. Yes. There was no wasting any more time. My goal was to get healthy and out of the hospital so I could marry the man whom I loved more than the air I breathed.

THE MOMENT I was wheeled out of the hospital, I insisted on standing up and walking. I felt alive. I'd spent another week in the hospital after I had woken up, and Colt never left my side. Most of the time was spent getting my strength back and that meant countless walks with Colt right there. Not once did he leave, only to get food. I wasn't sure how Gunner felt about Colt missing so much school, and Colt didn't mention anything about his conversation this morning with the head football coach at A&M.

Dropping my head back, I let the warm sun shine on my face. "Mmm . . . that feels so good," I said as I smiled.

Placing his hand on my lower back, Colt kissed my neck and chuckled. "Damn you look sexy as hell right now."

Grinning, I looked down at his lips. His soft plump lips that were begging for me to kiss them and suck on them. Oh, to have them kiss my body.

"Keep biting on your lip and looking at me like that, Lauren, and we won't make it to my truck."

Dropping my mouth open, I let out a moan. My body ached, but not because I had been lying in a hospital bed for over two weeks. I wanted to feel Colt's skin up against me. His lips trailing soft kisses along my skin. Oh Lord. I was going to go into a full-blown orgasm just thinking about it.

"Lauren, darling are you okay? Your cheeks are so flushed."

Colt winked as he turned and guided me down the

sidewalk to his truck as my mother walked alongside of us. "I am. I feel wonderful, Mom. I guess it's maybe from just moving about." I had insisted on walking to Colt's truck, even though the nurse had stood there and argued with me about it. I finally just stood up and walked a few steps away from the wheelchair. Figuring out I was not going to back down, she gave me a sweet smile and told me to take it easy and slowly build back to what I was doing before getting sick.

Feeling slightly light headed, I was regretting my stubbornness. "Colt?"

It was as if he knew what I was going to say. "Stay here with your mom and dad, I'll go get my truck."

Kissing me quickly on the lips, I watched Colt take off jogging toward the parking lot.

Feeling my father walk up next to me, I glanced up at him. Letting out a sigh, he said, "He loves you very much, Lauren."

Smiling, I nodded my head. "I know he does. I don't think he ever left the hospital once."

Letting out a soft chuckle my mother said, "No. He didn't. Gunner had to force him at one point to go eat."

Worrying my bottom lip, I wasn't sure how I wanted to say this without sounding crazy, so I just inhaled a deep breath and blew it out. "He saved my life."

"What?" my father asked.

Turning to me, my mother asked, "Who did, Lauren?"

Still staring straight out to where Colt ran, I decided I was going to tell my parents what happened to me. "Colt did. I felt him pulling me back."

My mother's voice cracked. "Pulling you back? What do you mean?"

Turning to look at her, I felt such a sense of peace. Smiling I said, "I saw Grandpa."

My mother's face fell and the color all but drained from it. "What do you mean, Lauren?"

Looking straight ahead, I inhaled a deep breath once again. This time I could smell rain in the air. Glancing up, I smiled when I saw the rain clouds. Oh, how I hoped it would rain. I wanted to sit in the barn and listen to it hit the tin roof. "I think for a few minutes, I might have been . . . gone. I was standing in a really bright room and Grandpa was there. Except, it didn't feel like I should go with him. I kept hearing Colt; he was calling out for me and his voice sounded so pained. Like he was in agony. Then . . . I felt his warmth and it was like he was calling me back to him and I couldn't leave." Letting out a soft chuckle, I turned to my mother. "Grandpa told me to open my eyes. That I needed to go back to Colt."

With her chin trembling, my mother pulled me to her and cried as my father wrapped both of us up in his arms. "Lauren, I don't know what we would have done if we had lost you."

With my father holding us tightly, we cried softly together. I'd never felt so loved before in my life. It was as if I could feel my parents' love pouring into me. I had to smile because I knew the moment they found out Colt and I were leaving to get married, they were not going to be so loving.

Hearing Colt clear his throat, my father dropped his hold on my mother and me. Kissing me gently on the cheek. "You ready to head home, sweetheart?"

Nodding my head, I turned to kiss my father, then my mother. "See you at home?"

Giving me that smile that has made me feel safe since I could remember, my mother said, "Be careful driving, Colt."

Reaching out, Colt shook my father's hand, then kissed my mother on the cheek. "Yes, ma'am."

Opening the door to his truck, Colt helped me up and buckled me in. Giving me that melt-my-panties smile, he placed his hand on the side of my face and whispered, "You're forever mine, Lauren Ashley Reynolds."

Becoming acutely aware of my own heartbeat, my fingers ached with the need to touch Colt. "Care to make that Lauren Ashley Mathews?" Colt's eyes turned dark as his mouth opened slightly. A shiver ran across my entire body.

"When?" Colt asked in a whispered kiss against my lips.

Slightly parting my legs, I internally begged for him to touch me. "As soon as we can," I stuttered.

Holding in his breath, Colt smiled as he pulled back and shut the door. Watching him jog around the front of his truck, I wiped my sweaty hands on my shorts. I wasn't sure how I was going to be able to make it without being with him. It felt as if our connection had grown stronger since I had gotten sick.

Jumping in, Colt reached over and hit play on this stereo. When his iPod started playing, I couldn't help but smile when I heard "Say You Do" by Dierks Bentley begin playing. Colt had played it the night we shared our first real kiss. Ever since then, I must have listened to it at least twice a day.

"I love this song," I said as I turned to Colt. Smiling, he nodded his head and looked back at me.

"I know."

Leaning my head back, I felt my body warm. Just being with Colt and knowing he was going to wrap me up in his arms when we got home had my heart fluttering. Closing my eyes, I slowly drifted off to sleep.

TWENTY-EIGHT

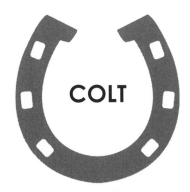

COLT

M Y FATHER AND I rode along the fence line in silence. I'd been waiting for him to have this talk with me since Lauren came home from the hospital almost two weeks ago.

Clearing his throat, I turned slowly and looked at him. His posture was rigid and I knew he had a lot on his mind. "Dad, I need to talk to you."

Nodding his head, he stared straight ahead. "I figured as much, son."

Letting out a long exhale, I decided the best thing to do was to just come out with it. "I'm not going back to A&M."

I held my breath while I waited for him to lay into me about how irresponsible I was being. Nodding his head, he kept riding as he stared straight ahead.

Clearing his throat, my father began to speak. "This morning I was thinking about when Alex left for college a few years back. The mistake I made by pushing my plans on her and what happened in the end."

Stopping my horse, my father turned to face me. "Dad, what happened to Alex was not your fault or Alex's fault."

Giving me a weak smile, my father let out a deep breath. "I know, Colt. But I vowed I would never step in and interfere with my kids' lives again. I'm not going to lie, I'm disappointed you're not going back, but at the same time I've never been more proud of you."

Pulling my head back in shock, my mouth dropped open. "Why?"

Letting out a gruff laugh, he continued to talk. "Why? Well for one, you knew what meant the most to you and that was Lauren. When your coach told you to either be at the game or lose your starting spot, and you picked staying with Lauren . . . well . . ." Shaking his head and smiling slightly, he said, "It showed how much you love Lauren and would do anything for her. Don't think Scott and Jessie don't know that, Colt. They know what you walked away from and they couldn't be more proud of you as well."

"I love her, Dad. The thought of losing her did something to me. It . . . I don't know . . . it changed the way I think about everything, not just football and college. Lauren getting sick and almost dying showed me that each day is a gift and I don't want to take it for granted. I don't want to miss a minute of anything."

Giving me a smile, he looked away as if he was thinking about what he was going to say next. Before looking back at me he asked, "Your plans?"

This was it. I'd already had this conversation with Scott and Jessie this morning with Lauren. Now it was time for my father. "This morning I spoke with Scott and Jessie." He nodded as if he knew this bit of information. "Lauren had already decided she was not returning to school. Scott and Jessie didn't argue with her at all. I think they're just happy she's here, ya know?"

"I can't even begin to imagine what that was like for them, so yes, I totally understand their thinking."

Fidgeting in the saddle, I ran my hand over my head and let out a sigh. *Holy hell. I was going to tell my father I wanted to quit school and work for Scott full time. What would he do? Laugh? Shout? Tell me I was out of my damn mind?* Taking in a deep breath, I slowly blew it out. "I'm going to work for Scott full time, Dad. I'm not going back to A&M. I've asked Lauren to marry me, and I honestly don't want to waste anymore time. I know what you're going to say, and well, I just hope that you and Mom will be able to—"

Holding up his hands to get me to stop talking, he laughed. "Colt, my gosh, will you give me a chance to respond before you go into full-blown defensive mode."

Shaking my head, I looked down to clear the thoughts running rampant in my head. "Right, of course. Sorry, Dad."

"May I talk now?"

Giving him a weak smile, I motioned for him to talk. "Your mother and I already saw this coming, Colt. Neither one of us can fault you for wanting to embrace each day as it comes. Would we like to see you finish school? Of course we would, but this is your life. The path you choose to go down is your own. I want you to know, your mother and I support Lauren and yours decision one hundred percent."

My eyes widened and I was at a loss for words. I'd never in a million years expected my father to be so understanding. "W-what about football, Dad?"

Tilting his head and looking at me like I'd grown another head he whispered, "Football?"

"Yeah, I know it was always your dream to have me play, and if I don't go back to A&M, that dream is over."

My father's eyes filled with tears as he quickly looked away and shook his head. "Colt, it's not about my dreams; this is about your life." Turning back to look at me, I saw the love in his eyes. My heart felt as if it would burst knowing just how supportive my mother and father were. "No matter if you go back and play football for A&M or stay on and work full time with Scott, I need you to know I'm so proud of the young man you've become. You inspire me each and every day, son."

Feeling my jaw tremble, I turned away to get my wits about me. I wasn't about to breakdown and cry in front of my father. Closing my eyes and getting a hold of my feelings, I glanced back at the man who I admired more than any other person on this planet. "Thank you, Dad. You'll never know how much your words mean to me."

Giving me a smile and a wink, he leaned closer and said, "So I'm going to safely guess that you and Lauren have planned a trip . . . Vegas maybe?"

Tipping my head to the side, I whispered, "How'd you know?"

Throwing his head back and laughing, he shook his head. "You don't think I was your age once? The idea of marrying your mother was so overwhelming, I can't even begin to tell you how many times I wanted to whisk her away and marry her. You're smart doing it this way. Plus it will save your mother and me the stress of another wedding."

Letting out a laugh, I followed my father as he kicked his horse to start walking. "Just do me one favor, Colt."

"Anything, sir."

Peeking over at me from under the brim of his hat, his blue eyes pierced mine. "Let the idea of Alex having a baby fully settle in before you and Lauren think of having any kids."

Letting out a chuckle, I nodded my head and said, "Yes, sir. We're in no hurry for kids right now. Lauren's gotten pretty much all of her strength back and is feeling normal again. I think our goal is to focus on each other."

Letting his shoulders drop into a relaxed position he laid his head back and sighed in relief. "Thank you, God."

LYING IN BED, I stared up at the ceiling. As much as I had been dying to make love to Lauren, I wanted to make sure she was feeling one hundred percent better. Being near her was beginning to take its toll on me. Lauren had come over to my parents' house for dinner tonight and every time she laughed, my dick jumped. The smell of her perfume caused my stomach to dip in that crazy way it does when you're on a roller coaster. The way she kept smiling at me with that adorable smile of hers was enough to keep me forcing myself to keep my hands at my side. Being with Lauren was more than a physical thing; she made me feel whole when we were together.

Closing my eyes, I could still taste her on my lips. It was almost as if they were still tingling from the kiss good-bye she gave me.

Reaching over to the side table, I grabbed my phone. Lauren should be back home by now.

Me: *Marry me.*

Lauren: *I'm pretty sure I already said yes.*

Me: *Marry me now. I don't want to wait any longer.*

Lauren: *If we left now, we could be married in twenty-four hours.*

My heart felt as if it leapt from my chest. Smiling, I hit Lauren's number.

"Hello there, handsome."

Grinning, I sat up. "Pack a bag, Ms. Reynolds. I'm taking you to Vegas."

"Mmm . . . I'm not sure. I mean, we aren't even twenty-one, what are we going to do there?"

Holding back my laughter, I said, "We can play strip poker in our hotel room after I make you Mrs. Colt Mathews."

I heard a noise and Lauren yelled out. "Shit! I stubbed my little toe!"

Laughing, I got up and walked to my closet as I grabbed a duffle bag. "Well?"

"Ouch. That really hurt, Colt!" Lauren whined.

"How about I kiss it for you?"

Lauren sucked in a breath of air, then let out a soft moan. "I'm packing right now. I'll be ready in a couple of hours."

The phone line went dead as I pulled it away from my ear and looked at it. Laughing, I shook my head and quickly packed a bag, then headed down to talk to my parents.

Holy shit. I'm going to marry Lauren.

TWENTY-NINE

LAUREN

R UNNING DOWN THE stairs I called out for my mother. "Mom! Mom!"

Stepping out of my father's office, my mother hummed as she made her way into the living room. "What's up?"

Skidding to a stop in front of her, I stared at her. *What's up? She wants to know what's up? Oh, just the man of my dreams is taking me to Vegas to get married and play strip poker! That's all! Okay, so maybe I won't mention the strip poker.*

Attempting to keep the panic out of my voice, I said, "I need a dress! Mom, I need a white dress stat!"

Well, so much for keeping the panic out of my voice.

A smile slowly played across her face. "Why white?"

Sucking my lower lip into my mouth, I felt my face flush. "Colt's taking me on a little road trip to Vegas."

Her face was blank. I couldn't read it at all and I wasn't sure if that was a good thing or a bad thing. "Lauren, I know you got the all clear from Dr. Cunningham, but are you up for a road trip, darling?"

My eyes widened as my father walked up and stood next to my mother. "Mom! Colt wants to marry me. Of course I'm up for a road trip."

Wrapping his arm around my mother's waist, my father chuckled. "Jessie, she's been home for two weeks, I'm sure she'll be fine. Where are you going, Lauren?"

Glancing over to the clock, I blew out a breath of air. Colt would be here soon. "Vegas, and I really need a white dress, Mom."

My mother's eyes began to water. I was slightly stunned they didn't seem more shocked. "You're eloping," my mother whispered as she placed her hand on the side of my face.

"Yes!" my father said with a fist pump as my mother turned and gave him a horrified look.

"Scott! Our baby girl is wanting to run off to Vegas and get married."

Looking at my mother and then me, my father shrugged his shoulders. "What? We knew they were going to be getting married soon, they both said so, and why can't they elope?"

Placing her hands on her hips, my mother gave my father an angry look. "Scott Reynolds, you just don't want to plan a wedding."

Laughing, he looked at me and winked. "Nonsense. I'll throw them the biggest reception ever thrown in Mason County."

Throwing myself at my father, I whispered, "Thank you, Daddy. Thank you for being so understanding." Pulling back, he kissed me on the forehead.

"You'll always be my little girl though."

Nodding, I whispered, "Always."

"Wait. Wait just a second. I can't . . . I mean . . . well—" Closing her eyes, my mother turned from me. When I heard her sniffle, I placed my hand on her arm.

"Mom?"

Turning to me, she wiped her tears away. "It's just I always dreamed you'd be walking down the stairs on your father's arm and getting married here, surrounded by your family and friends."

My eyes burned with the threat of tears. "Mom," I whispered, "that's your dream, not mine. The only thing I want is to start my life with Colt, and this is what we both want."

Nodding her head, she wiped her tears away. "I know,

Lauren. Will you at least let us throw y'all a reception?"

Quickly wiping my tears away, I smiled. "I'd love that. But what I'd love even more is if we could raid your closet for a white dress!"

Smiling, she took me by my arm and led me to her bedroom. Glancing over my shoulder I said, "Daddy, when Colt gets here, will you keep him entertained?"

Giving me a wicked smile, he chuckled. "Oh for sure. I have a few things I want to talk to my future son-in-law about."

Getting ready to protest, my mother pulled me into her room and headed to her closet.

Pushing some dresses out of the way, my mother smiled as she said, "I have the perfect dress!"

My stomach began flipping and dipping in every possible way imaginable as I thought about marrying Colt. My mother pulled out a white strapless lace dress and held it up in front of me. It was beautiful. The length and style of the dress was perfect. "Oh, Mom this dress is perfect."

Tears began to build in my eyes as I attempted to hold them back but couldn't. Turning to my mother, I lost it when I saw the tears rolling down her face. Pulling me into her arms, we both cried. "Lauren, I can't believe you're getting married."

Squeezing my eyes shut tightly, I mumbled, "I know."

Taking a step back, I held the dress up and shook my head. There was something about it. It was so simple, yet elegant. *Colt is going to love me in it and I bet my boobs are going to look amazing!*

"You know, when you were little, you used to put this dress on and line up all your dolls and teddy bear. Your father used to have to walk you down the aisle and then pretend to marry you to your Prince Charming."

Looking down at the dress, I smiled. "Oh my glitter! I remember that. Mr. Snuggles used to always be my Prince Charming."

Letting out a giggle, I looked at my mother who had a stunned expression on her face. She slowly brought her hand up to her mouth and let out a small sob. "What's wrong, Mom?"

Laughing, she dropped her hand and gazed into my eyes. "Lauren, do you remember who gave you Mr. Snuggles?"

Stopping to think about it, I looked away. My breath caught as the butterflies fluttered in my stomach when it hit me.

"Colt," I whispered.

My mother placed her hands over her mouth in an attempt not to cry again. With a disbelieving voice I attempted to tell the story of when Colt gave me the bear. "It was in our place, the treehouse, for my seventh birthday."

My mother nodded her head. "You wanted a tea party and we set it all up under the tree. After everyone left, Colt took you by the hand and led you to the treehouse, then gave you his gift."

Placing my hand over my stomach, I let my tears fall freely. "Oh my . . . the man was romantic even back then! I just didn't know it."

Letting out a chortle, my mother said, "You must have because you married that stupid bear over and over at least fifty times."

Looking into my mother's loving eyes, I was lost in the moment. My skin felt as if tingles were moving up and down my body, my heart was beating quickly and I felt breathless. "Mom, it's like everything has come full circle. Colt truly is my prince charming who saved me."

"Oh, sweetheart."

Walking into my mother's arms, we stood there for a few minutes and cried. It was then I realized my mother wouldn't be with me on the day I married my prince charming. My heart physically ached.

When I finally came to my senses, I heard Colt and my father talking. Chewing on my bottom lip I said, "I better go finish packing."

Lacing her arm with mine she nodded her head. "I'll help."

Racing through the living room, I yelled out over my shoulder, "I'll be a few more minutes!"

Colt and my father laughed as I heard my mother say, "We found the perfect dress."

"Baby girl, slow down," Daddy said as I raced up the stairs with my mother following closely behind me.

Thirty minutes later I was walking down the stairs with a suitcase in my hand and a smile on my face. Colt looked up at me and I had to catch my breath from the smile he was giving me.

Holy hell. Colt was so handsome. How in the world did I get so lucky to have those blue eyes look into mine with so much love? Oh my glitter. I could practically feel the heat coming off his body.

"Hey," Colt whispered.

"Hey back at you," I whispered back as I walked up to him. Taking the suitcase from me, Colt leaned down and kissed me softly on the lips.

I wanted to deepen the kiss so bad, but not with my parents standing right there. For a few brief moments, Colt and I were lost in each other's eyes. My father cleared his throat, causing us both to pull out of the trance.

"Colt and I were talking, Lauren. With both of you going to be working here, I thought it best that you stay with us when you get back. I'm going to have Aaron and Dewey look at getting the hunters cabin fixed up. Maybe add onto it and expand it some. I think it would make the perfect first home for the two of you."

Spinning around and facing my father, I ran into his arms. "Oh, Daddy! It will be more than perfect!" Burying my face into his chest, I took in a long deep breath. I loved how my father smelled. Anytime I ever got upset or sad, I would either hug my father or sneak into his bathroom and spray his cologne on my arms. "Daddy, I love you so much."

Holding me tighter, he kissed the top of my head. "I love you so much more princess. Now go on, you've been making poor Colt wait for what seems like forever I'm sure."

Colt and I both chuckled as I turned and made my way to the front door. This was it. When I walked back through this door I would be married. Mrs. Colt Hunter Mathews. *Oh holy shit. I'm going to Vegas. To get married. I'm going to puke.*

Taking my hand in her hand I felt my mother's breath against my ear. "Stop overthinking everything, Lauren Ashley." Looking at her I whispered, "I'm getting married, Mom."

Smiling, she pushed a piece of my blonde hair behind my ear and gave me a kiss on the cheek. "Yes you are. Send pictures and keep us updated."

Nodding my head, I whispered, "It's a long drive but—"

Colt cleared his throat, "Oh, we're not driving."

Snapping my head over to look at Colt, I asked, "What?"

Giving me that melt my panties crooked smile of his, Colt gave me a quick wink. "I didn't want Lauren to have to be in the car for that many hours, so I booked us tickets to fly there." Peeking over to my father, he was standing up tall and proud as he shook his head. I knew Colt's actions impressed the hell out of my father, but they touched my heart in more ways than I could ever begin to say.

"Oh my, this boy is good," my mother whispered into my ear.

Grinning, I nodded my head as I watched Daddy and Colt walk up to Colt's truck. "He is indeed. That's why he is the pop to my cherry."

Seeing my mother look at me, I realized I had just spoken those words out loud. "Lauren Ashley, that wasn't even funny."

Pursing my lips together to keep from laughing, I went on, digging myself deeper into the hole. "Um . . . the squirt to my bottle?"

Shaking her head she narrowed her eyes at me. "Not any better."

"The salt to my nuts? The hair to my beaver?" I laughed as she rolled her eyes and then glared at me.

Opening the truck door, Colt kissed me gently on the cheek. "What's so funny?" he asked as he helped me into the truck.

"Nothing, I'm giving my mother a hard time. I love you,

Mom. Daddy, I love you, too."

Both my parents gave me a kiss good-bye, and then my father shut the door to Colt's truck. "Take care of my baby girl, Colt."

Jumping into his truck, Colt smiled and said, "Yes sir! Thanks for everything." Colt and my father exchanged a knowing look. Almost as if they knew something and I wasn't privy to the information.

Colt put his truck into drive and we headed down the long driveway. "Are you ready to start our life together, sweetheart?"

Grinning, I reached for Colt's hand and held it tightly. "So ready."

Taking in a deep breath, I slowly let it out. *Oh my glitter. I'm marrying, Colt.*

THIRTY

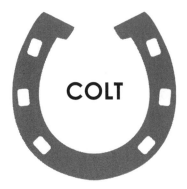

THE TAXI PULLED up to the Venetian as the valet opened Lauren's door and helped her out. I had been texting my parents and when I looked up, my mouth dropped open at the sight before me. Lauren spun around and smiled at me. "Colt! This place is amazing."

Nodding, I finished my text to my father.

> *Me: Pulling up now. Thank you for planning all of this for me and kiss mom. By the way, Lauren loves it so far*

My parents wanted to pay for our entire trip to Vegas. They said it was the least they could do since Lauren and I decided to elope. My father and mother made all of the plans while Lauren and I flew to Vegas. I was going to owe them big time since I'm sure they hadn't even gone to bed yet. Between talking to them and Scott and Jessie, my head was spinning. I knew how much this meant to Lauren, so it would all be worth it in the end.

After checking in, we made it up to our room. We were staying in one of the Prima Suites on one of the higher levels of the hotel. I smiled as I watched Lauren skip out of the elevator and to our room. Turning, she leaned against the door and looked at me. "We haven't been together in almost a month." Licking her lips, her eyes widened. "I think we should wait until after we get married."

My heart dropped to my stomach. "Huh?"

Nodding her head, she turned and slipped the key into the door and turned around to look at me as she pushed her back into the door and slowly opened it. "Yep, I think we should wait until after we get married."

Shaking my head to clear my thoughts, I quickly said, "Then let's go get married right now."

Laughing, she pushed the door opened and walked into the room. Throwing her hands up to her mouth she let out a gasp.

"Colt! Oh my glitter, this is amazing. Beautiful. Like nothing I've ever seen before."

As we walked into the foyer, there was a half bathroom to our left. Straight ahead led us right into the grand living room which featured a bar to the left, straight in front of us was a dining table that sat four and a little more to the right, was the living room. A sofa, three recliners and one of the biggest flat-screen televisions I'd ever seen finished off the room. The windows overlooked Vegas and I couldn't believe all the light coming into the room from the other buildings.

Lauren quickly made her way into the bedroom where she let out another gasp and then laughed as she jumped onto the king-size bed. "Oh it's so comfortable," she said as she wiggled her eyebrows up and down.

"Not funny, coming from the girl who just told me she wanted to wait until after we were married to have sex."

Biting on her lower lip, she batted her eyelashes at me, jumped up and skipped into the bathroom. "Oh, Colt! You have to see this."

When I walked into the bathroom, I was stunned by how huge it was. And beautiful. "Holy shit," I whispered. The giant jet tub had me thinking of all kinds of naughty things I wanted to do with Lauren in there. Adjusting my growing dick, I turned to the shower. Lauren was standing inside it. "It has two shower heads!" she said as she scrunched up her nose. Licking my lips, I smiled. "I know what to do with one of them."

Lauren's eyes turned darker. "Don't tease, Colt Mathews."

"Oh baby, I'm not teasing. Strip out of those clothes and I'll show you how serious I am right now."

Walking up to me, Lauren placed her hands on my chest. "Tomorrow at three you said, right?"

Nodding my head slowly, I bent down and kissed Lauren's neck. Running my tongue along her neck and up to her ear, I whispered into her ear. "I have a surprise for you, sweetheart."

Lauren's breathing picked up as I watched her chest rise and fall with each breath. Closing her eyes, she moaned lightly. "Does it involve kissing?"

Smiling against her ear, I whispered, "I hope so."

Swallowing hard, she asked. "Will we be naked?"

Attempting to hold back my laughter I said, "If we were it might be a bit embarrassing."

Turning, Lauren peeked up at me. Those beautiful blue eyes held mine as she said, "We won't be alone for this surprise?"

Spinning her around so she faced me, I cupped my hands to the sides of her face. My heart was racing as I stared into Lauren's bright eyes. Closing my eyes to savor the moment, I whispered her name. "Lauren. I love you so much."

Opening my eyes, I was met by her beautiful smile. My knees felt weak as I looked at the woman I would soon be making my wife.

"I love you too, Colt. So very much."

"Are you tired?"

Shaking her head, she sucked her lower lip between her teeth. "No."

Gently placing my lips to hers, I spoke softly. "Good, because I want to take you somewhere."

"O-okay."

Guiding Lauren back out into the living room, I had her sit down at the bar. "Want something to drink?"

Shaking her head, she took a seat on the bar stool. Turning, I grabbed my suitcase and Lauren's and brought them both into the bedroom. Setting mine down on the luggage rack, I opened it up and pulled the ring box out and pushed it into my pocket. The gondolas were now closed but somehow my future father-in-law had arranged for one once we got here. I couldn't very well marry Lauren tomorrow without asking her properly and giving her an engagement ring. Picking up the phone in the bedroom, I hit zero for the hotel operator.

"Hello, front desk."

"Um, hello. This is Colt Mathews in room thirteen twenty-seven."

"Yes, Mr. Mathews. We have that gondola waiting if you are ready."

My adrenaline immediately rushed through my body. This was the first step.

"Perfect, on our way now." Hanging up the phone, I dragged in a deep breath and held it for a moment in an attempt to calm my beating heart down.

Walking back out into the living room I reached for her hand. Giving me a sexy grin, Lauren slid off the bar stool and allowed me to guide her out the door. Making our way down to the plaza, Lauren snuggled into my side.

"Are you sure you're not too tired? I don't want you to overdo anything, Lauren."

Letting out a chuckle, Lauren shook her head. "I promise, I'm not tired. I'm too excited to sleep right now, and I promise if I get to feeling bad, I'll let you know."

As we made our way over to where the gondola waited for us, I wrapped my arm around Lauren's waist. Lauren went on and on about how Grace and Meg would go out of their minds with all the stores there. Nodding to the gondolier, he smiled and reached his hand out for mine. "Mr. Mathews? Ms. Reynolds?"

Lauren's mouth dropped open. "How did you know our names?" Lauren asked with a wide grin. Knowing how much Lauren loved surprises, I couldn't help but smile and fist pump internally at how happy she looked.

Holding Lauren's hand in mine, I helped her into the gondola. The gondolier got in and began taking us down the indoor river. As we moved about, the gondolier sang two songs while I held Lauren in my arms.

"Oh, Colt. This is so romantic."

Smiling, I placed my cheek against her cheek. "Grams and Gramps honeymooned in Venice."

Turning and looking at me, Lauren smiled. "Really?"

Shaking my head, I said, "Yep, they sure did. If there is one thing I want to do Lauren, it's make you happy for the rest of our lives."

Leaning her head back into my chest, Lauren closed her eyes and said, "Colt, you make me so happy. I can't imagine being any happier."

Having already taken the ring out of my pocket, I held it in my left hand. Lauren still lay against my chest with her eyes closed. Peeking up at the gondolier, he smiled and gave me a head nod. Reaching my hands out, I opened the box and held it in front of Lauren.

Brilliant round diamonds that extended down the bands surrounded the princess cut diamond. The light it was casting off was breathtaking.

"Lauren, will you do me the honor of making me the happiest man on Earth, and say you'll marry me?"

Lauren still had her head rested against my chest with her eyes closed as she let out a giggle. "I'm pretty sure I've already agreed to this, Colt."

Placing my lips to her ear, I whispered, "Open you eyes, sweetheart."

Opening her eyes, Lauren looked at me and smiled. Glancing back to the gondolier, she saw the ring and let out a gasp as she covered her mouth. Leaning forward, Lauren dropped her hands and whispered in a shaky voice, "Oh. My. Glitter. Look at it . . . glitter." Turning around in her seat to face me, she shook her head. "Colt, it's . . . it's beyond beautiful."

A single tear rolled down her face as I reached up with my thumb and wiped it off her face. "Is that a yes?" I asked with a wink.

Letting out a giggle, Lauren nodded her head. "Yes! Yes of course it's a yes!"

Taking the ring out of the box, I slipped it onto Lauren's finger as people surrounding us began to clap. I was glad it was in the middle of the night and not that many people were around. Lauren wrapped her arms around my neck as she began to cry. "Colt, thank you for making this so special. I love you. I love you so much."

Holding her tightly, I closed my eyes tightly and thanked God for not taking Lauren from me. "I love you so much too, Lauren. So very much."

We spent the rest of the gondola ride talking about our future. I would never take for granted the moments Lauren and I shared together. Not one single moment.

Lifting her chin and looking at me, Lauren smiled. "I'm exhausted. If you want me to be awake tomorrow when you marry me, you better take me to bed. Now."

The gondolier pulled over and Lauren and I thanked him for the amazing experience. I picked Lauren up and carried her back to the elevator as she nestled her head into my neck. By the time we got to the elevator, my princess was fast asleep in my arms.

Riding up in the elevator, an older couple smiled at me as the wife nodded her head and said, "Your wife?"

My heart about exploded. "Fiancée, we're getting married tomorrow."

The couple smiled and both said, "Congratulations."

Smiling, I said, "Thank you."

The couple got off one floor below ours. Trying to get the door open and hold Lauren proved to be difficult, but I somehow managed to do it.

Walking into the bedroom, I gently put Lauren down on the bed and brushed her blonde hair from her face. After carefully undressing her, I picked up one of the chairs and carried it over to the side of the bed and sat down. Smiling, I watched Lauren sleep. It was the first time since she'd been out of the hospital I could watch her sleep and not have this ache in my chest that she was going to leave me.

Tucking her hand up under her face, Lauren let out a soft moan that moved through my entire body, lighting it up until I felt nothing but pure love coursing through my veins.

"You will forever be mine, Lauren Reynolds. No one or nothing will ever come between the love that we share."

Moving slightly, Lauren opened her eyes and smiled as she gazed upon me with a loving look. "Colt," she whispered. "Please hold me."

Stripping out of my clothes, I crawled into the bed and pulled Lauren closer to me. It didn't take long for me to drift off to sleep. My dreams consisted of nothing but Lauren.

THIRTY-ONE

LAUREN

S TANDING IN FRONT of the mirror, I stared back at myself. I wasn't sure why I had tears in my eyes. There was nothing more I wanted to do than marry Colt. But now, standing here all alone, I felt so lonely. I wanted my mother here with me. I wanted her to fix my hair and do my makeup. Gush over me in my dress. I wanted Ellie to tell me how happy Colt was to be marrying me.

Turning around, I walked out of the bathroom and sat on the bed. Colt had gone down to check on a few things and hadn't been back yet. How were we both going to get ready in the same room? I wanted Colt to at least not see me until we got down to the wedding spot, which I still wasn't even sure where that was at. What if he sees me before the wedding? Isn't that bad luck? Closing my eyes I wiped the tear away.

Maybe this wasn't such a good idea. Running off without our parents here. Even Colt seemed to be off this morning when he mentioned something about his parents. He'd been texting with them all morning. Was it really fair we didn't include them in this? Colt seemed distracted all morning as he kept checking his phone over and over again. Maybe this was a rushed decision on our part.

Oh my glitter. What in the hell is wrong with me? I'm getting married today and being a Debbie Downer. Stop this Lauren.

Sitting up, I pulled myself together and was about to start putting my hair up when the there was a knock at the door. Smiling, I shook my head and let out a giggle. Colt must have forgotten his key. Opening the door, my mouth dropped open and I couldn't believe who was standing in front of me. I immediately broke down into tears at the sight of my mother and Ellie standing there. My heart felt as if it was going to jump from my chest.

"Mom! Ellie!"

Both of them quickly wrapped me up in their arms as we all stood there and cried. When I finally took a step back, Colt was standing behind them with the most breath-taking smile I'd ever seen. The ground literally felt as if it shifted under my feet.

"Colt? Did you know?"

My mother stepped off to the side as Colt walked up to me. "There was no way I could let us get married and not have at least our parents with us, Lauren. The moment I hung up with you yesterday, I called your parents and told them our plan. Then I told my parents and they all made plans to be here early this morning."

Turning to my mother, my mouth dropped open. "You knew the whole time you would be here?"

Nodding her head she placed her hand on the side of my face. "Colt wanted to surprise you, baby girl. While y'all flew here last night, we took care of arranging the wedding plans and the flights here this morning."

Standing there I was stunned into silence. Colt Mathews truly was a Godsend. An angel sent straight from heaven, who would always protect me and take care of me. He seemed to know my feelings and emotions before I did. He knew my wants before I even expressed them to him.

The only thing that would come out of my mouth was, "Mr. Snuggles."

Colt tilted his head and looked at me with a questioning look. "Huh?"

"You're my . . . my Mr. Snuggles."

Colt chuckled and said, "Okay. I'll take it."

Ellie and my mother both laughed. Ellie walked up to Colt and said, "Colt, honey, don't you remember Mr. Snuggles. You gave him to Lauren on what . . . your seventh birthday I think?"

Nodding my head, I couldn't pull my eyes off of Colt. His smile seemed to light up the entire room when it finally hit him who Mr. Snuggles was. Leaning down he gently kissed me on my lips and spoke softly against them. "Baby, I'll be your Mr. Snuggles for the rest of our lives."

Wrapping my arms around him I held onto him tightly. "I'm scared, Colt."

His arms wrapped around my body tighter as he picked me up and carried me into the bedroom. Setting me down he placed his hands on my face and looked deep into my eyes.

"Do you love me?"

Nodding my head, I whispered, "Yes, so very much."

"Do you trust me, Lauren?"

Swallowing hard, I felt my eyes burning. "With my life, Colt."

"Do you believe me when I say I'll love you until I take my last breath?"

A small sob escaped my lips as I whispered, "Yes."

Brushing his lips across mine, Colt kissed me passionately as my entire body filled with a warmth I couldn't put into words. Pulling back, he kissed my tears away. My body calmed down almost immediately. Knowing that our parents were here and knowing it was Colt who had brought them here had my heart wanting to burst from my chest. "I'll see you at three, sweetheart."

Biting on my lower lip, I nodded my head. "I'll see you at three."

Colt took my hand and led me out to the living room where he placed my hand in my mothers. Kissing his mother Ellie on the cheek he turned and winked at me. "I'm heading back to my parents' room to get ready. See ya soon."

Watching Colt walk out the door with his bag and the tux he picked up this morning, I wanted to call out for him, but I pressed my lips together. The door shut and I spun around. Looking at the two most important women in my life I took in a deep breath and blew it out.

"I don't even know where to start," I said with a nervous giggle. Ellie and my mother looked at each other and smiled before turning back to me with the most loving looks on their faces. Ellie pulled out the stool and motioned for me to sit down while my mother lifted her suitcase and placed it on the table. Giving me a wicked grin as she unzipped the suitcase, I let out a gasp when I saw all of the stuff she had packed. "Mom, did you bring your whole bathroom?"

Laughing she handed Ellie the straightener. "I haven't forgotten how to make those curls with this thing."

Before I knew it I was sipping wine while Ellie and my mother fixed my hair, and then makeup. I'd never laughed so much in my life. My heartbeat had steadied and became calm. As Ellie and my mother fussed over me I felt elated. The moment was perfect and one I would never forget. I couldn't contain my smile if I had tried.

ELLIE WALKED UP to me and smiled as she reached out for my hands. Looking down I noticed I couldn't keep them from shaking. "Take a deep breath in, darling, and slowly blow it out," Ellie said as she handed me a bouquet of red roses.

Doing what she said, I closed my eyes. "Why am I so nervous?"

Chuckling and dropping my hand, Ellie placed her hand on my arm and said, "Let me tell you a story."

Opening my eyes, I focused on Ellie. "Right before I married Gunner, I had a serious panic attack. I couldn't breathe and no one could calm me down except for him."

Grinning, I asked, "Really?"

Nodding her head, I watched as her eyes filled with happiness as she recalled the memory. "The way you're feeling right now, sweetheart, is so normal, but I promise you, the moment you look into those beautiful eyes of Colt's and he smiles at you, your fear will melt away. The nerves will disappear and you will feel nothing but contentment. A sense of peacefulness will wash over your body."

And I'll wanted to do was jump on him and probably hump his leg. I guess we had gone too long without sex. *What in the hell was I thinking? Why did I tell him I wanted to wait? Oh my glitter.* He's going to be in a tux. Colt in a tux. The last time he was in a tux was at Alex's wedding and it was all I could do not to attack him and undress him on the spot.

Shit. Shit. Double shit.

Placing my thumb in my mouth I began chewing my nail like mad. Ellie reached up and pulled my hand down as she chuckled. "Lauren, you'll be fine."

Standing up, I nodded my head. "Right. I'm going to be perfectly fine. I just need to not look at Colt, cause if I look at him I'm going to want to have sex with him and—"

Slamming my hands over my mouth, my eyes widened in horror. My mother walked up and reached with her finger to close Ellie's mouth that was gaped open. "I didn't need that visual, Lauren," Ellie whispered.

Closing my eyes, I shook my head. *Where is the closest rock?*

"Well, now that we know what's on my daughter's mind, shall we get her married off?"

Ellie attempted to hold in her laughter but lost the battle. Soon, all three of us were laughing as my father walked into the room. Stopping dead in his tracks, his eyes traveled over my body as tears began to form. "Lauren, my God you're beautiful."

Kissing me on the cheek, my mother placed her hand on the side of my face. "My baby girl, getting married. I don't believe it."

My mother's touch instantly warmed me. She always had a way of making me feel so loved. "Mom, I love you."

Pursing her lips together, she nodded as her voice

cracked. "I love you, too."

Ellie walked up and adjusted my blonde curls one last time before she kissed me gently. "Lauren, I'm so excited you're going to be my daughter-in-law. I love you, darling."

Oh no. The tears. The tears are coming. Move this wedding along before I lose all control.

"Ellie, I . . . I . . ." Lifting her hand up to my face she shook her head.

"I know, Lauren. I know."

My mother and Ellie both turned and left the room. Closing my eyes, I prepared myself to look at my father who I knew had tears rolling down his face.

Feeling his hand on my shoulder, I turned to him. *Yep. There they were. Tears. Keep. It. Together. Lauren. Mascara. Don't smudge. Don't look in his eyes.*

Placing his hands on my shoulders, I felt his body shudder briefly. Peeking up, I looked into his eyes and saw a single tear roll down his face.

Oh my glitter. Blinking rapidly I tried to keep my tears at bay.

"Oh, Lauren. You're the most beautiful bride I've ever seen."

Laughing, I rolled my eyes as I carefully wiped a tear away. "Mom would be really pissed if she heard you say that."

Letting out a strained chuckle he nodded his head. "Your mother was breathtaking. I can close my eyes and still see how beautiful she was."

"Daddy," I whispered.

"I need you to know something, Lauren. Before you walk down that aisle and become Colt's forever, I need you to know you were mine first and you'll always be my little girl. My life is for you and your mother and no matter what you need, I will be there for you. Always."

Throwing myself into my father's arms, I held onto him tightly. "Daddy, I'm so happy you're here!"

"Me too, baby. Me, too."

My father held me for a few minutes before there was a knock on the door. "It's that time!" came a muffled voice from the other side of the door.

Stepping away I turned to the mirror to check my makeup. My mother was of course a step a head of me. She used waterproof makeup.

Holding his arm out for me my father asked, "Shall we?"

Lacing my arm over his, I smiled. "We shall."

THIRTY-TWO

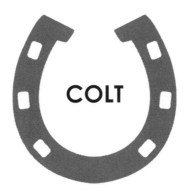

COLT

S TANDING NEXT TO my father, I attempted to calm my
beating heart. "Jesus, Colt. I can hear your heart from
back here. Take some deep breaths in."

Blowing out some quick breaths, my father laughed. "I
said deep breath in, son. Not blow all your air out in quick
bursts."

Taking in a deep breath, I looked around. The wedding was taking place on the terrace. It was simple, with
just a few decorations of white candles and red rose petals. I prayed Lauren liked it. The doors to the terrace were
closed as we waited. When the music played, I felt my
knees wobble.

"Breathe, Colt."

Not realizing I had been holding my breath, I slowly dragged in a deep breath and blew it out just in time
for the French doors to open. My eyes immediately fell
on Lauren. She was dressed in a lace gown with her hair
pulled up. Curls hung down and framed her beautiful face.
There was a lightness in my chest, and my senses height-
ened as I watched Lauren make her way to me. The smell
of her perfume engulfed me as I took a deep breath in.

As she got closer, I noticed my mother's daisy neck-
lace hanging around Lauren's neck. Quickly looking at my
mother, she smiled and wiped a tear away as she watched

Lauren make her way to me.

Stopping in front of me, Lauren smiled the biggest, brightest smile I'd ever seen. Scott turned to me and winked as the pastor asked who was giving Lauren away.

Placing Lauren's hand in mine, Scott said, "Her mother and I."

Lauren turned to face me, and my eyes moved across her entire body and back to her amazing blue eyes. "You look stunning, sweetheart. Absolutely beautiful."

A single tear rolled down Lauren's face as I reached up and wiped it away.

The pastor began the ceremony as Lauren and I held each other's hands. I wasn't even sure what he was saying; I couldn't pull my eyes from Lauren. Before I knew it, he was pronouncing us husband and wife and I was kissing my bride as our parents cheered us on.

Pulling away, I searched Lauren's face. Her face was relaxed and she wore the most beautiful smile I'd ever seen. It was her eyes that held me captive though. They were filled with nothing but love and desire. Leaning down, I placed my lips at her ear. "I've never in my life been as happy as I am at this very moment."

Placing her hands on my chest, her breathing picked up as she closed her eyes. "Colt. We need to ditch our parents. Fast."

Pulling back, I looked at her. She was totally serious. "W-what?" Jessie walked up and took Lauren in her arms as they both held onto each other. My father shook my hand, then pulled me in for a hug. "I'm so proud of you, Colt. So very proud."

Smiling at my father, I said, "Thank you, Dad. Thank you for everything you and Mom did to make this happen. I don't know how you did it all on such a short notice, but I'll never forget it."

Wrapping my mother up in my arms, I told her how much I loved her. Jessie waited patiently for my mother to step aside before she walked up and hugged me. "Take care of my little girl, Colt. I'm counting on you."

Giving her a reassuring nod and smile, I said, "Yes,

ma'am. Lauren will always be my number-one priority."

"Good, I'm glad to hear you say that."

Reaching out, I shook Scott's hand as he pulled me in for a quick hug and a slap on the back. I wasn't sure if he meant for the slap to be that hard, but when he pulled back and narrowed his eyes at me, I knew for sure he meant for it to be that hard. "You take care of her, or I'll break both your arms and legs."

"Um . . . I um . . . yes, of course I'll take care of her, sir." My mind was spinning as I let Scott's casual threat sink in.

After heading to the bar and ordering champagne, to which both my father and Scott said a little toast to, we headed to the Italian restaurant Levo and ate dinner. I loved watching Lauren soak in the attention, and the glow on her face made my heart feel so happy. Taking a sip of my tea, I began to daydream about making love to her. My dick had already begun to get hard the moment we sat down and she started running her hand up and down my leg mindlessly as she talked. I needed to get her back up to our room and quickly.

An Italian cream cake was served after dinner. Each of our parents took a turn giving us a few tips on keeping our marriage a happy and healthy one. Scott was the last to speak. His words of advice caused both Lauren and I to laugh and to cry. Soon our parents got wrapped up in their own conversations as Lauren and I sat there, the heat building between us until I couldn't take it anymore.

"Well, I think Lauren and I are going to head out and enjoy the evening . . . um . . . the evening—"

Lauren jumped in and tried to save me. "Air. We're going to go for a gondola ride, I think, and then maybe a stroll . . . outside."

Clearing my throat I spoke, when I probably should have just kept my mouth shut. "In the evening air. Cause the air is outside. To enjoy it you have to be . . . you know . . . outside." Lauren turned and gave me a dumbfounded look.

My father and mother stared at me as they pressed their lips together in an attempt to not laugh. Jessie turned to Lauren and smiled while Scott glared at me with evil lurking in his eyes.

"The evening air huh?" Scott asked as he looked at Lauren, then me. "I would really hope that you wouldn't be spending your honeymoon night with my daughter walking around the strip of Las Vegas, Colt."

My heart went up to my throat. "No! No, sir, I fully intend on taking her up to the room and—" Lauren dug her nails into my leg as I quickly stopped talking. Standing, Lauren smiled and let out a nervous chuckle.

"Dad, Mom, Gunner, and Ellie. I can't even begin to tell you how much it means to have y'all here. To spend this day with us was just amazing. Thank you so much for everything you've done for us. But, honestly, I'm not going to sit here and lie to you. I want to be alone with my husband, so if you'll excuse us."

Lauren grabbed my hand and pulled me up as I felt my face turn fifty shades of red. "Uh . . . thank you again!" I called out as Lauren walked off, dragging me along with her. "Dad, Mom, I'll see y'all tomorrow? Scott, Jessie thank you for everything!" I called back over my shoulder. All four of them laughed as I turned back to Lauren.

"Lauren, my God. Our parents know where we're going."

Laughing, she turned to me. "Oh my glitter, Colt. Like they don't know what we're going to be doing tonight. I've waited patiently, and now I'm done waiting. I want my husband to make love to me."

I want my husband to make love to me.

Yep. I've officially had all my dreams come true. Well . . . almost all my dreams.

THIRTY-THREE

LAUREN

C OLT'S EYES BURNED with desire as he gazed at me in the elevator. My heart had never beat so fast in my entire life.

Oh my. Wow. Just wow. I'm Colt's wife. Mrs. Colt Hunter Mathews. His. Forever. I'm pretty sure I just pissed in my pretty new lace panties.

Glancing at the people standing in front of us, I willed the elevator to go up faster. It stopped on the third floor and a family of three got on. The little boy turned and began hitting every single floor as Colt and I both shouted out, "No!"

The little boy jumped; the mom gave me a dirty look and the father apologized to us and the other couple in the elevator.

Colt reached out and pulled me over to him and placed me in front of him. "We have a long ride up, sweetheart."

Letting out a low whimper, I rolled my eyes and mumbled under my breath about never having kids.

Colt chuckled as he moved his hand up under the back of my dress. My entire body shuddered as my eyes quickly darted around the elevator. The mother and father of the little boy were both engaged in a conversation with the other couple about how kids will be kids.

Dropping my mouth open, I sucked in a breath of air

as Colt cupped my ass as he whispered into my ear, "A thong . . . I like it, Lauren."

Swallowing hard, I pressed my lips together to keep the moans suppressed. Slowly sliding his hand around to the front, he adjusted my dress and the position I was standing in so no one could see what he was doing.

Shaking my head, I couldn't speak. *He can't do this with all these people in here. There's a little . . . oh my glitter! His hand . . . is in . . . my panties.*

My breathing picked up and I could feel my face flush as the elevator kept stopping at each floor and the door would open, and then close.

Colt's fingertips left a path of hot tingles as he moved them further into my panties. Pressing my bottom into his hard dick, Colt hissed. "I want to fuck you right now, right here, Lauren."

My knees wobbled as Colt wrapped his other arm around my waist. "Colt," I whispered as I attempted to act normal.

His fingers massaged my clit as I struggled to gain some control of my body. *It's been too long. Oh dear God, it's been too long. I'm going to come in this elevator with four adults and one young child standing within inches of me.*

Squeezing my legs together, I attempted to get Colt to stop. Resting his chin on my shoulder, he was about to say something when the father of the little boy looked at us and smiled. "Did you just get married?"

Colt kept up the rubbing as I began to get dizzy with my approaching orgasm trying to build. "We sure did," Colt said enthusiastically.

Everyone turned and looked at us. *Are you freaking kidding me?* "Congratulations," was spoken by everyone at once.

Clearing my throat, I tried with all my might to sound normal. "Thank you . . . um . . . it's been . . . amazing . . . intense . . . really intense."

The mom started laughing. "Oh, yes. I remember those days."

I willed everyone to turn back and look forward, and somehow it worked. Looking over my shoulder at Colt, I widened my eyes at him as he smiled and winked at me.

That bastard. He's doing this on purpose . . . oh God. Spreading my legs apart some, my body was beginning to betray me. More. I need so much more of him.

Slipping his finger inside me, I felt my body beginning to shake. The two couples were back to talking. *What fucking floor are they all on? Shit. Shit. Shit.*

The doors opened on the tenth floor and everyone exited the elevator, but not before the father turned and winked at us. "Have fun."

The doors shut and Colt's fingers moved faster as my orgasm hit me fast and hard. Clenching my teeth together, I began pumping my hips as my body was overtaken by the glorious orgasm as it raced through my body.

Slumping into Colt's body, my breathing was erratic as Colt kissed my neck. "Do you feel better, sweetheart?"

Slowly nodding my head, I panted, "Yes."

Pulling his hand away, he reached down and picked me up. Wrapping my arms around his neck, I smiled at him. "I can't wait to tell Grace and Maegan what we just did."

Throwing his head back and laughing, he quickly kissed me. "I love you, Mrs. Mathews."

Heat radiated throughout my body at those words. *Mrs. Mathews.* I wanted to hear it again.

"Say it again," I whispered.

The elevator door opened to our floor and Colt stepped out as he carried me to our room. "Mrs. Mathews, I love you. I'll always love you."

Slowly sliding me down his body, Colt cupped the sides of my face as he lightly brushed his lips across mine. "I'm going to make sweet, passionate love to you now, Lauren."

The palms of my hands began to sweat as butterflies took off in my stomach at the thought of Colt's hands on my body, his lips kissing every single inch of bare skin. His face buried between my legs. His five o'clock shadow rubbing softly against my skin.

"Oh, God. Colt, I want you so much."

Colt gently rubbed his thumb across my sensitive skin. "I want you too, Lauren."

Nodding my head, I whispered, "Will you open the door then so we can go in? Or I swear I'm going to strip down in this hallway and beg you take me against the door."

Colt's eyes lit up with raw passion as he quickly took the key out and opened the door. Swooping me back up into his arms, he carried me inside the room and straight to the bedroom. Gently setting me down, he took off his tie. Then he slowly unbuttoned his shirt as he gazed into my eyes.

Licking my lips, I reached up and pushed his jacket off his shoulders, letting it drop to the ground. With shaking hands, I removed his shirt as Colt closed his eyes. I gently kissed his chest as Colt let out a low growl from the back of his throat, instantly causing a rush of wetness between my legs. Slowly dropping to my knees, I removed Colt's belt and then unbuttoned his pants. My heart was racing as I watched his hard dick spring from his pants.

I took him in my mouth and began to move. Colt moaned and quickly reached down and grabbed my shoulders, pulling me up to him. "Stop. I won't last one minute with you doing that."

Giggling, I took a step back. "Undress me, Colt."

Stepping up to me, Colt lifted his hands and I couldn't help but notice his hands shaking as well. Closing my eyes, I felt his hot breath against my neck as he slowly unzipped the back of my lace dress. Dropping it, the dress pooled at my feet as I heard Colt moan.

"Jesus, you look beautiful."

Opening my eyes, I watched as he gazed upon my body and licked his lips. Everything I had on was white. White push-up bra, white garter belt, and white lace panties. Dropping to his knees, he pulled me to him and kissed me, breathing his hot air through the lace panties that I was now wishing he would just rip off my body.

Unclasping the garter belt, Colt slowly rolled each stocking down. Carefully lifting each foot as he pulled them off. His hands moved lightly back up my legs as he removed the garter and tossed it to the side of him. When his fingers moved along the edge of my panties, my entire body was covered with goose bumps. Dropping my head back, I moaned in delight. My body felt light as it shook with desire.

Colt slowly pushed my panties down as I bit down on my lower lip and willed him to kiss me. Lifting my leg, he blew warm air on my clit as I let out a gasp. "Colt," I whispered. The desperation was so evident in my voice.

One quick movement and he was giving me what I desired. My hands rested on his head as I felt his stubble brushing across my sensitive skin. *Holy mother of all things. Shit! Shit! Shit! Oh, this is gonna be big. God, I hope my parents don't have a room on this floor.*

"Colt!" I cried out as my orgasm quickly hit me. My body was overloaded with all the sensations it was feeling. His tongue, his lips, the stubble. His finger gently pressed against my backside. It was all too much for me to take. My legs started giving out as Colt quickly stood up and pressed his lips to mine. Moaning when I tasted myself against his tongue, Colt unsnapped my bra and picked me up.

Setting me gently on the bed, I smiled as I stretched my arms above my head. "You're amazing, do you know that?" I asked as Colt kissed my stomach, then chest, until he finally captured my lips again with his.

"Please don't ever stop," I whispered against his lips.

"Never," Colt said as he moved his lips along my jaw and down to my neck. "Spread your legs for me, Lauren. I want to make love to my wife."

Oh. My. Glitter. How can one man be so sexy and so romantic at the same time?

Doing as he asked, I felt him push the head of his dick at my entrance. Arching my back, I prepared myself for him. It had been entirely too long to live without the feeling of Colt inside me. I needed this every day.

Slowly pushing in, we both let out a moan as Colt went perfectly still. I could feel him twitching inside my body. Wrapping my arms and legs around him, I felt my tears begin to fall.

I wasn't sure how long we stayed this way, just Colt inside me as we held each other tightly. As he slowly moved within me, my body quickly began that familiar build up.

Lost. I was completely and utterly lost in the way Colt made love to me. It was slow, passionate, and the most moving moment of my life.

Moving his lips to my ear, Colt whispered, "Lauren…I'm yours," as he pulled out and pushed back into me hard as he came.

Placing his hands on the sides of my face, Colt kissed me. Not just any kiss. A kiss that was filled with so much love I found myself sobbing as I kissed him back. My body shuddered with the feeling of love pulsing through my veins as I fell more in love with Colt.

Pulling out of my body, Colt rolled over and pulled me to his side as he held me. His heart was beating against my back as he wrapped his arms around me. A sense of peace filled my body and I couldn't help but smile.

Running my finger lazily over his hand, I stared out the window at all the twinkling lights.

"Colt?"

"Mmm?"

"I've never felt so happy in my entire life. I'll never forget this moment for as long as I live."

Pulling me tighter to him, he kissed my shoulder. "I'll never forget it either, Lauren. You've made me the happiest man in the world."

A tear rolled down my face as I smiled and said, "Tell me something."

"Anything, Lauren. I'll tell you anything you want to hear."

"Where is your favorite place to be?"

Feeling his warm body, he pulled me around to face him. Colt's eyes held mine as we looked into each other's souls. My heart had always and will always belong to this amazing man. Smiling that smile of his that made my stomach drop still, Colt kissed me gently on the lips as he spoke against them.

"My favorite place to be will always be right here, Lauren. Holding you."

The End

EPILOGUE

GRACE

G RABBING MY KEYS, I dashed out the front door, cursing myself for being late to class. I was already so far behind in all my classes since I missed over a week of school when Lauren was in the hospital. Turning, I pulled the front door shut and locked it. Spinning around on my heels, I went to walk down the stairs and was stopped dead in my tracks as I sucked in a breath of air.

Oh. My. God. Noah.

"What are you doing here?" I asked in a weak sounding voice.

Staring back up at me were those beautiful caramel eyes I found myself lost in on more than one occasion.

"I never got to finish talking to you. I'm glad Lauren's okay."

Fumbling over my words, I asked, "H-how did you know? I mean, yeah, Lauren's actually in Vegas with Colt. They're . . . um . . . they're getting married."

Noah smiled and my world rocked on its axis. *Lord help me, for his smile does things to my body even still.* Swallowing hard, I smiled back.

"That's wonderful. I'm really happy for them both. I haven't had the pleasure of meeting Lauren yet, but Alex was talking to me at the hospital and filled me in on Lauren's progress."

Yet? He hasn't met Lauren—yet?

Shaking my head to clear my thoughts, I asked, "Noah, why are you here? I mean . . . you're . . ." My heart hurt as I tried to speak the words that wouldn't form in my mouth. *He's married now. Just say it, Grace.*

Noah took a step up as I instinctively backed up. *No. Please don't come closer to me.* I wanted to beg him to stop. If he came any closer, I'd feel his pull and my heart couldn't take another break.

"That's what I wanted to come and talk to you about, Grace. You mentioned me being married."

Swallowing hard, I looked away so he couldn't see the tears forming in my eyes. It was my fault. I pushed him away. It was no one else's fault but my own.

Noah reached the top step. Taking in a deep breath, I smelled that familiar scent of his cologne and I whimpered silently inside. My eyes stung as I forced myself not to look at him.

Another step closer. My chest was rising up and down so fast as I dragged in breaths of air.

Noah stopped right in front of me. My body shook as I attempted to push away every memory of him. Every touch. Every kiss. Every romantic word he whispered in my ear as he made love to me.

My skin exploded when his finger touched my chin. Turning my face to him, his eyes locked with mine. "I've missed you so much, and I thought I'd lost you forever, Grace."

My mouth parted open as a single tear fell from my eye. "Noah, you're married and I can't . . ."

Leaning in closer to me, I sucked in a breath of air as his eyes landed on my lips. "Grace, my sweet Grace. I'm not married."

Widening my eyes, a sob escaped my lips. "You're . . . you're not? Are you sure?"

Noah laughed softly and nodded his head. "I'm positive, baby."

Baby. Jesus, Mary, and Joseph. He called me baby.

My mind drifted back to the girl. Who was the girl he

was with at the mall? At the hospital?

"But, I saw you with her. You were registering for your wedding."

Placing his hand on the side of my face, Noah looked into my eyes as he gently moved his thumb across my skin. "That's Emily, my sister, Grace. She's the one who got married. When I lost my phone and lost your number, I didn't know what to do. There were so many times I wanted to get in my car and come here. Please don't push me away, Grace. I need you. I need you so much."

My whole world stopped as I stared at Noah.

I need you so much.

Holy shit. Closing my eyes, I dropped my head back against the door and let out a sigh. His sister. All those texts I ignored. The phone calls I sent to voicemail because I thought he was with another woman. If I had just given him the opportunity to explain to me what I saw, I could have saved myself so much heartache.

My body jumped when I felt his lips against my neck. "Grace, I had to come find you. I needed you to know the truth."

Oh God. He came for me. Noah came for me.

Finding You
Grace and Noah's story
Coming September 2015

PLAYLIST

"Love You Like That" ~ Canaan Smith ~ Prologue

"Dancin' Away With My Heart"~ Lady Antebellum ~ Colt and Lauren at Libby and Luke's wedding dancing.

"Don't Happen Twice" ~ Kenny Chesney ~ Colt and Lauren leaving the reception to be with each other.

"My Everything" ~ Ariana Grande ~ Colt and Lauren making love.

"Wild Child" ~ Kenny Chesney ~ Colt and Lauren in library study room.

"Smoke" ~ A Thousand Horses ~ Will and Colt talking about Colt's feelings for Lauren and his fears.

"Waited Too Long" ~ Brett Eldredge ~ Grace and Lauren talking about Noah.

"Wastin' Gas"~ Dallas Smith ~ Colt and Lauren spending the evening together on the water tower and their spot the night before the girls' trip.

"Give It 2 U"~ Robin Thicke ~ Grayson dancing at the club.

"When I Look At You" ~ Miley Cyrus ~ Colt crying out for Lauren at the hospital.

"Say You Do" ~ Dierks Bentley ~ Colt and Lauren talking about their future after Lauren is out of the hospital.

"Love Me Like You Do"~ Ellie Goulding ~ Colt and Lauren getting married.

"Changed By You" ~ Between the Trees ~ Epilogue

THANK YOU

Darrin—Thank you for always being the cream to my coffee. The bun to my burger. The salt to my shaker. I love you.

Lauren—I'm going to have to insist now that you stop growing up. That is all. I love doo. And the Brother reference is for you.

Danielle Sanchez—Thank you for putting up with my crazy writing schedule and ideas. I'm not sure how I would be able to do all of this without you! You're the best publicist ever. I hope you know how much I appreciate everything you do for me!

Perfectly Publishable—Thank you Nichole and Christine for all you do!

To my friends and family—You know who you are. Thank you for your continued love and support. Love y'all to the moon and back!

To my readers—Thank you for your love and continued support. Thank you for every book bought, shared, recommended and reviews left. I appreciate it more than y'all will ever know! Without you, none of this would be, so THANK YOU! Muah!